An Epic Construct

AN EPIC CONSTRUCT

DAWN CUTLER-TRAN

THE PAPER HOUSE
PUBLISHING

This book contains fictionalized experiences of characters discovering their gender and sexual identities, based on real experiences many people in the LGBTQ+ community face. Some of the conversations and thoughts they have encompass gender and body dysphoria, internalized homophobia and transphobia, and feelings of imposter syndrome and inadequacy. If any of this is triggering or uncomfortable for you, please feel free to skip those sections of the book.

To Thuy and Leta, for standing by me through not just the process of writing this book, but everything else that came with it. You will never know how much your support has meant to me.

Contents

AUTHOR'S NOTE

Content Warning: This book contains fictionalized experiences of characters discovering their gender and sexual identities, based on real experiences many people in the LGBTQ+ community have. Some of the conversations and thoughts they have encompass gender and body dysphoria, internalized homophobia/transphobia, and feelings of imposter syndrome and inadequacy. If any of this is triggering or uncomfortable for you, please feel free to skip those sections of the book.

ONE

PENELOPE

"Maria!" Penelope yelled moments before her rainbow sock clad foot connected with Maria's bedroom door. The door flew open with a satisfying woosh followed by a slightly concerning crunch as it collided with the wall behind it.

Penelope supposed she could have just yanked the door open, but she feared ripping off the door handle. She'd done that the day they moved in together two years prior, and she'd had to call the fire department to come to release Maria from her new bedroom. It had taken four hours and a lot of tears and ice cream, but she was eventually released. The tears were Penelope's because somehow Maria had packed all of the ice cream into her suitcase, and it was melting all over the floor of her new bedroom. Maria did what any self-respecting twenty-six-year-old would do and ate all of it by herself while watching Netflix on her phone.

Penelope prided herself on never making the same mistake

twice, so instead of trying the handle, she had gone for a round-house kick today.

Maria yelled, "You crazy bitch! What do you want?!" as she lay sprawled on her stomach across her bed. "Also, great socks. Can I steal them?"

"Of course, but maybe not while they are currently on my body?"

"But you know how I like my clothes pre-warmed for me."

"Uhm. Ew."

Penelope flopped down on the bed, landing spread eagle on top of her best friend, who gave an indignant squawk in return.

"Okay, moving on. Look!" Penelope said, thrusting her phone into Maria's face.

"Oh my god, you're filling out another dating profile? I thought you said you were done with this."

Maria did a half push up, forcing Penelope to slide off her and rest on her stomach next to Maria so they were both facing the same way.

"Well, yeah, but this one is different—and also not the point! Look at the sexuality list!"

Maria glanced back at the phone, and her face lit up. "Oh, Poppy! They went all the way down to the P in LGBTQIAP+!"

"They went all the way down to the P!"

"Yay, the P!"

"The P!!!" Penelope shouted back, and then they both froze.

"Alright, we should never say that again," Maria deadpanned.

"Agreed," Penelope said gravely.

"Okay, well, that's seriously great! What site is this? Maybe I should sign up since they have the A as well..." Maria murmured, and she actually sounded like she was considering it.

Maria and Penelope had found each other on a different dating app almost seven years earlier when Maria thought she was a run of the mill lesbian, and Penelope thought she was bi. They had gone on a few dates and gotten handsy in their respective dorm rooms before they realized they were better off as friends.

As the years passed, Penelope had begun to think of her sexuality as less of a "this and that" and more of a "this and that... and everything else." She had stumbled across a pansexual flag at a pride event and had done some googling and instantly felt a connection. Maria, of course, immediately showered her in t-shirts, pins, bags, and posters adorned with the cute blue, yellow, and magenta flag, and it stuck. During that time, Maria had also come out as an asexual romantic lesbian, determining that she didn't experience sexual desire for anyone of any gender, but she did feel romantically towards women. Penelope had a great time flooding Maria with not one but two pride flags, and now her bedroom was a sea of purple, orange, black, and white.

Almost exactly two and a half years ago, Maria had made a big show of getting down on one knee and proposing to Penelope in front of all their friends. She had opened up a ring box, and on the soft pillow sat a pin made up of the pan and ace flags crossed at the hilt, attached to a note that said, "Be my roommate, so we don't die alone? JK, but seriously."

Penelope had laughed so hard she'd cried, and six months later, they had found this little fire hazard of an apartment and immediately fell in love with it. Aside from the obvious challenge with door hardware, the dishwasher only worked about half the time, and the fridge was so cold it was almost a freezer, and the freezer barely got to fridge temperature.

Their landowner was a charming older woman. Like *really* old.

So old that she had a walker, was almost entirely blind and had never once gotten their names correct. She had agreed to take half off the rent so long as Penelope and Maria took charge of calling in their maintenance orders and fed her cat.

Pogo was a three-legged cat who flitted between their apartment and their landlord's upstairs, coming downstairs every night to be fed and then meandering around the building after that. All in all, it was an incredible deal. So what if some of the floorboards felt like they would give out at any moment, and this morning Penelope's window had gotten stuck in the open position for four hours? She liked fresh air! She also enjoyed being able to afford an apartment in the hippest part of town, just a ten-minute walk from her job and a fifteen-minute walk from her brother's cafe.

"All right, let's see your profile then," Maria said, hip bumping Penelope and reaching for the phone again.

"It's nothing special..." she said, handing over the phone.

She wasn't very good at online dating. About once a year, almost every year since college, she would download a new app, get super invested and go on about a dozen dates before she inevitably became too disheartened and deleted it. She met a few men and women the old-fashioned way, at bars and through friends, but her last blind date set up had been a disaster. He had been pretentious and cold, and Penelope had ended up in tears, sitting on their apartment stairs petting Pogo until Maria got home to comfort her. After that, she had a no set-up rule. Well, at least until the dating app went so badly that she would inevitably institute a no dating app rule and be right back to meeting people in bars and getting set up.

"Aww, I love this picture of us," Maria said.

Penelope knew immediately which one she was referring to. The first photo on Penelope's profile was a pretty picture of her in a jean jacket and leggings, posing with a llama at their city's zoo. The second photo was of her and Maria at the top of a hike they'd done the previous year. Maria was as gorgeous as ever. She was about 5 feet on a good day, with a petite frame that had slightly rounded out as time went on, making her appear soft and like she would give great hugs—which she did. Her skin was golden brown, thanks to her Filipino parents. Her long silky black hair, which she got from her mother, was blue and orange in the photo.

Penelope was her opposite in many ways. For most of her life, she had been bordering on too thin, making her appear a little lanky even though she was of average height at just under 5' 5". Over the past few years, she'd started putting on weight in both muscle and fat. She blamed her second job working at a cafe, which included lifting an absurd number of heavy boxes, and then rewarding herself with free pastries. Penelope thought having a little more meat on her bones seemed to suit her pretty well, so she wasn't too worried about it. Her boyish frame and lack of any distinguishing features had bothered her when she was younger, but now she enjoyed the privilege of easy clothing shopping in both the women's and men's sections. There was another reason she liked her relatively indistinguishable figure, but that wasn't something she thought about a lot.

Her skin was peaches and cream and burned if she even thought about the sun. She would get a splash of freckles across her face and arms every year after only a day or two of Spring UV rays. In the photo with Maria, she had both a sunburn and freckles.

Penelope's hair was a dark auburn that would sometimes catch the sun in ways that made it look almost red. She usually wore it loose and not particularly styled around her shoulders, occasionally attempting a side braid or twist, but for the most part, she left it alone.

She'd experimented with different haircuts in high school but hadn't done anything fun with it in years. Maria had begged her to let her dye it last summer, so she was sporting blue side bangs in this picture, but it had faded, and they'd dyed it back earlier that year.

Maria continued to swipe through the photos. Next was a professionally shot photo of Penelope at a friend's wedding wearing huge goofy glasses, her arm wrapped around the bride. After that was a picture of her holding a pumpkin in a patch because she was *that* white girl. The second to last photo was one of her at Pride. She was covered in rainbow splatter paint and surrounded by their group of queer friends, all sporting various rainbow-themed hats, bandanas, shirts, bras, and undies. Penelope was wearing a t-shirt with a trio of blue, yellow, and magenta puppies lying on a stack of "pan-cakes." It was her favorite shirt, and she still wore it all the time even though it was dyed technicolor from the paint.

Finally, Maria got to the last photo, which Penelope hadn't been sure she would post. It was a photo of her on the beach, her back to the camera, or, more importantly, her scantily clad butt to the camera. Her hair was down, covering most of the tattoos adorning her upper back and shoulders, and it had the perfect saltwater wave. She had her hands up, running through her hair, and her face was turned towards the setting sun. She would never dream of posting a photo of her in a bikini if she was facing the camera, but maybe this one was okay?

"Is it... too much?" Penelope asked self-consciously.

"Uhm, your ass is phenomenal, and you take good 'looking wistfully off into the distance' photos, so, no. It's not too much. It's great. Let me just read your bio."

If the butt photo hadn't been the worst part, this definitely was. She never knew what to write here, so she usually went with blatant honesty. She changed the profile a little each time she downloaded a new app, but the gist was usually the same. This year it read:

Hi! My name is Penelope, and I'm just your typical twenty-nine-year-old, working two jobs and filling the rest of my time with family and friends. My life is whole, but it's not complete. I am looking for someone who will not just fit into my life but bring new energy, laughter, friends, adventure, and love to every part of my life. I promise to try and bring the same to yours.

Also, I would hope this goes without saying on this app in particular, but if the words "make America great again" resonate with you in any way, PLEASE swipe left. You will hate me. I will hate you. It will be awful.

Maria snorted but nodded appreciatively. "I think you should move the Pride photo and your butt photo up in the order, and then your profile is perfect!"

Penelope did as instructed, cringing a little at the butt picture, but unable to delete it under Maria's watchful gaze. The last step was to select what kind of profiles she was interested in seeing. She left all the gender settings on and set the age range as 28-32. She moved on to the sexuality setting. While she tended to mesh with them the least, she left the heterosexual men filter on, and after glancing down through the full list she swiped off Asexual and Aromantic and left everything else on. She loved Maria like she was part of her soul, but she was looking for a romantic and sexual partner, or at the very least, a sexual partner with the potential for romance down the line. She clicked submit, and suddenly a photo of a guy her age appeared.

"Oh, the first guy popped up!" she cried, and Maria crowded into her space to look at the screen.

The name at the top read just Riley since these dating apps never asked for middle or last names. His profile had a bolded "Qr" on it.

"Huh, Qr. Just... generally queer, I guess?" Penelope said uncertainly.

"Hm, I feel like I hear men use queer less than women do, but maybe he's a baby gay? Or... a baby bi? Baby pan?"

"Great, you think he's an infant. Got it."

"I just mean maybe he hasn't settled on a label or an identity quite yet. Or maybe queer is just how he identifies, and you'll have to ask him more about it when you get married."

"Wow, thanks so much for your help!" Penelope grumbled.

She scrolled down slightly to read his bio. It said a whole lot of nothing like most men's bios did, but he sounded like a generally nice guy.

She scrolled down a little more to see his photo gallery. He had what Penelope would describe as delicate-adjacent features. His brow was soft, with a slender nose, pouty lips, and a soft jawline. She would think his features were almost feminine if it wasn't for his eyes. His eyes had a deep intensity, and were quite striking. They were brightly colored, somewhere between blue and green, almost like aquamarine but slightly darker. She could just barely tell, but it looked like there was a little bit of yellow around the pupils.

He had what appeared to be fairly long hair, but it was tied up in a severe bun at the top of his head in every single picture. It was a dark honey color, with some blonde highlights and chestnut lowlights.

Maria leaned over her shoulder to get a better look. "Oh wow! Look at that hair!"

"I know, right? It's so pretty, even up in a bun. I wonder if he ever lets it down..."

He had tan skin with yellow undertones and a smattering of freckles across his nose and cheeks which softened his look even further, again, except for those intense eyes. Every picture was like he was staring into the camera, almost daring Penelope to swipe right.

So, she did.

Then... nothing happened. Her screen didn't light up with a "Congrats! You matched!" or whatever corny message this app would use. Instead, it just took her to the next profile. She groaned indignantly.

"Cheer up, buttercup, that was the first person you swiped on. Your account has also only been online for, what, ten seconds? There's probably no way he's even seen your profile yet." Maria flopped onto her back, but Penelope stayed where she was.

She thought Maria was probably right, but she decided to spend less time on the next profile so she wouldn't be quite as disappointed. Eventually, she found herself doing what she always did, which was just mindlessly swiping based on looks alone, making her feel crappy and alone, so she put her phone away.

"I'm bored. What should we do?" Maria whined.

She had pulled out a bottle of lime green nail polish and was painting her nails upside down above her face.

"Well... we could go see a movie?" Penelope offered.

"Nah."

"We could go out to eat?"

"Ugh, too much work."

"What about... a nice walk?" Penelope hedged.

"Oooh, how about takeout and Gray's Anatomy?" Maria asked, absently blowing on her wet nails.

"Oh, so you mean exactly what we do every other Sunday night because you never want to do anything else?"

Maria stared blankly at her.

"Yup, that sounds great. How about Thai food?" Penelope offered, rolling her eyes as she sat up.

"God, you know me so well. Do you think we're soul mates?" Maria sassed, returning to her nails.

Penelope rolled off the bed to find some takeout menus. While they were both self-respecting millennials who could quickly look up takeout menus on their phone, there was something comforting about having an entire drawer filled with the little paper menus.

She was rummaging through the drawer when she felt her phone vibrate in the back pocket of her jean shorts. It wasn't quite warm enough to wear shorts outside, but her Sunday routine included a lot of cleaning, lounging, eating, and not going outside, so jean shorts and knee-high socks it was. She was going to ignore the notification, but then she realized with a start that maybe she had gotten a match. She quickly scrambled for her phone, nearly dropping it twice, only to see that it was a text from her little brother.

> Frankie: Can I call? Reviewing inventory and can feel my eyelids closing. I just want to chat.

She had trained her brother so well. Penelope had low level—

okay, maybe mid-level to, on occasion, panic-attack-level anxiety. Her parents loved to text her ominous things like *Call now. Please call.* And the worst, *Why aren't you answering your phone? We really need to talk.*

Each time she got a text like that, her heart would end up in her throat, high-fiving her tonsils as she fumbled to return their call. Without fail, the reason for the text was always something benign like asking when she was coming home next, if she was already coming home, what she wanted for dinner, or why she didn't come home more often. Her stupid gremlin brain always jumped to the worst conclusions, though.

She had asked them time and time again to treat texts like emails and put the subject of the request in with the ask to call, but they still only did it about half the time. Thankfully, her baby brother, who wasn't a baby anymore at twenty-seven, had not only gotten but implemented the memo.

She dialed his number and pressed the phone to her ear while she finished rummaging through the drawer. The phone rang three times, and Penelope found the Thai food menu, grabbing it with one hand and her phone in the other as her brother answered.

"Lopi!" He sang over the phone.

"Frankie!"

"How goes it, big sis?"

"Not too bad little bro; how goes it for you?"

Their parents had named them Penelope and Franklin, which it turned out, were very hard for small children to pronounce. Franklin had dubbed Penelope "Lopi" when he was three, and he'd never stopped calling her that. It had led Penelope down a fun path of name shortening, nicknaming, and renaming herself over the years, but Lopi was the original nickname. She had been able to say

Franklin at her slightly older age, but he had begged her for a nick-name, so she'd gone with the easy-to-say Frankie, and it too had stuck after all these years.

"It's fine. Diego just left me high and dry to take care of all the inventory today so he can go 'pay our mortgage, so we don't get kicked out of this place you love to hate so much' or something stupid like that."

"Oh, how lame," Penelope said as she hip-checked the drawer closed and ambled her way back to Maria's room.

"I know, right? I'm way more fun than boring paperwork."

Diego was Frankie's thirty-one-year-old business partner and definitely-something-more-than just-business partner, but Penelope could never get him to admit anything concrete.

Frankie had come out as bi-sexual almost a decade before Pene-lope had. Their aunt had asked him what his favorite Disney movie was, and he had said Cinderella because he wanted to marry a prince, and when she asked, "What about Cinderella, wasn't she pretty too?" Frankie had looked her dead in the eye and said, "Well, duh, I have eyes."

She was one of their least favorite aunts, and they didn't see her much anymore. Once they had both moved out, they'd stopped speaking to many of their extended relatives. Their parents always tried to get them to reach out to them on birthdays or for holidays, but they didn't see the point. After a while, the reminders stopped coming and they'd never spoken of it again.

Frankie had met Diego when he was twenty-one, and Diego was twenty-five and they were both attending university in the town across the river. They were both working on business degrees, a BA and MBA, respectively. They hit it off immediately, and when they both graduated, they decided to go into business together.

They opened what they called an inclusive cafe that hired people from all different walks of life, served a diverse menu of drinks and foods, and flew Black Lives Matter and a smattering of different LGBTQ+ flags out front as well as within the cafe. They also hosted a drag brunch every Saturday and Sunday that had grown so much in popularity they were considering instituting a waitlist.

It wasn't until the cafe opened that Penelope learned Diego was trans. Penelope had bought Frankie a gay pride flag to pin to his lanyard, and the next day she had noticed Diego had pinned a trans pride flag on his. Penelope had nodded at the pin and smiled, and that had been that. She had been a little surprised Frankie never mentioned it to her during the two prior years, but he was very sparing in what he shared about Diego. About a year ago, she'd walked in on the two of them kissing in their joint office, and she hadn't said a word, just grabbed her backpack, gave them both a huge shit-eating grin, and walked out. They never spoke of that day but the way they had been kissing, Frankie's pale hand gently touching Diego's russet brown cheek, made Penelope think it wasn't their first time.

That had actually been her first day on the job. The cafe was generally well staffed, but Wednesday nights were always hectic for some reason, so she had agreed to pick up shifts to help Frankie out. They had arranged for her to be paid in take-home pastries and unlimited coffee every day of the week. She would have done it entirely for free, but Diego had nearly thrown a fit when she offered, so Frankie had compromised between them with the offer of food for payment.

Throughout their entire childhood, Frankie had always been the troublemaker, and Penelope had been the one who had to make peace and form compromises between him and their parents. As they grew up, though, Frankie settled into his life like he was made to be a coffee shop owner. On the other hand, Penelope had floundered around a bit after college, slowly finding her way into a career, a great friend group, and her sexuality. Frankie had become the sturdy one, and now Penelope often found herself leaning on him for support.

"So, how exactly can I be of service?" Penelope asked as she leaned her shoulder into Maria's door. Thankfully it was still open because she didn't think she'd be able to do another kick. She may or may not have pulled something with the first one. Man, getting old sucked.

"Oh, just prattle on about something. Truly I'm on my sixth coffee, and my eyes are closing. This inventory is going to be the death of me. If you find me under a stack of paperwork on Wednesday, you know what to write on my tombstone."

"Death by a thousand paper cuts?" she asked.

Maria looked up from where she was now bent in half, her back on the bed, legs above her face as she attempted to paint her pinky toe. She gave Penelope a weird look, as if her joke was the strangest thing happening in this room.

"Who are you talking to?" she mouthed. Penelope mouthed back "Frankie" as she handed over the paper menu.

"FRANKS!" Maria yelled loudly, and Penelope rolled her eyes and handed over the phone as well.

Maria put it on speaker just in time to catch Frankie yelling, "Mars! How's my favorite girl?"

Penelope rolled her eyes even harder and groaned, flopping back onto the bed.

"I'm lovely, as always. Thank you for asking, Franks. How are you? Dying via documents, I hear?"

"Oh, Mars-y, it's awful! Diego abandoned me to do the ENTIRE inventory. Do you know how much that is? It's ten pages long!"

That did sound pretty awful to Penelope, so she rolled over on the bed, maneuvering between Maria's arms and legs, to lie with her head on Maria's sternum. While Maria openly admitted she would be perfectly happy never having sex again, she was an absolute cuddling fiend. She admitted to Penelope once that perhaps it had taken her so long to realize she didn't have any sexual desire for others because of how much she loved the cuddling afterwards. She would pick her partners based on how good she thought they would be at cuddling.

Penelope also loved cuddling. She filled most of her cuddling needs with Maria, but she had a few other friends who would come over just to curl up with her in bed, reading magazines, listening to music, or watching movies. Since her dating life had been in the shitter for quite some time now, she wasn't getting physical intimacy in any other form.

"So, what I'm hearing is you want us to tell you some fun stories to keep you entertained? You know I'm the best at that, Franks; I'm not sure why you called Poppy and not me."

Penelope gave an indignant grunt.

"You're right as always. I just hadn't heard from Lopi in a while, and you and I just talked last night."

Penelope loved how close the two were, but sometimes she felt just the tiniest bit left out. Maria didn't have any other siblings, so it made sense she needed an adopted older sister and younger brother to fill the void, but still. Sometimes Penelope just felt very alone in general, hence her foray into dating once again.

As if reading her mind, Maria said, "Well, Poppy just started an

15

online dating profile! Do you want to help us review potential dates for her?"

"Oh my god, why does that sound like the best thing that's going to happen to me today? Yes. Absolutely. Hit me with the first one."

With a few flicks of her now bright green fingers, Maria switched the screen to the dating app and began reading out the first profile to Frankie.

Penelope snatched the Thai food menu back from Maria and selected three dishes for them, pointing at each item one at a time and receiving two nods and then a big thumbs up from Maria. She called in the order on Maria's phone as Maria continued reading out the profiles. Penelope figured if she were ever going to find a match, this would probably be how it would go—selected by her overprotective best friend and under protective brother.

Apparently, a few of the matches had already swiped right on her because a few times, the cheery "You got a match!" message would pop up on the screen, full of rainbows and actual unicorns flying across the screen.

They kept it up until there was a noise on Frankie's end of the line. Suddenly, his voice was muffled as if he had put his phone down and was talking away from the microphone. "Hi!... Yes, I did it all by myself! Or I mean, I guess not by myself... Lopi and Maria... yes, they're on the phone... okay... okay, I'll see you upstairs? We can make dinner... oh yeah, that pasta you like? Okay... you too."

Penelope and Maria stared at each other with raised eyebrows but said nothing. Maria was just as invested in prying into Frankie and Diego's supposed love life as Penelope was, and this was the biggest scoop they'd gotten in a while.

"Hi, sorry. Diego just got back from the bank. I think I'm good to finish up here, and I'm sure your food will be there soon. It was great talking to you both!"

"You too. Lots of love to you and Diego," Maria said.

"And from me!" Penelope chimed in right before the line went dead.

"Well, you are going to have a mess of matches to sort through, and honestly, some of them were not hot, but Franks liked the description, so... there you go," Maria said, dropping Penelope's phone into her hand.

Penelope rolled her eyes and went out to the kitchen to grab some forks and napkins for them, and the Thai food arrived a few minutes later. Pogo scampered inside, weaving between the delivery person's legs, and Penelope called to Maria to come feed him while she accepted the food and shut the door.

They settled on the couch together, wrapped in blankets, and dug into their food. Smelling more food, Pogo crawled into their laps and sniffed around the boxes. When Maria pushed his face away from her Pad Thai, he circled awkwardly on his three legs, plopped down, and promptly fell asleep.

Halfway through the TV episode, Penelope heard a strange ding and pulled out her phone to see that she had another match from the dating app. It seemed the app came with its own noise alert so everyone in the room would know that she was single and ready to mingle. Penelope wasn't sure how she felt about that but was too lazy to do anything about it. She tossed her phone on the couch and burrowed into Maria's chest instead. Maria laughed indulgently, pulled Penelope's hair out of its elastic band, and began combing her fingers through it.

They made it through another two episodes before calling it a

17

night. Penelope had a long week ahead of her, including a long shift at her brother's cafe Wednesday night, so she thought she might as well try to get some extra sleep. She brushed her teeth while thumbing through some work emails, trying to get a jump start on the week. The dating app let out a chorus of chimes to remind her that she was still single and only slightly ready to mingle. To her horror, when she opened the app, she saw fourteen matches waiting in her queue. She groaned and switched her phone back off. This was already feeling like more work than it was worth.

RILEY

Riley had absolutely no idea why he'd allowed Johanna to talk him into trying out this new dating app. Aside from a bone deep weariness around dating and dating apps in general, he wasn't even really sure he was ready to date right now.

Johanna had flown out to visit him for the weekend, and she'd used his phone a few times to call Ubers, place food orders, and play music. This in and of itself was nothing out of the ordinary. However, after dropping her off at the airport Sunday morning, he swiped his phone to pull up the maps app and saw a weird technicolor app sitting on his home screen.

He tried to call her when he got home, but she must have already turned her phone off for the flight, so he hesitantly opened the app. Its title screen read "Chasing Rainbows: An Inclusive Dating Experience." The title was self-explanatory, but he was curious about what made it so inclusive. He scrolled down through the intro text and found that it gave a large number of sexuality and gender options for users to select from for themselves and the profiles they wanted to see. He thought the idea was interesting but could be sketchy if someone used it to fetishize specific identities or sexualities.

He closed the app and didn't give it another thought. He went about his usual Sunday routine, cleaning his spacious two-bedroom apartment, prepping for a few meetings he had first thing Monday morning, and grocery shopping so he could make himself a quiet dinner. Sometimes he would go out for lunch with friends on Sundays, depending on what kind of mood he was in that day. Today, he was in the "put out from playing host to his overbearing big sister" mood, which meant he wanted to be alone.

He reveled in the silence until the early afternoon when his phone began to ring. He checked the caller's I.D. and saw it was Johanna, possibly returning his missed call.

"What is this, an intervention via a stupid app?" he sniped, beginning the call grumpy and already over the conversation they were about to have.

"Why yes, my flight went well, and I landed safely in the city of our birth. Thank you so much for asking, and yes, I did get some sleep. After sharing a bed with my obnoxious sibling for six days, it was actually quite relaxing."

"Hey! Not only do I have a pullout bed in the guest room, I even offered to sleep on the couch..." he grumbled, sinking back into said couch.

"That's true, you did. Oh, and since you asked, I ordered a sprite, and they gave us stroopwafels. Can you believe it? What a grand day it has been."

He put his phone on speaker and leaned his head back on the sofa, closing his eyes for a moment as she went on to describe the indie movie she had watched on the plane.

"Did you seriously call me just to ignore me?" she complained at a high enough volume that it caught Riley's attention.

"No, Jo Jo, of course not. I called to ask why you downloaded a queer dating app on my phone."

"Well, you're queer. And dating. So, I don't see what the problem is."

"I am... one of those things, yes," he sighed in exasperation.

"Well, you could be dating if you tried a little harder. Like, for example, by creating a profile, selecting your preferences, and doing a little swipe-y swipe. It's not that hard; you could be doing it right now instead of IGNORING ME."

"I'm not ignoring you now, so you can stop yelling. You know how I hate that."

He got up from the couch, assuming this would be a long conversation, and moved into his bedroom so he could sprawl out while listening to her lecture.

"So, what exactly is the problem?" she asked, and Riley didn't like the tone of her voice. This was the "serious older sister that cares about you but doesn't appreciate your shit" voice. He wished the "bothersome older sister" voice would return because he could ignore that and not feel bad. He couldn't ignore this, though, especially when she asked such a direct question.

"I don't know if I want to date right now."

"You spent almost the entire time I was there pining after couples we saw on the street. You took me to all these amazing places and multiple times said how nice they would be to take a partner to. That doesn't really sound to me like you don't want to date."

Riley rubbed at his sternum. Conversations like this always made him feel like he'd taken a too big bite of food, and it left a lump in his throat he could only just barely swallow around. "Is it stupid to say I want a partner, but I don't want to date to find that partner? I just... want someone to accept me. Like you accept me. Like a few of my friends out here accept me."

"It's not stupid, but it is unrealistic, Ry. You have to get out there to meet that person. They're not just going to appear in your life, fully integrated and ready to go. That's called a robot, and I know you don't want that."

He didn't want that. He didn't want someone who would just be absorbed into his tiny little life. He wanted someone who would expand his boundaries and push him out of his comfort zone. But he also wanted someone who would understand that some of his boundaries were non-negotiable, and some parts of his comfort zone were specially crafted to protect him.

"So... what if I want a partner right now, but I'm not ready to date right now. Where does that leave me?"

She was silent for several moments, and he heard the noise of a car door opening and closing and the muffled sound of her greeting someone he assumed was an Uber driver.

"Well, I guess you must ask yourself if you think you'll ever be ready to date. Or is this just something you're always going to want but think you can't have? If it's the latter, then... fill out a profile. Swipe on some pretty people, go out for coffee, or grab brunch. I know how much you love brunch, so don't even try to throw a fit about that."

"I do like brunch..." he grumbled, turning over to lie with his head pillowed on his arm and his knees tucked up to his chest, making himself as small as possible.

"There's also happy hour, a movie, a gig at a bar... I'd suggest dinner, but I know that would probably scare you, so... Maybe just try those others first."

"I could... probably do that."

"Hey, there you go! That's the spirit! And besides, I know that your closest three friends are all women. If you go on a date with a sweet girl and things don't turn romantic, maybe you'll make a great new friend!"

"Yeah, because women love being friend-zoned."

"Riley."

"Okay, okay, I'm doing it..."

"Perfect! You'll find I already went through all of your photos and expertly curated the six photos you should use."

"You WHAT?!" he shrieked, in a tone so high he was surprised his windows didn't shatter.

"Wow. I was joking; I just downloaded the six best photos from your Facebook, so they'd be the most recent photos in your camera roll. What the fuck is on your phone, Ry—"

"I have to go. Goodbye."

"I love you!"

"...I love you too."

"To the moon and back," she said, and this was the third voice she used with Riley.

"To the moon and back..." he responded, with the same instinct that told him to breathe in and out or to blink.

Johanna would use this third voice when they were kids to read him bedtime stories late at night. He'd crawl into her bed when the world felt too big and confusing, and his head and body just didn't feel right. She would read to him and stroke his hair; to this day, she and his two closest girlfriends were the only ones who he would let touch his hair. He had always imagined his partner would be the fourth and final person to get that kind of permission from him, but his dating life had completely stalled out.

Riley had been on dates before, but they'd never gone very well. He either admitted too much too quickly or not enough at all. His dates would then inevitably think he was clingy and emotional or distant and a jerk. This partly stemmed from the fact that he had challenges with his body and physical intimacy. The few times he had taken someone back to his dorm or college apartment, it had ended in frustrated tears, sometimes from both parties, and by the time he'd graduated, he'd pretty much given up on it entirely.

There had been a few good experiences since he'd moved here. One of them was actually how he'd met one of his now best friends, Kim. They'd met at a bar, and he'd taken a chance and asked her back to his place. They'd made out, and he'd asked if she would mind if he just focused on her for the night. She had been delighted, and they had a great time together.

Afterwards, they'd cuddled and talked all night, and he'd asked her to come over again the following weekend. She had agreed, and the same thing happened, but he'd shut down when she tried to reciprocate physical intimacy for him.

She'd cuddled him in bed again, and through whispered admissions and long stories, they had decided just to be friends since he clearly wasn't ready for anything more than that. Their friendship had blossomed quickly, and thankfully all sexual attraction faded, but they would still cuddle when one of them was having a bad day.

After Johanna hung up, Riley grudgingly opened the app again and closed his eyes in exasperation as the garish opening screen showed. When he opened his eyes again, he looked at a much more subdued menu that asked him for his name, age, sexuality, and gender. He put his usual answers, Riley, 30, Queer, Male, but was impressed by the range of options for gender. It then asked him for a bio, and he panicked, quickly switching to a texting thread with Johanna and asking her to write him a quick profile.

While he waited, he began slowly reviewing the photos Johanna had selected for him. He liked them all well enough, which was why they had ended up on his Facebook in the first place.

He was about to text Johanna again when she sent him a flowery, exaggerated bio with words like "attentive partner" and "emotionally involved." He groaned and deleted three-fourths of it, keeping just the bare bones structure. He knew if he spent too long on this, he was going to chicken out, so he only het himself read through it one time before he pressed submit. Immediately a gorgeous blonde woman popped up on his screen, and he had to put the phone down to get over his shock. He picked it back up again and saw that she was listed as As for asexual. He bit his cheek when he realized he hadn't changed his preference settings.

He spent far too long, for a semi-functioning card-carrying member of the millennial generation, trying to find the settings. Unfortunately, he was feeling frustrated when he finally found them, and the number of choices overwhelmed him. He ended up throwing his phone across the bed and deciding this was the universe telling him to take a break.

He made himself dinner and spent an extra hour watching TV, trying to avoid going back into his bedroom where his phone lay on his bed like Exhibit A in the case of his failed love life.

Eventually, it got too late to keep putting off reentering his bedroom, so he avoided his phone and quickly went about his nightly routine. He brushed his teeth with his back turned to the mirror, only turning around at the last moment to spit and rinse his mouth out. He turned off the lights and padded over to his dresser and grabbed the pajamas resting on top. He changed quickly in the dark and crawled under the covers.

He thought about what Johanna had said, questioning if he would ever be ready to date. He honestly didn't know if he ever would be, but he also knew the older he got, the more desperately he wanted a partner. His bed and entire apartment felt vast and empty, and he missed his sister desperately. It had been so great having her here.

He offered to make up the guest bed or sleep on the couch every night, but she never once took him up on it. Instead, they lay side by side like two logs, the way they had since they were kids. They would wake up sprawled across the bed, her elbow in his face and his cold feet jammed up against her exposed calves. They would tussle for the blankets and argue over why he never used a top sheet. The answer was that top sheets were stupid, but she didn't think that was sound logic. She said adults used top sheets, and once again, Riley was reminded of the fact that he was nothing like what he was supposed to be. He would then hit her in the face with a pillow, and all would be right again.

He rolled over and looked at his empty bed, and just like that, he made an impulsive decision and grabbed his phone. The intro screen flashed, and this time it automatically prompted him to change his preference settings, and he switched a few off without really thinking but then, on second thought, switched most of them back on purposefully omitting only two of the options.

He switched back to the swiping screen and was greeted by the same blonde woman as before. He swiped right on impulse, began slowly glancing through profiles, and swiped, mostly left, as he went. His eyes were starting to blur with sleep, and he was about to put down his phone when the next profile caught his eye. More precisely, it was the number of p's on the page. The first and second p were in Penelope's unique name. The third p was her sexuality, pansexual.

He had always been intrigued by pansexuality. It felt so easy and simple to be attracted to and have the potential to love everyone and anyone. His own sexuality was harder to describe, so he usually just didn't. For a long time, he just let people assume he was straight, but slowly, with the help of Johanna and his friends, he began to say he was queer, as it felt like the most accurate descriptor for himself.

He slowly began swiping through her photos and decided she was cute. More androgynous than feminine, but still with the softness Riley liked and somewhat envied. He was all rough edges and angles, but often wished for a softer look, some muscle, some fat, just the right amount of body. He glanced at her bio and laughed at the entry's final words. Before he could think any more on it, he swiped right.

TWO

PENELOPE

If Penelope had to write "per my last email" one more time, she swore she would gouge someone's eyes out with the business end of a staple remover.

She worked on the communications team of a mid-sized nonprofit. Those things meant she often had to be nonpartisan and unbiased and could not say what she actually meant in work emails. What she wanted to say was, "if you would be so kind as to open your fucking eyes, you would see that I already outlined everything you're asking for in the email I sent you yesterday—which I have gone to the trouble of reattaching below, so you realize how much of a jackass you're being."

"I love my job. I love my paycheck. I love my job. I love my paycheck," she repeated to herself as she pushed her chair back, pocketed her phone, and went to the coffee maker.

She put her chipped "I <3 NYC" mug into the machine and

pressed the triple espresso button. No milk. Just black. Like her mood.

Suddenly, a tall, impeccably dressed Black man around her age appeared in her peripheral vision. He came to rest with his back against the counter, so he was facing her. Greg was one of the few openly LGBTQ+ people in the office and the only one who worked on this floor with her.

When she had first started working here, she had walked by his rainbow-clad cubicle and immediately wanted to be his friend. She had always struggled with how to be openly out and proud at work when she hadn't ever been in a long-term relationship with a woman. She had been on multiple dates and had sex with a handful of women throughout the years, but there wasn't ever really anyone serious she could talk about at work or put photos of on her desk.

Sandra in IT had a wife and two children, and the head of their division, Jorge, had invited the entire company to his and his husband's destination wedding in Aruba. She had thought that was such a genius move, inviting the whole office knowing almost no one would actually go, but they would all feel obligated to buy them something off their registry.

For a while, Greg had an on-again, off-again boyfriend who would occasionally swing by to pick him up for lunch, so the whole office at least knew about him. That left Penelope in a strange no man's land of wanting to be accepted by her queer peers and seen as not-straight by the rest of her colleagues, but with minimal options to achieve either. Greg had been the one to befriend her. He had to walk past her desk to get to the kitchen, and they had begun chatting and grabbing coffee together her second month on the job. When he found out she was pansexual, he ordered a very tasteful piece of modern art for her desk in the pansexual flag colors that was a little phallic, a little sapphic, and a lot fantastic.

"Oh honey, who peed in your coffee?" he asked, taking in her glowering expression and tense shoulders.

"Well, first of all. My coffee isn't even ready yet, so that's not the problem. But to answer your question: at this moment, it's two of our vendors, one of our consultants, the entire IT department, and those stupid fucks over at the Facebook verification office."

"Oh no... still no blue check mark?"

"HOW CAN THIS BE SO HARD!" she whisper-shrieked, yanking her coffee mug out of the machine so hard she nearly spilled boiling coffee all over herself. If that had happened, she probably would have just given up and gone home, which honestly might have been for the best. She was feeling a little unhinged.

She'd been working with the team at Facebook for a month to help get her organization officially verified so she could improve their social media engagement and reach. She had been told on the phone multiple times that it would show up in the next few days. However, those phone calls had taken place over three weeks ago, so she had sent a nicely worded email earlier last week and had gotten the response today.

Evidently no one in their verification team had ever heard of her or her organization, so they would need to begin the verification process again. She had then sent a much less nicely worded email and nearly gnawed off the end of her pen. She would get that stupid blue check mark if it was the last thing she did. They could carve that shit into her gravestone.

Her other favorite coworker, Maya, walked into the kitchen and bumped her shoulder into Penelope's. "Troubles with Facebook?"

Maya's desk was two seats away from the kitchen. Because she was currently six months pregnant, she used any excuse, namely Greg or Penelope being in the kitchen, to get up and stretch her legs.

"God, my life has become the title of a bad news article," Penelope groaned and took a sip of her espresso.

She nearly gagged and decided she wasn't nearly edgy enough to drink this black. She dragged herself to the fridge and pulled out the first coffee creamer she could find. French Vanilla with a side of hydrogenated oil. Her favorite. She could feel Frankie cringing all the way across the city, but she had to get her caffeine fix somehow, and this was the fastest way to do it other than mainlining it directly into her veins.

All of a sudden, her phone chimed in that embarrassing noise again, and she could practically see Greg's ears perking up. "Is that what I think it is? Are you online dating again?"

"Oh, give us all of the deets!" Maya said, slowly making her way to the small kitchen table in the corner.

"God, yes, let us live vicariously through you. Please!" Greg followed behind Maya, pulling her chair out for her when she got to the table. He pulled out another chair and gestured for Penelope to sit down.

She could try to run. Maya would never be able to catch her, but Greg's legs were pretty long. She might just be able to make it back to her desk before he reached her, though, and there's no way he would make a scene about her dating life at her desk, was there?

She gave him an appraising look, and his expression turned from curious to impatient. "I will drag you over here, do not play with me. I have been staring at spreadsheets since six a.m. You can't avoid me all day, now that I know there's gossip, I will find it."

Well, that answered that question. She sighed in resignation as she brought her horrendous coffee to the table, pulled out her phone, and opened the app.

"There isn't all that much to tell, so you can stop getting excited. I created an account last night, and I did some swiping, Maria did some swiping, and Frankie did some remote swiping. Would you like to take a turn?"

Maya's gentle fingers took the device from her, and she placed a comforting hand on top of Penelope's as she squinted at the app. Penelope was always struck by just how sweet and maternal Maya was. She had grown up in a bustling Indian household where she and her older sister were tasked with watching after the four younger siblings. Since then, she had known she wanted to be a mother and often mothered Greg and Penelope even though they were only a few years apart in age.

Penelope didn't have any of those instincts; truthfully, babies scared the living daylights out of her. She was also less than thrilled with the idea of another person growing inside her, for a multitude of reasons. Maya made it look natural, though. She was glowing, and she'd begun showing them photos of the baby room she was decorating at their daily, and sometimes twice daily, kitchen hangouts.

"I don't want to swipe for you, but I will check out your matches—oh wow, you have eighteen matches!" Maya said, her voice turning impressed.

Penelope blanched. She was sure there hadn't been that many the previous night. This suddenly all felt too overwhelming. She briefly considered just snatching the phone away and deleting the app, but she didn't think snatching a phone out of a pregnant woman's hands was on her bingo card for the day.

"Shall we start at the top then, Peacock?"

Penelope smiled at Greg's silly nickname for her, and that, more than anything else, had her agreeing.

They worked their way slowly through the matches, several of which Greg immediately unmatched for her, if they were "hideous" or "too attractive, and they only have one photo, so they're probably a bot." Penelope would have liked a little more approval power in the process, but she also wasn't feeling significantly invested. She made Maya keep the four women she'd matched with, and they were nearing the bottom of the list when Greg said, "Oooh, Riley is a pretty name."

For some reason, Penelope felt something in her chest perk up, almost like Greg had when he'd heard that fateful ding from the app. "Hey, wait! I liked his profile, don't delete him!"

Greg was swiping through his profile and batted Penelope's hand away as she tried to reach for her phone. "Don't worry, silly; I'm not going to delete someone this hot. I mean, look at him!"

Penelope and Maya scooted their chairs closer to look over his blazer-clad shoulders. Penelope found herself smiling as she looked at Riley's photos once again.

Maya elbowed Greg not-so-subtly, and they both turned to look at her.

"What... do I have horrendous coffee on my face or something?" Penelope ran the back of her hand across her mouth and looked at them.

"Ah, damn, Peacock, you wiped away that adorable smile," Greg teased. Maya was practically beaming at her, and even Greg looked pleased.

"I don't know what you're talking about," Penelope scowled.

"I think he messaged you already—oh, I'm so sorry. Have to pee again," Maya announced, and she began to struggle to stand up.

Greg quickly stood up too and helped her out of her chair. Penelope reached out and took her phone back from Greg before he dropped it and/or Maya.

She glanced down at the photos of Riley and his intense eyes. She hadn't wanted to admit it to herself after she had swiped and not received a match, but he was almost exactly her type. When she was younger, she went for the more macho men and super femme women, but as she'd gotten older, she'd noticed that her taste had slowly shifted. She found herself attracted to men who were a little more feminine and women who were a little more masculine.

She clicked on the notification bubble and saw that Riley had sent her a message at 10 pm the night before. The message read *You have a very beautiful name.* Penelope laughed a little to herself since Greg had just said the same thing about him.

Speaking of Greg, he had escorted Maya to the kitchen door and was now sliding back into his seat next to Penelope.

"So, you going to message him back?"

"You know, I think I migh—" her breath caught as a work email popped across the top of her screen.

"OH MY GOD, they're escalating my request to the head of the department at Facebook! I have to go!" She nearly knocked her chair over as she ran out of the kitchen and back to her desk. She gulped the rest of her coffee in one acrid mouthful and slammed down the cup. She crammed the hideous headset onto her head, cracked her knuckles, and prepared herself for the caffeine-fueled rage she was about to rain down on Facebook.

It was a beautiful April day outside, and Penelope decided to walk home after work. She pulled out her headphones and started up one of her go-to playlists. She was about to put her phone back in her jacket when her eye caught on the dating app logo.

She considered it for a moment and then pulled up the app. She immediately navigated to Riley's page, looking at his photos once more before clicking on the chat bubble.

> Riley: You have a very beautiful name.

> Penelope: Thank you! I'm pretty fond of it, actually.

She stared at the chat and wondered if it was the kind that would show when the other person viewed the message. She was about to click out of the app when the little icon under her message changed to a pair of eyeballs.

She laughed out loud but then caught her breath when she saw the little bubbles pop up to show he was typing.

This was stupid. Penelope didn't freak out over simple text messages anymore. She was too old for this. However, it had been a long time since she'd been even slightly interested in someone. Her unsuccessful experience with being set up was preceded by a string of awful dates last winter when she'd tried another dating app that was supposed to be able to match you with your soulmate, but only managed to match her with two jerks and a ghoster. Her phone vibrated, and she let her eyes come back into focus over Riley's newest chat bubble.

> Riley: Do you ever let anyone call you by nicknames, or are you more of a purist?

Penelope: Actually, funny you should ask that. I have a thing about nicknames that started when my little brother couldn't pronounce my name when we were kids.

Penelope: I like to let people come up with their own creative nicknames for me, but they can only call me something if no one else in my life is already calling me that.

Riley: Oh, that sounds fun. Care to share an example?

Penelope: Sure! My roommate, and all-time best friend, calls me Poppy.

Riley: Oh dang, that's a good one...

Penelope: My little brother calls me Lopi, and my coworker calls me Peacock.

Riley: Two more good ones taken!

Penelope: I wish you the best of luck, but until then, Penelope works!

Riley: Alright, Penelope. It's lovely to make your virtual acquaintance.

Penelope: Same! So, what about you, Riley? Have any nicknames?

Riley: Well...

Riley: Riley isn't my first name, it's my middle name, so I guess it could be considered a nickname in and of itself?

> Penelope: Oh, that's cool. I have some friends who do that as well. Any particular reason?

> Riley: My first name has never quite felt… right.

> Riley: I don't know.

> Riley: It's too feminine for me or something.

Penelope tried not to flinch at the comment. He had every right to feel a particular way about his own name, but disliking things because they were too masculine or too feminine had always rubbed her slightly wrong.

He quickly glossed over it, asking her to tell him more about herself, so, not wanting to give up on him quite yet, she did. She arrived at her apartment building and walked up the stairs, describing her job in basic detail and mentioning her one-night-a-week stint as a waitress/barista/cashier/general helper at a cafe.

She let herself into the apartment and nearly closed the door on Pogo. On a whim, she snapped quick photo of him and sent it off to Riley. She set about making Pogo's dinner and tossed leftover Thai food in the microwave for herself as she waited for Riley to respond. He didn't answer for a while, and Penelope tried not to deflate as she rinsed out her dishes and put them in the dishwasher. Her phone dinged right as the front door opened.

> Riley: Wow, what a cute cat! Please tell me their name is something amazing like Triple Sec?

Penelope: Wow, if you put this much thought into naming my landlord's cat— that already has a name— I can't wait to see what you come up with for me!

Riley: Well, I promise to do much better than cheap alcohol for you.

Riley: Are you going to tell me the cat's name or is suspense part of your strategy to pique my interest?

Maria was barely out of her shoes before she launched into a story about one of her bosses at work. She worked as an accounts manager at a law firm that mainly worked on marijuana legalization. They were allowed to wear whatever they wanted into the office, and one of the partners had one of the most eclectic styles Penelope had ever heard of. Maria's favorite job at work was to catalog every piece of his ensemble to report to Penelope each night. Today it was a fisherman's hat, a vineyard vines t-shirt, bright red cargo shorts, and crocs.

Penelope managed to make it through the entire explanation without bursting out with her news. She enjoyed these shared moments with Maria, but she was nearly vibrating out of her skin with anticipation.

Maria had been bustling around the kitchen preparing her dinner while she spoke, but as she finished, she turned to face Penelope and seemed to notice her energy for the first time. "Poppy! What's going on? You look like you just ate a canary." All of a sudden, she gasped. "Did you get the blue check mark?"

Penelope snorted, but she couldn't stop a grin from spreading across her face. She didn't give herself time to think that if asked to guess what thing in her life would make her abnormally happy,

Maria's first guess was a work thing. She knew she needed a bit more of a life, but hey! She was working on it now!

"Ugh, not quite, but I'm so fucking close I can nearly taste that stupid little blue checkmark..." Maria gave her a concerned look, and she quickly pivoted. "Anyways... I matched with Riley last night, and we've been texting all evening!"

Maria's concern morphed into downright shock. "And... that's making you smile like that?"

Penelope's grin faltered then. "Wait, okay, why is everyone saying that today? Smile like what?"

Maria hesitated for a moment, then she walked purposefully towards Penelope and dragged her by the arm, through Penelope's bedroom and into her bathroom.

"What are you doing—"

"Okay, tell me what you just told me again," Maria interrupted, looking into the mirror to meet Penelope's eyes in her reflection.

"Uhm... I matched with Riley, and we've been talking all evening?"

"Hm... and how does that make you feel?"

Penelope faltered. "Well... happy, I think? A little skeptical, maybe?"

"You're not giving me much to work with, are you... oh! Okay, I know. Can you pull up his profile?"

It was sad that the finger movements were beginning to become routine, but Penelope was able to open the app and pull up his profile quickly. She was about to hand her phone to Maria when instead, she grabbed Penelope's wrist and lifted the phone in front of Penelope's face.

Penelope looked at the photo of Riley smiling softly into the camera, and she imagined maybe he was at home in his apartment, lounging at his kitchen table, or maybe on the couch texting her.

With a quick jerk, Maria pulled her arm down, and Penelope wasn't looking at her phone. She was looking at her smiling face.

It wasn't a bad smile. It was almost sweet, maybe a little wistful, with a dash of hope. She had to admit she didn't recognize it. She felt a pang of sadness suddenly that she'd let herself give up on finding love for so many years. There was no telling if this thing with Riley would go anywhere, but the fact that she could feel this much excitement meant that maybe it was time for her to get serious about her dating life.

"Oooh, I know this face!" Maria said, wrapping her arm around Penelope's waist. "This is the 'let's do this shit' face, and I am, as always, 100% down for whatever shit you're about to do."

"I just think it's time for me to get more serious about dating. The fact that just texting a new guy is making me feel like... like that," she gestured vaguely at the mirror, "I think it means it's time for me to try and find someone to be with."

Maria smiled softly in the mirror as she nudged Penelope's arm out of the way to give her a full hug. "Well then, what are you waiting for?" She released Penelope and lifted her hand holding her phone back up again.

They left the bathroom and Maria wandered out of Penelope's bedroom and off to her own room. Penelope flopped backwards onto her bed. Her bedroom was small but cozy, filled with baubles, little decorations, and memorabilia. It wasn't messy, per se, more like full of memories and the occasional sweater or pair of jeans flung over a chair. She pushed a stray sock off her pillow and pulled up her messages again. Just as she was typing out her response Riley sent another message.

Riley: Are you going to tell me the cat's name or is suspense part of your strategy to pique my interest?

Riley: Because if it is… it might be working…

She felt a blush ravage her cheeks. She hadn't felt like any of their conversation thus far had been even the slightest bit flirty; it had felt more like texting with Maria or even Frankie. She was pretty awful at text flirting, so she decided to go with blatant honesty. Maybe he would find that endearing?

Penelope: Sorry! I wasn't trying to leave you hanging. My roommate came home and wanted to tell me all about her day.

Riley: And this is roommate, all-time best friend, who calls you Poppy?

Penelope: Precisely! She's awesome, truly the best roommate/best friend I could ask for.

Riley: Tell me about her.

Penelope was a little surprised he would ask about Maria when they barely knew anything about each other, but for some reason, it pleased Penelope even more than if he'd asked her a question about herself. She bit her lip as she quickly typed out her best description of Maria and what it was like being her best friend. She tried to describe how it felt to have someone who could read her every move, predict her needs, and meet them in ways Penelope could never have imagined. Sometimes it was like Maria knew her thoughts before she even had the chance to think them.

Riley admitted that he didn't have any roommates right now, but he said he wouldn't mind roommates if they were as impressive as Maria sounded. Penelope counted that as a point in his favor. He then described his best friend Kim, who he said made him feel the way Penelope described Maria.

> Riley: Your profile said you hope we can bring friends and adventure into each other's lives. Does that mean you and Maria are a package deal?

> Penelope: Oh, we are absolutely a package deal, probably verging on codependency issues. I hope you can handle that.

Penelope groaned to herself. Why was she so blunt over text? That's not something she would have said out loud—or at least she hoped it wasn't. It wasn't that they were codependent. It just could appear that way from the outside. They were each other's support systems, cheerleaders, and tough love experts. They had been through some tough times as individuals and as friends.

Being friends with someone for as long as they had meant there would be growing pains. They'd had their fair share of disagreements, but they never delved into petty fighting the way some of Penelope's other friendships had ended over the years.

It was important to Penelope that Maria got to know someone she was considering as a life partner. Maria would never tell her not to date someone, but Maria's opinion mattered almost as much as her own did. On top of that, sometimes Maria saw things in herself and in others that Penelope either couldn't or chose not to see.

> Riley: I welcome the opportunity and the challenge.
>
> Riley: How long have you two known each other?
>
> Penelope: We've known each other for over seven years.

Well, that was the best response she could have hoped to receive about Maria. Bolstered by this, she pulled up her big girl pants and decided to finally just pull the trigger.

> Penelope: It's a bit of a long story, but maybe I can tell you in person sometime?

She hit send and then immediately regretted it. She frantically tried to see if she could unsend or recall the message and only succeeded in dropping her phone on her face. She let out an undignified little shout, and Maria popped her head into her room.

"Is there another mouse? Because I just let Pogo back up the stairs. Do I need to go get him?"

"No, no mouse... I just told Riley I'd tell him a story in person sometime soon. So... I think I just asked him out on a date?"

"Oh shit! Boys and girls and everyone else, guard your hearts! Poppy is on the loose!" Maria nearly howled the last few words, and Penelope threw a shirt at her. It didn't go very far and was rather unsatisfying, so she reached for a pair of socks and threw them instead. They bounced off Maria's cheek with a satisfying thwomp. That felt better.

"And what did our prince charming say in response?"

"He hasn't responded yet—" Her phone dinged next to her head, where it had landed after assaulting her poor nose. Maria gave her a wide-eyed look and gestured frantically. Penelope had to sit up for this one. She took a deep breath and opened the message thread.

> Riley: I'd really like that, Penelope. But I have a very serious request to make first, and if you can't meet it, I'm not sure if I can agree to see you.

"Oh, shit..." Penelope muttered, her eyebrows knitting together.

"Oh my god, he didn't say no, did he? Give me your fucking phone. I'm going to kill him!" Maria made as if to lunge for the phone and Penelope held her hand in a stop gesture as she watched the typing bubbles appear, disappear, and reappear.

> Riley: Can you please, for the love of god, tell me what the cat's name is?

Penelope burst out laughing and continued laughing until she felt tears prick the corners of her eyes. Maria lost patience with her and snatched her phone away to read the thread. She laughed softly, but when she looked up and made eye contact with Penelope, they both froze, and then they burst out laughing together. Big, robust laughs which sounded like excitement from Maria, and relief and anticipation from Penelope.

Penelope: That is a pretty serious request, sir. I will consider it.

Riley: Oh, how kind of you.

Penelope: Your request has been reviewed, and the company has decided to approve it.

Penelope: Please hold as we gather the correct information to fulfill your inquiry.

She quickly switched to her photo library and scrolled frantically back through two and a half years of photos of her, her and Maria, her and Frankie, and a few of Frankie and Diego she had forgotten she had taken during a vacation they all took the previous summer. She paused quickly to favorite those last ones and send them to Maria for their further investigation.

Finally, she found the photo she was looking for. It was a picture they had taken when they first met Pogo. Penelope was gently holding him up, so he was standing on his one leg and did indeed resemble a pogo stick.

Riley: Excuse me, ma'am. I have waited the appropriate 3-5 business minutes.

Penelope: Sorry, I had to make sure to do this right.

Penelope: Without further ado!

Penelope: His name is Pogo! [photo attached]

Riley: Wow. That's so perfect.

> Riley: I can't believe I'm saying this, but it was worth the wait.

> Penelope: You know, I'd like to believe I am as well.

> Riley: Well... While I'm sure that's true, I don't think I can wait much longer to meet you. How about this Thursday? Want to grab a drink?

Penelope looked up to give Maria the good news, but she had already returned to her bedroom. She tried to suppress her stupid grin, but she couldn't. She was going on her first date in almost eight months and was truly excited about it. They agreed on a time and a place, and they talked a little more, discussing cats, dogs, and childhood pets. Penelope fell asleep in her clothes with her face turned towards the soft light of her phone.

RILEY

Riley had felt so confident about this whole dating thing Monday night. After texting Penelope for over five hours, he was finding that he enjoyed their rapport, and when she hinted that she wanted to meet up, Riley pulled the metaphorical trigger.

By Tuesday morning, though, he was a ball of nerves and wondered if there was some way he could back out without coming off as rude or hurtful. He tried to keep his sister's words in mind throughout Tuesday and Wednesday, reminding himself that the worst thing that could happen would be that she got up and left the bar, and they never spoke again.

That shouldn't seem like such an awful thing to Riley, but

they'd been texting a fair amount, and he thought he might miss Penelope if she got up and walked completely out of his life. Well, it would probably be more accurate to say that Penelope was texting him a lot. She texted about random things happening in her day, funny things Maria said, and the weird antics of Pogo the tripod cat. Riley responded to every message diligently, but he had a more challenging time thinking of things to say to her. There was so much about his life that just seemed mundane and uninteresting, and some of the things that were more interesting about himself he didn't know how to share over text.

As Wednesday afternoon turned into evening, he thought he might feel better if he wasn't alone. He texted Kim and offered to pay for her favorite takeout if she came over with such last-minute notice. She showed up with a bag of pho and fried rice, and she shoved the receipt under his nose as she walked into his kitchen and began pulling out large ramen bowls and chopsticks. He kept them around just for Kim, who refused to eat pho in anything else.

Based on the smell, he could tell she went to the shop right around the corner. They used a unique combination of spices in their broth that Kim said was the closest she could find in the city to her mother's. She ate at other restaurants too, this was just her favorite. She ate pretty much any food except coconut. She had a deep hatred of coconut.

They sat at the kitchen table and slurped their soup, chatting amiably about this and that. Kim never pushed him to talk about anything he wasn't ready to talk about, and he didn't think he was quite prepared to talk about this yet. She took care of the dishes while he wrapped up the extra rice. He would have to make sure she took it home with her. She was always "accidentally" leaving food in his fridge, insisting she didn't need it anyways, and he should just eat it and maybe fatten up a bit.

He had tried to gain weight throughout his life, chasing even a hint of that elusive softness he saw in others, but he had never been successful. He'd tried lifting weights but hated how it made his angular body look even harder, so he just let himself be thin and gangly.

"So, darling, what should we do? Do you want to cuddle on the couch and pretend like you don't have anything important to talk about, or should we lie in bed and I can stare uncomfortably into your eyes until you decide if you feel like sharing tonight?"

She brought out two mugs of hot chocolate for them, and he knew that she meant business. Hot chocolate was his kryptonite; it was his favorite comfort food, happy food, and sad food.

He groaned indignantly. He had understood Penelope when she'd talked about having someone who knew her better than she knew yourself. For him, that was Kim, Ashley, and Johanna.

"I'm sure you know that I'd prefer the first, but—"

"That means we should do the second. Alrighty, come on." She nudged him gently with her elbow as she passed by, and he followed her into his bedroom.

They settled under the covers, mugs in hand, as they'd done hundreds of times before. He wasn't a big fan of spooning, not liking how it made him feel too big or too small depending on the person. Usually, they would curl up with their head on each other's chests and chat quietly, but on days when they had something important to discuss, they would sit side by side, legs tangled under the covers.

"Johanna downloaded a dating app, and I'm going on a date

tomorrow night," he finally burst out, his breath causing ripples on the surface of his cocoa.

Kim's perfectly shaped eyebrows disappeared under her fringe bangs. "Wow, that's big news! Did Johanna set up the date for you...?" she asked, sounding a little skeptical.

"No, uhm... she helped me pick out the photos and write the description, but I've been doing the uh—swiping and texting and stuff. I matched with a woman named Penelope."

"Wow, what a beautiful name!"

"That's what I said!"

"Did you... what did you put on your profile?" she asked cautiously. This was what Riley had wanted to talk about the least, but it was a valid question. "Not that there's anything specific you should or shouldn't put! I was just wondering," Kim added.

Riley smiled softly at her and reached into his back pocket to pull out his phone. He pulled up his profile and handed it to her, shrinking into himself a little as she perused the page.

"Aww, this is a cute profile. I'd have swiped right on you if I was single."

Kim was bi, and currently dating a wonderful woman named River, who was very much like her name. Her energy was soft and gentle and seemed to flow around the room, comforting everyone in its wake. Riley always knew his relationship with Kim, and their cuddly nature, would have to change when she got a partner, but not only was River completely supportive of their friendship, she would often join them on the couch or in bed to cuddle.

"I... know it's pretty vague," he said, placing the phone face down between them.

"That's okay, darling. You don't have to bare your entire self for the whole world—or the whole app to see if you're not comfortable with it. As you start to get to know Penelope for real, and if it seems like you have a real connection, I'm sure you'll open up to her naturally."

"... you think?"

"Yes, Riley. I know you're a very private person, but you opened up to Ashley and me. If Penelope is the right person for you, either romantically or even just as a friend, I'm sure you'll be able to open up to her."

He thought about this for a moment. He'd done virtually no opening up to her yet, and maybe that's why tomorrow felt so momentous and terrifying.

Kim must have felt his body stiffen because she reached up and placed her hand at the nape of his neck. This was one of his favorite places to be touched; it made him feel grounded, warm, and safe. He relaxed almost immediately and let out a sigh. He placed his almost empty mug of cocoa on his nightstand and sank under the covers. Kim followed suit until they were lying face to face.

"Is that why you're so nervous about tomorrow? You feel you have to spill your guts to her, or she won't like you?"

"Well, the last three dates I've gone on in the past four years ended like that. Because I couldn't open up," Riley said sadly.

Kim hummed thoughtfully. "I don't think the first date is the end-all-be-all for that, though. Just be yourself as much as you can and share when it feels appropriate and safe."

He nodded grudgingly. "I suppose I can do that..."

"Now, don't be stubborn. She agreed to go out with you and deserves your full, genuine intention and attention, or you shouldn't go. Do you not want to go?" Her voice was stern and reminded him of Johanna's big-sister voice.

"...No. I... I do want to go," Riley admitted.

"Well, that's settled then. Now! Can I see pictures of her?"

If someone could jump up and down with excitement while lying horizontally, that's what Kim did.

They spent the next fifteen minutes swiping through her photos, and Kim tried to psychoanalyze her description, but Riley just laughed and rolled onto his back. He pulled her to rest with her head on the meatiest part of him, where his shoulder met his torso. They stayed this way for an hour or so, talking about Kim's job as an art curator's assistant at a local gallery, and he asked for updates on River's most recent art project. They'd met when River had taken a class at the gallery on expressing sexuality via watercolors.

Kim told Riley about some of their latest adventures and said they were both doing very well, but she admitted she should probably be getting home.

She hugged him at the door and whispered, "I believe in you. All of you. You can do this. You deserve to be loved."

He hid his face from her as he quietly closed the door behind her.

THREE

Wednesday night was a whirlwind at the cafe, and Penelope found herself dragging Thursday morning. She realized making plans on Thursdays might not be the best strategy for her dating life, but she was committed to bringing her best self.

In an attempt to be fully caffeinated for the day, she walked all the way to Frankie's cafe and cashed in on three free coffees for the three days she hadn't come in that week. Frankie laughed as he filled her order and said he'd give her three coffees daily if she wanted. She kissed his cheek and waved to Diego as she ran outside to catch the bus across the city to work.

She drank her entire first coffee on the way there and put one in the fridge, nursing the second throughout the morning. Thankfully, after her tumultuous Monday, the next two days had been easier, and today was the same. She floated through tasks, letting her mind wander to her date tonight. She'd worn her favorite pair of black skinny jeans, a cute maroon sweater, and a cream-colored silk scarf. She had pierced ears but was too lazy to change out her earrings very often, so she was just wearing her usual cubic zirconia studs and a simple gold chain necklace. In other words, for Penelope, she was trying pretty hard.

By four-thirty, she was nearly vibrating out of her chair from the caffeine and anticipation, so she signed out early and headed to the bar. She wasn't set to meet Riley until five-thirty, but when she arrived at five, she thought a drink would do her some good, so she smiled, nodded at the hostess, and escorted herself to the alcohol.

Penelope had been to this bar only once for a work fundraiser, and she hadn't remembered the place being so elegant. She suddenly felt a little underdressed, but when she looked down at herself, she realized that the dim golden lighting was pretty flattering, and she looked quite nice. The room was filled with rich mahogany furniture and black and gold accent decorations. The bar itself was completely backlit, shining through the multicolored bottles of alcohol to cast a mosaic of colors across the back of the room.

A handful of people were already sitting on bar stools, so she slid into one of the only available seats and flagged down the bartender. She ordered a rum and coke, hoping the sugar would somehow calm her nerves, no matter how counterintuitive that might be. She was about to pull out her phone to fiddle away at nothing when a soft voice called her name.

She turned to look at the man sitting to her left and found he looked quite familiar. His sharp features were somehow muted in the bar light, but his eyes were still a striking green. His hair looked darker in this light than in his photos, but she could still catch little sparkles of blonde.

"Oh! Riley! You're—early!" she stuttered out, stumbling and tripping over every syllable, nearly shouting at the poor man.

"I am. I'm sorry. I was... a little nervous about being late and getting lost, so I thought I'd get her early and get a drink and relax."

She noticed then that he was wearing a crisp V-neck sweater over a button-down, on top of dark slacks. He looked much more put together than she felt, and she hoped her blush wasn't too visible.

On top of how nicely dressed he was, Penelope realized with a sinking feeling that his photos didn't do him justice. He was stunning, all long-limbed and slender. He reminded her of the elegant crane that sometimes frequented their local park.

"Oh no, please don't apologize. I was just plain nervous, so I thought I'd also get a drink and try to be less nervous, but that has clearly backfired. I mean—not that I'm not excited to see you, because I totally am, I just... you know... wasn't ready to do the whole talking thing. Except like. To myself. In my head."

Penelope knew she was rambling, and the bartender thankfully came to her rescue, sliding over her drink which she immediately brought to her lips so she wouldn't be tempted to speak again.

"Would you... I mean... would it be weird if we just took a few more moments to ourselves? I know we weren't supposed to meet until five thirty, so maybe we just take the next twenty minutes like we had both intended? I have to admit... I wasn't quite ready to socialize either."

Penelope noticed an endearing blush creep across his cheeks, which didn't bode well for the visibility of her own burning cheeks.

On Riley it was kind of cute, though. It helped release some of her tightly wound muscles.

"I don't think that would be weird at all. In fact, that would be kind of perfect. I think I only need ten minutes to get myself together, but I'm happy to give you twenty?"

"Ten it is," he said gently, raising his glass to her and then purposefully tilting his stool away from hers.

She settled into her seat and pulled out her phone to subtly check out her hair. She'd been planning to escape to the bathroom to do some last-minute primping right before their date, but she had been outwitted by their combined anxieties.

She smiled a little at that. It was nice to know she wasn't the only one not coming into this with the utmost level of grace and confidence. Although, come to think of it, Riley looked amazing sitting there, not a hair or fiber out of place. He had said he'd been nervous, but he didn't look it.

Penelope felt her spine begin to stiffen again as she wondered if maybe he was just pretending to be nervous so she wouldn't feel as bad for being so clearly frazzled.

Just as she was starting to really freak out, she felt her phone vibrate, and she thanked every deity she could think of that the sound was off in case it was that incriminating text tone again.

She flicked open the app and saw it was indeed a new message, but her heart skipped a beat when she saw it was from Riley.

> Riley: You look beautiful, by the way.
> Sorry, I should have said that before
> anything else.

Riley: Also, I guess I shouldn't be saying it over a message before saying it out loud to you. I'm clearly still pretty nervous...

Riley: I just thought you should know.

Penelope glanced over at his stiff back, his fingers tight around his glass as he stared down at his own phone. She melted a little like an ice cube in the summertime and quickly messaged back.

Penelope: Thank you, that's so sweet of you to say. You look amazing, too, by the way. Straight from work?

Riley: Yes, and to be honest, I even left early. I hate being late, but I also seem to be incapable of not getting lost. I tend to be an hour early or twenty minutes late without fail. Obviously, it didn't serve me well today.

Penelope: Oh, I wouldn't say that.

Penelope: This is the most unique start to a first date I've ever had. I don't think I've ever sat next to someone and texted them at a bar before. It's strangely nice. Like we really are just having a drink in our own little worlds, getting ready for our date.

Penelope took a longer sip off her drink and glanced at him again. The lean lines of his back had softened some, rounding out his shoulders as he tipped his own glass up to his mouth to drink. She watched as the amber liquid slid between his slightly parted lips, and she had to look back at her phone or risk reigniting her blush.

> Penelope: I think I might have moved on from nervous to excited. How about you?

Riley: I think I have as well.

Riley: Can I ask you for a favor? Would you mind playing along?

> Penelope: Sure, playing along with what?

Penelope felt a gentle hand on her arm and looked up to see Riley standing there, drink in hand, phone tucked away somewhere hidden from her view. He was grinning sweetly, and his eyes seemed to sparkle with a hint of mischief.

"Hi there. You must be Penelope? I'm Riley. I'm very excited to meet you."

Before she could stop herself, she released the full force of *that* smile on him. Everyone had mentioned the smile all week long. Even Diego had noticed it the night before.

Riley's eyes widened, and his smile grew as well. "Wow, you... have an amazing smile. Your pictures don't do it justice at all."

Penelope was grinning so hard she felt like a total idiot. So, naturally, she decided to blurt out the first thought that popped into her head. "Your pictures don't do you justice either. You're absolutely gorgeous."

His smile faltered for a second and then returned, but smaller.

"I'm sorry! Is... that too feminine a compliment? I know not all guys like that. I'm sorry..." she trailed off. As if an invisible thread linked their sudden anxiety, they both simultaneously bit their lips.

"No, no, it's... it's fine. It's nice actually, I—I've just never been called that before," he admitted shyly.

Penelope thought that that was a damn shame because it was true.

"Would you... like to grab a table? It's starting to get a little loud," he said, looking out around the bar.

Penelope had barely noticed, but while they'd been texting and chatting, the bar had begun filling up. They returned to the hostess stand and were seated at a high-top table against the front windows a few moments later.

Penelope unwound her scarf and laid it on the back of her chair with her jacket, and Riley rolled up the sleeves of his sweater and shirt. This revealed slim arms with the lightest smattering of blonde hair across them, and Penelope had to force herself not to stare. Jeez, it had been a long time since she'd been with a partner. Getting hot and bothered over forearms.

Their server arrived a moment later with glasses of water for them both and asked if she could get them each another drink, which they both eagerly agreed to. They asked for a few extra minutes with the menu to look at the food, and when the server left, they bent their heads over the single menu in the middle of the table. Penelope noticed the soft scent of cinnamon and something else wafting off Riley. Maybe vanilla? It was a little muskier than vanilla, though, almost as if he had applied something vanilla to himself, but his natural pheromones had turned it a little darker, a little spicier. This, too, was highly distracting for Penelope, so she pointed to the first appetizer she saw, which turned out to be soft pretzels. They went back and forth on the second appetizer to order and settled on flatbread.

They chatted about work, and Penelope learned that he worked for an investment firm which explained why he was dressed more formally. Their server returned and took their order, and at the last second, Riley sheepishly added a lava cake to their order, admitting he sometimes had a wicked sweet tooth. Penelope laughed loudly and admitted she was the same way, and they smiled at each other.

As they continued chatting, something in Riley's body changed, almost like a heaviness had returned after their sweet moment at the bar. Maybe after she'd blurted out that she thought he was gorgeous?

As if reading her mind, Riley cleared his throat.

"So... at the bar, something you said reminded me... I was wondering if I could clear something up? I've been feeling weird about it for days now..."

Penelope blinked at him in surprise. "Sure, what's up?"

"When I said over text... that I don't go by my first name because it's too feminine, that's not entirely what I meant." He gulped his drink and stared down into the glass for a moment.

"It's not that I don't like it—actually, I do like it, but... even though my parents technically chose it together, my mom was the one who pushed for it, and it turns out my dad always thought it was too feminine. That's why he chose Riley for my middle name. I guess he just always wanted me to go by Riley." He cleared his throat again, looking out the window and across the street. "He made it very clear he thought my first name was no name for a real boy and wouldn't call me anything but Riley even... even today if I ask to be addressed by something else, he refuses. So, I've settled into Riley even if it doesn't always... fit."

Penelope looked at him in shock. "Would you like me to call you by your first name? Or something else entirely?"

He grimaced and kept looking out the window. "No—I don't know... If I completely change my name, it's almost like I'm changing myself. I feel like Riley is part of who I am now, even if it still doesn't always feel right. I don't know if I'm ready to be someone else entirely, though."

Penelope could understand that feeling. When she was with other people, she often felt like she was a slightly different person depending on who she was with. It was actually why she loved to let people give her nicknames. It helped her settle into the person she was with them and only them.

When she was completely alone, she felt her most Penelope, but it wasn't as if she lost herself when she was with others. Instead, it was like she got to flex herself and be different things for different people. A support system, a sister, a daughter, a friend, and hopefully, one day soon, a lover and a partner. Riley was dealing with something different, though. The outside world was trying to define him, and he was clearly chafing under that definition.

"Well... I'm really sorry that your dad doesn't respect your wishes. You just let me know if you ever change your mind, okay? I'm happy to flip names whenever you want, or even if you want to go back and forth between names, that's all fine with me."

He finally turned back to look at her and gave her a quizzical look. When she just returned the gaze steadily, he finally nodded gratefully. Their food arrived a few moments later, and Riley changed the subject, asking about her hobbies, which included calligraphy and collecting old pens, and their conversation flowed smoothly from there.

Riley was a very attentive listener and an engaged conversation partner, so there weren't any awkward pauses or fumbled silences. However, Penelope slowly began to realize that almost all of the conversation was focused on her. Riley was just asking questions and probing for details with her stories. Most people she knew would interject with their own stories or relate to something in their own life, but Riley didn't seem to do that. It was like his entire focus was on her, and while it was pretty flattering, she didn't feel like she was getting to know him any better.

She tried to get more information from him on hobbies and things he liked to do, but he admitted he didn't have many hobbies aside from watching some pretty trashy television.

The flow of the conversation finally changed when, with some prodding from him, she told the full story of how she and Maria had met. Riley had laughed and engaged fully with her story, but when she finished, he hesitated for a long moment, taking a slow, measured bite of the flatbread.

When he lowered the other half back to his plate, he immediately brought a napkin to his mouth and patted it thoughtfully as if he was about to make a big decision.

He finally locked eyes with her and admitted, "That's actually how I met my two best female friends as well. I dated one of them and hooked up with the other, but both ended up as best friends instead."

Penelope wasn't going to give up an opportunity like this to better get to know him, so she asked a few follow-up questions until he finally relented. He told her a few scant details about their dates and hookups but went into deep details about the women and their eventual friendships.

Penelope found she actually learned a lot about him from how he described Ashley and Kim. He clearly wanted to be seen and understood, and he seemed to value kindness and empathy above all else. He looked very uncomfortable as he admitted they had been two of just a small handful of relationships he'd had in adulthood, and he looked a little ashamed when he said none of them had gone well.

She admitted her past relationships hadn't been much better. She told him a funny story about a guy she met at a bar who had accidentally set up two dates at once, and when the other girl arrived halfway through their date, he had run, pumping arms and all, out of the bar. Penelope and the other girl had a lovely chat, ordered a few drinks on his tab, and went their separate ways.

Riley seemed to lighten a little as she spoke, the shape of his shoulders changing to softer slopes but not the peaceful, relaxed valleys she was hoping for.

"Also," she said suddenly, "I don't think your hookups and dates with Kim and Ashley were failures. Even though you couldn't connect in one way, you did in another. And now you'll be in each other's lives forever, as opposed to if you tried to force the relationship and ended up not being able to stay friends after that. I know Maria and I are a little different because she wasn't sexually interested in me *at all* but... still. I feel like those are still two very successful relationships!"

He gave her a funny look out of the corner of his eye as he delicately placed the last piece of his flatbread in his mouth.

She felt her stomach drop as she realized something. "Is this story your way of friend zoning me? Because I have to be honest, it wouldn't be the worst way someone has gone about it. Your friends clearly adore you, so you must be a pretty good friend to have. So... if that's how things end up happening between us, I guess it wouldn't be that bad?

Riley nearly choked on his drink. "No I... I just... well..." He fiddled with the end of a pretzel.

They had eaten their food in reverse order, devouring the lava cake, then moving on to the flatbread and ending with the pretzels.

The server had brought their check, but neither of them had made a move for it yet.

"Okay, I guess... maybe I wanted you to know it was an option. In case you decide I'm not right for you after today, but... if you still wanted to be friends, I—I would like that."

She smiled softly over at him and hesitantly reached across the table to touch two fingers to the hand still playing with the pretzel. He stilled immediately but didn't retract his hand. She noted briefly that his skin was soft and almost the same temperature as hers. Sparks didn't fly from where their skin touched because this wasn't fanfiction or a fairytale. This was just two slightly awkward people getting to know each other.

While deep down, she thought she might be starting to like this particular awkward person, for some reason, she wasn't ready to admit that yet.

"I don't think I've decided one way or another about whether we're right for each other but thank you."

He was staring at her fingers, so she slowly withdrew her hand, and his eyes followed her back across the table, slowly coming up to meet her own. She gave him what she hoped was a comforting smile. He still looked a little reticent, so she chanced saying a little more.

"That is great to know, though. If we don't end up being right for each other, I think I would very much like to stay friends and, if nothing else, that will have made this whole 'taking a shot at dating again' thing worth it," she concluded.

Suddenly she saw that sparkle in his eyes again. It reminded her of that silly smile she'd seen in the mirror, excitement sprinkled with a bit of hope. "Does... that mean you would want to do this again? You can decide if you want it to be a date or not a date, but... I think I'd be pretty happy with either."

He wasn't like anyone Penelope had ever met before. He seemed to be a rather private person. While she was an open book, he was like a scavenger hunt. She felt like she had to find one clue just to be able to know where to start looking for the next. At the same time, though, he would randomly open up to her and admit big things before withdrawing back into his turtle shell.

She knew without a shadow of a doubt she wanted to keep hanging out with him and keep getting to know him, but a small voice in the back of her mind wasn't sure if they were in fact a good match. They both seemed to have some anxiety, and she wasn't sure if what Riley needed was someone who could gently help him open up. She was not a notoriously gentle person. She tended to bumble her way through conversations and relationships. She sometimes hit others' exposed nerves in conversations and sometimes stepped right into one of her own emotional sinkholes, as if forgetting they were there in the first place.

"Not that I think I'll need long to make the decision, but do you think I could get back to you on what the hangout should be?" Penelope hedged, hoping to buy herself a little more thinking time.

He nodded, and she could tell by the tightening in his shoulders he was about to look away again, so she quickly blurted out, "Sorry, I should have said first—yes! Absolutely yes, let's do this again really soon, okay? But... I don't want to give you a knee-jerk reaction now on whether I think it should be a date or not a date, and then feel different tomorrow or the next day and have to take it back."

Riley gave a short laugh that was barely more than an exhalation of breath, but at least the distance between his ears and shoulders increased again. "I completely understand feeling different from day to day. Take as long as you need; I'm happy to follow your lead."

"And... you don't have a strong opinion one way or another?" she pressed.

He contemplated her question for a second, and when he spoke, his words came out slowly like he was choosing them very carefully. "I do not have a strong sense of whether or not I am what you are looking for. But... I do know I would like to see you again."

They hadn't talked much about what they were looking for in a partner, and by "much" she meant at all. Aside from their initial compliments, it was more like they had been playing twenty questions, just trying to get to know each other as individuals before getting to know each other as potential partners. Perhaps this was because neither of them were particularly experienced at dating. Maybe that would be what their second date could focus on.

She saw the server walking towards them in her peripheral vision and realized she only had a few moments to make her signature move. Penelope didn't mind it when men, or women, paid for their dates if they were the ones who did most of the talking. While Penelope was a pretty avid talker, in the past, she often seemed to get bowled over on dates, and so she had started a practice of only fighting for the bill when she felt adequately involved in the date. This date had been different, though.

"I have plans this weekend, but... how does Tuesday sound? I'll get back to you on details by Sunday?" Penelope asked, drawing out her words a little.

While Riley was distracted listening to her question, Penelope reached forward and snatched up the bill. He looked slightly alarmed as she did a quick behind-the-back maneuver to hand the bill and her card to the waitress as she passed by.

"That... was... very impressive, but completely unnecessary. At the very least, we could have split it, but I would have been happy to—"

Penelope placed her hand on top of his again, and he clamped his mouth shut.

"I got it, Riley. I feel like I did a lot of the talking today, and you made me feel really... heard the entire time. I like to split dates where I feel like I was an active participant, but I feel like today was mostly focused on me. Maybe we can shift the focus to you next time, and then you'll get to pay." She winked at him, and he gave her a perplexed look.

"But... while I do not mind paying, that doesn't sound like a good incentive to get me to talk more. So, what's the motivation in it for me?"

Penelope smirked at him. "Well, I feel you're like me and might feel guilty when other people pay for you. So, I think it will bother you until you decide to do something about it and make sure you get to pay one of these days."

Riley's eyes widened, and he looked a little impressed. After she got her card back, they walked to the front door together.

There was an awkward moment where they weren't sure if they should hug or kiss or maybe awkwardly shake hands until one of them fell into a sinkhole of embarrassment. Okay, perhaps it was only Penelope who was worried about the sinkhole. She was a hugger, but she'd noticed Riley's hesitation with touch and didn't want to pressure him or risk doing the wrong thing.

"I... like hugs? But only if you like hugs," she fumbled out.

To her surprise, Riley smirked at her. "So... if I say I don't like hugs, then suddenly you won't like hugs anymore?"

She scoffed. "Riley, nothing on this planet would convince me not to like hugs. I meant we don't have to if you don't want to."

His smile softened. "Noted... A hug would be great."

She went for a more casual hug, wrapping her arms around the middle of his back instead of behind his neck. She leaned forward slightly, curving her shoulders forward, so her cheek pressed against his shoulder, but there was a solid amount of room between their stomach and hips. He wrapped his arms around her shoulders and also kept the rest of his body away from hers.

She was momentarily surprised at how solid his chest and shoulders felt, despite how thin he was. She could feel the slight shift of muscles in his back under her fingers and felt the obvious tendons in his forearms around her shoulders.

It was a shockingly nice hug, given that it was sort of only half a hug. She found herself not wanting to let go, but she thought it would be best if she didn't make him step away first. After one more moment savoring the feeling, she managed to pry herself away from him.

"I'll see you Tuesday, Riley," she called as she turned and headed home.

RILEY

Riley would feel that hug for the rest of the week and into the weekend. It wasn't like he was starved for touch, but her hug had just felt different somehow.

He ended up having another cuddle session on Saturday with Kim; this time, River and Ashley joined as well. Ashley and Kim knew each other only through their friendships with Riley. They had very little in common, but they had become best friends through their connection and love for Riley.

Ashley was straight, and her most recent boy, Asher, was unanimously not invited to the cuddle puddle. Ashley didn't seem to mind, though, preferring to keep her romantic life separate from the rest of her life. This was the complete opposite of Kim, who would only date someone if they could seamlessly integrate with her friends.

Where Kim was soft but firm with Riley, Ashley was brash and pushy. However, she would easily back off if told to, whereas Kim would hold steady, like a rock in a stream, refusing to yield until Riley bent to her will or completely maneuvered around her.

Penelope had been right about his relationships with them. He and Ashley had nearly messed things up by trying to stay together longer than they should have. Riley figured out pretty quickly that they weren't right for each other, but Ashley had kept pushing until Riley nearly broke. Finally, he opened up to her about why he didn't think they were right for each other, and she immediately backed off and did an impeccable job of friend-zoning herself. In the end, she fully agreed they weren't right for each other, and they became lifelong friends, just as Penelope had asserted.

He had been worried that Penelope would learn just a few things about him and run screaming. Instead, she seemed to latch onto every morsel he gave her, sinking her teeth in, refusing to let go until she had learned everything there was to know about that flavor of Riley. Unfortunately, now Riley had a new fear developing. He was now worried she would figure things out about him faster than he could come to terms with admitting them to her.

As he fretted about this, he rested his head in Kim's lap while his legs rested in Ashley's. River sat on the floor at Kim's feet, gently rolling Riley's left wrist. Her slightly calloused ebony fingers were working out tension Riley didn't even know he carried in his hands. She always claimed her impeccable massage skills were just a product of her time at the easel, paintbrush in hand, but it was more than that. River seemed to have a knack for pinpointing stress points in people's bodies and helping them work to relieve them. A few weeks ago, she had spent nearly two hours teaching them all how to release tension in their ankles.

"I'm sorry you're feeling so down today, darling. Is there anything we can do besides hold you and stuff cookies in your mouth?" Kim asked.

Ah yes. That was why they were all here. Riley had sent a panicked message to the group saying he was having an off day. At first, they'd asked if he was having a "not-Riley" day, as he sometimes called them in his head. Sometimes, Riley would wake up, and he didn't feel like himself, like he was someone else entirely, someone he was only just beginning to get to know.

Today, he was very much Riley. A very much depressed Riley.

He'd suffered from anxiety and depression since he was a child. He hadn't known what they were until he was sitting in his freshman elective psychology class in college and several pages of the DSM felt a little too close for comfort. He had gone to the free school counselor a few times and had been officially diagnosed with both. He wasn't interested in medicine or therapy, or more accurately, he wasn't ready for treatment, so he had just tucked diagnosis away and ignored it.

He reasoned that his anxiety was low, and he could function pretty well with his few coping mechanisms. The depression, however, was different. There were days when he couldn't get out of bed, shower, or feed himself. They were rare, and when they did hit, he tended to drop pretty low for a day, recover the next day and move on like nothing had happened the day after that.

Because of this, it was hard for him to convince himself to find a therapist. When he was depressed, he was incapable of the executive functioning needed to find, investigate, call, and schedule a first appointment. Then when he was better, he didn't feel the need to see a therapist anymore. He knew it was a vicious cycle, and he promised himself he'd get help every time he felt like this. The problem was that he knew a therapist would want to talk about things he just didn't want to talk about yet. Or possibly ever.

He knew he couldn't be a functioning partner or friend when he was like this, though. Meeting Penelope had made him realize that, even if their relationship just ended in friendship, he wanted to be better. Not *for* her, but maybe a little bit *because* of her. He had felt something when he saw her standing at that bar and then when she'd given him the space to sit in his own mind for a few minutes and had even entertained his rambling text messages while they sat less than a foot apart. He had felt seen and accepted by a virtual stranger, and it had sparked a hope in him he hadn't felt since he was a small child. Back then, he had thought everyone would always love and accept him the way his family did. The problem was that his family, really just his father, hadn't loved and accepted him for very long.

He felt himself spiraling too deep down that road of thought, so he forced himself to blink up at Kim. She was currently stroking her fingers through his long hair while reaching for the box of cookies she had brought.

Sometimes he wondered why he never agreed to move in with her. She also had a two-bedroom apartment all to herself. While she was currently using the second bedroom as a part plant sanctuary, part yoga studio, part office, she insisted she would be happy to make room for Riley. The problem was that he didn't want her to make room for him in her house or her life. Kim wanted to get married one day and have children, and it would be hard to do that with Riley uselessly hanging around. He liked the tiny corner of her life that he occupied now, which would have to be good enough for him.

Ashley had also offered him a room in her apartment. She lived in a sprawling apartment she had inherited from her late uncle. The flat was situated above the bar she owned, which had been her father's, and when he'd died, he'd left his share to Ashley. She worked at the bar with him until he too unfortunately passed away two years ago and left her the flat and the bar. Her Uncle had taken impeccable care of both, and Ashley had made it her mission to keep the bar running, which meant she needed a lot of staff. Sometimes her staff would fall down on their luck, and Ashley would be there to pick them back up. She had sparsely furnished the apartment just enough to turn it into a crash pad for anywhere from two to six other bartenders at a time.

Behind her gruff exterior, she had a heart of gold, and Riley found himself loving her a little more each day because of it. All this aside, there was no chance he could handle the chaos of having an ever-changing cast of roommates, so he had pretty much settled on living alone.

"No... you ladies, just being here is all I could ask for... thank you..." Riley sighed.

He closed his eyes again and let himself sink into their warmth, soft touches, and sweet smells. There was some sitcom playing on the TV Kim had insisted she wanted to watch, but Riley had a sneaking suspicion it was just on to give Riley some cover from the silence. That was the most challenging part for him when he was depressed and living alone—the cold and the silence.

Thankfully there was none of that in his apartment tonight. They all slept over, crashing on his bed in a puddle of cuddles. He woke up the next day feeling a little better, and after Ashley made them all a greasy breakfast with extra coffee, he was feeling even better. The final piece slotted into place when he got a message from Penelope.

Everyone in the room glanced over as his phone made the now familiar chime. Riley felt like he was becoming Pavlov's dog, his heart skipping a beat anytime he heard that sound. He had gone back through his other matches, and after briefly considering each, he'd decided he could only pursue one relationship at a time. Even if it amounted to nothing, he wanted to give it his all, so he'd deleted the other matches and had stopped swiping altogether.

He opened Penelope's thread and read the message.

Penelope: I've decided our date is going to be doing something super fun, and I'm going to come prepared with a list of questions so I can get my money's worth out of you.

The following message was just an address, but Riley had to take a moment to catch his breath. She had called it a date and wanted to ask him questions. The first part made his heart soar, but the second part made him feel like it was not just soaring but flying. Right off a cliff.

For some reason, though, it seemed to help him shake off the remnants of the depression. He had something exciting happening this week; even if it filled him with equal parts anticipation and dread, it was at least something to do.

He wondered if his low-level excitement was a step in a new direction or at least an admission that he was giving this a real shot.

Having all of his friends here, surrounding him with love and acceptance, made him itchy to see if there was someone else out there who could also learn to love him. Maybe that person could be Penelope?

His friends seemed to read his mood change, and they put on one of their favorite Japanese game shows and reconvened on the couch. They sprawled across each other to laugh, yell, and throw popcorn at the TV as their chosen contestants tripped, slipped, and folded their way to victory. He was feeling so much better that he forgot about his fear over the impending questions and failed to look up the address she had sent him.

FOUR

PENELOPE

Penelope was glad she had chosen Tuesday for their date because early Tuesday morning, she got a text from Frankie asking her to work a full shift the next night, as well as warning her that Diego had a huge favor to ask of her, that she could *"totally turn down, but I just wanted to warn you, so you'd be prepared."*

Penelope had a soft spot in her heart for Diego and an even softer spot for her brother, so there was a very high probability she would agree to whatever they asked. If that meant she ended up sorting inventory until two in the morning or staying up until four to receive the newest shipment of whatever new ingredient Frankie had ordered for their new menu, then so be it.

None of that mattered now, though, and Penelope was genuinely excited as she got off the bus for their date. She walked the half a block to the venue and found a perplexed looking Riley standing at the front door.

"I thought when you said you wanted to get your money's worth out of me, you meant it was going to be an expensive place?"

They both turned and looked up at the huge arcade bar that spanned an entire city block in the northern part of the city. "Uhm, you've never seen me play arcade games. You're going to need to cash in an entire paycheck to supply me with enough quarters to be satisfied."

She was waiting for him to make some kind of joke with the word satisfied, but instead he surprised her by saying softly, "I've never actually been to an arcade... I've always wanted to go."

She felt her heart melt a little, and she reached forward and grabbed his hand, pulling him into the bar behind her.

Penelope had been right in her earlier assessment. It hadn't taken her long to conclude that she wanted a second date. She had made up her mind before she had even gotten the chance to do a postmortem on the first date with Maria. Her decision was solidified as she described the date and her wish to get to know him, his interests, and his desires better. She figured that wasn't something she would want from someone she just wanted to be friends with. So, Penelope decided to ask for a second date. If she could dig just a tiny bit deeper into Riley, find out what he was looking for in a partner and see if there was any chance she could be that for him, she thought the date would have been worth it and would probably even warrant a third date.

They got in line to order drinks and convert their money into quarters, and she felt a small thrill that Riley hadn't removed his hand from hers.

"So... if I understood you correctly... If I talked for most of this date and hogged most of the conversation, then I would pay for the date. But we're about to decide who's paying for the date before we've even started talking."

Penelope had already thought this through. "That's true. So! I've thought of a new system!"

Riley gave her a skeptical look but kept in step with her as they moved up a spot in line.

"Whoever wins each arcade game gets to ask the other person a question, and they have to answer it to the best of their abilities. The person who won can also answer the question, but it's up to them. I think this should make it easier for us to take turns being the focus off the conversation."

"Okay, but what about-"

"Oh, and since it was my idea, I'll pay!" she said, whipping out her credit card and shoving it into the machine as they stepped up to the counter.

"... I'm starting to think you just want to pay for everything and are making up rules to accomplish that," Riley grumbled under his breath, but he spoke up to order himself a drink anyways.

Penelope ordered her own drink and requested $5 worth of quarters to start.

They took their drinks and bucket of quarters, and Penelope led them to the corner of the arcade. "Okay, so this is one of my favorite games—"

"Wait..." Riley said, pulling her to a stop with their linked hand. "You've been here before, haven't you. This feels like cheating. Does that mean you're going to win every game?"

Penelope laughed and squeezed his hand. He squeezed back, but if a touch could be skeptical, his was.

"If you'll let me finish!" she said while laughing and throwing back a big gulp of her drink. "This is my favorite game, even though I'm atrocious at it."

Riley squinted at the game as if trying to piece together if she was lying or not. She wasn't. The game was blaster-style, and she had terrible hand-eye coordination when it came to video games. She loved it though because it was very physical. To do even remotely well, she had to jump up and down, duck, and move back and forth to avoid getting shot by the enemy, aka her partner.

They took their places in front of the game. Unfortunately, they had to unlink their hands to do so.

Riley wasn't good by any stretch of the imagination. He admitted halfway into the game that he didn't like violent video games, so while he was totally fine playing this with her now, he was probably worse than she was. That was true all the way up until the end when she jumped to the left when she should have jumped to the right and ended up blowing herself up on her own land mine. She could barely breathe, she was laughing so hard, and even Riley began to chuckle after a few moments of watching her antics.

"Alright, sir, what is your question?" she asked as she led them to a high-top table, plopping down their quarters and taking a big sip of her drink.

"What are you looking for in a partner?" he asked, not missing a beat.

Penelope nearly spit her drink all over him. "Shit, Riley. Really coming out of the gates strong. Damn."

He gave her a look that was far too knowing. "Tell me with one hundred percent honesty that it wasn't going to be your first question."

"Oooh, too bad, you were close. It was going to be my second."

76

Riley laughed. "Really? Darn, I was going to offer to answer the question too since I thought it would save you your first question, but I guess now we'll just have to wait until you can beat me twice to get my answer."

He smirked over the edge of his drink at her, and she couldn't help but respond in kind, smiling back over the top of her glass. Something had changed in him since their last date. She couldn't put her finger on it, but he seemed just a little more confident in his own skin. He wasn't flirting, so much as lightly teasing, but it made her chest tingle all the same.

"Don't threaten me with a good time, Riley. I'm more than happy to beat the crap out of you two times in a row just out of principle."

Riley laughed but said nothing else, staring meaningfully at her. She had prepared for this question, planning to answer it herself when she asked it as her second question.

"I'm looking for someone who I can form a life with. Not their life or my life but a new life, where we take everything that makes us *us*: our friends, family, apartments, hopes, dreams, and just... put them in a big shaker bottle and shake," she mimed roughly shaking a shaker bottle and Riley smirked at her, "then we pour it all out and see what goes well together with the future we see for ourselves."

He tilted his head at her in thought. "Can you... say more about the kind of person you think would be able to do that with you?"

"Well... I guess they would have to be open to change, able to learn and grow on their own and with me. I think they would need to be kind, to fit in with my friends, a little adventurous to fit into my future travel plans, and willing to love and be loved by my family—well, mostly my brother, but also the family we would form together."

He tapped his fingers on the table as if in thought, squinting at her over the top of his cup.

"You... talked about your future, friends, and family, but... what about just you, Penelope. What would make a person perfect for just you?" he asked.

She took a small drink, letting the fizzy liquid sit on her tongue, cold from the ice but with a burn from the alcohol. "I think it's not about being perfect for me. It's more... being able to accept me even though I'm not perfect and me being able to accept them even though they're not either. Because no one is, and I don't think I'd even want perfect if I could get it. I don't want to feel embarrassed for having a panic attack because they've never experienced a moment of anxiety. I don't want to feel ashamed if I have a bad day, and I don't want to feel unlovable if I fuck up sometimes. I also don't ever want to be made to feel like a burden. I'm not incredibly high maintenance, but I have needs and desires, and some of them are non-negotiable."

Riley raised his eyebrows but said nothing, gently reaching across the table to take her hand in his again. They stood in silence for a moment before Riley slowly began to speak. "I think I'm looking for something similar to that last point you made... I mean, I resonate with a lot of what you said, but I have... a lot of needs, and quirks and—... well, while I think I *am* a little high maintenance and sometimes I *do* feel like a burden, I don't think I could handle someone else making me feel that way. I have anxiety and—uh, depression, and I think it can be hard to be around me sometimes. I used to think everything about me that makes me who I am totaled up into this person who was..." he stopped and looked away, eyes landing on one of the racing games in the opposite corner.

His hand seemed to tighten unconsciously around Penelope's,

and she changed the configuration of their fingers so she could better squeeze his hand back. When he didn't finish his thought, Penelope very gently began stroking her thumb over the back of his hand. His breath caught at the movement, but he still didn't say anything for another moment. Penelope wasn't always good at being patient, but she had a feeling she needed to wait this one out.

Finally, his eyes came back to meet hers, and he said, "For a long time, I thought I was unlovable. I don't think there's any point in being with someone who makes me feel like that again. And... if that means there isn't anyone out there for me, then so be it."

Penelope felt her own breath catch, and she had to take a moment to process her thoughts. "And... just to clarify. You don't feel that way anymore?" Penelope asked softly, stepping around the last part of his admission. Penelope couldn't promise someone was out there for him, especially if it wasn't her, so she wanted to let him be honest about his feelings without trying to comfort or cajole him.

"Well... I don't think I would be here if I did."

His gaze was steady on her in a way that should have intimidated her, but for some reason, it didn't. She stared back at him, and that's how she noticed something very subtle shift in his eyes.

"That... being said. Just because I don't think that I myself, as a whole person, am unlovable... there are parts of me I love but think others will struggle to accept, and there are parts of me that even I still struggle to accept, and I think there are even parts of me that I might hate... So, I can stand here and tell you that I—" he stopped talking for a second, and Penelope saw his throat bob a couple of times as he tried to swallow.

She glanced down and noticed that his glass was empty, so she nudged her own over to him. He gave her a grateful smile and lifted her glass to his lips.

He cleared his throat and finished his thought slowly, holding some of the words in his mouth longer as if he wanted to make sure their shape felt true. "I can tell you that... I think I am worthy of—of love. But it can still feel almost impossible to show others some of those parts of myself that... maybe I'm worried they won't or shouldn't love."

He brought her glass back to his lips, and for a moment, she wondered if in her passing him her drink, maybe the glass had shifted, and his lips were touching the place hers had. Like they were sharing a secret kiss.

"Thank you for sharing that with me, Riley. I have only known you for a short time, but I can promise you that you are absolutely worthy of love."

She still wasn't sure if that love was going to turn out to be hers, but with every explanation and every admission, she found herself more and more interested in finding out.

A slow smile started in his eyes and spread to his lips and into the way he held his head up and took his next deep breath. "I think... it's my turn to get the next round. Did you want to pick out the next game for us?"

"Oh, honey, I have the next twenty games picked out for us, don't you worry," Penelope said, flashing him a big grin.

Riley laughed over his shoulder at her as he made a beeline for the bar to grab their next round of drinks. Penelope really couldn't afford to get wasted tonight, but he had drunk almost half of her drink so she figured she could do one, possibly two more, especially if they stayed long enough to get some food.

They played the racing game Riley had been staring at before, and she won with flying colors. She asked him if he had any siblings. He blanched and immediately apologized for not having told Penelope about his sister Johanna sooner. He filled up their next two games with stories of her, and Penelope refused to implement the question rule while he was being so forthcoming with information.

She kept count in her head that they had each won one game each, and as they settled into their third game, he snapped his mouth closed with a soft blush. "I'm so sorry. I'm doing that thing that makes you let others pay for your dates, aren't I."

She laughed as she placed her hand on the joystick of the Mr. Pacman machine. "It is so totally fine, Riley. I like listening to your stories, so I changed the rules for you. I bet you could probably write a biography about Maria at this point from how much I've talked and texted about her."

She stuck her tongue out in concentration as she began abusing the joystick and buttons. She could see Riley watching her out of the corner of her eye, but she was feeling competitive now, so she didn't turn to meet his gaze. "You won the game before last. Do you have a question?" she asked, not breaking concentration for a second.

He asked her about her brother, and she told him a little more than just the basics, but not a huge amount. Frankie, his cafe, and Diego were the few things she was a little more private about in her life. He had gotten a lot of shit when he was younger for being bi, and she had little insight into Diego's life, and if he'd experienced any discrimination or bigotry.

She hoped that someone who identified as queer would be accepting of all people and all things queer, but she knew that wasn't always the case. Riley had given her no sign that he would have any sort of negative reaction, but the overprotective big sister thing was just part of the deal with her.

They switched out players, and Riley ended up destroying her score. She laughed, and they moved on to the next game and the next question. They volleyed questions and answers back and forth for the next hour and a half, stopping to order corn dogs and chili cheese fries. They discussed favorite tv shows and had a few sitcoms in common and favorite foods and found out they had a lot more of those in common.

Some questions turned silly, like least favorite color for a row house front door, to slightly flirty, like favorite place to be touched. Penelope asked that question and was only a little surprised when he said, "Actually... the nape of my neck? I just find it comforting and sort of grounding."

She had been curious to see if he was uncomfortable talking about physical intimacy or if he was just uncomfortable with some specific acts of intimacy. His response didn't quite answer the question, but she didn't think they were ready for that full conversation just yet.

She felt like she needed to clarify just a little more before deciding if she was going to proceed forward. She said she loved it when a partner would bite, lick, or even just whisper in her ear. Riley turned a deep shade of red, but he didn't look away. Instead, he bit into the plump middle of his bottom lip and seemed to focus on her ears. That was almost enough of an answer, but she knew she had to ask just one more question.

She lost the next four games in a row, and she forced herself to be patient as she answered questions on favorite dessert, city, music, and movie. Finally, deciding to cheat just a little, she led Riley to her second favorite game in the arcade, a huge version of galaxy attack. She and Frankie had played this almost religiously as a kid, so, as she suspected, she wiped the floor with Riley.

She must have been a little too intense, because suddenly Riley seemed a little wary. She led them to a corner table, and the tightness was back in his shoulders. The longer she spent with him, the more she could trace how he held anxiety in his body. It would start in his eyes, jaw, and neck and would run down through his shoulders into his forearms and all the way to his fingers. He would drum them on the table and even tense them into soft claws on his arms when he was stressed. Right now, his fingers were still so she counted that as a good sign.

"Okay Riley, this is where I want to emphasize that you only have to answer to the extent you are comfortable, but I feel like we've reached a point where I should ask."

His fingers turned to claws on the edge of the table, and, on instinct, she reached across the short space between them to take one of his hands in hers. He obliged immediately, releasing the stress in his fingers, but he seemed to channel that arm's stress into his other hand, which turned to a fist he quickly shoved into the pocket of his slacks.

"When I was... filling out my profile on the app, I chose my settings based on the fact that I am ultimately looking for love but... I'm also looking for physical intimacy and sex because they are both important parts of a relationship for me."

She was a little startled when he actually pulled his hand out of hers. He put his elbow on the table and leaned his chin into his open palm. His eyes were still locked on her, urging her to continue, but she was a little shaken by his response.

"Uhm... I know that you listed yourself as queer on the app. I've noticed you're a little sensitive about touch, and you've alluded that physical intimacy is challenging for you. And—shit, sorry. I should have said first, before anything else—I'm less worried about myself and my needs being met, and more worried that I could... accidentally make you uncomfortable or even hurt you because I don't know your boundaries."

He continued to look at her, seemingly still waiting for more. There was a little more, but she wasn't sure if she should outright ask the question or not.

She took a steadying breath and decided to just go for it. "Are you... ace?"

He blinked, and some of his tension seemed to bleed away. He lifted his head out of his palm and said, with a surprising amount of conviction, "No. I'm not. I am very sexually attracted to you."

Penelope's eyes flew wide, and her head jerked back. Some of the tension flooded back into him, and Penelope could have kicked herself for her reaction.

"Sorry—I—I didn't want you to think that... that I wasn't. But there are parts of—of sex that are..." Riley stuttered out.

His visible hand turned into a fist, and he pressed his knuckles into his lips, effectively silencing himself. She reached out and grabbed his sleeve, not touching his body but just wanting to grab his attention before he tried to say anything else.

"Hey, it's okay. We don't have to talk about it now, because... honestly, there is a real chance that we don't get that far. I don't want to make you talk about something you're uncomfortable with for no reason when you don't even know me that well. I—I just wanted to know if your sexuality meant you were even open to the possibility."

He nodded slowly.

"I do... just want to ask a clarifying question. You are sexually attracted to me, but could you ever see yourself having sex with me? In whatever capacity you're comfortable with, on your timeline, with all of the grace you would need to get there and all that. But... if we were together, would that be a part of our relationship, or is it not a possibility?" Penelope asked, feeling like she was possibly pushing too hard but needing to know the answer.

He swallowed hard but slowly lowered his arm, so his wrist fell into her hand. She held onto his arm slightly awkwardly, but she didn't dare break that connection between them.

"I do want that. And I think it is possible that sex could be a part of our relationship, but—I think there is an equally real possibility that we try and... I find out that it can't be," Riley's words were halting, but at least they didn't seem to be too horribly stressful for him to say.

She nodded earnestly. "Okay. Okay, that's—... thank you. That's all I wanted to know, just if it was a possibility."

He nodded tightly, but his eyes drifted away from her. She didn't want to chase him too much, but she felt she had one last thing to say.

"Riley?" she called softly, turning her hand to slide it down his arm, so their hands were linked again.

His jaw flexed, but he slowly brought his eyes back to meet hers.

"I just want to let you know how insanely brave I think what you just did was. I think that was probably the hardest question I asked you, and you answered it perfectly—I mean... not that your answer was perfect, but the fact that you were so honest. That's really all I can ask of you. Thank you, Riley."

He sealed his lips into a thin line, but his eyes betrayed a kaleidoscope of emotions.

"And..." she continued, "I am also very attracted to you. And I only asked such a hard question because—well, I would want to be intimate with you if we were dating."

He blushed scarlet and squeezed her hand almost painfully tight. "Thank you, Penelope."

Suddenly, his entire demeanor shifted, and her heart tripped a step at the smile that broke across his face.

"Oh! I thought of a nickname for you! I can't believe I forgot until right now."

Her eyebrows shot up. "Oh yeah? Let me hear it! And remember, it has to be unique, so don't be offended if it's already in use."

His grin turned lopsided. "Oh, I will be, don't worry. But I'll just have to get over it."

She laughed, and then when he paused, she made a come-on gesture with her free hand.

"Nels," he said, the s coming out somewhere between a soft s and a soft z.

"Oh..." she breathed, letting the soft sounds play across her mind for a moment, "can you use it in a sentence?"

He quirked an eyebrow at her but said, "Okay... I think I'm starting to really like you, Nels. As a friend, but... also maybe more if that's where this takes us."

The way he said her new nickname was almost a purr, and it ran down her spine like a chill and then back up as a spreading warmth. That was before his words sank in. Once they did, they spread like fingers through her chest, sliding in between her ribs and sinking in.

Then, as if Penelope wasn't already a little wobbly and a little melty, he lifted their joined hands and his eyes closed for just a second as his lips brushed across her knuckles. Screw melting a little, she was an actual puddle on the floor.

"Riley..." she whispered, and he lowered their hands back to the table.

"Does that mean... I get to call you Nels?" he asked softly.

She nodded and laughed, and it was a light, breathy thing that didn't sound like it belonged to her, but somehow it did, and so did this stupid smile that seemed to be taking up permanent residence on her face.

They didn't have a tab to close, so they slowly walked hand in hand together out to wait for their respective buses. As Penelope's bus pulled up, he reached down and kissed her hand again, and Penelope had to stop herself from doing a lot more. She couldn't stop herself from pulling him into a tight hug. It was quick, and there was no room between their bodies this time, but as she turned to make her bus, he captured her wrist for a moment.

"Can I see you again?"

"Of course," she said because it didn't seem like much of a question for her anymore. "Saturday for lunch?"

He smiled and released her wrist, raising that same hand to wave. "Saturday."

Penelope was feeling very conflicted.

On one hand, she would do anything for her brother and Diego, but on the other hand, she had just made plans to see Riley this Saturday.

She was sitting in their office after closing time on Wednesday and anxiously tapping her fingers on Frankie's desk. She wasn't sure if this was a habit she had before or if she was starting to pick it up from Riley. She pulled her hand into her lap to still her fidgeting and turned back to look at the two men.

Their usual MC for their weekend drag brunch had quit yesterday morning, and they'd spent several hours today trying to find a replacement with no luck. So, here they were, asking Penelope.

As she looked at their expectant faces, she had to admit that her third date with Riley wasn't the only reason she had to think twice before agreeing to their offer. The MC had to dress up in drag for the show as well, and in Penelope's case, that would mean dressing as a drag king.

Penelope was about 99% sure she wasn't a trans man. She had never wanted to be or felt like she could be a man. However, she had never associated strongly with being a woman. In the past several months, she had started to believe that maybe she just didn't fit into the gender binary.

If anyone ever asked her to pick her gender off a spectrum, she would probably choose somewhere between female and neutral, and sometimes she felt much more strongly towards the neutral. However, no one *had* ever asked before, so it wasn't something she talked about. This drag king business felt a little like she might be asking herself a question she wasn't sure she was ready to answer.

She glanced between Frankie and Diego and thought of all of the times Frankie had come through for her, and she made up her mind.

"Okay, fuck it, why not. I'm in. I will have to reschedule a date though, so I expect my compensation to be upped to include Bellini's after the show. Fucking love those things..."

"Penelope," Diego's gravelly voice cut through her internal

musings about peach-tinged alcohol, "this is too much to ask for free. We're going to pay you for this."

Seeing she was already beginning to protest, Frankie cut in, "At the bare minimum, the MCs usually receive tips for their performance, so you'll keep those. We can reassess after the first show if you feel adequately compensated by tips and fruity bubbly?"

She found her affectionate smile mirrored on Diego's face, and she tucked that away into her mental filing cabinet under "reasons she loved Diego," which sat conveniently right next to the folder on "reasons she thought her brother might also love Diego."

They spent another two hours, with free pastries for Penelope, discussing the logistics and the full plan for the brunch. By the time she got home, it was too late to message Riley, so she drafted up the message and left it in the chat box to remind herself to send it in the morning.

RILEY

Riley woke up Wednesday morning feeling happier than he had in a long time. So naturally, he was immediately skeptical of the feeling and called Johanna to update her on his date with Penelope the night before.

She was ecstatic with how much progress they'd made in just two dates, but she also commended him and Penelope for taking things as slowly as they were. In Riley's mind they weren't moving slowly at all, but he knew a lot of people had at least kissed by their third date. Riley, however, didn't think he could be any happier with the speed their relationship was developing at.

He was convinced that they could be amazing friends, but he was also very aware that friendship only made-up part of a successful relationship. He was genuinely concerned about the sex aspect, but in addition to that, he was still unsure if they met each other's needs. He thought they had a lot in common and seemed to want a lot of the same things out of life, but while for Penelope the path towards those things seemed relatively straightforward, it wasn't quite so clear cut for Riley.

As Wednesday wore on, his excitement turned into a low level of happiness that kept him warm as he fell asleep alone in his apartment. Thursday morning, he woke up feeling cold and a little off. Well, maybe more than just a little. He knew what the feeling was, but he hoped perhaps it would pass.

He opened the dating app, intending to reread some of Penelope's older messages. He knew it was a little ridiculous, but it made him smile, and few things in this world did that without fail for Riley, so he decided to lean into it. That was, of course, until he opened the app and saw the typing bubble pop up.

He paused, not wanting to scroll up to read old messages and miss her new message. He waited about ten minutes and when nothing came through, but the bubbles kept typing, he closed out his phone and decided just to get up and get going for work. He went about his routine quickly and didn't think about the bubbles again until after lunch.

He was sitting at his desk trying to ignore his work email when he remembered the bubbles. He went into the chat again, and they were still there. He knew this could happen from something as simple as a space left at the beginning of the chat box, making it appear as if there was text in it. However, for someone with anxiety like himself, it could mean that the person had drafted a message but hadn't hit send.

Whether she just forgot, hadn't finished the thought, or felt uncomfortable sending the message yet, Riley's brain did a fantastic job of spinning out a series of disastrous possibilities. He closed his phone and locked it in the top drawer of his desk for the rest of the day so he wouldn't be tempted to check it.

He only took it back out when he was heading home, and there were still no missed messages. He made it halfway home before he caved into his anxiety and sent her a simple *Hope you're having a good week* message and immediately hated himself for doing so. Maybe it would prompt her to send the message that she had typed out, or perhaps it would just go ignored if she wasn't ready to send whatever message she had been working on. There was, of course, still the possibility that there was no message at all, and Riley had just single-handedly derailed his entire day, but that possibility had left his mind when he had locked his phone in the drawer.

Finally, around seven, as he stared dejectedly into his fridge, not feeling hungry but knowing he should probably eat, he heard that blessed beep, and then he heard it three more times. Well, usually it was blessed. Today it sounded more like the imperial death march to his jangled nerves.

He opened the message and was immediately relieved, disappointed, and relieved again.

> Penelope: Hi! Oh my god, I'm so sorry. I meant to message you last night, but then I overslept and missed the bus. Then, I tried to chase the bus and ended up tripping into a puddle, so I had to go home, change, then I missed the next bus…

> Penelope: Anyways, that was not what I needed to tell you.

> Penelope: I'm so sorry to have to do this, but I think I told you how I help my brother with his job sometimes? Well, he needs me to fill in for someone this Saturday and Sunday, and I'm going to have to ask if we could reschedule our date.

> Penelope: Monday? Tuesday? I'm happy to do any day but Wednesday! Whatever works for you. I'm so sorry again. I can't wait to see you, though!

He imagined Penelope falling into a puddle and then going home to change, just to miss her bus again. He felt his cheeks warm at the image as he realized just how adorable he found the entire situation. Very unfortunate and totally inconvenient, but also utterly adorable.

So, in the end he had been partially right. She had probably drafted a message to him last night and forgotten to send it. One of his disaster scenarios had been that she was canceling their plans on Saturday, but it hadn't been for anything as noble as helping her brother out at work. He let his eyes linger over the last few words for a while before responding that he'd love to grab a coffee after work on Monday. That was going to be his suggestion for Saturday, so it felt easy to just stick with that. She immediately agreed and said there was a place she had wanted to scope out near her apartment, so they planned to meet up right after work, and Riley put his phone away for the night.

He was feeling better, but that other feeling was still there, and it was growing more insistent as he went through his bedtime routine. He forced his eyes closed as he brushed his teeth, not allowing himself even the briefest glance in the mirror tonight, deciding he'd just deal with whatever happened in the morning. He curled up in his dark bedroom and tried to lull himself to sleep with thoughts of Penelope's warm hand in his or the way the back of her hand tasted on his lips.

Unfortunately, this led him to think about what her lips might taste like, and he groaned as anxiety gripped his stomach the same way it had during their terrifying conversation about sex. In the end, he thought the conversation had gone alright, but he had no doubt actual sex wouldn't be so easy. He rolled onto his other side, shoving a pillow over his head, and he prayed for sleep.

FIVE

Penelope's week was not going well. After #Puddlegate, she got in a fight with Facebook on Thursday and spent all of Friday panicking about not having a Drag King name figured out.

Thankfully, late Friday night she and Maria had an epiphany.

Penelope was in her bedroom practicing calligraphy. She was working on her own name with a new quill and inkwell Frankie had bought her when Maria wandered in.

"Is your trusty pen and ink helping with the drag name dilemma?"

Absently Penelope began doodling the words pen and ink under her name as she complained to Maria for the umpteenth time that if she was doing Frankie and Diego such a huge favor, the least they could do for her was come up with her drag name.

She flung down her pen and groaned, threading her fingers

together and placing her head in her hands. She glared down at the paper, and suddenly it came to her in a rush.

"Oh my god, it's perfect!" she cried.

"What is...?" Maria glanced down at the paper. "Pen and ink...?"

"No!" She crossed out the 'a' and the 'd' to get n' and then added a 'w'.

"Pen n' wink. Pen like Penelope, Pen and ink like—well obviously like what it is, and wink to make it a fun, flirty drag name!" Penelope nearly shouted in excitement.

Maria jumped up and down, squealing, so Penelope assumed that meant it was a winner.

So here she was on Saturday, still a bit sleep-deprived and a bit of a stressed-out mess, but at least she had a name. She also had an outfit courtesy of one of the drag mothers who had taken one look at Penelope and pulled her into the bathroom along with her entire trunk of drag gear.

She ended up in a gaudy pinstripe suit and a frilly, Victorian-style men's dress shirt. Her hair was up in a tight bun underneath a matching pin stripe top hat, and her new drag mother, Sham Pain, helped her contour her face and draw on a fake mustache with slow, patient brushstrokes of an eyebrow pencil.

Penelope had to say, it wasn't quite as impressive as those gender-bending Tik Tok filters, but it was still pretty good. She didn't look a thing like herself, and the feeling was a little thrilling. Sometimes those filters left her feeling a little confused, but this just made her feel, well, hot. She loved how the masculine-cut suit hid her chest completely but accentuated her legs. Those were, respectively, her least and most favorite features about herself.

"You like?" Sham Pain asked as Penelope shifted back and forth in the mirror, appreciating the outfit more and more the longer she was in it.

"Yea, it—I mean, it looks amazing but... it also feels really good? Like it's so not me that it somehow is me, just... another me?"

Sham Pain's eyes crinkled, and it caused the pink gemstones glued to her brow to catch the garish light of the cafe bathroom. "That's exactly how I've always described the feeling I get when I do drag. The performance is great, and you gotta love the eyes of a hundred men, women, and others on you, but it's the feeling I get in my own skin that makes me keep coming back for more."

Penelope wanted desperately to hug Sham Pain, but she didn't want to mess up either of their outfits. "Will you... help me tomorrow too? Are you doing both shows?"

"Hmmm, I wasn't planning on it, but I can come as a civilian and help with your outfit and makeup. Don't you worry your handsome little face about it, doll."

The word handsome didn't hit Penelope in a particularly good or a particularly bad way. Unlike this outfit which was hitting in a *very* good way. She filed that away in the "figure this shit out later" filing cabinet in her brain, and they exited the bathroom.

Diego had helped her craft an intro speech, and she'd practiced all of the drag queen's names in the mirror at home last night until she could barely tell if she was speaking English anymore. She was about as ready as she was ever going to be, so she signaled to the queens and to Diego that she was ready to go, and she took the stage.

The show went fairly well, it took her a little time to get her bearings, but once she did, she found herself having a lot of fun. She would never have noticed the woman in the back corner of the cafe if it wasn't for a slight play of the light.

She hadn't told Riley about the drag show because she wasn't sure how much she was ready to share about her brother, his business, and her whole slightly questionable gender thing. Just as she was introducing the last queen, she caught a flash of honey blonde hair out of the corner of her eye. She played it cool, finishing her introduction and stepping into the backstage wing. She managed to wait a whole ten seconds before opening a small slit in the curtain to glance at the back of the room.

She couldn't explain the flippy-floppy feeling her stomach was doing at the thought that Riley might be in the audience. It was between nerves, excitement, and what felt a little like an intense high school crush.

However, it wasn't Riley. Instead, it was a breathtaking blonde woman sitting next to a tall black woman with braids, both around Penelope's age. The black woman was watching the stage with a rapt expression, similar to many other attendees, but the blonde woman was glancing between the drag queen on stage and almost exactly where Penelope was hiding. Penelope pulled back from her little peek-a-boo spot with a sharp gasp. Frankie hissed a shush at her from where he was standing to the side, supervising the beginning of the backstage cleanup.

Penelope barely heard him, though. The blonde woman's eyes had locked directly with Penelope's, and she had felt her heart stop for a moment.

She was even more beautiful than Penelope had noticed at first glance. She was wearing stylish, large, white-framed glasses over what looked like either blue or green eyes. It was hard to tell through the glasses, as well as the bright flashing lights of the stage. Her hair was wavy and fell in cascades to mid-bicep. She was wearing an incredibly soft-looking purple sweater with a puffy gray vest.

It wasn't just that she was beautiful, though. Penelope didn't believe in love at first sight, and she didn't believe in soul mates, but when their eyes met, Penelope had felt something deep in her chest, like what she imagined a premonition would feel like. Like the universe was telling her something, like maybe she had known this woman in another place, in another lifetime.

She didn't have time to dwell on the feeling, because the final queen was sauntering her way towards the exit from the stage, which meant it was her queue to close the show. She did so with as much grace as possible, but she couldn't help glancing into the corner a few times, and each time, she found the blonde woman's eyes riveted on her.

Penelope exited the stage to raucous applause from the queens and she was swept up into the post-drag show celebration and had no space left in her head for thoughts of the woman.

That is, until the next morning when she stepped out onto the stage for the Sunday morning show and saw her sitting in the same seat as the previous day, but this time she was alone. Penelope felt that same feeling in her chest, but as they made prolonged eye contact, the feeling morphed from a sharp pinching feeling to a deeper ache, like a hook or a snare had caught her heart and was slowly pulling it towards the woman across the room.

She managed to get through the first half of the show, only stumbling once when she had let her gaze linger on the woman for a beat too long, and she'd missed one of the steps on the stage.

Sham Pain had decided to attend the brunch as an audience member, but in full-drag attire. Everyone sitting next to her fawned over her and asked for selfies, which she happily agreed to. When intermission started, she stepped up onto the stage to check on Penelope.

"How are you feeling, sugar? You're doing great except for that tiny, baby stumble, but that's alright!"

"It's going really well! Uhm... can I ask you a random question you totally don't have to answer if you're not comfortable?" She glanced for a second over Sham Pain's shoulder and saw the blonde woman looking down at her phone.

"Of course, ask me anythi—"

"Do you know the woman in the back right corner of the room?" Penelope interrupted in an urgent whisper. "Is she a regular? I know sometimes you interact with the audience. I wasn't sure if maybe..." her whisper faded as Sham Pain turned around to subtly sweep her gaze over the room.

"Oh yes, I met her a few months back. Her name's Taylor. As far as I know she's not a regular. I think I've only seen her once or twice before this, but she approached me after a show and asked me a few questions about drag, where I shopped for some of my outfits, and then we had a lovely conversation about what drag meant to me. We actually—" she stopped talking, and Penelope snapped her eyes back to meet Sham Pain's.

"You actually?" she asked.

"... you've got a look on your face, doll. What's happening? Are you crushing on her?"

"Oh god, I don't know, I just... we made eye contact a few times and... I don't know. I hate to say I felt something..."

"But you felt something?" Sham Pain asked, quirking a perfectly manicured eyebrow at her.

"... yeah."

Sham Pain hummed for a moment, and then to Penelope's absolute please-just-kill-me-now horror, she turned on her six-inch heel and waved wildly at the blonde woman, catching her attention. Penelope would have paid every penny in her bank account for the floor to open up and swallow her whole. She didn't care what was waiting for her underneath. She'd take snakes, rats, or even primordial ooze if it meant she didn't have to be here right at this moment.

The blonde woman, Taylor, raised a very tentative hand in a wave, and Sham Pain began to mime to her. She held up the universal symbol for a phone, thumb and pinky extended next to her ear, then she pointed aggressively at Taylor, and then, because of course she did, she pointed at Penelope.

Taylor seemed to hesitate for a moment before slowly nodding in a slightly exaggerated way, so they'd be able to see it from across the room.

"Thirty seconds!" Diego called frantically as he rushed past them. "Sham! Off the stage! Hang out with your drag son after the show!"

Sham Pain winked at Penelope and quickly exited the stage.

Penelope finished the rest of the show in a daze, and when Sham Pain found her after the show, she was considering just running for it.

"Pen! You were fantastic! So much frenetic energy. You really owned that stage. Am I to assume you were putting on a good show for Taylor?"

Penelope looked down at her sock-clad feet, trying to find that elusive sinkhole that never seemed to show up when she needed it.

"Okay, don't tell me, but I do love a good meet-cute story. Tell me all about how it goes next weekend." Sham Pain took Penelope's phone out of her hands and quickly typed in Taylor's phone number. Before Penelope could stop her, she went on to type out a quick message and hit send. "There you go. Now she'll have your number too."

Penelope felt like she was going to throw up. Or, more accurately, she felt like she was going to smash her phone and promptly throw up on it. Sham Pain was oblivious to her internal struggle, and she sauntered away to talk to Diego and one of the other queens.

Penelope finished changing and stumbled her way home where she immediately crawled into Maria's bed and told her about the entire crazy day. Maria stroked her hair while she tried, and failed, to describe that insane feeling she'd had when she'd locked eyes with Taylor the previous day and again that morning.

Maria admitted she really couldn't relate, but it sounded like she needed to text Taylor right now. Penelope finally pulled up her texts and saw that Sham Pain had sent the following message: *Hi, this is Pen n' Wink's number. Sham Pain thinks we should connect.*

All things considered, it was a very tame message and not anything to freak out about, but that didn't stop Penelope. She freaked out so badly she threw her phone across the room and into Maria's laundry basket and refused to retrieve it. Instead, they ordered Indian food and curled up on the couch to cuddle through four full episodes of Grey's Anatomy.

When she finally did retrieve her phone, or more accurately Maria retrieved it and chucked it in the vicinity of Penelope's bed, she didn't have a single missed message. Penelope's heart stuttered as she realized she hadn't thought about or texted Riley all weekend, and he hadn't messaged her either.

Suddenly, that feeling she'd gotten when looking at Taylor that she had thought was important, so important she'd cornered Sham Pain to ask about the source of that feeling, didn't seem so important anymore.

She remembered the way Riley made her feel. Warm and soft and full of potential. She was fairly sure she'd much rather feel that way than this near panic she was feeling thinking about Taylor.

She allowed herself a few more moments to think about Taylor. She pictured her the way she had been dressed today, in a bright red, chunky, cowl neck sweater, her glasses perfectly balanced on her long narrow nose, and her blonde waves expertly framing her face. She felt her mouth go dry, and she nearly threw the phone across her own room this time.

Finally, she opened her chat with Riley. It took a few more moments for her to figure out what to say, but as she sat with her thoughts, she realized she knew exactly what to say.

> Penelope: Is it too much to say I think I might miss you, and I'm really excited to see you tomorrow?

Sadly, she didn't hear back from him that night.

TAYLOR

This was why Taylor didn't go out much. When she went out, shit like this happened. Well, shit exactly like this had never *actually* happened before, but since there was always the possibility, she just tended not to go out.

She sat cross-legged on her bedroom floor, staring at her phone. She hadn't even wanted to go to that first drag brunch on Saturday. She'd been twice in the past and had a surprisingly good time, but she hadn't been in the mood to be in public surrounded by gawking strangers this weekend. Her friend had convinced her to go, so there she was on Saturday, minding her own business when the gorgeous MC had walked out in full Drag King regalia. He'd introduced himself as Pen n' Wink, and it was either his first day, or he was just terribly nervous.

Something in Taylor had fluttered at the way he stumbled over the beginning of the show and then slowly came into his own as the morning progressed. Taylor also thought his drag name was incredibly sweet.

This in and of itself should have been a warning, because aside from the fact that Taylor rarely made new friends, she was also a lesbian suddenly attracted to a drag king. She knew that many drag queens and kings identified as one gender, but performed as another, but she wasn't one to make assumptions. Until told otherwise, Pen n' Wink was a man to her. However, that didn't stop Taylor from watching his every move throughout the performance.

She had watched him scurry off stage during the final performer's set, and when she'd glanced at the curtain behind which he had just disappeared, she could have sworn they made eye contact. It was like something was drawing her eyes around the room to follow him.

She tried to brush it off, and when she finally left the brunch, she was sure that would be that. Just a strange Saturday experience she would soon forget about and go back to her regularly scheduled programming. Not that anything about Taylor's life was regular, but that was beside the point.

Unfortunately, she did not return to any semblance of normal when she woke up Sunday morning feeling curious and a little bold. Maybe there was more to her strange feelings from the day before. So, on a whim, she decided to go to the cafe's second drag brunch that morning.

She threw on a cuter, more curated outfit and added some texturizing product to her hair. Bless her friends for gifting her precisely the types of makeup, product, and clothing that fit her style. If it were up to her to dress and style herself, she'd probably end up in a paper sack.

She got to the brunch almost on time to be early. In other words, she was only fifteen minutes early when she'd hoped to be much earlier than that to get the perfect seat. Somehow though, the gods of whatever the hell it was she was getting herself into smiled down on her, and her same seat from the day before was unoccupied.

She spent the entire brunch following Pen n' Wink with her eyes, and when intermission started, she got the insane idea to approach him. However, right as she was about to stand up, she saw Sham Pain join him on stage.

Funnily enough, the last time Taylor had gotten the wild idea to approach one of the performers during intermission, it had been with Sham Pain herself.

They had chatted amiably, while Taylor tried to memorize every one of her answers. Taylor had been attempting to update her wardrobe and thought perhaps going straight to one of the most fabulous sources she could think of would help her to do that. She learned many new clothing brand names but didn't quite get what she was looking for. Right as Sham Pain was about to walk away, Taylor blurted out, "But how do you know what makes you feel like you the most if you don't know who you are?"

Sham Pain had frozen and turned around to look Taylor very carefully up and down. She immediately regretted asking such a personal question, and she shrunk into herself, hoping maybe Sham Pain would just huff and walk away. Instead, she reached out very gently and took Taylor's hand. Usually, this kind of gesture would have had her reeling, but Sham Pain's overheated hand on hers made her feel grounded.

"Sugar, I do drag because it's the only way I can feel like myself, but it took years and years for me to realize that. It's not about the clothes for everyone, but for me, they sure did help. I started very tame and worked my way through androgynous to this ultra-femme princess in pink you see before you now. You obviously don't have to do anything quite as extreme as me, but," she looked down again at Taylor's sweats and t-shirt, "you could try experimenting with masculine, feminine, or androgynous streetwear and see if anything feels right for you. Sometimes makeup and hair are all it takes. I can wear a full face of makeup and a men's suit, and I will feel almost as fabulous as I do right now, but that's just me, doll. You gotta walk before you can fly."

Taylor had been blown away by her answer, and she'd desperately asked if they could exchange numbers and keep in touch. Sham Pain had immediately agreed, taking Taylor's phone from her hands, typing in her number, and texting herself.

After that, Taylor had convened a focus group of her closest friends, and they'd gone on a shopping spree together. Her friends had been ecstatic, but Taylor had stood in the corner of almost every shop they went into, back against the wall, feeling terrified and exposed. Despite this, her friends had managed to build her a nice capsule wardrobe that fit her needs perfectly.

She had to admit; the clothes were a game changer for her. And the accessories. There was something about putting on her accessory glasses in the morning and sliding on a pair of properly fitted skinny jeans or leggings that made Taylor sort of sink into herself. For once, her body felt like hers. Like she had found the worn groove in the couch that was perfectly molded to her body's shape, and she could just sit in it for a moment.

Taylor had slowly begun to venture out of the house more, wearing her new amazing wardrobe, sometimes for brunch or to go to bars. She was a huge sucker for brunch, so that was often the easiest way her friends got her out of the house. It had become her thing by the time this weekend rolled around, and that was the only reason she had agreed to go to the show in the first place.

The show where she had, once again, sat in the corner of the room, back pressed tightly against the soft fabric of her chair, unable to move or speak or do anything as she watched Sham Pain and Pen n' Wink very clearly whispering about her on stage. Taylor felt a flash of sheer terror as she wondered if Sham Pain had seen more and understood more about Taylor than she'd let on, and was telling Pen n' Wink all her secrets.

She tried to shake herself out of it because there was no way she'd been that obvious, and she truly didn't think Sham Pain would do that. When she waved over at Taylor, Taylor gave one of the world's most awkward waves back, and when Sham Pain mimed giving Pen n' Wink her number, she said yes.

She then proceeded to regret that decision for the rest of the day.

She had read the text message a dozen times, but she didn't

know if Sham Pain had really just thought they should connect, maybe trying to provide her with the opinions of a drag queen and king, or if Pen n' Wink had been the one who wanted them to connect.

Taylor had felt safe when speaking, and on rare occasions texting, with Sham Pain, so she thought it must mean Pen n' Wink was a reputable person.

All of this would be much simpler if Taylor knew how she felt about Pen n' Wink. If she knew she just wanted to be friends with him, she would just text him back. There was something in the way their eyes met, though. She couldn't be sure, but she felt like she had felt this way before, but she had no idea how that was possible since she'd never been interested in a drag king, or queen for that matter, before. She was rarely interested in anyone, to be honest. She'd been with a few women over the years, but physical intimacy had always been challenging for her, and relationships were even harder. She barely had enough time to figure herself out, let alone figure another person out.

Why, then, did she suddenly want to figure Pen n' Wink out? She wanted to know his story and map out the similarities and differences between them, like comparing notes for a hard test Taylor never felt like she'd studied well enough for.

She was lying in bed, phone resting on her stomach, when she felt it vibrate. She quickly glanced at the screen and felt a wave of disappointment when she saw it wasn't Pen n' Wink. She didn't even bother looking at who it was actually from. That poor person didn't deserve her disappointment right now. A disappointment she couldn't even really trace the root of.

With a groan of frustration and confusion, she tucked her phone away in her nightstand.

She quickly got undressed and redressed in a soft shirt and baggy sweatpants and dove under the covers. She would just wait and see how she felt in the morning. Things changed overnight for Taylor quite frequently, and she wasn't sure if she would be ready to deal with the consequences in the morning if she did something reckless like texting Pen n' Wink back.

Six

Penelope had hoped the anticipation and excitement for her third date with Riley would eclipse her uncertainty from the day before. Unfortunately, when she woke up that morning, she found that none of her clothes fit. Everything was clinging too tightly to her chest, felt too low cut, made her legs seem short and wide, and she just felt like a lump made up of the wrong flesh.

Maria walked by her door as she sat slumped on her bed, staring angrily down at the sweater she had worn on her first date with Riley. It was the only thing that felt even remotely right to her today, but she couldn't wear the same outfit twice on only three dates. He was going to think she just didn't own any clothes, which at this point was beginning to feel true.

Maria took one look at her and seemed to know exactly what she needed, because no more than 60 seconds later, she returned with a color-blocked sweater. There were three stripes of color, black, slate gray, and a deep burgundy, arranged in a very flattering V-shape design. Somehow, it seemed to flatten out her chest in a way that reminded Penelope of how she'd felt as Pen n' Wink.

"Maria, how do you always know me better than I know myself? This is absolutely perfect."

Maria just smiled at her, but there was a crease between her eyebrows Penelope didn't understand.

The weather was glorious today, and it was warm enough to not only not wear a jacket, but Penelope thought she might even eat outside for lunch. She left the house without packing anything to eat, deciding to treat herself to a nice lunch outside as a reward for working seven days in a row. She realized she might be doing that a lot moving forward if Diego and Frankie couldn't find someone else to MC.

Penelope floated through the morning, looking forward to lunch and starting to look forward to her date tonight. Unfortunately, that was precisely when she got a message from Riley.

> Riley: Nels, I'm so sorry to have to do this, but I think I might need to be the one to reschedule today. I'm not really feeling like myself, and I think I just want to take some time to unwind after what turned into a surprisingly long and challenging weekend. Could I get back to you on rescheduling? Maybe Thursday or Friday?

> Penelope: Of course! Please let me know if there's anything I can do.

She felt her heart sink at rescheduling their plans, but she also felt a sharp ache from the fact that Riley had utterly ignored her previous message about missing him. She knew that was silly. She wasn't some heart-sick teenager that needed her boyfriend of two weeks to tell her he missed her.

Hell, Riley wasn't even her boyfriend. They were just starting to go on dates, and she wouldn't even say they were dating per se. More like they were engaged in the slow dance predators would do while trying to figure each other out. Except that wasn't quite right either since she and Riley were probably two of the least predatory creatures on the planet. On the upside, their combined anxiety could probably power a small town if harnessed correctly.

She was about to pocket her phone when two things happened simultaneously. Another chat message popped up from Riley, and her eyes landed on her texting app, where she knew there was still an unanswered message to Taylor.

Her thumb swiped across the screen as if of its own volition, and Penelope wasn't sure what direction it would go until it clicked on Riley's message. Good. That was the right thing to do. That felt like the safe, sound plan, even if she was slightly disappointed.

It turned out her thumb had been completely correct, because his new message read:

> Riley: And I miss you too. Please do not ever think that you or anything you say or do is too much. I think you are the perfect amount.

Penelope decided this was her happy cue to get herself some lunch. She wandered down the sidewalk feeling airy and comfortable in her borrowed sweater. She was a little disappointed Riley wouldn't be able to see it, but maybe she'd wash it and rewear it when they went on their next date. Or perhaps she should get some new clothes. Her mind flashed to Taylor, sitting in the back corner wearing two different outfits that bordered on androgynous, but somehow simultaneously made her look like a feminine goddess.

She sat in a nearby park and ate her sandwich as she considered her next move. She was allowed to make new friends, and heck, she was pretty sure she was even allowed to date new people. She and Riley weren't exclusive, and she could honestly say if Riley was also seeing other people, she wouldn't be too upset. The goal of their slow, measured dating was to determine if they were truly right for each other; they had both agreed on that, and that meant also figuring out if someone else was right for them.

She realized it was pretty likely Riley was seeing other people. He was on the same dating app Penelope was on, and just because Penelope had completely given up swiping on it didn't mean Riley had.

She was getting way ahead of herself though. She wasn't even sure if Taylor would text her back, if she was interested in women, or if she was even slightly interested in Penelope. Also, she pretty much knew next to zero about the woman. It was possible they wouldn't end up liking each other anyways. Just like with Riley, the idea of even being friends with her made a smile creep across her cheeks.

She pulled out her phone and sent one of her classically awkward texts and then proceeded to try to drown herself in the park's pond. Okay, she didn't actually do that, but she did nearly trip into it and had to relive #Puddlegate all over again. She didn't think she'd forgive herself though if she damaged Maria's gorgeous sweater.

Penelope began to, carefully, walk back to work, uncertain how one person was expected to weather this level of emotional ups and downs in one day. As if she had tempted fate with the thought, her phone buzzed in her now sweaty hand.

> Penelope: Hi, I wasn't sure if it was weird to have the only message you ever received from me not be from me so. Here I am! Pen n' Wink in the virtual flesh.

> Taylor: Hi Pen n' Wink. Is that how I should denote you on my phone?

> Penelope: Actually, you can feel free just to call me Pen if you'd like!

> Taylor: What a lovely name! So I don't make a mistake, do you have preferred pronouns?

Penelope froze in the middle of the sidewalk, and she was roughly jostled as the midday foot traffic parted around her. Penelope was a very femme-presenting person. Even when she wasn't dressed in particularly feminine clothing, her hair and feminine face usually meant she was perceived a certain way. She had a moment where she really considered asking for they/them, but she just didn't feel quite ready to take on new pronouns if she wasn't even really sure if she was nonbinary. Heck, until this moment, she hadn't ever even thought of the word nonbinary in relation to herself. She'd seen the flags at pride, and done a bit of research over the years, but that was as far as she'd ever gotten. With a surprisingly heavy heart, she responded.

> Penelope: Thanks so much for asking! I guess I'm not used to being asked that question; this was my first weekend as a drag king. You can use she/her pronouns for me, I think.

> Taylor: Okay! But... if you ever change your mind, let me know? I promise I'm happy to switch to anything else.

Penelope felt something unfurl inside her ribs, like a metamorphosed butterfly's soft translucent wings. She hadn't even asked for new pronouns but somehow, the acknowledgement that maybe one day she would want them had the butterfly wings inside her flapping happily.

What was it Riley had said to her? He wasn't ready to be someone else entirely? That almost perfectly summed up how Penelope felt. It was as if she had just booted up a new video game, because yes, Penelope actually loved video games even though she sucked at them, and they'd asked her to choose a gendered character. However, instead of the usual lightly veiled threat of "this decision cannot be changed later on," it instead said, "Please choose one now but feel free to change your mind later on. Maybe even a second time? How about a third? Why not! Gender is a construct anyways."

Okay, so there was about a 0% likelihood that any game would say all of that, but the thought of it lifted a weight Penelope didn't even know she had been carrying off her chest.

Penelope had expected the week to drag by slowly as she waited to hear back from Riley, but she and Taylor ended up texting a lot. Like, a *lot*. Like, they texted all Monday afternoon and night and all throughout the day Tuesday and into Tuesday night. She didn't want to say it was a welcome distraction because it was more than that, but Penelope did notice a hole missing without her usual daily texts from Riley.

By Wednesday night, she had texted him two "just checking in, miss you" texts, to which he had sent a very kind response but provided no information about himself or sent any additional messages after that.

Frankie and Diego had insisted she take Wednesday night off since she was on the schedule to MC again that weekend. So instead of working, Penelope made a huge batch of spaghetti with Maria, and they curled up on the couch, alternating between chatting and mindlessly watching TV while scrolling through their phones.

"So... I thought maybe you'd like to know that I matched with two asexual women on Chasing Rainbows," Maria said out of the blue.

Penelope nearly fell off the couch as she threw herself onto Maria.

"Oh my god, Maria! You've been letting me prattle on like an asshole about Riley and Taylor all week, and you've just been swiping away? I didn't even know you had a profile!"

Maria laughed fondly as she nuzzled her cheek into Penelope's hair. "Well, your love life is much more interesting to talk about. Me and one of the women have been in a five-day debate about the perfect starter Pokémon. The second woman and I tried to set up a meeting at a coffee shop, but then we got in a six-day conversation about what the city's most overrated coffee shop is and have yet to pick a not overrated one to meet at."

Penelope glared at her. "Excuse the fuck out of me!"

Maria blinked at her for a second and then blanched. "Oh, no! She lives on the north side, so everything we're talking about is up there. That's a good idea, though. I should bring her to Frankie's café! Are you going to work next Wednesday? Maybe I'll set it up for then."

"Awesome! I will totally stalk the shit out of your first meetup. Awww, Maria, I'm so excited for you!"

Maria patted her head affectionately. "Alright, let's not get too excited now. Anyways, I feel like we're both not here for this show right now. Shall we squirrel away in our bedrooms to text our ladies and maybe your gent?"

Penelope frowned sadly. "Probably not my gent. I mean, he's definitely not my gent, but he probably isn't going to text me back today... I am texting Taylor, though... we've been texting a lot. Do you... think that's bad?"

Maria shook her head vigorously. "Not at all. You and Riley aren't exclusive, right? I mean, I'm texting two women right now too, and honestly, I'm still swiping, so if I match with any more women, I'll probably text them as well."

Penelope nodded against her friend's chest. "I don't feel like I'm doing anything wrong. I just... wanted to make sure..."

Maria patted her cheek softly. "Well, you know I just want whatever and whoever is best for you. And that means I want you to get to know both of them so you can find the right person." She smoothed her hand gently down Penelope's back. "I can already tell you're starting to like Riley. So, if you end up dating him, I support that. Or if you find that Taylor is better for you—or maybe not even better, but if Taylor is different and it's the kind of different you think you need? Well, then I am absolutely all for her then. I do demand to meet them, though, and since you've already been talking to Riley for weeks, you should just feel free to invite him over any day now. I'll be ready." She flashed a huge Cheshire grin, and Penelope let out a loud guffaw.

"For some reason, that doesn't inspire confidence in me..."

Maria huffed indignantly. "You know I'm just joking, Poppy! I would like to meet him, and I'll be nice, I promise."

Penelope sat up and smiled fondly at her. "I know... I'll try to see if we can arrange something in the next week or two? Even if we don't end up being right for each other, I'd like to be his friend, so you might as well meet him sooner rather than later."

They untangled themselves from each other, the blankets, and the couch itself, which liked to try and suck them into its comfy clutches for hours at a time. Penelope meandered into her room and got herself ready for bed. She pulled out her phone and saw Taylor had asked her a question about psychology, oddly enough. They texted back and forth and eventually turned to the topic of grade school.

Taylor alluded to high school being very hard for her and that things had only gotten a little easier in college. Penelope was always so bad at talking to and flirting with women. She had what she liked to call negative gay-dar. She never minded when someone else inquired about her sexuality, but she had no idea how to bring up others' sexuality. With this in mind, she thought maybe her best strategy was to do what she did best. Over sharing.

Penelope: I think I was pretty lucky in High School, actually, because it was almost like I didn't know what I didn't know? I knew that I had what I would call "friend crushes" on several of my female friends, especially (please don't laugh, I know it is so stereotypical, but it's completely true) on the captain of my softball team. She had short blonde hair and a super athletic build, and I just found myself gravitating towards her whenever we were on the field. She was a senior, and I was a freshman, so she didn't even notice I existed, but I noticed her.

Penelope: I feel like I can never know now, but part of me wonders if it was internalized homophobia just from growing up in our society or if I didn't have enough queer women in my life, but I truly had no idea what I was feeling wasn't "hetero-normal" so I didn't even think to question it. Then I went to college, and I was suddenly around all of these queer women, and I kept trying to figure out if I wanted to be them or be with them. It turns out it was both.

Taylor: Wow. I don't know if I've ever heard a truer statement than that. That's how I finally realized I was lesbian when the "I want to be you" so clearly turned into "I want to be with you."

> Penelope: But it was almost more than that, right? It was also like "I want you to notice me. Please notice me as one of you. I am one of you." Except, of course, I was bi, and now I think it's more accurate to say I'm pan, but either way, I wasn't quite one of the lesbians I was so interested in being and being with.

Penelope let out an actual whoop, and Maria texted her asking for an explanation and if she needed to come in there. She quickly shot her a text confirming that Taylor was, in fact, queer. Maria sent a "no duh" emoji back, and Penelope switched back to her chat with Taylor.

Penelope went on to explain how it helped having a bisexual brother. She thought she would feel that typical guilt she always felt when talking about her brother, as if it was her job to shield him from the sometimes-cruel eyes of the world. He was a very open and proud bisexual man, though, and Penelope knew she probably needed to dial down the overprotectiveness.

Taylor agreed it had helped having a loving and supportive sister and a mostly supportive mother. All she said about her father was that they were no longer on speaking terms. Penelope hesitated for a moment before her thumbs flew across the screen.

> Penelope: I'm so sorry to hear that. I can't imagine what it must be like to cut ties with a family member because they don't accept you.

Penelope: I guess my situation is a little different. My parents were very supportive when my brother came out, but it's been a little different for me. Over the years, it's like I've had to come out to my mom multiple times, like she just sort of conveniently forgets.

Penelope: I remember the first time I came out so clearly. I was sitting on the floor in my college dorm. My roommate was having sex with her boyfriend, so I was in the hallway, just sitting there staring at my rainbow knee-high socks. They were the first LGBTQ+ article of clothing I ever owned. My mom just so happened to call at that exact moment, and I answered and somehow, it just all came tumbling out. She was... supportive in some ways and unsupportive in others. It was like she was supportive at that exact moment, but then it was like she just forgot.

Penelope: She would gift my brother bisexual flag t-shirts and hoodies, and he never even wore any of them. Instead, he'd give them to me. I'd wear them when I was at school because it was like I didn't want them to see I'd gotten his hand-me-downs (hand-me-ups? How does that work with younger siblings?) even though I so desperately wanted them to see... well me. All of me.

She wasn't even entirely sure her father knew she wasn't straight, even though she had alluded to it in many conversations over the years and was pretty sure she had outright told him once over the phone. Her parents never brought it up, though, making a big show over the few men she'd dated and told them about, but never asking if there was anyone else. It felt almost as if her sexuality wasn't legitimate unless she was in a committed relationship with a woman. Since she had never been in one of those, had never been able to bring a girl home for thanksgiving or send her parents a photo of them to put on the mantle, it sometimes felt like she wasn't gay enough to wear the LGBTQ+ rainbow.

That, of course, was not even considering the fact she was beginning to suspect her gender wasn't as cut and dry as she'd once thought. That felt like too much to unpack tonight though.

She explained her family dynamic and imposter syndrome to Taylor, leaving out the bits about her gender. For some reason, Taylor took a long time to respond. Penelope wondered if she'd fallen asleep, since they had been texting for almost six hours. Penelope was suddenly reminded of the hours and hours she would spend on instant messenger in middle school. She would sit there, hunched over her Windows 2000 computer, typing away late into the night like she and her friends were philosophizing about life's big questions when they were just chatting about emo bands and softball practice.

Penelope was considering going to sleep herself, since it was nearly two in the morning, when Taylor finally responded.

> Taylor: I feel like I already know you so well, Pen, even though we've only been texting for a few days. You are clearly a strong, confident woman who knows who she is on the inside. Don't let anyone or anything outside of yourself tell you who you are or who you love. I have to admit, I fall victim to that a lot, and it is a constant struggle for me, but I'm trying to work on it.

> Penelope: Maybe we could work on it together?

Penelope nearly threw her phone across the room. She was really spoiled by her industrial-strength phone case, as it was the only thing that kept her phone from absolute destruction on a near daily basis.

She had meant to ask, or at least imply, that they could keep talking about some of these deeper topics. She talked to Maria, Frankie, and maybe one or two other friends about stuff like this, but they all had different experiences. It felt like she actually had a lot in common with Taylor, and she wanted to keep getting to know her because it felt like the more Penelope was getting to know her, the more she was getting to know herself.

Unfortunately, her sleep-addled, hormone-driven brain had typed out that dumb question instead. Her stomach dropped when Taylor's next text finally came in.

> Taylor: I think maybe I should clarify something before we continue texting.

> Taylor: I really don't think I'm looking for a relationship right now, and I'm truly sorry if I did anything to lead you on.

Taylor: You're really funny and interesting, and I would love to get the chance to keep getting to know you, but I think friendship is all I can really offer right now.

Penelope sighed a little sadly. It was probably best she found this out now as opposed too much later on, but she was still disappointed. Actually, this entire week had been disappointing. She wasn't upset with Riley in the slightest for needing to take some time to himself, but she was beginning to miss him terribly.

She had then thrown herself, maybe a little too eagerly, into her conversations with Taylor. She hadn't even decided if she was interested in her yet, and then in one conversation, she found out Taylor was, in fact, interested in women but not in Penelope. Or at least not right now. She seriously considered not responding, but deep down, she knew that was the absolute worst way to handle disappointment, so she took a few minutes to compose herself and her text.

Penelope: I completely understand, and please don't apologize. You've done absolutely nothing wrong. I admit that I might have had the tiniest interest in pursuing more than just a friendship with you. You're quite possibly one of the most beautiful women I've ever seen, and I love talking to you. I know it's only been a few days, but it feels like I've known you forever. It seems like we might have a lot in common, and I find myself just wanting to know more and more about you.

Penelope: But I completely respect your decision not to want to pursue anything further with me. I'd really like to be your friend though, if that's alright?

Taylor: Wow, you are so incredibly sweet. Yes, let's absolutely be friends. I am so sorry to quash your "tiniest bit of interest" in me, though. I hope you survive the devastating heartbreak that is soon to follow.

Taylor: ;)

Penelope burst out laughing and thought that maybe the week was turning out alright after all because at least it seemed like she had made a friend.

RILEY

Riley still wasn't feeling quite himself by Thursday morning, but he also wasn't feeling much of anything. He wasn't depressed, but he also felt detached somehow, like he was his own shadow, merely following behind his body as it went about its daily tasks.

Strangely, the only thing he wanted to do, the only thing that felt like it would ground him at all, was talk to Penelope. He pulled up the dating app and noticed for the first time there was a telephone icon in the upper corner of their chat. Could he call her through the app?

Before he could think better of it, he hit the button. It asked if he wanted to do a video or audio call, and he slammed his thumb into the audio button so hard it almost launched his phone right out of his hand. There was nothing worse on this planet than receiving an unexpected video call. Suddenly, he realized that receiving an unexpected audio call wasn't much better, and he was about to hang up in a panic when the line connected.

"... hello?" Penelope sounded a little breathless and uncertain as she picked up.

"Hi Nels, it's... well, it's Riley, but I just realized maybe I shouldn't have called you out of the blue like this... if your anxiety is anything like mine, this probably just took a few years off of your life."

Penelope's laugh was ethereal, and Riley drank it up through the phone line.

"No, it's totally okay. I just wasn't sure what the noise was. I've never received a call on the app before. My phone was halfway across the room, and Maria and I thought it was some kind of alarm going off in our apartment—oh! I'm not sure if I've told you all of the fun features our apartment came with, ranging from doorknobs that also function as paperweights to fridges that are actually freezers and vice versa. We thought maybe this was some new alert to something in our house catching fire or somehow breaking down."

Riley slowly sank onto the bed while he listened to Penelope talk. He thought he could listen to her talk for hours, maybe even days. He didn't often notice people's voices except when they were particularly memorable. Ashley had a deep gravelly voice that seemed to massage deep into Riley's muscles, while Kim's voice was as soft as a cloud. Penelope's voice wasn't incredibly unique, but she spoke with such animation, inflecting aggressively in some parts of her sentences and rushing through others depending on the emotion she was trying to convey or perhaps the emotion the words elicited in her. He found it rather intoxicating.

He figured she thought he didn't volunteer more information about himself because he was a shy, possibly closed-off person, but it wasn't just that. It was definitely partially that—okay it was mostly that—but he also liked listening to her speak.

"Hey, is there a reason you called on the app?" Penelope asked.

"Oh, I... I don't know. I opened it to send you a message, saw the phone icon, and just kind of pressed it. I guess... I just wanted to hear your voice?"

Penelope was silent for a beat. "That's... really sweet, Riley. Uh, I actually meant why you called on the app and not via a normal phone call but—I like your answer to my nonexistent question much better." She laughed quietly, but it wasn't at Riley. It was somehow with him even though he wasn't laughing. Well, now he was laughing, just as softly as she was.

"I don't have your number."

"Would you like my number? I do think we've passed the point where you've earned it," she said sweetly.

He liked the way that sounded, like he'd earned some level of trust from her, but for some reason, he found he didn't want the number. The trust, yes, absolutely, but not the number. He thought about this for a second and then came to a funny conclusion.

"Er... so this is a little embarrassing to admit, but... I've kind of become fond of the text noise this app makes... is that weird to say? I think if it's alright, I'd rather just keep using the app for a while?"

Penelope was silent, and he felt like he'd said something wrong. He played back his words in his head and realized he might have messed up.

"Oh, Nels, I... I meant I like the noise it makes for you when you text me—I mean, I know it's not unique to you, but—to me, it feels like it is because I'm only talking to you on the app. I'm not even swiping; I just use it to message you—"

"Riley, Riley!" She called over the phone, and he could almost feel her small hand grabbing his shirt sleeve again like she had at the arcade bar. "It's okay! I was just thinking I felt the same way, that's all! Also... we've never talked about being exclusive or anything, so I mean, if you are talking to or even dating other people, that's okay. Until we—I mean, if we decide to enter a committed, exclusive relationship, only then would it be a problem for me if you were getting to know or seeing other people."

Riley didn't have to give that much thought. He had absolutely no interest in trying to date anyone else, but he had to admit, it was less because he knew Penelope was the only one he wanted to be with and more that he just didn't think he had the capacity for that.

"I... am probably not going to try and date anyone else while I'm trying this out with you, but that's more a me thing than anything else. I just have a lot going on, and I am very content to get to know one person at a time. Maximum, maybe two, but... even that feels like a lot."

Penelope laughed. "I'm the same way. One, maximum two." She paused for a moment before continuing. "Well, that's good to know. I'm glad we've talked about this now! Good to set expectations and all that. Uhm... I... well, I try to only be physically intimate with one person at a time. So, I would probably want to be pretty sure about the person before sleeping with them."

"Oh uhm... me too," Riley admitted.

"Okay, so we'll have a conversation about it if the time ever comes? It won't just be some drunken decision?"

"A conversation sounds perfect and—oh god, no. That is an absolute recipe for disaster for me. I need to be very sober and—

well. I have some needs we could... discuss further if the time comes for it? Maybe?"

He held his breath as he waited for her response. He couldn't believe how open they were discussing this now. Even just saying the word sex to Penelope last week had nearly given him an ulcer. He knew he had overreacted a little at the arcade bar to Penelope's line of questioning about physical intimacy. It was just that the night had been going so well, and the change in conversation had scared him. He felt like he was about to lose her before he even got to have her.

This conversation didn't feel stressful though. In fact, he was feeling better than he had all week, more grounded, just as he had suspected he would feel when talking to Penelope. He knew there was some added safety in having the distance talking over the phone offered as opposed to face to face, where he felt pressured to try and school his emotions and his reactions. But it felt like more than that.

"That sounds like a great plan to me, Riley."

They continued to talk for over an hour, and as Riley began to get ready for bed, he had a strange idea. He put the phone on speaker while Penelope began telling him some story about a cafe she worked at part-time. He could barely hear her, though, as he began to hear the familiar rushing in his ears as he slowly pulled his shirt over his head and forced himself to stare into the mirror.

Penelope's sweet voice was like a tether, keeping him tied to the here and now, and he didn't feel the usual anxiety and sometimes detached depression he got looking at himself in the mirror. Instead, he just saw... well, himself. Lanky limbs, honey blonde hair, slim shoulders, a flat chest, and flatter stomach. He had the slightest outline of obliques, creating the infamous "v" some people were crazy about. He didn't see the appeal, but he didn't hate it the way he hated some other parts of himself. In a way, it was kind of nice, giving his hips a little definition where they dipped below his pants.

He heard Penelope mention something about drag queens, and he wondered if she'd switched subjects to a tv show or something. He stopped staring at himself in the mirror and grabbed up his phone again just in time to hear her say, "So yeah. Unfortunately, I might be working weekends for quite a while until Frankie can find someone else to take over the job. I'm sorry about that... I know it will limit our potential date times, but I totally don't mind continuing to meet up after work?"

"Oh, uh, yeah, no, that's fine, Nels. No worries at all." He had definitely missed something from her monologue, but it seemed like he'd tuned back in right on time.

He glanced one last time into the mirror and turned his back on it like he usually did, leaning back against the counter. "Hey uh... Nels... would you want to hang out tomorrow by chance? I know it's last minute, so please feel free to say no—I mean, you probably already have plans, so it's okay— "

"Riley!" She called over the phone again, her laughter turning his name into three syllables, "I would love to hang out, but I have plans to do a three-movie marathon with Maria. Although... She was just bugging me to invite you and... I don't think she was joking... actually, let me ask—"

There was a brief shuffling noise and a muffled shout, and before Riley could protest or even process what was happening, she was back on the phone. "Okay! Maria would love to meet you, but if you meant you wanted to hang out like on an exclusive date, and this doesn't sound fun, then I'll have to push back our date again, maybe to early next week?"

His stomach did an interesting little dip and hitch at the thought of meeting her best friend. The same best friend who apparently had asked to meet him? He felt anxiety creep over his bare skin, so he quickly exited the bathroom and yanked a pajama shirt over his head.

He knew he had to give her an answer. Even if they didn't end up dating, it was okay for him to have met her friend, right? Because if they stayed friends, she might become his friend too?

"I had meant as a date, but honestly, after the week I've had, that sounds amazing—if you're sure it's okay with Maria, of course!"

Penelope's voice got soft all of a sudden. It felt like the first time he hugged her, gentle and tentative. "Do you... want to talk about it? I know you said you weren't feeling like yourself. I—well, I kind of felt a little like that this week too, so—I mean, not that I'm saying our feelings are the same, I'm sure they were very different experiences! But, anyways, I'm sorry. That you felt that way and that the week was hard. I'm here if you want to talk or vent or anything."

Again, with the gastrointestinal rollercoaster. The fact that she cared enough to ask and somehow also experienced feelings even a little similar to his own made him feel a little swoony. But he wasn't ready for this conversation right now. Especially not over the phone, when he had just started feeling like himself again.

"Thank you, Nels, that... truly means a lot more to me than you probably know. But I think I'm doing much better now, and I'd prefer to just move forward into tomorrow if that's alright. I'm excited to see you again, and I can't wait to meet Maria."

Well, that wasn't entirely true. He felt the claws of anxiety settling into his back and chest, but he definitely wasn't going to admit that and risk worrying Penelope. He just hoped he and Maria would get along. He liked to think he was a pretty palatable person. He was just sometimes hard to get to know on a deeper level. He was trying, though, he was really trying. For himself, and now maybe a little bit for Penelope too.

SEVEN

PENELOPE

Besides a brief good morning text, Penelope and Taylor didn't text on Thursday, and Penelope tried not to worry, but she wondered if there was some residual awkwardness left over from their conversation about not dating.

Friday flew by in a series of last-minute work meetings that resulted in Penelope getting assigned to a new project to help the company revamp its current, decrepit website. By the time she realized she hadn't heard from Taylor all day, she was on the bus home, texting with Maria about what they should order for dinner before Riley came over for movie night.

She checked her phone one final time when she got home, but when there was nothing from Taylor, or Riley for that matter, he shot Riley a "can't wait to see you soon, here's the address again!" message and put her phone away.

They ended up just ordering pizza, and Penelope shoved a few slices into her mouth as she scurried around the apartment. She was anxious-cleaning things that didn't need to be cleaned and ignoring the bigger problems like the ceiling tile that was about to fall out in the kitchen and the rug they hadn't vacuumed since they moved in.

She spent half an hour in the kitchen fumbling around with her best attempts at a charcuterie board. In the end, it turned into a bowl of popcorn sitting on a cutting board, surrounded by store-bought chocolate chip cookies, chocolate-covered raisins, sour gummies, and cheese puffs.

She wandered out to the living room with the board, planning to straighten the couch cushions for the tenth time, when she saw a sight that really should be surprising but wasn't in their household.

Maria was balancing precariously on a chair, attempting to hang fairy lights over the window in the living room. She had a roll of tape in her mouth and was holding the untaped end of the lights up to the wall but was just slightly too short to reach it.

Penelope hurried to put down the board and rush back into the kitchen to grab her own chair. She hobbled back over with the chair and climbed up next to Maria. She gently pulled the roll of tape out of her mouth and took the lights from her hand.

"Just... out of curiosity," Penelope said, grunting as she stretched to reach the correct height for the lights, "why did you feel like *now* was the correct time to hang up these lights you've wanted up for two and a half years?"

Maria gracefully jumped off of her chair, nearly knocking Penelope off in the process, to run across the room

"Oh wow, that's crooked," Maria mused, laughing happily and completely ignoring Penelope's question.

"Okay... so how can I fix it?" Penelope grunted.

"Oh, no, I meant the window itself."

Penelope banged her head against the wall, and Maria chortled. "Do you think we should hang the lights crooked as well? Would it make it more or less obvious that our apartment appears to be slanted..."

"Okay, I told you that *last year* when water bottles kept rolling across the floor, and you said—"

She was interrupted by a knock at the door, and Penelope threw Maria a desperate look.

"Coming!" Maria sang, running for the door, in the distinct opposite direction from where Penelope was now trapped, holding up fairy lights with no direction.

Penelope could hear Riley's gentle voice from their entryway, but she couldn't quite see him yet from where she was standing. "Oh. Hello. You must be Maria?"

"The one and only! You must be the gorgeous Riley I've been hearing so much about," Maria trilled in response.

Penelope was almost certain if she unlatched the window with her foot, she could probably just barely fit through the opening and make her escape. That is, if she could properly land the two-story drop to the cement pavement below.

"Now... is that Nels' observation or yours?" Riley asked.

"Nels? Damn, that's a good one; I haven't heard that one before —but of course, I guess that's the point, right?"

They laughed together this time, and Penelope was just hooking her toes under the window handle when they walked in. She was sure she made a glorious picture, standing with one foot on their rickety kitchen chair, the other balanced on the window handle, one arm still extended in the air with the lights, and the other holding tape uselessly by her side.

"What... are you... doing?" Riley asked, rather unhelpfully, gawking up at Penelope.

"Poppy wanted the room to be pretty for you," Maria said, as she skipped over to her side.

"Hey, could you do me a favor and just open this window all the way so I can throw myself out of it?" Penelope asked, glancing down at her horrendous best friend.

"You didn't have to go to any trouble..." Riley said from where he had come to stand below her, his blush apparent in the setting sun.

"Oh, believe me, this wasn't my choice. I've been hoodwinked," Penelope grumbled.

"I'm sure I have no idea what you're talking about. Now, Riley —" Maria grabbed his arm and wheeled him back from Penelope so they could look up at the lights together, "it has recently come to our attention that our window appears to be crooked. Do you think the lights should complement or contradict the slant?"

Penelope had to count to ten in her head, so she didn't throw the roll of tape at Maria's head. She would probably end up missing and hitting Riley anyways.

Riley brought his hand to his mouth as if thinking hard, but even from here, she could see the barely contained laughter in his eyes. She glared petulantly at both of them as her outstretched hand began to fall asleep.

"I suppose the question is what is going to make you happier. Having crooked lights that make your window seem straighter, or straight lights that make your window seem crooked?" Riley asked.

"You know Riley, we're not a big fan of straight things over here, so Poppy, what if you make the lights crooked but in the other direction?" Maria called.

Penelope blinked at her and slowly raised her hands up until the lights were at an acute angle to the window. "You have five seconds to change your mind before I tape them here."

No one said a word, so Penelope ripped a piece of tape off with her teeth, tossed the roll to the floor, and slapped a piece of tape over the end of the wire.

She hopped down and walked over to stand with the others. She turned back to look at the lights and burst out laughing. It looked horrid.

"Wow, that's quite awful," Maria murmured.

"How can it look that bad?" Penelope groaned.

"Yeah, I'm not sure if I can look at that all night," Riley added.

Penelope and Maria both turned to look at him. "Thank you so much for volunteering your services, Riley. How did you know we needed a tall glass of water like yourself to help us hang fairy lights tonight?"

Maria grabbed him by the arm again and pulled him towards the chair. Riley blushed and blanched simultaneously, and Penelope face palmed. It was obvious from their dates that Riley had reservations about being touched, and Maria had spent the last ten minutes manhandling him all over the place.

Maria managed to get him up on the chair, and she skipped back to Penelope's side. She took Penelope's hand as they both watched Riley awkwardly try to balance on the chair. He was probably the most casually dressed she'd ever seen him, having likely had time to go home and change after work. His hair was up in its usual bun, and he was wearing one of those baseball shirts where the body was white, and the arms were navy blue, overtop of a pair of light-washed skinny jeans.

Penelope realized, with a sudden tightening in her stomach,

that he had an amazing ass. Strike that. He had an amazing everything, and as he stretched up to reach for the end of the lights, his shirt rode up, revealing a small strip of his flat stomach. Penelope felt her mouth water. It had apparently been *that* long since she'd been this attracted to another person.

Penelope suddenly got a sneaking suspicion. She glanced down to see Maria looking up at her with a very smug expression.

"You didn't..." Penelope murmured under her breath.

"I know. I'm the best roommate ever. You're welcome."

"Uhm... any suggestion on where I should move it to?" Riley asked shyly.

Penelope looked back up, and her eyes met inquisitive green ones, and her breath caught. He was so gorgeous, and he was in her apartment, balancing dangerously on a chair they found on the side of the road two years ago, all because her crazy best friend had concocted an evil plan to let Penelope ogle him. Before she could open her mouth and say something stupid like "I think you are the sexiest person I've ever met" or "our apartment has never felt so much like home to me until this exact moment with you in it," Maria opened hers and said something much worse.

"Just follow your heart, Riley. I'm sure it won't lead you astray."

Riley gaped at her and nearly toppled off the chair in surprise. Penelope rushed forward, cursing every life decision she had ever made that led her to this moment. Having little other choice, she grabbed ahold of Riley's hip and placed a steadying hand against his chest. He didn't say anything, but his entire body went rigid under her hands.

She wanted to pull back, but she thought he might actually fall over if she let go. "Sorry, sorry—I just—" she tried to apologize, but he cut her off breathlessly.

"No, no, thank you. I think I was going to fall," Riley said, surprisingly calm based on how tight his muscles were flexing under her hands.

"I think just a little more to the left, Riley, and that should just about do it!" Maria called from across the room, and they both turned to glare at her.

With Penelope's steadying hands, Riley was easily able untape and retape the lights. When they gathered back on the other side of the room, she had to admit they looked pretty nice.

"So, tell me Riley, is this or isn't this the best third date you've ever been on?" Maria asked as she disappeared into the kitchen to grab them all drinks.

"Well..." he said, turning to look at Penelope, "I do feel like I was able to accomplish the mission of the date within the first ten minutes of being here."

"Oh?" Penelope said, raising an eyebrow at him.

"Yeah, I mean, I feel like the third date is when you want to prove how much you're interested in the other person and... I did just risk my life for your home décor."

Penelope blushed so hard she thought her face might be approaching purple.

"I can concur! Passing with flying colors thus far!" Maria called from the kitchen.

"Oh my god, I am so sorry about her," Penelope groaned.

"Are you really?" Riley said, and his tone was light, but his eyes held something serious.

Penelope looked directly into his eyes and took only a second to think before saying, "No, I'm not. She's amazing and a little over-protective, but I love her more than anything in this world. The fact she's teasing you so hard means she's already decided she likes you, so... no. I wouldn't change a thing. About her or our night thus far."

Riley's smile was breathtaking. "I'd never want you to feel the need to apologize to me for someone loving you the way she does. Also," he said, turning to face Maria as she emerged holding three cocktails, "I think I might adore you."

"The feeling is mutual, buttercup." She handed him a drink, and they all clinked their glasses.

"You know, when Penelope described some of the crazy things about your apartment, I was a little bit worried, but... it's quite lovely. You guys have done an amazing job with the place." He looked around but then turned back to Penelope with a slight pout.

Her brain nearly short-circuited at how adorable he was. "I have to say, though, I'm a little disappointed... I thought I would be meeting the infamous three-legged cat."

Penelope and Maria glanced at each other in horror. "Oh fuck-" Maria said as she turned for the door, but Penelope got there first, yelling, "POGO NO!" as she ripped the door open.

As expected, he was sitting on the floor, one paw raised lazily in the air from where he was scratching his claws down the door. He did this anytime he wasn't let in when he wanted to be, and every month their landlord would leave a can of paint at their door for them to fix it. Recently, however, he had begun to get past the paint and into the wood, and they were starting to worry they wouldn't just be able to slap some paint on it this time.

"You fucking heathen," Penelope growled, scooping up the demon spawn and closing the door.

Riley was on her in a second, pulling the cat out of her arms and holding him up in the air like they were in the fucking Lion King.

Penelope gawked, and Maria fake swooned as Riley began baby-talking to the cat.

"Hi angel! I've heard so much about you! Aren't you just the cutest thing I've ever seen. Oh my goodness, look at your little paws—and you've got three of them! That's more than I have. Did the mean girls forget to feed you? I'll feed you, don't you worry. We're going to be great friends. Look at your little nose!" He walked off into the kitchen, and Penelope mimed slapping herself to pull herself out of her shock, and Maria nearly keeled over laughing.

Penelope managed to compose herself enough to follow Riley into the kitchen, where he was gazing around curiously, not seeming too bothered with actually finding the food. Pogo had curled himself onto one of Riley's shoulders and was kneading biscuits in the back of his shirt with his two front paws. If Penelope had thought Riley's pout earlier was adorable, her heart nearly exploded now.

"I didn't know you loved cats so much," she said, gently moving him and Pogo out of the way with her hand on his back. She wouldn't have felt comfortable touching him like that before today, but after holding onto him while he hung the lights up and seeing how comfortably he received Maria's touches, she was feeling a little bold.

He didn't flinch or recoil from her hand, so she added that to the list of okay touches. "I really like animals in general. We weren't allowed to have any growing up. My father... didn't like many things, and animals were one of them."

She bustled around the kitchen quickly, fixing Pogo's food, but the cat and his new best friend didn't seem bothered by the wait. Riley gently stroked his hand down Pogo's back, and Pogo was purring so loudly that Penelope could hear it from across the kitchen.

"Wow, I think he's in love with you. It took us months to even be able to pet him, let alone hold him."

"Oh, I'm sure you've just warmed him up for me," Riley said pleasantly as he continued to stroke the cat.

She took Pogo's food bowl and their drinks back into the dining area. "Have you thought about getting a cat yourself?"

"Oh, I..." Riley said, glancing a little hesitantly at Maria, who just raised both of her eyebrows expectantly. "I told you how I... suffer from depression sometimes? Well... it can get to the point where I stop eating and caring for myself. I wouldn't want to subject an animal to that kind of neglect."

"You know..." Maria said, purposefully averting her eyes to watch Penelope place the food bowl on the ground. "Poppy and I are pretty good at keeping our little friend here alive. If you ever decided you wanted to get a cat, one or both of us could always stop by on days when you needed a little extra help around the house."

Penelope wanted to throw her arms around Maria. It wasn't the kind of offer Penelope would have had the guts to make, but she had been thinking almost the exact same thing.

"I... I could never ask that—"

"Oh, you wouldn't be asking. I'm telling you. We will be there for you. And your feline companion, whenever or if ever you need us," Maria said, looking directly into Riley's eyes. "My friends, Penelope included, saved me from some dark times. I will spend the rest of my life trying to pay that forward, and I don't appreciate people who get in my way of doing that."

Penelope didn't like to think about that time in their friendship, not because it had been hard for her to be there to support

Maria, but because it had been so painful for Maria. Coming out as asexual hadn't been a walk in the park for her, and there were some rough nights of Penelope sitting on the floor outside of Maria's closed apartment door, just letting her know she was there.

Maria's struggle with depression was actually one of the main reasons Penelope had agreed to move in with her. By then, Maria was doing much better. She'd found an amazing therapist and the right dose of antidepressants, but every now and then, she'd have a rough day, and Penelope was so glad she was only a door away, not halfway across the city.

To Penelope's surprise, Riley didn't shy away from Maria's gaze. Instead, he looked steadily at her for a few beats and then nodded slowly, as his hand buried in Pogo's fur. "Okay. I hear you. Maybe I'll... start looking around at shelters this weekend..."

"Oh my god, can I go with you?! There are so many cats that need to be petted!" And just like that, Maria was back to her happy-go-lucky self.

Riley laughed, a little surprised by either the offer or the drastic tonal shift in the conversation. "You're both welcome to come this weekend—or—oh, you said you're working weekends for a little while?" he asked, turning to Penelope.

"Yes, let Poppy go work her boring job, and you and I can go get our dopamine on with some fluffy kitties," Maria said, grinning a little wickedly.

Penelope would hardly describe a drag brunch as boring, but when she'd described it to Riley on the phone, he hadn't seemed particularly interested or engaged, so she let the subject drop.

"I'd love to go with you, Maria. Just pick a time, and I can find a few shelters we can get to within walking distance of my apartment," Riley said, finally releasing Pogo to the floor to eat his dinner.

"Oh my gosh, why is my life so amazing!" Maria said, latching onto his arm and dragging him to the couch.

"Do not come home with an animal, Maria! I swear to god!" Penelope yelled as she went to turn off the lights in the kitchen and dining area.

"I can't hear you!" Maria called back.

"You're literally ten feet away."

"We're going into a tunnel! Riley, can you hear anything?"

"Riley. Do not let her come back to our apartment with a creature," Penelope deadpanned.

"Hey, don't make me choose sides! She holds the future of my cat in her hands, and you hold the future of my romantic life in yours," Riley whined.

"Interesting. Are you implying that those have equal weight?" Maria asked curiously, and even in the dark, Penelope could see Riley turn red down to his shirt collar.

"Okay, okay, enough teasing poor Riley," Penelope said. She nearly tripped over Pogo as he did his awkward scramble up onto the couch to curl up in Riley's lap.

"Oh wait! Poppy before you sit down. Riley, are you a cuddler?" Maria asked from where she was still latched onto his arm on the couch.

"Uhm... I like cuddling. Why?" Riley asked a little hesitantly.

"Because I have a daily quotient of cuddles I have to reach, or I turn into a pumpkin, and if you can't meet those needs, I will get them filled somewhere else."

"Oh... I guess? I mean—we just met, but I could probably—"

"No, no, I've already decided. Here, scoot over." Maria shoved a little uselessly at Riley's shoulder until he acquiesced and moved seats, so the only seat left open was the middle seat.

Penelope shot Maria a "for fuck's sake" look but gingerly took the seat in the middle. Funnily enough, though, she knew Maria was only half doing this for Penelope's sake. Maria always requested near-constant touch when she was watching movies, and if Riley wasn't comfortable cuddling with her, there was no way she would make it through the movie without physically climbing over him to get to Penelope.

"Uhm... maybe next time, Maria?" Riley called softly over Penelope's head. "I promise I... I do actually like cuddling, just..."

"Hey, no need to say anything more, Riley. I am a pretty intimidating person, I know. You'll come to see, though, I'm just as warm and soft as Pogo there." It was probably the most ridiculous thing she'd said all night, but Penelope appreciated her letting him off the hook so easily.

They all settled into the couch, Riley holding a dozing Pogo and Penelope holding Maria. As Maria reached for the popcorn bowl, Penelope turned on the movie.

"Oh, Riley, Penelope made us snacks because she's far too good to us," Maria said through a mouthful of popcorn.

"She is..." Riley agreed as he reached for a cookie.

Penelope kept her eyes straight on the TV and refused to look at either of them as they tried to embarrass her to death.

The famous intro music began to play, and they settled in to watch the first in the series of three movies that were on the docket for the night. She didn't know if Riley would stay for all of them, but she hoped he'd at least make it through the first one.

He made it about thirty minutes in before he began to shift uncomfortably next to her. She turned to him and saw him biting his lower lip. He turned to meet her gaze and smiled sheepishly. "Are you guys a... no-talking-during-movies household?"

"Poppy is because she sucks, but I love talking during movies, buttercup, you can talk to me!" Maria called out.

"Hey! I only don't like when people talk through a movie we're watching for the first time. We've seen these a hundred times; you guys can talk," Penelope grouched.

So, they did. Riley and Maria took turns adding poignant, sometimes snarky, sometimes hilarious commentary throughout the rest of the first movie. When the credits began to roll, everyone got up to stretch, use the bathroom, grab fresh drinks, and Penelope let Pogo out to return to their landlord for bed.

"Are you in it for the long haul with us, Riley? We weren't sure if you'd make it through all three," Maria asked as they all made their way back to the couch.

"Oh yea, I mean, I've only seen this series twenty, possibly thirty times. What if there's something important I missed about the ending?" he said, smirking over at her.

Not for the first time that night, Penelope imagined what it would be like if this were a regular occurrence for them, if Riley came over for their Sunday Greys Anatomy nights or random movie marathons. It sounded pretty fantastic to her.

As they settled back into the couch, Maria hip-checked Penelope, so she ended up pressed up against Riley on the couch. She sighed internally but didn't try to fight back. Maria would just make a scene, and it would probably embarrass Riley. To her surprise, he gently rested his hand on her knee, which stayed there for the rest of the second movie. The same shuffle happened at the end of the second movie, but they all switched to warm, comforting drinks, including tea and hot chocolate. When they retook their seats,

Maria put her foot up on the armrest to bodily shove Penelope practically on top of Riley.

"Oh my god, I am so sorry, and this time I actually am apologizing for Maria. I think she would like us to cuddle. Please feel free to tell her to kindly fuck off, because she's clearly not listening to me." Penelope managed to right herself, so she was sitting pressed up against Riley's side, but Maria didn't let up with her pressure on Penelope's other side.

"Oh, I mean... I wouldn't mind? I mean, so long as you wouldn't mind..." Riley said, glancing hesitantly down at her.

She blinked up at him for a second. "Fine by me, but remember you can always withdraw consent at any point."

"We practice safe cuddling in this house," Maria chimed in. Penelope rolled her eyes at the thinly veiled comment, but Riley actually bit his lip and looked away.

"That's... good to know," he said, and his voice held a gravity that surprised Penelope.

Nothing more was said on the matter, and Riley lifted his arm up so Penelope could slide against his side. Maria grabbed one of Penelope's expertly fluffed couch cushions and leaned it against Penelope's leg. She then proceeded to curl up on her side with her head on the pillow, reaching up to grab Penelope's hand and place it in her hair. "Yes, alright, goodness," Penelope said affectionately as she began to stroke Maria's hair.

"I'm very happy," Maria announced, and Riley whispered "me too" into the darkness.

Maria made it about fifteen minutes into the movie before falling asleep. Penelope extracted her fingers from her hair and grabbed the blanket off the back of the couch to drape over her. She shifted in her sleep, and Penelope scooted slightly closer to Riley to give her a little more space. And yes. That was the only reason she scooted closer. Not because she loved the way Riley's scent had completely enveloped her senses and the way his warm chest against her side made her chest all fluttery.

Unfortunately, in shifting positions, she found herself slightly off balance. The last thing she wanted to do was freak Riley out, but she was on the verge of tipping over.

"Sorry—just for balance," she whispered as she placed a steadying hand on Riley's thigh.

They both fell silent for a moment, and then Riley whispered, "That feels nice. You're very warm."

She got a lot warmer after that, and she could barely concentrate through the next twenty or so minutes of the movie, hyper-aware of all of the places their bodies were touching.

Her head was resting against his chest, which was only a few inches away from his face. With frightening clarity, her mind conjured up what it would take to turn her face up to his and kiss him. She knew in her gut that if she did it too quickly, Riley would probably throw himself out the window she had so kindly scouted out for him earlier that evening. His long, lithe body meant he'd probably have no problem sticking the landing and making a run for it.

She made it approximately two more minutes before her bad ideas got the best of her. She tilted her head up to look at him and whispered his name so softly she wasn't sure if he would hear.

He slowly turned to look down at her, and their mouths were only a scant inch away from each other. His warm, chocolatey breath ghosted across her lips, and they parted unconsciously. She watched his eyes trace over her mouth, and when he whispered her nickname, she closed her eyes and tilted her head, so this time it was his lips, not his breath, that ghosted across her mouth.

On his next inhale, which Penelope could feel from where their sides were pressed together, he dipped his face just enough so he could softly press their mouths together. Penelope felt a warmth pool in the bottom of her rib cage.

She slowly let her tongue come out and caress his lower lip, and she felt him shift against her as he raised his free hand to her face. His hand was as gentle as falling snow as he cupped her cheek and parted his lips for her. She brought her left hand up to rest in the crook of his elbow, where it bent up to touch her face.

Slowly, always slowly, she brushed her tongue against his lip again and then slid it into his mouth, savoring the velvety softness of his tongue as it met hers. She felt him take a sharp inhale of breath, but she didn't stop, just continued to slowly caress his tongue with hers, inviting it to play.

His hand moved around to the back of her neck and pulled her deeper into the kiss. He pressed her tongue back and then chased it down with his own, sliding into her mouth and filling it with chocolate, hints of buttery popcorn, and that dark vanilla she had come to associate with him. She knew they had to be quiet, so she silenced a moan in her throat, but she let the vibration of it slide into his mouth, and she felt it travel down his chest and into his arms. His fingers shook and trembled where they cupped her nape, and with a flash of intuition she remembered one of their questions at the arcade bar.

She moved her hand tentatively from his arm to his shoulder and then up to the back of his neck. He broke away from the kiss and sighed against her cheek, leaning his forehead against hers. Their eyes both slid open simultaneously, and she could see a whole new spectrum of green in his eyes from this closeup. His irises had hints of a well-tended lawn in the middle of summer and the ripest avocados on millennials' toast. She smiled at the silly thought, and when he smiled back, she felt herself melt into him a little more.

"Nels..." he whispered again, and she leaned forward to drink the sound off his tongue, pulling him back into another round of kissing.

She would feel exceptionally rude for doing this right next to Maria, but she had once had a forty-five minute make out and grind session with a boy in the same room as Maria on a beach trip. Maria had insisted over and over she couldn't care less. Still, though, she would never do anything more than just kissing in such close proximity to Maria while she slept. She felt okay with the kissing, though, since she would without question kiss Riley in front of Maria if she was awake. Well, maybe she wouldn't kiss Riley quite like *this*. But still.

This was a slow, sensual dance between their tongues, and when she grazed her teeth over his bottom lip, she felt his thigh quiver beneath her fingers. She was beginning to realize that she wanted to do very filthy things to Riley. She knew he had a lot of hesitations with sex, so she refused to let herself play out any of the scenarios that her mind was presenting her on a silver platter. She would only allow herself to fantasize about things she knew for a fact he was comfortable with, so for now, it would just have to be this deliciously slow kissing.

Riley's entire body was trembling when they pulled back for air again. She applied a gentle pressure to his nape, and with a few steadying breaths, he stilled again.

"God, Nels... you... you do something to me..."

She smiled because damn did he do something to her too. "Me too, Riley. Me too."

"It's... a little scary..." he whispered, laying his confessions at her feet in their dark living room.

"It's okay. We're just going to keep on going slow and steady, alright? We're going to figure this out together."

"But... what if... I can't. Figure it out, I mean. Does us kissing mean we couldn't be friends anymore?" Riley asked, and there was utter heartbreak in his words.

"No, sweetheart, no." Penelope brought her hand around his neck to cup his face. She had no idea where the endearment had come from, but she felt a blush rise up under her hands, so she took that as a sign it was well received. "Hell, Maria and I did more than just kiss, and we're still friends, right? And you and Kim, and you and Ashley?"

He nodded against Penelope's forehead. "I... don't want to stop... but... if we have to... to figure things out, I could—"

She pressed their lips together again, collecting his anxiety with her mouth and trying to breathe reassurance back into his lungs. He welcomed the kiss and opened his mouth to her tongue for another few minutes of exploring.

She pulled back to whisper, "I kind of feel like this is a pretty essential part of us figuring things out."

He nodded again and didn't say anything else. They stayed like that, foreheads pressed together, for a few breaths before he made the first move this time. He cupped her neck and pulled her back in for another deep kiss.

They kissed for what felt like hours but was probably only a few more minutes. Something slowly shifted with the kiss. She thought it might be his confidence. He moved his mouth with more assurance and pushed into her mouth with his tongue to take instead of just to give. Penelope nearly groaned, but she trapped it in her chest right at the last moment, causing a shiver to run through her body and into Riley's. His fingers tightened on her neck, and he shifted uncomfortably under her hand, so she pulled back.

"I... I think I might need to stop... just for now," he said, panting slightly. She nodded because she thought she probably needed to stop as well.

As if the cinematic universe agreed, the black credit screen began to roll, plunging the room into a more total darkness.

"Can I call you an Uber? To thank you for an amazing night?" she asked, searching around in the dark for her phone.

"No, Nels, I got it. Thank you... for everything. Do you need help getting Maria to bed?"

"Nah, I got that one down to a science."

They slowly stood up, stretching out slightly stiff arms and legs. She walked him to the door, where they paused for a moment. They glanced down at his phone, and it said the driver would be arriving in two minutes.

"Is that enough time for... a goodnight kiss?" she asked quickly.

He smiled down at her in the glow of his phone, and captured her mouth with his own. She had been hoping for a full-body hug-kiss combo, but this was a perfect way to end the night. Sweet and warm.

"I... am assuming a goodnight kiss means I've earned a fourth date?" he asked tentatively, sliding on his shoes.

"Of course, and I don't think you're working to earn dates anymore, sweetheart. I think you can assume they're just another essential part of how we will figure things out between us, okay?"

He bit his lip around a grin and nodded. Penelope opened the door, and he surprised her with a final peck on the lips before he disappeared down the stairs.

Penelope came home from the drag brunch the next afternoon feeling pretty worn down. Riley and Maria had been texting her adorable photos from the animal shelter all day, and only some of the cuteness was from the animals.

She loved the photos and was truly ecstatic they were bonding, but she had felt a little sad to be missing it. She had also really hoped to see Taylor at the drag show today, but Penelope had fallen asleep last night too late to message her and ask if she was coming. This morning had been a whirlwind of drag prep, and she hadn't been able to ask her then either.

Penelope walked into her apartment and immediately noticed a strange smell, kind of like summer back home. She walked into Maria's room to ask her about it and nearly tripped over something soft. She looked down and just about lost her shit.

There was a fucking rabbit nibbling hay in the middle of Maria's room.

She whipped out her phone so fast Maria didn't even have a chance to give an excuse. Her fingers flew across the keyboard as she sent the traitorous bastard a message.

> Penelope: YOU LET HER GET A FUCKING RABBIT?!

> Riley: Well, I hope it hasn't been fucking. Did you know those things tend to have large litters of babies? Sometimes as many as 15?

> Penelope: How much swiping do you think you'd have to do to re-find me and match with me again if I unmatched us?

> Riley: Oh my god, please don't do that! I'm so sorry.

> Riley: Here, does this make it any better?

Riley had attached a selfie of himself pouting into the camera, his chin resting on top of a black cat with a patch of white on its chin and tummy. Penelope nearly swooned on top of the rabbit, who was still just munching away at her feet, looking up at her with big, knowing eyes.

Penelope already knew they would keep the stupid rabbit, but Riley would have sixteen rabbits and a cat on his hands if she ended up with fifteen baby bunnies.

TAYLOR

Taylor was having a rough hump day. Work had been ridiculously hard, and she despised the business clothes she had to wear all day. She threw them into an angry pile across the room the second she got home.

Unfortunately, she hadn't accounted for the furry creature she chose to cohabitate with, who took the flying clothing as a threat to his domain. Before she could react, he launched himself across the room at her ankles. Thankfully he was a loving overlord, and instead of clawing her, he began to wind his slinky body around her legs. He continued to do this as she attempted to make her way to her dresser to change into something comfier.

She chose a well-loved pink t-shirt and a pair of leggings to lounge the rest of the night in, accepting that they somehow came out of her drawer already covered in cat fur. She grimaced as the leggings caught on some of her leg hair as she slid them on. She'd been feeling lazy recently and hadn't been shaving as frequently. Also, she just despised shaving. She wasn't very good at it. She didn't understand how some women could shave their legs dry at a moment's notice. She was blessed by soft, downy blonde hair that didn't curve or cause razor burn. However, if she wasn't careful when shaving, she'd nick the ever-loving crap out of her ankles and knees and end up bleeding all over the place like a victim of a mauling.

Speaking of mauling, her cat was attempting to climb up her leg, so she reached down and picked him up, flipping him over like a baby in her arms. She carried him into the kitchen to feed him, and the second food was offered he became completely disinterested in her. Fickle creature.

She pulled out her phone from her legging pocket. One of her friends had bought her these for Christmas, and she would never be able to go back to leggings without pockets. She immediately opened her text messages and pulled up her chat with Pen.

Their last conversation had been Monday night when Pen opened up about feelings she'd been experiencing since starting to MC the drag brunch. How she described her feelings about her chest sounded very much like gender dysphoria to Taylor, but she had no intention of shoving anyone out of the closet or even making them aware that they might be in a closet. Pen seemed very settled into her sexuality, so Taylor figured it was probably just a matter of a few more weeks of these brunches before Pen figured out her gender for herself.

There was something so refreshing about Pen's emotional intelligence and how she seemed to be aware of her own weaknesses and insecurities. Instead of ignoring them, she pressed into them like a bruise, trying to explore them and suss them out.

Taylor enjoyed running from her problems, and she had become quite good at it over time, but as she got older, she knew this was not a lifelong solution. She felt herself opening up to Pen in ways she had only ever done with a select few friends and her beloved sister.

She had meant what she said when she told Pen she wasn't looking to find someone new to date, but she couldn't deny that Pen made her feel some kind of way. Sort of safe and seen even if Taylor was only showing Pen a fraction of herself. The parts she *was* showing were always accepted, no questions asked. It had Taylor considering how she could be more open with a future partner. She hoped one day she would be able to be as open and raw as Pen had been since day one.

She glanced down at the message box again. She wasn't sure how it happened, but she and Pen had almost become sort of queer pen pals. They rarely, if ever, talked about their days or their friends and family, instead, every conversation seemed to have them sharing things about themselves, their pasts, and even sometimes their futures.

Tonight though, she was tired, and she didn't want to talk about anything too serious. She stalked around the house looking for her cat and tried to take a cute picture of him, but he was not having it. The best she could muster was a photo of the white tip of his tail as he disappeared behind her couch.

She decided that would probably be a nice conversation starter, so she shot off the text and made herself some dinner. About an hour later, Pen responded.

Taylor appreciated that they had created a precedent where they didn't have to respond to each other right away. Taylor could go days where she didn't feel like talking to anyone, and Pen never pressed her for a response.

Pen: I didn't know you had a cat!

Taylor: Yes, he is probably the only man I will ever truly love.

Pen: Wow, my heart is breaking for the men of earth.

Taylor: I wouldn't waste your time on them. I feel like they're doing just fine without me.

Pen: Well, they wouldn't know what they were missing, would they?

Taylor: Actually, there is one man out there, at least I hope he's still out there, poor bastard, who knows exactly what he's missing.

Pen: Uhm, that sounds like there's a story in there somewhere.

Taylor: Hardly. I was still trying to figure out my sexuality, so I figured I might as well give dick a shot, but we didn't even get past kissing. It was gross.

Pen: Harsh. I've always wondered if I lean more heavily one way or another, but I find vaginas and dicks equally stressful and terrifying, so maybe not.

> Taylor: Interesting, but you do like having sex with men and women?

> Taylor: Now that you mention it, I think vaginas are rather enchanting.

> Pen: I think I like the sex, not the organ?

> Taylor: Is that a cousin of hate the sin, not the sinner?

> Pen: Hmmm, could be.

Taylor was toeing a line, she knew, between trying to open up a little with Pen and being cagey with her. Sometimes she would admit things and immediately regret opening up that particular drawer in her head. She never felt good outright slamming the drawer shut again, but sometimes she'd find ways to use humor and snark to move through a conversation that became too hard for her to engage with.

She was also finding herself beginning to toe the line between playing and flirting. She liked seeing how Pen reacted to some of her jokes and jabs, but she didn't want to lead her on. Taylor liked flirting but was scared to be flirted with and liked to give, but not receive physical affection. There was an entire paycheck's worth of therapy bills in that one sentence, and it had truly been on Taylor's to-do list for years to find a good therapist, but somehow, she was unable to find the time or will. So, she had a cat instead and thought that would just have to be it for now. That and her hours and hours of texting Pen.

They texted for several more hours that night before Taylor fell asleep with the gentle weight of her cat on her chest.

EIGHT

PENELOPE

Penelope did her best to balance a lunch date with Riley on Tuesday, work at the cafe and casually stalk Maria's date on Wednesday, and stay up late into the night texting Taylor on Thursday.

After their weeks of texting, Penelope had come to realize that both Taylor and Riley tended to stop responding to her for several hours and sometimes a day or two at a time. Very rarely would they both stop texting her at the same time, though, so she felt like she was constantly glued to her phone or thinking about the two people she connected with via her phone. She asked Taylor if she wanted to meet up in person, but Taylor had admitted she was going through a hectic time. She didn't think she was up for anything on weeknights, and since Penelope wasn't available on weekends, they decided just to be texting pals for the moment.

The problem was, the more Penelope got to know Taylor, the

less she felt like just a pal. It was a strange feeling. Not quite infatuation, more like fascination, and when they were in the middle of
one of their texting marathons, it verged on intoxication. That was
far too many "-ations" for Penelope, and as if having confusing feelings for one person wasn't enough, she was also still trying to get to
the bottom of her connection with Riley.

She had enjoyed kissing him more than she thought possible,
but she desperately wanted to respect the fact that he had been
crystal clear that sex wasn't a given for him. She forced herself to
focus on the other aspects of their relationship, even though sometimes she could swear she could still feel his lips on hers.

It was also hard to focus on the more cerebral and emotional
parts of her relationship with Riley because he still seemed to be
holding himself back from her. Penelope thought of herself as
pretty open and transparent. She'd basically word vomited all over
Taylor for weeks and in return she'd opened up to Penelope more
and more each day. Riley was just a much harder nut to crack. His
disappearing acts didn't help either, but she reminded herself not to
fault him for that.

Adding fuel to the dumpster fire that was Penelope's mental
state right now, she was also having almost non-stop thoughts and
questions about her gender. It had been in the back of her mind for
years, but as her participation in the drag shows continued, she
started to seriously question all of her preconceived notions about
gender. The previous weekend, Sham Pain had casually stated she
had noticed a change in Penelope. On a whim, Penelope hesitantly
asked her if they could stay after the next drag show and talk, and
Sham Pain had eagerly agreed.

Saturday rolled around, and the show was a roaring success.
Penelope had gotten the hang of the showmanship part of the gig

and was finding an inner confidence on stage she'd never known she possessed.

"All right, Sugar, lay it on me," Sham Pain said.

They were sitting at one of the cafe tables with steaming mugs of coffee in front of them. Penelope was still in her drag outfit. This weekend it consisted of a bright magenta suit over a black men's button-down. She wore a sports bra under it all and, again, she enjoyed how the outfit caused the eye to skim over her flattened chest and instead focused on her legs. She wasn't sure how to say all of this to Sham Pain, so she just blurted out her first thought.

"So, I think I'm starting to enjoy doing drag, not just as a way of dressing up to be someone different but... almost like dressing up to be myself?"

Sham Pain nodded but didn't say anything, letting her silence urge Penelope on.

"I've been researching the different kinds of gender identities, and I think I've been able to cross off most of them pretty easily." She'd been doing this in between texting with Taylor and Riley, wanting desperately to talk about what she was finding with Riley, but instead engaging almost exclusively with Taylor on anything related to sexual or gender identity. She just seemed to understand Penelope in a way no one else ever had.

"I'm certain that I'm not a man." Penelope continued, glancing up quickly to gauge Sham Pain's reaction. She quirked her lip but continued to say nothing. "So... I think that means I'm not trans or bigender. I also think I'm probably not gender fluid because I don't think I really 'flow' or 'slide' between genders or change genders."

Sham Pain took a sip of her coffee and nodded.

"But... I don't think I'm agender, either. I do feel like a woman in some ways, like... sometimes I look in the mirror when I'm wearing, I don't know, a nice sweater and cute jeans, and I'm like, 'wow, I'm kind of pretty,' or I catch my reflection in a shop window and I'm like 'oh wow she's pretty' and—... god that sounds pretentious doesn't it..."

Sham Pain snorted. "Sugar, do you think I'd spend five hours getting dressed like this if it wasn't so I could look in the mirror and say, 'Damn, that's one gorgeous piece of ass right there.' You are not only encouraged but required to be able to hype yourself up in this life."

Penelope smiled and took her own sip of coffee. "But... then there are times where I don't specifically *feel* like a woman, but it's not like I feel like anything else. Like... when I'm alone, at no point am I ever like, how does that song go, 'damn, I feel like a woman?' I just feel pretty neutral. But then there are also times that I feel... uncomfortable being a woman. Not just like being a woman in society is hard, so I'd rather just not be one. More like..." she stopped and looked down at her hands.

Penelope felt like she was on the edge of a precipice.

As if she could sense this, Sham Pain reached forward and took Penelope's hand in a solid grip.

For years, Penelope had the whispers of thoughts and the hints of feelings that she'd never been able to put words to. Taylor had been gently guiding her through some of her thoughts over text, but earlier this week she'd stopped them mid-conversation and sent Penelope a link to a book. It was a graphic novel, something Penelope would never have chosen for herself, but the title piqued Penelope's interest. She downloaded the eBook copy and read the entire book that night. She ran to her local bookstore, thank god they still had one of those, and picked up a physical copy the next day and she'd spent that night dog-earring almost half of the pages.

When she was done, she laid back on her bed and just let herself... feel.

She took a deep, fortifying breath and, just like that night, made the conscious decision to step over the edge of that cliff. "Sometimes I hate my chest. I look in the mirror, and it's like these foreign objects are there screaming at me that I'm some kind of phony. It's like—they're this dirty reminder I'm supposed to be something I don't feel like I've ever been. I didn't realize until recently, but I've spent my life trying to hide any hint of cleavage, and I try not to draw attention to my chest in any way, and... there have been moments of intimacy where I find myself getting angry. When someone tries to—to interact with them. Like, why do you like them when I—hate them so much." Penelope choked on the word hate.

Sham Pain squeezed her hand even tighter, still saying nothing. Penelope realized that she had never been around Sham Pain and not heard her rich voice filling the space. It was strangely reverent. Like she was sacrificing her voice so Penelope could have one.

"So, all this to say... I guess I've never given any of this any thought before because I've always known I'm not a man, so I thought those were the only two options because..."

"Gender is a binary?" Sham Pain suggested flatly.

"But... it's not binary, is it..."

"Not in the slightest, sugar," she said, smiling her killer smile at Penelope.

"So, I've done a lot of research on what it means to be nonbinary, and something in my chest just opened up. It felt a little like when I found the pansexual flag. It was like..." Penelope trailed off, trying to figure out how to say what she was thinking.

"Like you've been trying to think of a word you've forgotten your entire life, and when you remember it, it's this huge relief?

162

Like you've been blindly trying to fit a square peg into a round hole your entire life, and suddenly you find the square hole, and it just slots right in?" Sham Pain murmured softly.

Penelope didn't realize she was crying until Sham Pain reached forward and wiped her cheek with a napkin. She lifted her coffee cup to her lips and took a large drink. This most recent shipment of beans had a slight vanilla flavor, and thoughts of Riley immediately flooded her head, and she had another thought.

"But... Okay, so... what if—uh... What if I don't mind being called she/her? Like, it doesn't bother me in the slightest. How do I... should I still tell people I might be nonbinary? Like, does it even matter then, I guess? I'm kind of seeing someone, and I'm not sure... how to tell them," Penelope stammered out.

Sham Pain smiled softly. "Taylor?"

"Oh, uh, well... I'm talking to Taylor a lot! I like her, and... might even *like* like her a bit, but she's not interested in dating. And actually, I'll probably tell her soon. That one doesn't feel hard. It's... no, it's a guy named Riley. I think I really *like* like him but... I've never told him anything about this. We haven't even really talked about my sexuality and definitely not my gender..."

Sham Pain's brows pulled together and she bit her lip. "Is that because he makes you feel unsafe?"

"No! No, not at all, I... honestly, I'm not sure why. I feel like we just haven't connected in that way quite yet? But we've connected in other ways. I'm not sure why I'm finding it so much easier to open up to Taylor than to Riley. I don't think it's because of their genders. I don't really care what gender they are to be honest."

Sham Pain tipped her head at that. "Well, just because you like people of different genders doesn't mean you'll connect with everyone in the same exact way. When I look for partners, it's imperative that they accept every single part of me. I don't think I could ever be with someone who wasn't accepting."

Penelope thought about that for a few moments, the scent of coffee and vanilla surrounding her. She had the niggling urge to ask Sham Pain more probing questions about herself, both in and outside of drag, but this chat wasn't really about her, it was about Penelope.

"To answer your other question, your pronouns are your choice. They don't need to be a message to the world, even though they can be if that's what you want them to be. But if you like she/her and that feels right, then by all means don't change them just to be recognized as nonbinary. You can tell those that it feels important to tell. But... if you want to try out they/them, you can always ask a close family member, friend, or partner to use them and see how it feels. You can also always use the pronouns 'she/they.' It's a bit of a nod to you being nonbinary and a way to say you are okay with either."

Penelope had to stop and let that one sink in. "Would... would you use they/them pronouns for me? When I'm in drag? Just... just to try it out?"

Sham Pain beamed at her and nodded her head fiercely.

Penelope's pulse raced and she was excited for this new development but she knew there was someone else she wanted to share this with.

"Sham Pain... thank you so much. I'm sorry to dump all of this on you—"

"Oh honey, please. I'm just so happy you're finding joy in this experience in your own way." She gestured at Penelope's outfit. "Also, you look phenomenal in a suit. You might think about incorporating more androgyny into your daily wardrobe. You might find you can look as happy as you do up on that stage all the time."

"Thank you..." Penelope said as she stood up, and they hugged tightly.

Penelope hurried to change, grabbed her backpack, and headed for the street. She decided to walk home so she could talk on the phone and not disturb any of her fellow bus-dwellers. Her fingers hit the button, and she held the phone to her ear.

The phone picked up on the third ring, but there was a strange buzzing noise on the line. "Pen?" Taylor's voice was garbled as if she was talking underwater or in that imaginary tunnel Maria liked to pretend to be in sometimes.

"Taylor? Can you hear me?" Penelope called into the phone.

There was what sounded like a laugh. "I can hear you, but you sound hella weird."

"So do you," Penelope said, laughing. "Or, well, I mean I've never actually heard your voice before. Maybe this is just what you sound like."

"If it's anything like how you sound, I'm going to say it's probably a hard no," Taylor said with what sounded like a groan but could have easily been a loud sigh.

"Perfect. Do you think it's the connection?" Penelope checked her phone and saw she had full service.

"Well... my cat did one of those bip-bip things where he decided to throw my phone across the room this morning... the screen didn't crack, so I thought I was good, but this is decidedly *not* good."

"Oh shit, I'm sorry. Stupid cat," Penelope said, laughing.

"Yeah, he's an absolute asshole, but what can you do."

They fell into a buzz-filled silence for a moment. "Well, I had kind of wanted to talk to you about something a little serious, but... maybe now's not a good time," Penelope said with disappointment evident in her voice.

"Not gonna lie. I'm laughing at everything you're saying in my head because you sound a little like a gremlin."

"Fantastic," Penelope groaned sadly.

"Aw hon... okay, okay, it's fine, don't worry about the weird sound. I'm here, and you're here, and it's amazing to get to talk to you on the phone. I can't believe we've never done this before!"

"It seems like maybe the universe is trying to keep us from talking," Penelope said with a laugh.

"Well, fuck the universe. What's going on?"

She told Taylor about the conversation she'd just had with Sham Pain, leaving out the part about her breasts, as that felt too much for their garbled phone line. She also left out everything about Riley. She hadn't told Taylor about Riley, and she wasn't sure if she was going to until things felt more certain. She hated to admit it, but a small part of her was still hoping Taylor would change her mind and want to try things out with Penelope one day. She just felt like Taylor understood a side of her that no one else ever had. As they continued to talk about gender, it felt like a part of Penelope had been sitting in a dark room for so long, and Taylor had come in and turned the light on.

"Would you like me to call you they/them? I'm happy to do so, but I feel like your pronouns don't come up often in conversation because I'm typically not talking about you in the third person."

Shit. That was true. Penelope hadn't even thought about that. "I asked Sham Pain if she could use they/them for me in drag. I could probably ask Maria to try it out too... or, I don't know. Honestly, I think I like the idea of she/they? Sort of just letting the chips fall where they may, I guess?"

"I think both of those sound like good plans. And just so I understand, is roommate code word for lesbian lover?"

Penelope burst out laughing. "No, no, not at all—" Penelope froze mid-step, nearly causing a biker to careen off the sidewalk.

"Pen? Are you still there, or did my phone finally fully crap out?"

"Oh my god, I'm sorry, I just had the funniest realization. My brother lives with his business partner. I'm almost 100% sure they're seeing each other, and I just realized what an unbelievably queer cliche that is."

"'They were roommates!' That's amazing!" Taylor's laugh came through the line in a moment of clarity, hitting Penelope deep in her chest. Her hand tightened on the phone, and she felt a similar tightening under her ribs. She knew this feeling; it was how Riley had made her feel on Friday night. How could two people make her feel the same thing but in such different ways?

They continued to talk across phone lines, underwater, and in tunnels as Penelope walked into her apartment. She nearly tripped on the goddamn rabbit again, and when she saw Maria smirking up at her from the couch, she wished Taylor a good rest of her day and hung up.

She scooped up the blasted creature and brought him to the couch. "Hey, can I, uh... talk to you about something quickly? Actually... I don't know why I said that. It's not going to be quick. Do you have approximately two hours for me to dump on you, or do you have somewhere to be?"

Maria frowned at her watch. "Shit Poppy, I have to go in ten. I'm meeting the other girl, Crystal, from that dating app."

Penelope's eyes flew up, "Oh, you didn't tell me that! I really liked Natasha from Wednesday. Are you just as excited to meet Crystal?"

Maria smiled a fond little smile. "I am. They both seem to bring very different things to the table, and I think they'd bring a very different energy into my life. I want to try and get a feeling for which one is what I'm looking for." She gave Penelope a meaningful look as she stood up. "Could we co-op Grey's Anatomy tomorrow night for whatever you need to talk about?"

Penelope scrunched up her face at the thinly veiled reference to Penelope's confusing love life, but she nodded as she stood up. She placed the rabbit back on the floor, where it apparently now lived, and wandered into the kitchen for a drink that didn't taste like the guy she was dating—speaking of. She pulled out her phone, and since it had gone so well last time, she pressed the phone call button in her chat with Riley. The line rang, but he didn't pick up.

She sadly looked down at the screen and sent a quick message asking if they could see each other soon, proposing Monday. A few moments later, her phone chimed, and it was Riley saying he was doing pretty well, and he said he had plans with Kim and Ashley to try a new recipe for dinner on Monday, but he asked if she would like to join. Before she could stress about the implications of meeting his friends, she quickly agreed.

About an hour later, she was sorting through her closet when her phone rang. She saw it was Taylor, and felt a sudden jolt of happiness, breaking her out of the funk she'd been in since Riley had refused to answer her call.

"Hi, is your phone fixed?" Penelope asked cheerfully as she put the phone on speaker so she could continue sorting through her things. She had already found several sweaters, flannels, and t-shirts she thought encapsulated her style, but she wanted to use them as building blocks, not the only things she wore.

"Ugh. That's why I was calling, actually. I wanted to see if this at-home fix I tried worked, but... nope, apparently, it's gotten worse." Taylor now sounded like she was standing on top of a jackhammer, and her voice was coming in undulating waves. The buzzing noise in the background was gone, though, so Penelope could hear her more clearly. It was just what she was hearing was super bizarre.

"Oh, yeah, like way worse. But I can hear you better, so... I guess we can still talk if you want?"

"I'd love to, hence why I called you silly."

Penelope smiled into the mirror, and she realized it was that stupid smile she got when she had first started messaging Riley. Well. Wasn't that interesting.

"So, what are you doing?" Taylor asked.

"I'm sorting through my closet right now, trying to find all my androgynous clothing and see what I can do with it or what I need to buy to add to it."

"Oh, that's fun! I did the opposite a few months back, pulled out my most feminine clothing, which was like two things, and started building a capsule wardrobe around it. Then I told my friends what I was doing, and they pretty much filled in the rest."

Penelope looked at the items she'd taken out thus far and realized they were all tops. She walked over to her drawers and began shuffling through pants.

"It's awesome you have such supportive friends. I couldn't talk to my roommate, aka best friend, tonight, but we're going to talk tomorrow. Maybe I'll also ask her about clothing."

"So, what have we got so far?"

Penelope described the items on her bed and then threw in a few pairs of skinny jeans and straight-leg slacks.

"I think I want to get a really nice suit. I wore one for drag this morning—which of course, you would have seen if you'd come! But I've seen some queer and nonbinary people wear them online and... wow."

"Oh, god, that is, like, so my type," Taylor groaned over the line.

Penelope's ears perked up. "Oh really?"

"Really, really. I mean, part of me finds them insanely intimidating. Because, like..."

The line fell silent for a moment. Penelope stopped shuffling through her drawer to glance at her phone. It still displayed Taylor's name, and the speaker was still on.

"Well. I think maybe I'd look good dressed like that too, but... I've spent the past year feminizing myself, so it feels almost counterproductive to try and make myself more androgynous now, but... I don't know. Gender is hard." Her voice had gotten soft and a little sad at the end.

"It's an epic construct," Penelope agreed.

Suddenly that laugh sounded through the line again, and Penelope's heart lifted. "I think those are two separate phrases: it's an epic clusterfuck, or gender is a construct."

"Oh... well, you know what, I like it's an epic construct."

Taylor laughed again, but Penelope's mind had stuck onto something she'd said.

"I totally understand what you're saying about wanting to be feminine but also able to play with androgyny. I think I'm the exact opposite; I want to be androgynous but maybe still play with femininity?"

"Sounds like we should just share a wardrobe. Would be cheaper," Taylor joked.

"How tall are you?" Penelope asked absently.

"I'm around 5' 7"? Maybe a little under."

That was just about Riley's height, and Penelope almost snorted. Blonde, slightly androgynous, and a little taller than herself. Glad she had a type.

"Do you ever wear heels?" Penelope asked, eyeing her death trap shoes in the corner of her closet. She was coming to realize that all of her feminine clothes made her feel like she was playing dress-up—badly. Heels, makeup, dresses, purses. It all felt the same.

"No, absolutely not. Fuck heels. They're a construct."

Penelope laughed and picked up her heels and threw them in the trash. "Done. They're gone. I'm throwing them away."

"Good for you, Pen! You fucking tell them, you nonbinary gender-neutral royalty."

"Wow, that was a mouthful, wasn't it," Penelope said.

"Yeah, but how did it feel?"

She thought about it for a moment. "Can I get back to you?"

"Of course, Pen, you take all the time you need."

"... can I ask your advice on something else?" Penelope hedged.

"Always."

Penelope hesitated for just a moment and then decided to take the metaphorical plunge yet again today. "So... I'm kind of slowly starting to date this guy, and... I haven't told him anything about this yet. I think he'd be understanding—he did say he was queer, but we've never actually talked about it, and I know just because you're queer sexually doesn't mean you understand or can relate to genderqueer or gender nonbinary or all of that but... I guess my question is, should I tell him?"

The line went dead silent for almost a full minute. "That's... a really hard one for me to answer, Pen. Of course, I'd like to say that person should make you feel safe and comfortable enough to open up to them about something like this, but it's not really about them, is it? It's how comfortable you are talking about it, having them see you that way, and how ready you are to have to educate them about it if they don't know anything about gender or gender identity. That can be... terrifying. And it can change the way a person sees you—I mean, of course it's going to, and sometimes... Sometimes it's like you just want them to get to know you as a person without your gender, but gender is so important in our society and with dating and..." she trailed off at the end, the line falling silent.

"Epic fucking construct..." Penelope whispered.

"Yeah... right? So. I don't think I can answer that for you, Pen. Is it... sorry I—I don't know if I should ask this..."

Penelope glanced at the phone as if she could telegraph her feelings over the line. "You can ask me anything, Taylor."

"Does it... affect how you engage sexually with him?"

Penelope froze. Well, she had said anything, hadn't she.

"I... don't know. I've never really thought about it in this way before, but... I've had some bad feelings when my chest has been touched or looked at by men—...Is it weird though, that I don't mind quite as much when women look at me like a woman, but I'm starting to think I don't like it as much when men see me as a woman? Something about the female gaze makes me feel... seen? Like I'm not just a sex object or a boob squeeze toy?"

Penelope sank down on the edge of her bed and put her chin in her hand. "Sorry... does that all sound crazy? I know that was... a lot. I can be a lot."

"No, Pen... it doesn't sound crazy at all, and please... Do not ever say that to me. You are not. A lot. You are just the perfect amount."

That struck a chord in Penelope. Riley said almost the same thing to her a few weeks ago. Why was this coming up in two completely separate conversations? Did she think that she was a lot?

"I mean... this is a lot, though, isn't it? I don't just like men or women; I like everyone, but I've only ever seriously dated men, so what if I'm being overly dramatic with my sexuality? Now it's like I'm not entirely a woman, but I'm not a man, so maybe I'm non-binary, but if I don't mind the female pronouns, then why does it even matt—"

"Pen!" Taylor shouted through the phone, and Penelope stuttered and then stopped talking. Her heart was thundering a million miles a minute from her litany of rapid-fire confessions, and the shout scared her for a second.

"Fuck. That. You are not a lot, and none of that is a lot. You deserve to be your entire huge self regardless of what anyone else thinks, and... Pen... you are so worthy of being seen and loved, and anyone who thinks differently or treats you differently can go to hell. I wish... I'm not the right person to give you that Pen but, maybe this guy is? Because if he has a fucking clue, he will see how amazing you are and how deserving you are of love."

Penelope sat their frozen, still clutching a pair of leggings to her chest. She couldn't speak for a moment, just absorbing everything Taylor had said.

"... Pen? Shit, I—I didn't mean to yell. I'm so sorry. I know that... that can be triggering for some people. I know I don't handle being yelled at well; I can't believe I just did that—" Taylor said, her voice rising through several octaves, discernible even through the garbled phone line.

"Hey, no, it's fine," Penelope interrupted, "that isn't a trigger for me or anything. I was just trying to absorb everything you just said —I mean hell, even what I just said I... I've never told this to anyone before."

"... Pen—" she was interrupted by a shuffling noise, a large crash, and a shout. "—shit, I'm so sorry! This stupid fucking cat just ate an entire loaf of bread I have to go—text me? I'll text you? We'll text! I'm texting you right now. Bye—and... thank you. For trusting me like this."

The line went dead, and Penelope felt a little shaken but somehow like another piece of the weight that had been sitting on her shoulders all these years had lifted. She got a text from Taylor and an update on the cat, and she began to put her clothes into piles of love, like, probably not, and—well, the last pile was actually the trash can. She pulled out the bag to ensure there wasn't any actual trash in it, and she designated it as the goodwill bag.

She stayed up until two in the morning texting and sorting, and she knew there would be hell to pay in the morning, but she wanted to finish what she had started.

RILEY

Maybe allowing the chaotic best friend of the girl he was dating help him choose a cat to live with was not the best life choice Riley had ever made.

Oreo was an absolute love muffin, wanting constant attention and pets, but he also loved getting into trouble. With a start, Riley realized he had brought Maria home with him in cat form, and it all made a lot more sense.

Case in point, the cat was currently chewing on a lamp chord.

"For fucks sake, Oreo. They're going to be here any minute. What am I going to do if you break my only—" as he reached down to pick up the beast, he bit down one last time, and the lamp cord snapped into two.

"SHIT!"

Just then, he heard a knock at the door. "Ohhhh Rileyyyyyyy! We have arrived bearing gifts and one absolutely beautiful lady!" Kim called through the door.

"It's me." Ashley's gravelly voice came through the door.

"Well, it's also Ashley, but noooo it's Penelope!"

Damn. He had thought he'd have a few minutes to debrief with his friends before she arrived, but they were all arriving together just as his demon cat destroyed the only lighting source in the room.

"Shit—sorry—one second!" he called as he chucked Oreo into the guest room, turned on the working lights in there, thank god, and closed the door.

He answered his apartment door feeling a bit disheveled, and there Penelope was, looking as stunning as ever in an olive green off-the-shoulder sweater. It came all the way up to her neck on one side and slanted down, completely covering her chest but coming to rest halfway down her opposite arm.

He had never seen her shoulder before, and there was something soft and trusting in it that he couldn't describe.

"Wow... you look beautiful," he breathed.

"Thank you!" Kim trilled.

"Always so kind," Ashley grumbled, as they walked into his

apartment, gently bumping him with their shoulders as they passed.

Penelope stood in his doorway, looking at her boot-clad feet. She wore a pair of tight black jeans, and he let himself appreciate her legs for just a moment.

When he looked back up, she was smirking at him. He smiled crookedly right back. "You're always so pretty," he said reverently, the words slipping out before he could stop them.

"Yes, she's an absolute gem. Now, will you let her into the apartment or not?" Ashley teased. Riley quickly stepped back and welcomed her into his house.

"Riley, darling, why is it so dark in here?" Kim asked.

"Are we about to have an orgy? Because I have to say, as the only straight one here, things are not boding well for me," Ashley said, grimacing.

Riley's eyes shot to hers in alarm. He and Penelope still hadn't talked about his sexuality, aside from the fact that he definitely wasn't ace, and he didn't really think now was an appropriate time to do so.

Thankfully Kim was quick to jump in. "Well, especially since Riley's your ex."

In typical Ashley fashion, instead of rolling with the save, she decided to pile on top. "Which is a great topic to discuss the first time we meet each other, huh Penelope?" Ashley teased, wiggling her eyebrows.

Riley felt like he was watching a game of ping pong, and the ball was the future of his relationship. This had been a mistake. Of course their relationship was too new to be exposed to this level of stress. He should have known better.

His eyes slid back to Penelope, and to his surprise and immense relief, she smiled and laughed her amazing laugh. "That's alright, my roommate is *my* ex, so." She shrugged, and the sweater slipped slightly farther down her arm.

"Yes, the wonderful and amazing Maria who, in one day, convinced our Riley to get a kitty! Something we've been trying to do for months!!" Kim said, clapping her hands together.

"Where is the elusive kitty cat?" Ashley asked, glancing around the room.

Penelope followed her gaze, and her eyes landed on his couch for a second. She seemed to squint at it for a beat. Then she looked away. Damn, had he missed a stain or something? He'd spent all Sunday cleaning, so he thought he'd gotten everything.

He took a deep, steadying breath. "The kitty is in timeout because he chewed through the only lamp I had in here. Which is why it's so dark in here. Not for an orgy, which was just a wonderful question. Really. Thank you so much, Ashley, for coming over today, but you know what? I think you can both just go now so I can attempt to salvage any part of this date with Nels." He gave them a wide-eyed look, but he was smiling slightly.

"Ry, she definitely only agreed to come because she wants to meet us. I bet she already knows she likes you, so she's just here to see if she can like us too." Ashley's smile was confident, and Penelope gave an "aw shucks" shrug and smiled back at her.

"I guess *you* could leave and let us have this date with Penelope?" Kim chortled.

This was hell.

"I'm in hell," he said and walked out of the living room and into the kitchen.

"Wow," Penelope said as the others slowly followed him, "this is an incredibly clean bachelor pad. It even smells nice."

"Here's hoping he's not a bachelor for much longer," Ashley said quietly under her breath, but not so quietly that Riley missed it.

"I think it smells like Riley. Like Christmas cookies and warm milk," Kim said, and he whirled around to shoot daggers at both of them.

They just stared back at him innocently, and Penelope smiled warmly at him as she said, "Yeah, it's like... a spicy vanilla. Like if vanilla had a naughty friend."

Riley blushed crimson, almost as dark as his maroon V-neck sweater.

"Wow, that's pretty spot on," Ashley said, laughing as she came up behind Riley to rest a hand comfortingly between his shoulder blades. "Sugar and a little bit of spice."

"He is also quite nice," Kim said, with an air of zen Riley was sure he wasn't going to be feeling today.

Kim bounced over to the kitchen table, presumably to get out of Riley and Ashely's way. She had learned early on to avoid the kitchen when he and Ashley were cooking together. There was a definite splatter, and possibly "stabbed in the hand with a knife" zone around them when they cooked together.

"Yeah, I've noticed," Penelope said, gazing over at Riley.

"Oh, god, will it be this adorable all night? Because I might die," Ashley said, grabbing an apron out of one of Riley's drawers.

"Be nice, Ash. We're very excited to meet Penelope and are hopeful their relationship continues to blossom into something as beautiful as our dear Riley deserves."

"Oh, I'm truly ecstatic, but I'm also a hangry bitch so let's start cooking!" Ashley said with a big grin, and she shoved an apron at Riley and gently handed one to Penelope.

Riley began counting his breaths, one long in and two short out. He could do this. He could bear all of the teasing, jabbing, and praising, that last one primarily from Kim, if it meant his friends and Penelope had the chance to get to know each other.

"Can I rescue the kitty?" Kim asked, and Riley gestured with his hand at the extra bedroom.

She returned a moment later with Oreo in her arms, his long black and white capped tail swishing happily against her leg.

Kim sat at the table, and Penelope alternated between helping Ashley and Riley, which mostly meant just supervising their chaos, and sitting with Kim. She took a turn holding Oreo, and the cat climbed up onto her shoulder and hugged her for a while. Good kitty.

Dinner was shrimp pasta with garlic bread, salad, and a chocolate torte for dessert. He had noticed Penelope had almost as much of a sweet tooth as he did, so he'd asked Ashley if they could make this dessert specifically for her.

It was an absolute joy for Riley to be around her, as always, but Ashley and Kim seemed to feel it too. They followed her lead for conversation, and soon they were joking about shared women's experiences, like how small women's pants pockets were and the line for the bathroom at a concert Ashley had just gone to.

"Oh yeah, I took the gender signs off our bathrooms at the bar," Ashley said. She'd done it the same day she'd taken over full ownership of the bar. "There are just stalls in both. Literally, what is the point of gendering them? It can cause dysphoria for some, stress for others, and an unbelievably huge line that fucks up the aesthetic of my bar."

Riley had pretty strong opinions about the subject, but he didn't want to steamroll over the women getting to know each other. He thought gender-neutral bathrooms should be an option in every building built moving forward, and old ones should be updated to meet the times. If it was some kind of funding problem, he thought the government should help fund it as well as educational programs for people who couldn't understand the necessity of inclusivity and safe spaces.

Penelope turned to him as if about to ask him something when the timer went off for the garlic bread. He got up to switch out the bread for the torte, signaling dinner was ready.

Everyone helped bring plates, drinks, and food to the table, and then they all sat down to eat.

The conversation blossomed from there, and his friends inquired gently about Penelope's life, dating history, friends, and family, and Penelope flowed through the conversation gracefully. Whenever the opportunity arose, she would pull Riley into the conversation and pepper him with soft compliments and praise. He had a constant blush on his cheeks, and he searched under the table with his foot, accidentally nudging Oreo, until he found her leg. He gently rested his foot against hers, and she sent him a sweet smile in return.

After dinner and dessert, they adjourned to the couch, and the conversation continued. Penelope sat on Riley's left and Ashley on his right. Ashley tucked her legs under her so she could turn sideways towards Penelope. Meanwhile, Kim was lying on the floor with Oreo on her chest, taking a cat nap.

"So, Penelope," Ashley said sharply, and Riley bristled. Penelope's hand found his, and they laced their fingers together. Ashley clocked the movement with her eyes but continued. "If Kim and I could answer just one question for you about Riley, that would help you get to know him a little better and maybe decide if you guys are right for each other, what would it be?"

Riley stared in horror at Ashley, but she didn't so much as blink in response.

To Riley's surprise, Penelope didn't even have to think before asking, "How does trust work for Riley? How will I know when I've earned it, what can I do to earn it, and how can I be sure I can trust him?"

Ashley's eyes widened slightly, and Kim sat up, grasping onto Oreo, so he didn't slide off of her.

"Is trust crucial to you, Penelope?" Kim asked.

"Well, yes, but... I think you asked the question so that you could get a sense of what it's going to take for us to take our relationship to the next step? Well, I think one: it is probably just a little bit more time, but two: I think we need to have a few more hard conversations, and I think trust is going to be absolutely essential for those conversations to take place," she said succinctly.

"What a lovely question then," Kim said, stroking absently at Oreo's fur. "I think I'll take the first shot at it. Riley is a very private person. Some of that, I do believe, is due to being afraid to trust new people, but I think it may also be out of fear of being a burden." She stared directly at Riley while she spoke, clearly gauging his reaction. He couldn't argue with anything she was saying, even though he probably wouldn't have ever been able to voice it out loud.

"As women, I know we are often made to feel as if we cannot take up space in this world. Men, particularly white cis/het men, take up space innately as if it's their god-given right. Riley... does not." He glanced slightly to the side to check Penelope's expression; she looked thoughtful and nodded. "I think what others could possibly view as a lack of having earned Riley's trust is more that the more he gets to know and begins to care for a person, the less he wants to burden or bother them. So, what can you do about that? Just constantly provide a safe space for him to feel seen, heard, and loved—er, cared for." She quickly amended, not stopping for Riley's flinch but continuing forward. "He will open up to you more and more as he begins to trust not just you but himself around you."

Ashley chimed in next. "As for how can you know you can trust him? Well, I guess I think that might depend on what it takes for *you* to trust someone. I can say that Riley knows more about me than any other person on this planet. He has never once made me feel judged, misunderstood, or vulnerable. And believe me. I do not like to feel vulnerable. Riley has a way of... listening without any judgment. Like I could tell him I just put salt in some guy's drink because he was hassling a girl at my bar, and he wouldn't even bat an eye," Ashley stated, smirking at the end. She had done that, multiple times, which was not something Riley thought she should be admitting to a virtual stranger but. Alas.

The room fell silent, and Riley marveled at his friends. They, of course, knew almost everything there was to know about him and saw him as a whole, not just as the parts Penelope was slowly beginning to see of him. He was working almost every day to build up the strength and bravery to show her the rest of himself; he just wasn't quite there yet.

"I concur completely with Ashley. I tell Riley all of my dirty secrets, past struggles, and embarrassing stories. He has never so much as uttered a word of condescension or derision. Does that answer your question, Penelope?" Kim asked.

She smiled slowly. "I think it does, yes. Thank you."

She hesitated for a moment, wrapping a strand of her hair around her knuckles. "Is there... any one question you want to ask me?" She glanced between his friends, and then her eyes came to rest on him.

"I have one," Ashley said, and Riley stiffened. Penelope stroked her thumb over the top of his hand the way she had in the arcade bar.

"I know Riley has shared with you some of his... reservations about sex. Will you leave him if he can't have heteronormative sex with you?"

"Ashley!" he gasped. His back and legs clenched so hard it nearly brought him up off the sofa. In a flurry of movement, there were three hands on him, Ashley's strong ones pressing him back onto the couch, Kim cupping the back of his calf with her hand, and Penelope, her grip strong in his.

"I'm sorry, Riley, I would never try to embarrass you or degrade you in any way. But Kim, Johanna, and I are your only support network. I want to know going into this if that's the case."

"I... I don't know if—we can't know yet if—" Riley's voice shook as he tried to force himself to take deep breaths, but his diaphragm fought him every step of the way.

"Riley," Penelope said softly, bringing her other hand to rest on his thigh, "would you like me to answer the question? I know this is very private so I'm not going to answer if it would make you uncomfortable."

"I—I don't want *you* to be uncomfortable," he said. What he wanted to say was "I don't want you to leave me before I ever really had you," but he couldn't get the words out. Instead, he just clung desperately to her hand like it was a lifeline.

She smiled, crinkling the space around her eyes, and it was like a ray of light breaking through the clouds. "I'm doing perfectly fine, sweetheart. I am more than happy to answer the question if it would provide you with some relief, but," she looked over calmly at Ashley, "I will not say anything that is going to upset you just because I've been asked to."

Out of the corner of his eye, he saw Ashley nod once, but she said nothing further.

"You can... answer," he said quietly, focusing his attention on their joined hands. He didn't want to watch her face as she admitted that yes, she would probably leave him. Sex was important to her, she had said as much. Obviously she would want a relationship with a happy sex life; hell, Riley wanted that too. He wanted it so desperately. He just didn't know if he could have it.

"Well... sex is important to me. I think it's one of many ways we can connect and show ourselves to our partners. That being said, I am not heteronormative and therefore do not subscribe to only heteronormative sex. Just like everything else we do, we would have to figure it out together. What would make me leave is... if I found out you were doing something just to make me happy, meanwhile you were unhappy or uncomfortable. That would not be something I could get past. But... you told me you are interested in intimacy with me. I think that just means we have a lot to figure out. Together." She hadn't addressed her comments to Ashley the way she had the first question. Instead, she was speaking directly to Riley, as if she was trying to address his inner most fears.

Ashley stood up abruptly. "Well. That's great then. I'm opening another bottle of wine," she said and walked out of the living room. Penelope glanced in concern between him and Kim.

"Did I... upset her?" she asked.

"No, I don't think it was you, Penelope. Riley, why don't you go check on her?" Kim patted his knee.

He gave Penelope's hand one last squeeze before getting up to follow Ashley into the kitchen. He found her standing with one hand on a wine glass filled almost to the top and another on the now open bottle of wine.

He approached her carefully, the way he was learning to do with Oreo when he was trying to pull something stupid out of the cat's mouth.

"She's fucking perfect for you, Ry. I hope you see that," she said to her wine glass, apparently having seen him approaching from the corner of her eye.

"I am starting to believe that might be the case as well, yes... but I don't think that's why you're in here." He gently wrapped his hand around hers, where it clutched the wine bottle.

"I just... she's so intuitive with you. It's like she already fully knows who you are even though she doesn't even know half of it. It's like she knows exactly what to say and do around you while I... I fucked up our relationship. I pushed you too hard, and—you were trying to tell me with your mannerisms, your veiled references, and even your body, and I chose not to hear any of it. I really could have hurt you, Ry. It's just... hard. Seeing her as everything I wasn't and can't seem to be. I'm so rough with the men I like, and it means I keep ending up with equally rough men who shape up and then decide they don't need a rough girl like me anymore and... well, anyways. None of this is about you or her; this is allllll about me."

"Ash..." he breathed around a sharp pain in his chest. He had no idea she'd been carrying this around for so long. They always talked about him and his needs and his feelings, but never about how she had felt.

"Please. I don't want you to comfort me or make excuses for me right now, Ry. I just... wanted a glass of wine and a moment."

"Well... I'm happy to give you both, but... How about... my

forgiveness as well? I think I tried to give it to you over the years, but maybe I've never been clear enough. I was equally as clueless as you were back then. I barely knew what I needed or wanted, and we bumbled around together and... yes. It wasn't good, but it was equally not good for the both of us to continue together when we knew it was wrong. I have forgiven you, Ash, and I've even forgiven myself. I'm so grateful every single day that I have you in my life. I hope that you can forgive yourself too."

Ashley threw her arms around his neck and hugged him gently, leaving ample space between their bodies. Riley let out a huff and pressed his hand gently to her lower back bringing their bodies flush together. He preferred leaving space between their bodies, but he knew this was how Ashley preferred to hug. Full on and aggressive, just like she was. Riley could tolerate it. For her.

"I love you, Riley. And I don't think you could have found someone better suited for you than Penelope. She's phenomenal, and I'm so excited to see what happens between the two of you."

Riley smiled into her hair and nodded. "Me too."

NINE

PENELOPE

Penelope had no idea what overtook her, but at nearly eleven, after Riley closed the door behind Kim and Ashley, she nearly threw herself at him. She had her hands on his neck and face, lips on his mouth, and knees bumping and brushing his as she leaned up into him.

"Hi," he breathed between kisses.

"Hi," she whispered back. "I've wanted to do this since the moment you opened the door." It came out like a purr, and it wasn't a lie, but it also didn't sound like her. Her voice was low and had hints of that spice that seemed to permeate around Riley, as if she'd spent so long with it on her skin it had seeped into her blood, making her a little raw, a little wild.

"Well, please don't let me stop you." His lips curved into a smile as he slid his tongue into her mouth.

She got lost in the feeling for a few minutes, just reveling in his taste and feel. His hands were on her, but they stayed on her head, neck, and shoulders. It felt like just enough contact and she liked it, so she did the same for him. She particularly liked the way his warm hand felt on her bare shoulder.

On Sunday, after she'd given Maria the entire rundown on everything gender that was happening in her life, Maria had dived in headfirst to help her revamp her style. They'd spent several hours online shopping, with Grey's Anatomy blaring in the background, as they tried to flesh out her new androgynous capsule wardrobe. Since it would take several days for the clothing to start arriving, she'd borrowed this sweater from Maria and, based on the way Riley kept looking at her shoulder like it was a work of art, she didn't think she'd be giving it back any time soon.

"I think... I like you," he whispered against her mouth, and a blush spread across his cheeks like spilled wine.

"I think I like you too."

"I think... I really like you."

"Oh Riley... me too," she sighed and she pressed their mouths together for a slow kiss.

As she pulled back, she smiled and stood up on her tiptoes to kiss his forehead, gently brushing a stray bit of hair away.

"Do you ever let your hair down?" she asked and noticed his eyes tighten, and his fingers stiffen on her shoulder. "Okay, hey, no problem. It's your hair, sweetheart. You do whatever you want with it. I just... think it's quite beautiful, and if you ever want to share it with me, I'd love to see it. But for now—" She gently tilted his head down to kiss his hair sweetly. "I'm quite fond of your man bun."

She poked the bun teasingly, and he laughed, nodding his head, so it bumped against her hand.

She wanted to pull the elastic out and bury her face in his long hair. She wanted to bury her entire self in him, just open him up and crawl inside. See what all he kept stored inside his soft, guarded heart.

"Do you... want to... sit down?" he asked haltingly, gesturing at the couch.

"Oh, I don't know. We kissed sitting down last time, thought standing up might be a nice twist this time," she said, pulling him in for another long kiss.

When they broke away again, he laughed nervously, and Penelope tilted her head to the side in question. "Does that mean... next time it has to be lying down?"

His eyes skittered away from her face. Some of the heat that had been building in her stomach dampened to a low warmth as she settled took a step back to look up at him.

"Nothing ever *has* to happen between us, Riley. If we keep our relationship to just making out—standing up or sitting down for a while, that's okay with me. I think we need to have one or two of those tough conversations at some point, but there's no rush or anything from me, okay?"

He nodded and then hesitantly reached down to rest his hands on her hips. She smiled up at him and laced her arms behind his neck. "This is nice too," she said, swaying softly back and forth as if to music.

"Everything feels nice with you," he said, dipping down to kiss her again. God, this man was making her melt. She could feel it already; she was just a puddle on the floor, masquerading as a person.

"Do you want to talk now or...?" His voice was sincere, but she could see in his eyes, and feel in her bones, that it had been a long night for both of them.

"Honestly, I'm enjoying this, and I have an early morning tomorrow. I promised to bring the office coffee to launch the new project I'm leading, so I have to haul my ass all over town before 8 am."

He hummed sympathetically and pulled her in closer, so she was just an inch or so away from him. "Well, you don't have to ask twice for me to delay a hard conversation and keep kissing you."

She laughed, but before she kissed him again, she said, "We will need to talk soon, though. There's something I wanted to talk about —" at Riley's slightly panicked expression, she quickly added, "About myself!" She should have known not to say something so vague to someone with anxiety. "And I'd like to do it... maybe in the next week or two?"

"And... it does seem like we should probably further discuss Ashley's question of you tonight. Maybe... sooner rather than later," Riley said hesitantly.

Penelope nodded and brushed the backs of her fingers over his jaw. His eyes lowered to half mast, and Penelope reveled in how openly he was accepting her touch tonight. She was being very purposeful with her movements, only touching areas of his body she'd already touched and received positive responses to. She gently traced her fingertips down his neck, stopping at his slightly exposed collarbone to run her hand back up his neck. His head lulled slightly to the side, giving her further access.

Slowly, she leaned forward and pressed her lips to the side of his neck, and he lifted his arms to wrap around her shoulders. He nudged her head with his chin, and she turned, so it rested against his chest.

He dropped his chin on her head and hummed happily. Penelope could feel it rumble through her own rib cage as if she had made the noise herself. Actually, maybe she had. Maybe she was sighing happily too, as they fell still in each other's arms for just a moment.

Penelope could have stayed like that all night, even if her back and knees would probably hate her in the morning. Riley pulled away first and nudged her to gather her things so she could get some rest for work. He insisted on calling her an Uber and wouldn't take no for an answer, so ten minutes later, she found herself cozied up in the back of a car, daydreaming about Riley's kisses.

She barely had time to think, let alone daydream over the next week. Her project had launched successfully, thanks partly to the copious amounts of her brother's coffee she had plied the staff with. This most recent batch didn't have the same hints of vanilla, which was disappointing but at least it allowed Penelope to concentrate on her work.

This new project was much bigger than hounding Twitter. She would be doing work that would be visible by the entire company, including the higher-ups. She was excited for the opportunity, but it meant she didn't even check her phone until the end of each workday.

She texted with Taylor and Riley sporadically after work. She had a brief, still garbled, phone conversation with Taylor that Thursday night. They discovered they had a similar infatuation with speakeasy-style bars. Taylor tentatively invited her to come with her to a friend's bar the next night since their friend group would often go there on Friday nights. Unfortunately, Penelope already had plans to finally meet Crystal.

Maria had invited Crystal over for drinks and takeout, and Penelope was looking forward to it. Taylor promised her a rain check, and they didn't speak again until Saturday morning when Penelope texted to see if she wanted to come to the drag brunch, and Taylor said she was too busy being hungover.

Penelope tried not to feel too let down, and she resigned herself to the fact that Taylor probably wouldn't come to another brunch. As they continued to grow closer and closer, Penelope still hadn't been able to let go of her interest in the woman, but Taylor had made it very clear she wasn't interested back.

Penelope put her phone away, forgetting to text Riley good morning, and threw herself into a good drag show. Sham Pain came to check on her after the show. She'd used they/them pronouns for Penelope the entire show and she found she liked it, but it wasn't as much of a game changer as she had thought it would be.

"Love your suit, sugar. Did you take my advice?" Sham Pain asked.

Penelope was wearing a new royal blue suit. Maria had helped her pick this one out, and she loved how it hugged her hips and ass. She was giving Sham Pain a brief rundown of some of the other styles she wanted to start incorporating into her regular wardrobe when she felt a gentle hand on her shoulder.

She turned to see Diego standing with a tray of coffees and a plate of scones in his hands. "So sorry, Sham, but I must steal Pen from you. Your brother and I want to discuss something with you."

Penelope raised her eyebrows at him but followed him out into the empty cafe. They sat at the table right near the window, which Penelope had come to think of as the "serious" table, used for "big conversations." There had only been a few of these over the years. Once when Diego's mother was dying, and he had to take a leave from the shop. Penelope had taken on some of the workload while he was gone and also provided emotional support to Frankie as he fretted and worried about Diego. The next time was when Penelope came out as pansexual.

She briefly wondered if they had somehow figured out she was exploring her gender identity, but she wasn't sure how they would have since she had only just put words to the feeling in the past few weeks.

"So," Diego began, "we think we've found a full-time MC to replace you, but we wanted to give you the option to keep the job fully, keep it some of the time, on rare occasions, or hand it over completely."

"Oh!" she said, surprised. "You brought me to the serious table to talk about that? God, guys, I thought something was—...okay, what are those faces?"

Diego and Frankie were making the same hesitant face at her until she brought it up, and then they both widened their eyes innocently.

"Okay, seriously? Do you guys think you developed the exact same facial expressions by living and working together every day, or are you finally going to admit you are star-crossed lovers in my favorite fanfiction?"

To her surprise, they didn't laugh, scoff, or brush her off. Instead, Frankie said, "You're right, Lopi. Of course you're right. We are together, and we've been together for a while now."

Penelope very nearly fell out of her chair.

"That is about—uhm, half of why we're sitting at the serious table," Diego said.

"But now we're doing the whole thing out of order because you are a nosy nelly who couldn't wait for us to finish our well-curated speech!" Frankie said, taking a fake angry bite of his scone.

Penelope could feel cool air passing over her tongue, and she realized her mouth was hanging open, gaping like a startled fish.

"You're... together. You've... been together. And this is how you wanted to tell me? In relation to a drag brunch—Oh my god! Are you both okay?! Is everything okay with you, is—are you leaving? Are you eloping and selling the shop and the new drag MC host is going to take ove—"

"Oh my god, Lopi! No! It's fine! Everything is fine! Actually, everything is amazing. We are healthy and so happy, and we're not going anywhere. Can you. Just. Hold the fuck up, please?" Frankie said, but he was smiling, and Diego was smiling, and something was glinting on Frankie's left hand.

"Oh my god, you absolute fucks, are you married?!" Penelope nearly shrieked.

"PENELOPE! LET ME DO MY SPEECH! PLEASE!" Frankie shouted, barely containing his laughter.

Penelope was shaking her head no, but her mouth was saying, "Fine, fine. Go ahead. Come on, what are you waiting for!"

"So..." Diego started again, trying to temper down his smile. "We wanted to ask you about your continued interest in the drag show because... well, we've noticed a change in you the past few weeks while you've been doing it. You just..."

"Come alive," Frankie said wistfully, "like I don't think I've ever seen you before. And we don't want to take that away from you, so you have the next four days to decide what kind of schedule you want to work out with the new person. They're ready to start next Saturday but said they'd be very happy to defer to you and your wishes first."

Penelope nodded. She'd have to think about that, but she knew more was coming, so she didn't say anything yet.

"So... on that note—" Diego said.

"The note of how amazing you have been at MCing and how much of a stage presence you have—" Frankie interrupted.

"We wanted to ask—" Diego said, laughing as they spoke over each other.

"If you'd be in my wedding party and give a speech at our wedding because YES, WE'RE ENGAGED!" Frankie shouted, and they both held out their hands, showing matching thin silver bands.

"OH MY GOD, YES, HOLY SHIT!" Penelope cried, launching herself across the table at her brother and her brother's freaking fiancé. She proceeded to sob on them for an embarrassingly long time.

Frankie patted her hair, and Diego rubbed her shoulder.

"You absolute assholes. Okay. Start at the beginning."

So, they did.

"Okay, so you remember how I volunteered for a while as a scribe in college, taking notes for other students who needed extra assistance in class? Well..." Frankie bit his bottom lip and looked at Diego.

"I had just gotten top surgery, and I was pretty out of it for several weeks, but I didn't want to have to retake any classes," Diego said, providing his personal details that Frankie seemed unwilling to divulge for him.

"So, I became his scribe, and it was for a class on starting your own business," Frankie continued. "And I mean... we just really hit it off, but we hit it off in a 'let's go into business together and not fuck each other senseless on this desk' kind of way—which I *know* is what you thought when I first told you about him! But it wasn't like that, at least not for the first few years."

"Welllll, it was a little bit like that for me, to be honest," Diego said, smiling at him, and Penelope blushed, but it was a happy blush. "I was still dealing with... well, to be frank, a lot of gender dysphoria at the time, and I just wasn't ready to burden someone else with that, so I held back."

"You and all of your feelings are never a burden, love," Frankie whispered, taking Diego's hand on top of the table.

Penelope felt her lungs constrict painfully, at both Diego and Frankie's words, but she just nodded.

"And you know most of the story of the next several years," Frankie picked back up. "We started the cafe, moved in together, and... I mean, seriously, it was like a dumb Rom-Com Lopi. I don't know what else to tell you. It was stolen glances and brushing fingers, forced proximity and friends to lovers... and it was great. But it was... slow. We took things slowly because, first and foremost, we were business partners," Frankie said, and the way his face lit up as he looked at Diego was something Penelope tried to snapshot in her brain so she could pull it back out at their wedding— oh man, their wedding! How crazy was that?!

"So, we didn't tell anyone. Not until my mother died. It was the first time I saw most of my family in years. Most of them didn't even know I was trans. For the most part... it went about as badly as I thought it would, but a few of them were accepting. I very slowly started to tell one person at a time in my life about Frankie, and it was... tough. Many people weren't understanding because of one thing or another. Because we were business partners, because I was trans, because Frankie was a man which meant I was a *gay* trans man, and... so on and so forth. Eventually, I just stopped telling people. Frankie had wanted to wait to see how it went with my family, and since it went less than stellar, we decided to just... wait," Diego admitted. His expression was one Penelope had never seen before, sort of sad but accepting.

She reached across the table and placed her hand on top of their still joined hands.

Diego smiled at her, and Frankie picked the story back up. "But things have changed! We're not just business partners anymore. Now we are first and foremost—well... fiancés!"

His eyes grew misty and he turned and kissed Diego softly on the lips. Penelope almost swooned her way onto the floor.

"And so... we decided it was finally time to tell people. And if they want to judge, then so be it, but this is real, we are real, and we love each other and want to spend the rest of our lives together. Possibly in this same apartment over this same cafe, maybe somewhere else entirely with another business or living on a ranch somewhere I don't know, but... We're going to do it together. And we want people to know," Frankie said with conviction.

"And you're the first person we're telling," Diego said, turning his hand out of Frankie's to grasp her hand.

Penelope took a deep, shaky breath. "Wow. That is so much to absorb and also if I'm going to give a speech at your wedding, I'm going to need about one million percent more details than that but... Wow, I... can't even express how happy this makes me. You're going to be my brother-in-law!" she said, and then she was crying again. Not just from happiness, although that was most of it, but also from the pain she felt over the challenges they had to overcome to get here—both on their own and together.

They talked for a while about the wedding and the plans they'd started to scrape together about what, where, and when. They shared a few more stories with her, that she'd been adjacent to but never a part of, about how they had found ways to navigate their relationship in private, out of the eyes of their families and the cafe patrons. They had told a few select friends, so at least they had that support, and Penelope was grateful for that.

"You can be my... best... maid of honor?" Frankie said, screwing up his face in concentration. "Maid of... best man..."

"How about: best person? Nice and gender-neutral," Diego suggested, and there was something knowing in his eyes and in his tone as he gazed across the table at Penelope.

She looked across the table at her soon-to-be brother-in-law and felt a burst of courage. Maybe it was their open, honest admissions, or maybe it just felt like this was too good of a time to pass up.

"Soooo... speaking of gender neutral... you said you've noticed a change in me since I started doing drag?"

They both nodded seriously, and so she began to tell them everything she'd come to realize about herself in the past few weeks. She talked about her conversations with Sham Pain, the discoveries she was making on her own and through her friendship with Taylor, and finally, her hesitations in telling Riley.

Diego held her hand throughout her explanation. As she finished, he squeezed her hand tightly. Frankie looked between the two of them and then quickly excused himself to grab them more coffee and some actual sustenance, as it was now approaching 6pm, and they'd all only had scones for lunch.

"It is sometimes a little harder to decide when to open up when there's nothing external forcing your hand. For me, it was like I didn't have a choice for a long time. Before the T took effect and I got top surgery, I basically outed myself in every conversation and relationship I had just by existing. That's changed over time, and nowadays I often pass as cis, which means I get to control who I come out to, because the gender I am is the gender I'm presenting as. For you, you are currently very femme-presenting. You could, of course, change your look, your hair, et cetera, but in our society right now, it's hard to look nonbinary, so you will probably be misgendered as a woman."

"Well... it's not even like it's misgendering necessarily. I think I am... kind of a woman. I'm also kind of neutral. It doesn't bother me to use she/her pronouns, but... I do think I... kind of like they/them. She/her doesn't bother me, but something just feels..." Penelope tried to think of the right words.

"It feels like somehow this part of you that you thought only you knew existed is finally being recognized by the world?" Diego supplied gently.

"Yes!" Penelope exclaimed. Love and affection swirled behind her ribs as she looked over at this amazing man who would soon be joining their family. She wished she had come to both Frankie and Diego with these feelings earlier. It was clear to her now that they would have not only accepted her but understood her, just like how they had understood her sexuality.

An idea struck her and she squinted down at the polished tabletop as she tried to piece together her thoughts.

"I guess... it also feels a little like coming out as pan. Like, obviously straight wasn't right, but bi-sexual didn't feel quite right either. It's not this stark difference, like being straight and lesbian, or cisgender and transgender, but... it still feels significant to me?"

"That's all that matters, Lopi," Frankie said as he returned to his seat with fresh coffees and sandwiches. "Whatever makes you feel happy and fulfilled. If you want us to try using they/them pronouns, or if you want to borrow some of my clothes to play around with styles, or want to go shopping with me or—"

"Honey," Diego interrupted gently, placing his hand on Frankie's cheek to silence him. "We love Penelope very, very much. You dress like a 19-year-old who just got his first credit card. Please stop offering her anything to do with fashion." He turned to look at Penelope with warmth overflowing from his eyes. "You are welcome to borrow *my* clothing and *my* fashion sense anytime you want."

Penelope burst out laughing and had to agree with him. Frankie didn't dress badly; he just dressed like he had discovered vineyard vines, polos, slim-fitting button-downs, and straight-legged chinos and had decided to call it a day. Diego dressed in beautiful, expensive clothing. She'd learned over the years that he was a master thrifter and had built out an amazing wardrobe that was professional, a little androgynous, and incredibly stylish. Penelope could feel herself salivating at the thought of getting her hands on any of his clothes. They weren't quite the same size, but their top halves were close enough, and his clothes weren't ever form-fitting so it might work out for her.

"I... yes, please," Penelope said, nearly burning her tongue as she took a huge gulp of coffee.

"You're welcome to come up after work tomorrow. I'll pull some things out for you."

Penelope's eyes got watery again. "Best. Brother-in-Law. Ever."

"You mentioned... you don't know what to tell the man you're seeing?" Diego nudged gently.

"Uh, yeah... It's not that I don't want to tell him. It's just that I feel like I'm still so new to all of this I wouldn't even know how to answer most of his questions. Is that... bad? To not tell him? Is that like I'm lying to him?" she asked, a little uncomfortably. She didn't know Diego's dating history and didn't want to imply that any decision he had made in his past was good or bad. She was just genuinely uncertain.

He shook his head vehemently. "No, it's not lying. Many straight couples go on dozens of dates before opening up about things as serious as their gender, sexuality, preferences in bed, things to be avoided in bed, et cetera. Just because your—well, all of the above is different from the person you're dating or is different from how you outwardly present doesn't mean you owe them an explanation right away. I can only speak to my experience, but I don't think you need to discuss genitals and your conformity with or against them when you first meet someone. If you want to have that conversation when you get more serious and are physically intimate with them, that's completely fine."

"Does he seem... accepting?" Frankie asked. There was a protective edge to his voice that Penelope had rarely experienced.

"I—I think so? Yes... I think he would be," she said, her conviction growing as she spoke.

"Well, then it's just up to you to bring it up when you think you're ready. And remember, you're not doing it because you owe him anything. You would be doing it because you owe yourself the chance to be loved fully and completely for who you are. All of you." Diego emphasized his words by waving his panini, and a piece of pepperoni flew out and landed in his coffee.

They all laughed, breaking the serious mood, and Penelope urged them to change the topic, so they returned to wedding planning and talked for another several hours.

On her walk home, she tried to call Riley, but once again he didn't answer. She bit her lip and sent him a shot in the dark text.

> Penelope: Hi, I hope your weekend is going well. Is there any way I could come over and we could talk tonight? I know it's a little last minute, but I would love to see you and think we should talk.

> Riley: Sorry, I don't think I can tonight. I would love to see you; I'm just god-awful hungover.

> Penelope: How about Thursday?

> Riley: Perfect. Miss you, can't wait to kiss you.

Penelope was a little annoyed that he didn't pick up the phone but responded immediately to her text, but she could understand being hungover. It seemed like she was the only one who hadn't had a crazy night yesterday. She, Maria, and Crystal had ordered Indian food and spent a solid twenty minutes laughing at how crooked the fairy lights were in the corner.

They'd ended up on the couch watching a movie, and Penelope continually tried to excuse herself to give them more privacy, but Maria had spread herself out across both of their laps and refused to let her leave. Crystal held Maria's hand throughout the entire movie, chatting amiably with them both. While it nearly killed Penelope to admit it, she was ecstatic that Maria had found her own movie talker.

Still feeling like she needed to debrief on her conversation with Frankie, she dialed Taylor's number. She also didn't pick up, and Penelope groaned.

Taylor: Sorry, still SO hungover. Can we
text?

Penelope agreed, and they spent the rest of her walk home and another solid hour texting about whether or not Penelope should continue performing as a drag king or not. She took a break from texting to tell Maria the amazing engagement news. Maria demanded to see all of Diego's clothes when Penelope got them on Wednesday.

She still hadn't unboxed the most recent shipment of clothing she and Maria had ordered. Feeling inspired and a little excited, she texted Taylor about both the package and her future access to a Diego's wardrobe.

Taylor demanded photos now and Wednesday, so Penelope began assembling and photographing outfits on her bed. She sent them slowly to Taylor, loving her running commentary and appreciating that they could share this. She imagined what it would be like to do this with Riley, and she thought they might get there one day, if Penelope handled this conversation about her gender correctly. It was just hard that she already had this with Taylor.

The gender conversation wasn't the only one she needed to have with Riley. They had also promised to talk about sex soon. She had meant what she'd said to Taylor before. Both penises and vaginas intimidated her to equal measure. When Ashley asked about heteronormative sex, she assumed she meant part a inserted into part b type sex. Penelope had never gotten a huge amount out of that kind of sex, so truly, she didn't mind if that was the smallest or even a nonexistent part of their sex life. But she still needed to be sure they could have a sex life.

As she continued chatting with Taylor, she flopped back onto her bed and scrolled back through all of the photos she'd just taken. Taylor seemed to love the androgynous look, but she wondered if Riley would like her style as it changed to more androgynous. She hadn't dressed super femme in years but maybe Riley would prefer if she did?

She rolled over and continued scrolling until she hit the photo Riley had sent of him with Oreo. If she were looking in a mirror, she would probably see that goofy grin again, and she turned off her phone and went to bed with it still on her face.

RILEY

Riley blamed Kim. She was the one who had insisted they go to Ashley's bar Friday night, and she was the one who ordered them five tequila shots in a row.

Riley didn't like liquor, preferring wine and ciders. When he did have liquor, it was usually a fruity cocktail. He used to feel embarrassed about this, but as he neared thirty, he stopped caring what other people thought of his alcohol preferences. Ashley had a cosmopolitan ready for him on the bar when they arrived, and Kim had proceeded to smash a hole in his plan for a nice quiet drink with his friends.

He blamed the hangover for agreeing to "talk" with Penelope on Thursday. He would have agreed sober, but he would have probably asked for it to be earlier in the week, so he didn't spend the entire week stressing about it. He also probably would have done so without the dorky rhyme. The hangover did nothing to ease the immediate anxiety he experienced after agreeing to talk that week, and he barely slept Saturday night.

He felt out of sorts on Sunday as well, and he blamed the alcohol, but somewhere in the back of his mind, he worried it might be something else. Monday, he could tell it wasn't alcohol but more than likely depression seeping in, like water through the cracks in the sidewalk, slipping in amidst his anxiety when he wasn't looking.

By Tuesday, he felt awful. He called out of work and spent a few hours on the phone with Johanna. She tried to talk him down from his anxiety and up from his depression, but he was so anxious trying to explain to her why he was so anxious he threw up and fell asleep on the floor of the bathroom.

He knew logically that whatever Penelope wanted to talk about, that she had said was about her and not him, was probably nothing bad. His brain didn't listen to logic, though, and his depression just laughed at him.

On top of that, no logic on earth could make him think the sex conversation would go well. Maybe, just maybe, they'd get through whatever Penelope wanted to talk about, but when they got to his part of the conversation, things were probably going to fall apart.

Thankfully, he had the wherewithal to dump a mountain of food in Oreo's bowl Monday morning, so he was still being fed throughout the week. He momentarily remembered Maria and Penelope's promise to take care of Oreo if he fell into a bad depression. Unfortunately, somewhere in the midst of his misery, he managed to lose track of his phone, and he didn't find it again until Wednesday afternoon.

When he finally found it, he considered messaging Maria and Penelope for a split second before his helpful brain reminded him that he probably shouldn't ruin things with Penelope the day before they were going to have the conversation that might very well ruin things anyways.

So, instead of messaging her or responding to any of her messages, he opened his texting app. He ignored the other missed texts there and called in reinforcements, texting his group chat with Kim and Ashley. All he could manage was a selfie of himself curled up on the couch in his favorite pink t-shirt. His hair was loose and knotted around his shoulders, and fresh tear tracks were visible on his cheeks. At least Oreo was asleep against his chest, having not abandoned him quite yet.

They were there an hour later, and he reiterated the anxieties he'd shared with Johanna. They too assured him that as long as he was open and honest, the conversation would probably go well, and their relationship would be stronger because of it. Ashley made him soup while Kim prodded him into the shower. She sat on the floor outside the open bathroom door and talked to him, trying to keep his mind off how much he loathed showers.

He scrubbed his favorite vanilla-scented shampoo through his hair, lathered up his vanilla body wash, and shaved as smoothly and quickly as he could. He always felt light years better after shaving, but sometimes it was hard to find the will to do anything when he felt like this.

Kim gave him privacy to change, then placed him on the living room floor in front of the couch. She disappeared into the kitchen for a few moments and returned with hot chocolate. She sat down behind him and began to comb out his hair while he drank the hot drink.

"Do you... think it was too much alcohol? Did I do this to you?" Kim asked, her fingers soft on his scalp as she massaged a leave-in conditioner into his hair.

Riley had considered this as well. Sometimes if he hit a terrible low while drunk or high, back when he used to smoke, he wouldn't be able to pick himself up out of it.

It felt pointless to say that now, though. It was too late, and he was a consenting adult who could have said no to the alcohol. He didn't blame Kim or Ashley—or Penelope for that matter. His depression was an illness that took no prisoners.

"No, don't be silly. It just happens sometimes... I'm sorry you always have to take care of me..."

He pulled his knees up to his chest, balancing the mug on one knee.

"You know," Ashley said, as she brought over three bowls of soup, "maybe this is a good opportunity to let Penelope see a little more of you? You don't have to tell or show her everything, but maybe show her a little sliver of this part of you? Because it is a part of you, and if she's going to love you, she's going to have to love this part of you as well."

"God, how are you even talking about love right now? We're not even talking about sex, we're talking about *talking about* sex, and I'm a disaster. There's just... no way this is going to work."

"Darling, you don't know that. In six months, this could very well be Penelope combing your hair, making you soup, and holding your hand through a rough day. She's already admitted to you that she has anxiety, right? And she wants to talk to you so she can tell you something about herself? I'm sure there are ways she needs you, too," Kim said gently.

At the thought of Penelope seeing him like this, his stomach clenched, and he had to take sharp, shuddering breaths in through his teeth until the wave of nausea settled. He just couldn't believe that she'd still be here with him in six months after learning everything about him.

"Do you think... I should have just told her everything from the beginning... instead of trying to tell her everything tomorrow?" Riley asked miserably.

Ashley forced a bowl of warm soup into his left hand, removing the mostly empty mug from his right, and he began to eat absently.

"I think you would never have done that. If you had tried to make yourself share everything up front, you probably would have ghosted her," Ashley said.

He paused mid-bite to think about this and decided she was probably right. He had multiple times today thought about canceling their hangout tomorrow, and it wasn't even necessarily going to be a conversation about him.

"But," Ashley continued as if reading his mind, "you're in too deep now to ghost her. First, because that would be awful of you. But also because you have actual feelings for her now."

He put the spoon back in his half-empty bowl and placed it on the coffee table in front of his face.

"I know this is scary, darling, but try to concentrate on how amazing it is that you have feelings for her at all. This is farther than you've let yourself get with someone... ever?" Kim asked, beginning to braid his hair. Normally he would worry about it getting too wavy, but he would just take another shower tomorrow to work out all the kinks.

"What does it matter though if it just blows up in my face because I can't open up, or if when I finally do open up, she... leaves."

"I think maybe you should give the girl a little credit. She rolled with every single thing we—or, well, mostly I threw at her last week, and it seems like your reservations about sex aren't going to be a deal breaker," Ashley said.

"Yeah, but what about when I tell her why I have those reservations?" Riley said, and both women froze.

"Is... that what you think is going to happen tomorrow? I didn't think when you said, 'Tell her everything' you meant'—" Ashley said nervously.

"Everything?" he interrupted a little petulantly. "Yes. Everything. Should I have told her *everything* from the beginning? Would it have been better for her to leave me then, when it was just that she couldn't handle everything I am before getting to know me, but... now she knows me, at least a big part of me, and... what if she still leaves."

"Then you will come to the bar on Friday, and I will keep you well stocked on fried food and fruity drinks, but only two fruity drinks, and we will get through this together. You. Me. Kim. And Oreo," Ashley said, picking Oreo up from where he had been asleep under the coffee table and placing him in Riley's arms.

"Actually, if it goes well, you should come too," Ashley amended. "I'm working a triple, and I need the company either way —and so do you. If it goes well, just bring her!" Ashley asserted, already looking ahead to Friday like Riley's world wasn't going to collapse tomorrow.

"I think... maybe this is a mistake," Kim said softly, having only just started stroking through Riley's hair again. "I think she wants to talk to you about something, and you both want to talk about sex, and now you want to tell her *everything*? I think it's too much. Honestly, Riley, if you're still like this tomorrow, I think you should just be honest with her and talk about your depression, and maybe whatever it is she wants to talk to you about. But I think you're putting a huge amount of pressure on yourself with this, and I think it's why you're buckling under that pressure. The conversation has no chance of going well if you're like this."

Ashley squinted at her for a moment. "Do you think?"

"Yes. I mean, honestly Riley... you were an absolute mess when you told me. And it was hard for both of us. That's not what you want this conversation to be. You at least want to be in a good place to start the conversation."

Ashley nodded aggressively. "You know what, I think she's right. You were also... not in a good place when you told me. I think you're right to want to tell her soon. Maybe it's just part of the larger sex conversation you have before you get intimate?"

Riley had resigned himself to have one, huge, "Fuck me up" conversation, but what they said made some sense. It did mean prolonging this hell, though, because Penelope still wouldn't know everything. Maybe it would give him more time to get his shit together, though.

"So... no matter what happens tomorrow... I'll see you both on Friday?" he asked hesitantly.

"Yes. And we can have a sleepover on Ashley's floor if we need to. One of your roommates just moved out, right? We can drag their mattress over," Kim suggested helpfully.

"Well, that might be taking your life into your own hands, but sure! Whatever makes you happy, Riley," Ashley said with a wry smile.

Right now, he sort of felt like nothing was going to make him happy, but at least he had a plan. Sort of. Get through tomorrow, and be open and honest, but not about *everything*, just some things. Then fall into his friends' arms on Friday. He thought he could probably do at least one of those things.

TEN

PENELOPE

Penelope couldn't shake the feeling that it was somehow the end of January.

Every new year, she would start off with great intentions, resolutions, and promises to herself. Then the weeks would pass, and her plans would slip, and by the end of January, she'd have forgotten why she had even set the resolutions to begin with.

That was how she felt as Thursday morning dawned.

She'd fallen asleep Saturday night feeling confident and excited to share her full self with the world. She'd felt buoyed by Frankie, Diego, and Taylor's support and was hopeful she'd get Riley's support on Thursday. She imagined them talking about her gender identity, discussing his hesitations with sex, and coming together amidst all of it. She imagined holding his face in her hands, kissing him, and happily sinking into his arms.

As the days passed, he went completely silent on her, only

211

responding a few times and then not at all on Tuesday and Wednesday. Taylor also disappeared around the same time, and Penelope used the time to make a decision about being the drag brunch MC.

She had loved every moment of the experience, and it had brought Taylor into her life and helped her discover herself, but she didn't want to do it every single weekend. If things with Riley were going to get serious, she wanted to be able to spend more time with him. In addition, Maria was spending more and more time with Crystal, and Penelope wanted to get out of their hair by potentially spending the night at Riley's on some weekends.

Ultimately, she decided to do one brunch a month, agreeing to work with the new MC to coordinate their schedules.

She told Frankie and Diego Wednesday night, and she tried to get excited to look through Diego's clothes, but by the time they finished closing the cafe, she admitted she just wasn't feeling it. Diego and Frankie invited her up to their apartment anyways, and they sipped tea while watching a sitcom on their couch.

Penelope had only been to their apartment a handful of times, and she could see now how the two men had braided their lives together in their décor through the photos on the wall, and even their monogrammed blankets tangled together on the couch. There was so much love here, and Penelope momentarily wondered if she'd ever have something like this.

Thursday morning arrived, and it was cold and raining and actually did feel like the end of January. She trudged through the workday and got a message from Riley asking if she was still coming over that night. She still hadn't heard from Taylor, and she was beginning to wonder if she'd done something to upset her. So much of their recent conversations had been focused on Penelope. Maybe Taylor was just getting tired of it. Tired of her.

Penelope laid her head on her desk, feeling dejected and like she just wanted to go home and go to bed. She felt a large, warm hand on her back, and a cup of coffee swimming with hydrogenated-oil-packed creamer was placed in front of her nose.

Maya had switched to remote work to finish out her pregnancy, so it was just Penelope and Greg for the next few months. Penelope had been so busy with the new project that they hadn't talked much, but Greg seemed to sense when she needed him, and he'd bring her a coffee or a crappy pastry from their downstairs shop.

Suddenly, she imagined telling him that she was nonbinary, and she knew he'd be immediately supportive. He might even buy her some new artwork. She didn't have the energy to do it today, but maybe one day soon.

As she trudged her way through the rain to the bus stop, she wondered if she had the energy to tell Riley today. She huddled underneath the bus sign and considered getting on the bus that would take her to her apartment, not his. She pulled her phone out and sheltered it from the rain with her arm.

If she could just talk to him, she thought she would know if it was better for her to call today a wash and try again later or if she would feel better after speaking with him.

She pulled up the app and called him. He again didn't answer, and she wanted to throw her phone on the ground, but it would probably end up in a puddle, and then she'd be sunk.

She let her annoyance carry her onto the bus and stewed in it all the way to Riley's apartment. Why couldn't he just answer the phone today and those other times when she'd just wanted to talk to him and open up to him? Why couldn't he just open up to her a little bit more so that she knew she could trust him fully with herself? Why couldn't he just fucking read her mind already and know that there was nothing he could tell her, short of being an axe murderer, that would make her not like him, and could he just get on with it already?

By the time she got to his apartment, she was feeling more than a little combative. She knocked aggressively on his door, making sure to drip all over his front doorway.

"Is there a reason why you refuse to answer my calls?" Penelope demanded the second he opened the door.

Riley blinked down at her. He had been smiling tentatively when he answered the door, but his face fell at her question and her appearance. She could only imagine how she looked right now. She was soaked through her clothes, and she felt like a drenched cat. An angry drenched cat.

"Did you... get stuck in the rain? And... try to call me?" Riley asked and he pulled out his phone. He looked down at it in confusion and then back up at her. She felt a drop of water run from her hairline down to the tip of her nose and then drop onto the carpeted hallway. Something about that seemed so absurd to her that she did the only thing she could think of. She shook out her hair and body like a wet dog, and when she stopped her little shimmy, she had gotten a fair amount of water all over his hallway wall and him.

She felt just a touch better.

"Can I come in now, or..."

"I'm so sorry— yes! Please come in! Can I... get you some fresh clothes? Do you... want to take a shower? I could dry your clothes—"

Penelope watched every single one of his stress signals come out one after another as he spoke. He was even wringing his hands around his phone, which seemed like a new one.

"I think I would like you first just to tell me why you refuse to answer any of my calls." She wasn't sure why this was the hill she was choosing to die on today, but it had just been the last straw for her fraying nerves.

"I..." Riley said, biting his lip as he pulled up the app and opened his chat with her. "It doesn't... say I missed a call from you," he said tentatively as if knowing that if he tried to mansplain technology to her right now, she might actually throttle him.

"Do you... mind... calling me now? I just want to see what I did wrong," he asked, completely chagrined as he glanced down at her.

"Well, it's not just this time, Riley. I've called you several times over the past few weeks, and you've never answered," she said as she pulled out her phone. She swiped to the app on muscle memory and pressed the call button. It showed up as a call on her screen, but his screen remained on the chat.

They both stared at his phone, and Penelope felt her shoulders start to loosen, but a small kernel of embarrassment began to settle into her chest. There truly wasn't anything showing up on his screen.

"Maybe... I'll try calling you..." Riley mumbled as he reached over and softly pressed the end call button on Penelope's screen. He then pressed his call button.

A warning popped up on his screen: "Unable to connect to audio. Please check speaker and audio settings."

Riley's shoulders slumped in defeat. "Oh no... I've been having trouble with my phone since Oreo chucked it off the counter a little while back, but I thought it was only related to my cellular phone calls. I had no idea it had somehow disconnected the app from my audio... Shit, Nels, I'm so sorry. I... would have loved to talk to you."

He looked over at her, and she finally noticed the dark rings under his eyes. His hair was freshly washed but somehow lacked its usual luster, and he looked a little gaunt in his cheeks.

Even though he was several inches taller than her, in that moment he looked small and so, so sad. Penelope felt the wall she'd been shoddily constructing around her heart the past few days crumble. She threw her arms around his shoulders with no regard for her sopping wet clothes.

Seemingly equally unbothered about the precipitation she had brought into his warm, sweet-smelling home, he wrapped his arms around her waist.

"Shit... Riley, I'm so sorry... I got here and immediately jumped down your throat like an asshole. I think I'm just wet and cold, and... it's been a long, lonely week, and I just really missed you and felt a little sad—which I then turned into anger because I hate feeling sad and... weak."

He gently nudged her back a few inches to look into her eyes.

"I'm so sorry you felt that way, Nels. I promise I wasn't ignoring your calls. But... I told you how sometimes I..." he fell into silence as he bit his poor, abused lower lip again and looked away from her.

She reached up and cupped his cheek, gently urging his teeth off his lip with her thumb. "Were you..." She wasn't entirely sure how to ask someone with depression if they had been depressed that week. She knew for many people with depression it was a constant low-level hum that sometimes surged into something unbearable and then leveled back out. She'd seen it for years with Maria.

"Were you in a bad place this week?" she finally asked.

He went to bite his lip again, but she traced her thumb over it once more, not allowing him to bite down. She stepped back into his space, leaned into him, and replaced her thumb with her mouth.

He wasn't expecting the kiss, so it was more just a brief brush of lips, but it was sweet and soft, and it made Penelope's heart ache.

"You don't have to answer... and actually—before you answer..." she hedged, taking a step back from him, "is there any way we could... start over? Redo my horrible entrance?"

His smile was just barely there, and it didn't even attempt to reach his eyes, but he nodded.

She placed her bag gingerly on the ground, and before he could stop her, she rushed out of the apartment, closing the door behind her. She could imagine his surprised face, so she quickly straightened out her clothing, turned to face the door, and knocked gently.

There was a brief shuffling noise, and then the door opened.

Intellectually, Penelope knew this was fake. It wasn't like they'd be able to forget her awful behavior of the past ten minutes, but when she saw him open the door, she was truly struck as if seeing him for the first time today. His eyes widened comically in surprise at her appearance, putting on a pretty impressive show.

"Hi," she said happily.

One of his eyebrows raised. "Hi... you're all wet."

"Yeah, I sort of got stuck in the rain," she said, picking up a piece of damp hair and letting it flop back onto her chest with a splat.

"Wow, well... thank you for still coming over. Please—come in!" he said, pivoting to give her space to enter.

"Thanks and of course I came over! I missed you terribly and I'm so happy to see you."

"I'm happy to see you too," he said quietly as he closed the door.

They turned to face each other, and she involuntarily shivered.

He frowned. Whether part of the act or his actual response to her discomfort, she wasn't entirely sure. "Can I get you some warm clothes and maybe a hot chocolate?"

"That sounds amazing. Is there... any chance I could take a quick shower too?" she asked, remembering his earlier offer, and feeling like if anything was a hard reset, a shower was.

"Of course! This way," he said, leading her into his bedroom.

She followed him obediently but hesitated briefly in the doorway to his bathroom. She had been expecting the hall bathroom. There was something intimate about using the shower that he used. She stood a little shyly behind him as he fiddled with the dials, and when he turned around, there was a slight blush across his cheeks.

She took a tentative step towards him. "Thank you, Riley... is there... any chance I can get just one more thing?"

"Of course," he said, his hands resting softly on her hips as if he already knew what she was going to ask for.

Maybe he did because he was already bending his head when she said, "Just one kiss?"

"Always," he whispered as he captured her mouth. This kiss was light years away from their first of the night. It quickly turned from the soft slide of lips to the brush of tongues and crash of teeth as he pulled her against him, and she wrapped her arms around his neck, pulling herself up to meet him more fully.

For the first time, she leaned against him during the kiss. She could feel the steadily increasing heartbeat in his chest and the rise and fall of his lungs against her sternum. The way she was tilted, their contact ended right at her navel, where it pressed against his flat stomach.

He lifted one of his hands to card through her wet hair as he deepened the already deep kiss. His fingers snarled in tangles, but she didn't care, and neither did he. She took and gave, he pressed back, and she would have sworn it was them fogging up the mirror, not the hot water from the shower.

They finally pulled back from each other to gasp for breath, and Penelope didn't need the mirror to know she was smiling like an absolute idiot.

"Wow..." he said, reaching up to touch his now kiss-swollen lips.

"Well... I did only ask for one, so... had to make it count, right?" she said with a slight smirk.

"I mean... I guess, but you can have as many as you want; I'm just not sure how many of those I have in me tonight." He gave her a self-deprecating smile, but it turned sweet as he pulled her back to him by her hip. His arms lifted to wrap around her shoulders. "Maybe, like, ten more?"

She laughed and squeezed her arms around his back.

"I'm so happy to see you," she said again into his chest.

"As am I... even if you have pretty much soaked my shirt."

She laughed and plucked at the wet fabric at his rib cage. "Yeah, I'd say sorry, but..."

"I don't want you to," he finished, which wasn't what she was going to say, but she liked it better.

"If you want to leave your clothes on the counter, I can throw them in the dryer for you. I think I—uhm, I might have some clothes that should fit you." He stumbled slightly over the offer. She wasn't sure if he was nervous about her wearing his clothes or what, but she just nodded.

He left, closing the door quietly behind him, and she stripped down quickly, pulling off the wet fabric like shedding a layer of skin.

The hot water was glorious, and she felt all the tension leave her body. That is until she heard the door open and she became suddenly aware that there was only a thin shower curtain between them, and she was completely naked. She listened to the wet noise of him lifting up the clothes, and then there was a soft plunking noise as he deposited the fresh clothes on the counter. Then there was silence. She wasn't sure if she'd missed the door clicking shut again. If she concentrated hard, she thought she could hear him breathing softly.

"...thank you, Riley," she said softly, her voice almost completely drowned out by the water.

"O-Of course," he stammered, and then she heard the door shut.

She finished showering quickly and changed into Riley's soft sweater and joggers. She tried to finger-comb her hair, but all she managed to do was tangle it. She looked around briefly for a brush and found one in the first drawer she opened.

Unfortunately, the brush wasn't much better. She would be in here for over an hour if she wasn't careful. Maybe he'd let her brush her hair on the floor in front of the TV, like she used to when she was a kid.

She walked to the living room just as Riley placed two mugs of steaming hot chocolate on the coffee table. He looked questioningly at her as she scowled at the brush in her hands.

"Sorry, this is so embarrassing... is there any way I could brush my hair out here? I'll try to gather up any hair I shed, I just... it might take a while, and I didn't want to squirrel away in your bathroom the whole time."

He bit back a smile at her evident annoyance and nodded, but then his expression changed, turning hesitant but a little hopeful.

"I could... brush your hair out for you? If you want? I do have a fair amount of experience with it myself, and—I mean, I like it when someone else brushes my hair. It feels nice—but I mean—if you don't, that's okay—maybe it's silly. Obviously you know how to brush your hair—"

"Riley," she stepped forward and placed a hand on his arm. "That sounds wonderful. Maria does that for me sometimes, and you're right. It feels nice. Should I sit here?" She gestured to the floor in front of the coffee table.

He snapped his mouth shut and nodded, taking a step back so she could maneuver into a sitting position between the coffee table and the couch.

He sat down softly behind her, placing his knees on either side of her shoulders. He reached for something she hadn't noticed on the side table—a bottle of leave-in conditioner spray. He tilted the bottle so she could read it, "Would you... like any of this?"

"Sure, I've never used it before, but honestly, I'll try anything at this point."

He hummed his understanding and placed his hand on the edge of her hairline, catching the extra spray as he sprayed it onto her hair. She was hit by a wave of emotions that seemed to come one after another. There was a deep nostalgia for when she was a kid, and her mom would brush out her hair for her. It was followed by an ache that always accompanied innocent memories, back before life got hard and complicated. Then came the warmth that enveloped her when another person cared for her. This warmth settled in her stomach, and turned into a low, rolling burn because it was Riley.

He began slowly working the brush through her hair, starting at the ends and methodically working upwards. "You know it's...

funny. I was sitting here yesterday, and Kim was doing the same for me." He kept brushing, his fingers gentle but firm on her scalp, giving him a little leverage to pull the brush through knots and snares.

"I... wasn't doing very well. So, she and Ashley came over to make me food and... they made me take a shower and then Kim brushed out my hair and Ashley sat next to me, just talking and being there for me..." His voice was soft, almost hypnotic, as he made this deep admission to Penelope. She understood the significance of the moment, so she didn't speak, barely even breathed.

"Kim said something to try and cheer me up. At the time, it didn't work, but now... well... She said that maybe in six months' time, it would be you sitting here, brushing out my hair while I... dealt with depression or anxiety or... whatever the issue of the moment was. Maybe you would be here to make me something warm and... tell me everything was going to be alright." His voice stopped and started, but his hands never stilled, not even for a moment. It was as if whatever well of confidence he was using to brush her hair wasn't the same one he accessed to make this admission to her.

"And now... here we are, not even 24 hours later, but the roles are reversed... Do you think Kim is, like, a really bad psychic?"

Penelope laughed indulgently but still said nothing. She'd learned this trick from Maria. Sometimes leaving a silent space for the other person to fill was the best way to coax them to open up.

"... I was... scared. About today. I mean, it wasn't just that. That would have just caused anxiety, but I also fell into another depression spell and, well, apparently my phone is broken, then I also managed to lose it for an entire day and when I found it I—" He paused, and his hands stopped moving.

His knee was starting to jiggle next to her. On instinct, she threaded her arm between his leg and the couch and gently wrapped it around his calf, providing a gentle pressure she hoped might be grounding. His leg stilled, and he took in a deep breath before continuing.

"When I found my phone, I saw your messages and was so close to calling you. I remembered that Maria said if I ever needed you— either of you to take care of Oreo while I was depressed... you would come."

Penelope nodded her remembrance of this promise.

"I... I wanted to. I wanted to so badly, but I distinctly thought to myself..." he paused, and Penelope felt like whatever he said next was quite possibly going to be the most important thing he'd ever shared with her. She could feel the moment's gravity pressing down on her, rooting her to the spot.

"I thought, 'Riley, don't ruin this today. Let there be just one more day where you still... have her. You're probably going to r-ruin this tomorrow. When you... talk about sex and all of the reasons it's challenging for you and—... when you tell her everything she would need to know to make a final decision about you, just... let me have one more night, one more morning waking up with the hope that maybe this thing between us could work out.'"

His voice was ragged and wet, and even her strong grip on his leg couldn't stop his trembling. She wanted so desperately to turn around and take him into her arms. Just pull him down onto the floor with her and hold him. But she could feel there was more he wanted to say, and she wasn't going to stop him now.

"So... I called them, and they came... and they sat with me and helped me see that maybe I was putting too much pressure on today. You had said there was something you wanted to talk about,

about yourself. And I have something I want to talk about, about myself. And we want to talk about us and—sex. But maybe it's not wise to do that all at once, so they said maybe we should only talk about one thing at a time and so... I guess I wanted to ask... do you want to go first or..." He slowly began to brush her hair again, and Penelope felt herself deflate as some of the tension left her body.

She sat there for a moment, thinking through everything he had just said. She turned her head enough to see him, but not so much that he had to stop brushing the strand he was working on.

"Riley," she started, squeezing the leg she was still holding onto, "I am... so sorry you felt so anxious about today. That was never my intent. I thought giving you a heads-up that I wanted to talk would be better than springing it on you, but if that's not the case, I won't ever put this kind of pressure on you again. Truly, I had no idea you were having such a hard time with it this week."

He said nothing, so she guessed it was her turn to monologue. "I did want to talk today. I want to share something with you, solely about myself, but... honestly, it's been a tough week for both of us. I tried to call you today—" she felt him wince, and she soothed her hand on his knee, "To cancel because I didn't think it would be fair to try and have a conversation when I wasn't in the right headspace and I can tell you aren't in it right now either. Again I... I'm so, so sorry, Riley. I never wanted this to be a stressful thing."

He momentarily shifted his eyes away from her hair, searching her face for something, but she wasn't sure what.

"It's not your fault. You have nothing to apologize for. I worked myself up all on my own," he murmured as he went back to staring intently at her hair.

She pursed her lip and looked down at where her hand was wrapped around his leg. "What would be the best way to have these conversations? Do you want to pick the time, place, venue, et cetera? Do you just want to wait until it comes up naturally?"

He hummed thoughtfully. "Maybe... if I get to pick—well, all of those things you listed—maybe that would help? I also think picking a day closer instead of farther away gives me less time to stress about it."

She nodded. "Okay, all of that works for me."

"So... maybe—oh shoot, you're working weekends. Uhm... maybe—"

"Oh, actually, I changed my schedule to be only once a month! I'm free on weekends moving forward," Penelope said, flashing him a dorky thumbs up.

He smiled, his first smile since their conversation began. Before Penelope could even enjoy it though it faded as he said, "Okay. So... Saturday, maybe?"

"Saturday works for me," she said as she began rhythmically rubbing his leg up and down. A small smile returned to his lips, so she kept doing it. Her neck was starting to get stiff, so she turned back around and reached for her cup of hot chocolate. It was surprisingly still pretty hot.

"Riley, I... it makes me really sad that you thought that with just one conversation, we would be done. I feel like, at least for me, it would probably be at least a few conversations as we worked through everything together. If, in the end, it truly isn't the right thing for us, I told you, I still want us to be friends. I... I don't want to lose you. So, unless you push me away... I'm still going to be here." Her breath made waves in the hot liquid as she spoke, and she watched them crest and fall in her cup.

"I mean... truly, Riley. There is very little you could tell me short of you hurting other people, animals, or... I don't know that you scream at every server you interact with... there's nothing you could say that would make me get up and walk away after a conversation. There are serious things that maybe we would have to work through, and if we couldn't, then... Then at least we tried. But, I don't like that you think it would be so easy for me to leave you."

He had finished about half of her hair and gently ran his fingers through the finished portion, checking for any final knots. The feel of it made her shiver, and he stilled for a heartbeat before doing it again and then again.

"Hey—that's cheating. You don't get to just—melt me like that and not respond to what I said," Penelope complained.

He leaned over her and very gently turned her chin to look back at him.

"I... melt you? Like how you melt chocolate?" he asked, a little skeptical.

"Yes, Riley. You make me melt. When you stroke my hair like that, when you kiss me, when you hug me, and... well... when you look at me the way you are now," she said as firmly as she could, needing him to hear the truth behind her words. Even if she was internally cringing at using such a silly word as "melt." At least she hadn't said swoon.

A small breath escaped his lips. "I... make you melt? When I..." he stopped and just blinked down at her.

"Yes, sweetheart. You do. And surprisingly, it seems that I like melting. So. As I was saying... you're not going to lose me over an open, honest conversation about yourself, about sex, or—I mean... I hope that what I have to tell you about me won't... make you leave me either."

His mouth set into a soft line. "No... I mean, as long as you're not going to tell me you're, like, a secret bigot who burns rainbow flags on the weekend or something."

"Oh, but all my axe murdering of bigots is okay? Cause I mean, it's a recent hobby of mine, but, oh how I enjoy it," she said teasingly.

She didn't miss the specificity of his example, but she promised herself she wasn't going to push him, so she slotted that away in her Riley filing cabinet for the moment.

"Well, it's good to have hobbies, so I don't want to take that away from you. I guess if we're going to be together, I'll just have to get good at axe—er—cleaning?" His brows knit together adorably as he pieced together his joke.

"Axe cleaning... together?" she asked softly. It was the first time either of them had said anything other than "figuring it out."

He purposefully started working the brush through a new section of her hair.

"Is that what you want, Riley?" she pressed when he didn't answer.

"Yeah, I—I think I've passed the 'just want to see if I'm interested' stage... I am interested, and I... I want to be with you. It just... god, it feels like there are still some huge hurdles to get through, and it's really... really scary." His eyes fell closed for a moment, and his head bowed as he took a deep, shuddering breath.

She squeezed his knee comfortingly. She turned her head to look more fully at him and waited until he opened his eyes again to speak. "You're not going through this alone, though, Riley. I'm right here with you, and we're going to face those hurdles together."

She wasn't sure when she had developed real feelings for Riley, but she knew now that she wanted to be with him.

He smiled softly and nodded. He gently turned her head to

look forward again and began working through the biggest knot left in her hair. They sat silently for a few moments, and Penelope sipped the hot chocolate. It was nothing compared to the warmth already in her chest from this conversation, but it felt nice all the same.

"I think I need to get my phone fixed... maybe I'll go on Sunday? You're usually busy on Sundays, right? With—oh, well, I guess not with work, but you watch Grey's with Maria?"

"Yeah, that's our Sunday tradition. Sometimes we do movie marathons on Fridays, like the one you came for, but—oh! I don't know if I told you? Maria is seeing someone now. I think movie marathon Fridays might be becoming a thing for them. She insists that I can join, but it does feel a little awkward when it's just me. Maybe... I mean, probably not tomorrow if we're also going to do Saturday—that might be a lot of me in one week for you, but maybe you could come over for another movie night? Like a... double date night?"

Riley threaded his fingers through the tangle-free portion of her hair, clearly meaning it as a comforting gesture. "I don't think I could ever have too much of you in my week. I do have plans tomorrow, though—and actually, you might have to compete with Ashley for Fridays. She's trying to get us to make Friday's an official thing at her bar, but her bar is exactly what fucked me up last Friday, so... I'm not too sold on it. Your idea sounds much, much better."

For some reason, this tickled a memory for Penelope, but she wasn't sure why. Bars on Friday? That couldn't be it; that was a pretty common occurrence. She thought about it for a moment but then gave up.

"Well, maybe we can do an every-other-Friday sort of deal? I'd love to see Ashley's bar," Penelope said, taking a larger sip of her drink as it started to cool down. She hadn't had anything to eat since lunch, and she was starting to get a little ravenous.

"I like the sound of that— oh okay here, last one," he said, picking up the final lock of her hair to pull the brush through. "Alright..." he continued, a bit absently to himself, "so Friday bar, Saturday Nels, Sunday fix phone... I can do that."

Penelope smiled to herself. She would often do the same thing in her head, usually multiple times a day, just trying to solidify plans in her mind.

"Maybe I can finally get your number, hm?" she teased as he finished with her hair.

He laughed. "Yeah, it does feel like it's time, doesn't it... let me get my phone all fixed up and see if they need to give me a new one with a new number. Then I will happily delete the app and give you my number."

He gave her a hand up from the floor, and she took the brush from him and handed him his hot chocolate. He took a deep sip and then said, "Wow, I didn't realize how hungry I was until I gave my stomach something close to food but not quite food."

She snorted at his phrasing. "Yeah, I was just thinking the same thing."

"We could order something, but it might take a while... any interest in leftover soup? Ashley made it, so it's delicious."

Penelope was glad she wasn't a jealous person. She knew that two ex-girlfriends coming over to comfort her boyfriend, brushing his hair, and making him "really good" soup could be something others would be jealous of. Well, he wasn't technically her boyfriend yet, but it felt like maybe they were finally heading in that direction. Regardless, she wasn't a jealous person, and actually, she was kind of excited to eat Ashley's cooking again.

Riley settled their mugs of hot chocolate on the table and reheated the soup. He also pulled out some crusty bread, and her stomach growled as he set it and the soups on the table.

They ate in companionable silence, occasionally sharing small anecdotes and comments about their week. Penelope began to feel sleepy from the warm soup, as well as the warmth and the relative silence of the apartment. Oreo had come out of the other bedroom to join them, and he sat amiably next to Riley's chair, occasionally looking up as if requesting food. Riley gave him a mouthful of chicken and then shooed him away.

Riley reheated the remainder of their cocoa after they finished their soup and bread. Once they were done with those, they cleaned up quickly and then stood in momentary awkwardness as they both considered what to do next.

"So... we could..." Riley started a little awkwardly.

In a rush, Penelope interjected, "Pretend to watch a movie, but really just make out on the couch?"

Riley laughed, a little startled, but then he nodded.

They walked around opposite ends of the couch and met in the middle. Almost perfectly in sync, they reached for each other, and suddenly they were kissing. Riley's hands were a little bolder this time, running through her now silky-smooth hair and down her back, coming to rest right in the curve of her spine. Penelope allowed her hands to wander down his shoulder blades and across the slight musculature of his sides.

Riley tried to pull them down neatly onto the couch, but they ended up in a tangle, half on and half off the couch. They broke the kiss to laugh and rearranged themselves, so they were lying facing each other, Penelope pressed up against the back of the couch and Riley lying in front of her. His couch was fairly wide, so this wasn't a challenge, but Penelope couldn't help but laugh at the irony.

"What's so funny?" he asked softly, dropping soft kisses on her cheeks and nose.

"Didn't we say last time we would probably end up horizontal kissing?"

"We did indeed... maybe we're both really bad psychics too?"

"Oh yeah?" she said, nipping at his lower lip. "How did you see this going then?"

"Oh, I mean, it's making out with you so... amazing?" He leaned down to catch her mouth in another kiss.

They kissed for a while, their legs slowly tangling together as their hands explored each other's faces, shoulders, and backs. Unfortunately, all of the warm, floaty feelings Penelope was experiencing came to a crashing halt when Riley brought his hand around from her back, just as she turned her shoulder, and it brushed across her breast on its way up to her face. She had given Riley her bra to dry because it had been soaked through by the rain. The gentleness of the touch took her almost as much by surprise as the dual feeling it shot through her. It was a combination of pleasure and revulsion. She gasped audibly, and it wasn't a good gasp, more like a gasp she would make when seeing a cockroach scuttle by.

Riley froze immediately and pulled back so fast he almost toppled off the couch. She grabbed for his shoulder, and his hands went up in the air between them as if in surrender. "Oh gosh—are... Are you okay? Did I... hurt you?"

Penelope felt a little shaken, so she shook her head while she tried to regain composure. She realized with almost crippling clarity that the feeling was not a new one. It was the typical response her body had to being touched there; she was just now finally examining it. It was like a heat ran down into her stomach, but then an angry electricity shot back up her spine, alerting her brain that something was wrong. While her body's natural response to stimulus was pleasure, her brain's response was a black, oily discomfort that sometimes sparked into a flash of anger.

"No, no, you didn't hurt me you... just brushed my chest and..." Penelope tried to explain, trailing off awkwardly at the end.

Riley's eyes turned confused, but there was still a sheen of concern in them. Penelope felt immediately guilty for not having brought this up already, but she had wanted it to be part of one of the other conversations they were going to have. She wasn't sure how to explain it now, though.

"I... don't like being touched there... I don't think..."

Riley's eyebrows shot up, but he nodded frantically. "I'm—I'm so sorry. I promise I didn't mean to. I would never touch that—that part of you without asking first. You... You said you wanted to talk before we got intimate. I promise I wouldn't—"

"Hey, hey, it's okay," Penelope interrupted, taking his outstretched hands in hers before he could really freak out. "I know, Riley. I know you didn't do it on purpose. It was an accident. I just... wanted to let you know why I reacted that way. I'm sorry. I didn't mean to freak you out. I... probably should have said something before, but I was planning on mentioning it today when we talked."

Penelope was momentarily, ever so slightly, annoyed with Riley for making her have to comfort him when she was the one who was upset. She understood that he would probably feel a bit freaked out if he felt he'd been accused of touching a woman inappropriately. Then again, she'd had many hookups where the guy wouldn't even ask permission. They'd just go for a touch or feel while making out, and Penelope usually just accepted it. She knew Riley, and she knew he wouldn't have done something like that on purpose though.

"No, please. Don't apologize; I was just... well, surprised doesn't sound right. I was... shocked? And maybe a little scared and—wow, I made this entire thing about me, didn't I? Shit, Nels, I'm sorry..." Riley said, scrunching up his face.

She smiled a little wryly at him. He smiled back ruefully.

"Uhm... Is there... any chance you'd give me a do-over?" he asked sheepishly.

Penelope's smile turned to a soft laugh. "Well, you gave me one today, so I think it's only fair."

"Okay," Riley said, his smile turning hopeful, but then disappearing just as suddenly. "Oh gosh, I mean, I'm not going to... do that again! I just meant—uhm... could you maybe just say what you said again?"

Penelope stifled another laugh and then immediately sobered. "Uhm... Riley. I don't think—I mean—I have discovered recently that I don't like to be touched there, I think... maybe there's room to explore it more, but for now I'd appreciate it if you... uh—didn't." Well, that was a mess. She'd have to work on her "sex talk" before their next conversation.

Riley nodded emphatically, blessedly ignoring her awkwardness. "I'm so sorry I made you uncomfortable. I promise it was just an accident. I would never have touched you that way without your permission. Even so. I'm sorry it happened, and I promise I'll be much more careful in the future."

Penelope's eyes went misty, and she threw her arms around his shoulder, pressing her face into his neck.

"Thank you," she whispered into his ear.

His hands came around her back and gently stroked her shoulders.

"We're going to figure this all out together, Nels. We'll talk more on Saturday, okay?"

She nodded, and he kissed her temple, continuing to stroke her back.

They kissed a little more, but most of the steam had left them, so Riley went to fetch her clothes from the dryer. She changed quickly in his bathroom again, and when she met him at the door, they hugged and kissed one more time before Penelope headed out into the still-rainy night.

Her day and their night hadn't gone even remotely as planned, but she was pretty happy with how things had turned out. Riley had handled her admission with anxiety, which seemed to be his normal setting, but then had shifted into grace. She thought there was a high likelihood that their conversation on Saturday would go well, even if there was still some anxiety. She wanted to talk this out with someone, and the idea struck her to call Taylor later that night.

Taylor

Taylor was exhausted.

She'd had a rough week and hadn't slept well in days, and Thursday night was no exception. She had tried to go to bed early but just tossed and turned for hours. She finally gave up and crawled out of bed around one a.m. She checked her phone and saw she'd missed a call from Pen at eleven, but it felt too late to call her back, so she tossed her phone back on the bed and left her room.

She ended up pacing around her apartment until three a.m. with her cat following her, looping in and out of her legs as she walked. Her eyes drifted to her couch each time she passed it, and she was tempted to curl up on it, but she didn't want to accidentally fall asleep there and royally mess up her back.

After a dozen or so more laps she finally did collapse onto the blasted couch and fell into a dreamless stupor, only to wake up with a headache and an aching back.

Pen sent a follow-up text early Friday morning asking if they could talk. She said she had a small update on her gender exploration, and she was feeling anxious about an upcoming conversation. Taylor was touched that Penelope kept coming back to her repeatedly to talk. Taylor hesitated, though, because her phone was still broken, and she didn't think she could be fully present in any conversation about gender today.

Ultimately, Taylor decided to use her phone as an excuse, and she asked if they could just text throughout the day.

Pen seemed anxious to talk, though, and she even asked if they could meet up that night. Taylor almost considered inviting her to the bar she was going to with friends, but she thought better of it at the last minute. This week wasn't the right time to meet Pen in person. Partially because Taylor was beginning to resemble a raccoon, the circles under her eyes were so dark, but also because she was distracted and a bit out of sorts. So much so that she got on the wrong bus for work.

She had to run across town in her stupid, stuffy suit, and by the time she got to work, she wanted to rip her clothes off and maybe also her skin underneath it. Perhaps she could just shake it out and put it back on, and it would fit better than it had this week.

She watched the clock religiously, counting down the minutes until she could get home, get out of this stupid costume, let her hair down, and see her friends. She drummed her fingers on the table so loud during a staff meeting her coworkers all glanced at her with concern, and she didn't care in the slightest.

Thankfully, around one p.m. a coworker pulled her into a meeting on an error he'd found in a spreadsheet, and that used up a good chunk of time. The instant the second the clock struck four p.m., she was out of her seat and out the door.

Her knee jiggled on the bus ride back to her apartment, and she realized she had never texted Pen back about hanging out tonight. She threw some leftovers in the microwave and stripped out of her work clothes, tossing them in the corner, narrowly avoiding her cat yet again. She let her long blonde hair tumble out of its rubber band and fluffed it with her hands as she slid on her glasses. They were just for style, but it always felt like she was putting on her face to go out into the world, the way other women put on makeup.

Taylor had never quite figured out makeup, but she had been meaning to do more research into the brands Sham Pain had suggested for her a few months back. Her friends were constantly offering to help, but she just couldn't seem to take this final step into her femininity. So, for now, the glasses would have to suffice. She rummaged through her closet until she found a green cowl neck sweater that hid her flat chest and hugged her slim waist. She paired it with skinny light-wash jeans and ankle boots.

She shot a text to her friends that she was on her way and her eyes lingered on the unanswered message from Pen.

At the beginning of their friendship, Taylor had been uncertain what it was that Pen wanted from her, whether it was friendship or something else, possibly something more. After she'd admitted she wasn't looking for a relationship right now, Pen had been amazing in backing off and never bringing up her interest again. She'd loved getting to know Pen and helping her explore her own gender had solidified a few things for Taylor as well.

She paused in front of her bathroom mirror to take in her "feminine armor" as she liked to call it. She could admit to herself that she'd been holding back from fully opening up to Pen. She hadn't purposefully meant to keep her at arm's length, she was just a private person who took a while to open up. Maybe she could work on that.

Could she be brave enough to meet up with Pen tonight, listen to what she had to say about herself, and help her prepare for whatever conversation she was going to have tomorrow? Yes.

Could she be brave enough to finally open up to Pen in return? Maybe someday.

She took a deep fortifying breath, sent Pen the address of the bar, and headed out of her apartment.

ELEVEN

PENELOPE

Penelope returned home from Riley's house Thursday night and spent an hour on the couch with Maria debriefing on everything that had happened and planning the conversation she was finally going to have with Riley on Saturday. While Maria had tried to be supportive, she was also actively falling asleep, so Penelope eventually shooed her off to bed.

She had tried to call Taylor, but she hadn't answered. Instead of going to sleep, Penelope spent several more hours thinking about her relationship with Riley and her friendship with Taylor. She was still harboring feelings for Taylor, but she knew it was time to let it go. She fell asleep rereading her messages with Riley.

She woke up Friday full of nervous energy and an almost desperate urge to talk to Taylor about Riley and the gender conversation they would have in less than twenty-four hours. Perhaps this was a good sign that her crush on Taylor was receding. Unfortunately, when she'd asked Taylor to meet up, she received no response.

Even so, she was in a much better mood than she had been on Wednesday. So, when Diego texted to ask if she wanted to swing by after work to look at some of the clothing he'd pulled out for her, she happily agreed.

She spent about an hour trying things on and had found three shirts and a jacket when she got Taylor's text. It was just an address for a bar with no additional information, but Penelope made a game-time decision and changed into one of the shirts she'd taken from Diego. It was a green button-down overlaid with a black velvet floral pattern. She rolled the sleeves up to her elbows and left the top two buttons undone, revealing just a hint of collar bone.

She felt amazing and looked almost as good. She folded up the other items, slid them into her backpack, and headed for the bar. It was close by, only a five-minute walk, so she had a few minutes to gather herself before meeting Taylor.

The bar was a speakeasy-style joint with dark lighting, gorgeous cherry wood paneling, and a dimly lit bar with barrels as bar stools. She was immediately in love with the decor and added this to her list of go-to bars, right up there with the arcade bar. She approached the bar and saw a surprisingly familiar face working behind the counter.

"Ashley?" Penelope asked as she came to stand next to an equally familiar-looking woman on her side of the bar. "Kim?" she asked, turning to the shorter woman.

They both looked at her in shock, and then Ashley's expression turned quizzical. "Hi, Penelope... what are you doing here?"

"I'm meeting a friend here actually—wait, is this your bar? It's gorgeous!" she exclaimed.

Ashley cast a meaningful look at Kim. "It is, yes, and thank you. You're too sweet. Can I... get you something while you wait?"

"Sure, rum and coke?" Penelope asked, pulling out her phone to see if she had any additional texts from Taylor or anything from Riley. She didn't.

"Coming right up... So, is your friend a regular? I tend to see mostly the same faces around here," Ashley asked nonchalantly as she flipped a cup across her knuckles and began pouring coke from a fountain gun. Penelope couldn't help but grin at her and Ashley smiled back, but it looked a little pained.

"Yeah, actually, I think she said she comes here every Friday with friends. Maybe you know her? Her name's—"

"Taylor," Kim breathed, but she wasn't looking at Penelope; she was looking at someone as they approached from the door.

Penelope whipped around to see the beautiful blonde woman she had first seen at a corner table at her brother's cafe. She was just as ethereal as she remembered, if not even more so. Her hair was falling in undulations down her back, and her glasses seemed to amplify her startling green eyes, soften her slender nose, and emphasize her soft jawline. She was wearing a cowl neck sweater which accentuated her slim waist and sharp hip bones.

She didn't seem to notice Penelope as she walked up to the bar, which didn't surprise Penelope since Taylor had only ever seen her in drag.

"Ugh, work was so long today. I could really use a drink—but! Let me be very clear, that does not mean I want five shots of tequila again—" Taylor came up short as her eyes came to rest on Penelope.

Penelope's lips were forming into a smile, but they froze when she heard Taylor's confusingly familiar voice. She saw confusion slowly dawning into panic in Taylor's eyes and imagined she was probably making a similar face.

"Penelope?" Taylor's voice was painfully familiar as it formed the shape of her name. Her full name. Which Taylor shouldn't know.

Penelope pushed every thought and every feeling to the back of her mind so she could say, "Yes, but... you know me as Pen?"

Behind her glasses, Penelope saw Taylor's eyes, her gorgeous, too familiar green eyes, widen impossibly large.

Penelope remembered the feeling she had had the first time she laid eyes on Taylor. She had stupidly wondered if it was a familiarity across time and space, but apparently, it was just a familiarity in the here and now.

"You were... in drag, I—... Nels?" Taylor's words were little more than a whisper, but they hit Penelope in the chest like a punch.

All Penelope could do was blink back at her. Each blink felt heavier than the last, and suddenly she was overcome with a bizarre feeling. It was as if the entire world tipped on its axis, and the floor came rushing up towards her. She would have made contact with the floor, except a strong arm wrapped around her waist, holding her upright against a solid, lean body. She didn't recognize this body. Somewhere in the back of her mind, she realized it probably wasn't Taylor.

Penelope blinked blearily and saw that it was Ashley. Ashley, who she met through Riley, who clearly also knew Taylor and was also quite clearly livid.

"Both of you. Need to go upstairs. Right now. Whatever 'come to Jesus' talk you're about to have obviously needs to happen, but it's not going to happen right here. And you—" she said, addressing her harsh words to Taylor and then jerking her head at Penelope, "Need to sit down."

She led Penelope up a back flight of stairs and into an apartment. Penelope felt like she was drunk or high or something else because she didn't feel like she was entirely there. It felt like they were floating, not walking, and when she came to rest in a chair, her head went all woozy, and she bent over to try and get the world to stop spinning.

There was near silence in the room for several minutes as she took in long, shuddering breaths. The only other noise in the room was another set of lungs breathing heavily near her, but she didn't know if it was Ashley or someone else. Someone she knew all too well and simultaneously not at all.

From underneath her lowered eyelids, she could just barely make out the sparsely furnished apartment, and she remembered a conversation about how Ashley lived above her bar and offered rooms to her staff. The room was clean but felt empty, making the silence somehow deafening.

Finally, a quiet voice whipped across the small space, shattering the silence.

"How... long have you known?" Taylor asked. Her voice was cold and harsh, a voice Penelope had never heard before.

"Uhm, I'm sorry, what?" Penelope croaked in an equally cold voice.

She slowly sat up straight and took in Taylor's hunched over posture as she leaned against the wall by the front door. She was so beautiful, and so distinctly Taylor, yet there were hints of Riley in her posture and the anxious ticks in her fingers.

Penelope was vacillating between hurt and confusion and back again. As they continued to stare at each other Penelope felt the confusion turn to venom in her mouth and her voice shot up an octave and about fifty decibels as she practically shrieked, "How long have I *known*? Approximately five fucking minutes! How long have you known?!"

Her last words rang in the air so loud it hurt her ears. Taylor visibly recoiled from her, pressing herself back against the wall.

"...Well, I'd say approximately four minutes and fifty-nine seconds then." It wasn't just Taylor's voice that was shaking; it was her entire body. She clutched tightly at her arms and visibly ground her teeth together.

In an instant, all of the confusion, hurt, and anger that had been turning to bile inside Penelope vanished. Because in that instant, she remembered Taylor's garbled voice telling her over the phone that she was triggered by yelling and Penelope had just outright screamed at her.

"Oh, god, Taylor, I... I'm so sorry. I shouldn't have yelled. You told me and... I didn't think I—I forgot. I'm so sorry, oh no—" Penelope babbled helplessly as she stood up and reached a hand forward in the air.

Taylor's shoulders began to shake, and big fat tears started to roll down her cheeks. She was trembling so hard her teeth began to chatter, and her knuckles were white where they were clawing into her arms.

"Taylor, I—It's me. It's just me. I'm so sorry I yelled, I... can I hug you? Can I... do anything? Please, I'm sorry—"

Before she could finish, Taylor was across the room and in her arms.

"Okay... okay... It's okay. You're safe. You're always safe with me. It's okay. I'm so, so sorry. I was confused, and out of it, I raised my voice, and I'm so sorry. You're okay. I promise everything is going to be okay," Penelope uselessly soothed her hand up and down Taylor's thin back.

"Is it?" Taylor's voice was broken, and oh god, it was so achingly familiar, and yet actually a little different, like the way she was inflecting her words was different. There was a slight lilt and almost breathiness to the words as if she held them inside herself longer before releasing them. Penelope wondered if it was purely the garbled phone lines to blame or if she actually wouldn't have been able to recognize Riley's voice when Taylor spoke over the phone.

Hesitantly, remembering what Riley had once told her, she reached up and placed two gentle fingers against the nape of Taylor's neck, carding through her long, gorgeous hair to do so. Taylor's knees buckled, and Penelope stumbled under her weight for a moment before stabilizing them.

"Okay... see? It's okay. I've got you." Taylor was taller than Penelope, but somehow she seemed so much smaller with her shoulders hunched down and her head resting on Penelope's shoulder.

"Here, why don't—why don't you sit down."

Penelope turned them around so she could gently lower Taylor onto the chair. She kneeled down in front of Taylor, so they were at eye level again. Taylor's gorgeous eyes were bloodshot, and she refused to meet Penelope's eyes, staring down at her jean-clad knees instead.

Penelope's mind was racing a million miles a minute, images and thoughts flashing through her mind too quickly for her to keep track of. A cat's tail, the corner of a sofa, a broken phone, similar patterns of disappearing and reappearing, a nameless sister, a horrible father—

"Your name is Taylor Riley," Penelope said suddenly, remembering one of the first messages they'd sent to each other. "Your... father thought your first name was too feminine, so you... go by your middle name, and even today, he refuses to call you by anything else even though—oh god." Penelope had to tip her head back to look up at the ceiling to stop her own tears from falling. She fiercely blinked them away. This already tense situation would go straight to hell if they were both crying incoherently.

"But I've always really liked the name Taylor..." Taylor whispered, and Penelope looked back at her, but her head was still bent down. "It's like the same feeling I get when someone uses the right pronouns—"

Taylor's head snapped up so fast she almost smacked Penelope in the chin. Penelope only just managed to lean out of the way, or she would have ended up on her ass.

"Oh my god, Nels... you're nonbinary?"

First, that name, Riley's name for her, and then the question at the end tore through Penelope like a knife. Penelope did fall backwards then. Thankfully, she didn't have very far to go. She just ended up sliding down onto her butt, so she was sitting at Taylor's feet.

"We've... talked about so much together..." Penelope whispered. "Oh my god, I asked *you* for advice on telling *you* that I was nonbinary. I came here today to get *your* advice on how to have a hard conversation with *you* tomorrow—"

Penelope's stomach roiled violently. She fell forward onto her hands and knees and had to bite down on the inside of her mouth to keep from breaking into sobs. This was all just too much for her.

"So... is that... what you wanted to talk about tomorrow?" Taylor asked, and Penelope laughed at the absurdity of it all, but then it finally did turn into a sob.

"Oh god, Nels... Pen... fuck, I—" Taylor dropped to her knees, and her hand came to rest on Penelope's back, rubbing in slow frantic circles. They stayed like this for a few moments until Penelope slowly sank back onto her butt. Now they were both sitting on the floor.

"Okay. Maybe we should be clear right now—I mean, starting right now—" Penelope gave a miserable hiccup, "—from now on, just call me Nels. I'm not even really doing drag anymore, so Pen is... gone."

Taylor nodded. "Did you... want me to use they/them or—okay; this is not a good time for that conversation. Got it," Taylor said, holding up her hands as Penelope gave her what must have been a desperately panicked look.

"Should I... only use she/her pronouns for you from now on and call you Taylor? Do you... do you always go by that, or...?" Penelope hedged uselessly.

There were still a thousand thoughts flying through her head. Was Taylor trans? Had she been misgendering and dead naming her by accident this entire time?

Taylor took a huge breath in and let it out in a woosh. "I... am sometimes a woman, in which case I go by she/her and Taylor. And sometimes—well, more often than not, I am a man, and I go by he/him and Riley. And finally... sometimes I am a fucked-up mess of somewhere in between, but that's called depression, and sometimes in those moments, I'd prefer they/them, but it also doesn't really matter what you call me then."

Penelope blinked rapidly. Somehow, she could recall a website, back from her early research days, with a scale on gender and sexuality. She squinted at it in her head, and the term came to her in a rush.

"You're... gender fluid?" Penelope asked, remembering clicking on that link and then sending it to—"oh fucking hell, I sent you a link on your own gender identity and asked you to discuss it with me, like a fucking asshole. Oh my god—"

Penelope had to take in a deep gasping breath as she bent over, placing her elbows on her knees, and her head in her hands.

Taylor's hands flapped desperately over her and finally came to rest again on her shoulder. "Hey, you... You didn't know because—because I'm a fucking piece of shit who didn't tell you..."

Taylor said, her voice cracking several times throughout the sentence.

"You... You did tell me something, though, didn't you?" Penelope said, raking through her brain frantically as if she could pull out the files from her mental filing cabinet.

She imagined taking the Riley drawer and the Taylor drawer, throwing them all to the floor in a chaotic heap, and frantically scrabbling through them until she found the one she needed. "You said... you understood if I found it scary telling people my gender identity because... I would probably want them to get to know me as a person without my gender. You told me those exact words about my gender but you—you were talking about yourself, weren't you?"

It was as if Penelope had finally been given the secret code-breaking glasses necessary to decode the mystery that had always been these two strange, wonderful, lovely people in her life. She imagined putting them on and looking down at all the files spread at her feet, and suddenly she saw so much more than she could have imagined.

"Oh god—" Taylor gasped, and her breath turned into another shaky sob, "you... You told me about your gender dysphoria and—and I couldn't even tell you about mine. I—you were so open and so honest with me on the phone and then last night—" a sob broke through her words and her body heaved, slender shoulders shaking violently again, "I accidentally touched you and—I didn't even know, and you didn't even know, and oh my god, I'm a horrible person."

"Taylor—" Penelope breathed, her heart shredding at the words, "please don't say that—"

"How—" she gasped, bringing her hands up and digging her nails into the skin at her temples, "How are you still sitting here with me? How can... how can you even look at me—"

"Because you're so impossibly, heartbreakingly beautiful," Penelope said, grabbing Taylor's wrists to stop her from clawing at her face. She yanked Taylor's hands away and accidentally knocked off her glasses.

Her eyes were even brighter without the glass distorting them. They sparkled with tears and pain and—god, so much fear.

"Because... I really *really* like Riley and I... I was absolutely enchanted by Taylor and... I still am. I really, really like you, and I am enchanted by you and—"

"You like a lie," Taylor said, and her voice was suddenly scarily devoid of emotion. "I mean... you like two lies! Holy shit—I just..." Taylor pulled her hands back from Penelope's grasp.

"But it wasn't a lie. *You* are not a lie, Taylor... You opened up to me in every way you could. Please..." Penelope said, suddenly feeling some of the fear she saw in Taylor's face.

"No, Nels—no. I can't—I can't do this." Taylor stood up sharply and started walking towards the door of the apartment.

"No, Taylor, please! Wait!" Penelope was on her feet, and even though the room spun, she tried to take a step forward.

"I can't do this, oh my god, I can't fucking do this..." Taylor continued to mumble as she walked towards the door, and Penelope panicked. She panicked as the two people—who were actually one person—one unbelievably complex, wonderful, amazing, lovable person, walked away from her. She was walking out. Out the door and possibly out of Penelope's life. So, Penelope did the absolute worst thing she could do.

"Riley, please!"

She was sobbing again. And yelling. And she felt the floor rush up towards her again as she fell to her knees.

Taylor took one look back at her over her shoulder and whispered, "how can you call for him... when you don't even know who he is..."

And then she left.

Penelope knelt on the floor for what felt like minutes but might have been closer to an hour before the door to the apartment opened, and Ashley tentatively stepped in. Behind her was probably the only person Penelope wanted to see more than Taylor Riley right now.

"Oh, Poppy..." Maria ran across the room to her and fell to her knees, pulling Penelope into a tight hug.

"Riley gave me Maria's phone number before he left..." Ashley said.

Penelope was momentarily confused by the name and gender shift, until she realized that Maria only knew Taylor Riley as Riley, so of course Ashley had to use his name when talking to Maria.

"Please... Penelope, Maria, stay as long as you need," Ashley said as she slowly shut the door behind her.

Taylor must have told Ashley some of what happened because when she'd carried Penelope up the stairs earlier, she had looked furious, probably assuming this had been some insane catfishing setup. Now, she just looked incredibly sad as she shut the door.

Penelope felt like the biggest idiot in the entire world. She had literally been accidentally catfished and had accidentally catfished someone else. She choked on a laugh, and Maria pulled her in tighter, perhaps interpreting it as a sob. Or maybe, as her best friend, she interpreted the laugh for what it was—the edge of absolute hysteria.

"We can stay here as long as you need, Poppy, but just so you know, Frankie and Diego are out front in their car, probably double or triple-parked illegally. Do you need a few more minutes, and I'll tell them to circle around a few times?"

"I—" Penelope said, and even though she was on the ground, she felt her knees give out, and she collapsed sideways. Maria caught her and brought her head forward to rest on her chest.

"Okay. Okay... it's alright. Everything is going to be okay," she cooed.

That was what Penelope had said earlier to Taylor. Because she had truly believed it. Yes, this situation was insane, and if it had happened to anyone else, she never would have believed it. But it *had* happened, and it had happened to her.

Even still, though. She had thought, maybe naively, that they could work it out together. Penelope adored both sides of Taylor Riley, and she had thought it would be enough. Yes, there was probably six years' worth of fodder for a couple's therapist to work through with them, but Penelope thought they could have done that together.

As she sat there on the hard floor, though, she realized there was no way Taylor wasn't going to run. From everything she'd learned about Riley, he ran from everything hard. She'd seen him try to do it right in front of her when they'd first talked about sex. She'd watched him run into himself and slam the door closed, the same way she'd felt Taylor run from her since the moment they met. Taylor had told Penelope she wasn't interested in a relationship while Riley had been dating her. Penelope couldn't reconcile that in her mind. She couldn't reconcile many things, like why it had been Taylor hiding things from her this whole time, but then when it all came out, she was the one who ran away. Didn't Penelope deserve an explanation, deserve the chance to say her piece?

"Poppy... I'm so sorry... just—what should I tell Frankie?" Maria asked as her hands tenderly stroked Penelope's hair back from her wet cheeks.

"I... let's just... go," Penelope mumbled, and took a deep, fortifying breath. She sat up straight and finally met Maria's gaze. "Let's go, but I want to talk to Ashley before we go." She wasn't sure where this conviction was coming from, but she wanted to ask Ashley to tell Taylor Riley something.

Maria helped her up and slowly led her to the door and down the stairs. Ashley was standing behind the bar again, her eyebrows and mouth set in tight lines. When she saw Penelope, she actually looked almost frightened.

"They left," she said quickly as Penelope approached the side of the bar, and Penelope wasn't sure if she meant Taylor Riley and Kim or just Taylor Riley. "I'm sorry. I don't even know what to say—hey, please don't—" Ashley yelped as Penelope reached behind the bar, but all she did was grab a napkin and snatch a pen off of a closed check holder on the bar.

251

Penelope glanced sidelong at Maria for a moment and decided to stick with Ashley's earlier use of he/him pronouns.

"I know Riley was going to get his phone fixed on Sunday... if something happens and he loses my number, here it is." She handed the napkin to Ashley, who took it gingerly as if it was a sacred text that could be damaged or broken. "And can you... can you just tell him one thing for me?"

Ashley didn't even hesitate before nodding.

"Can you tell him..." she drew in a deep breath and tried to remember everything she'd learned from her conversations with Sham Pain and Diego, her endless texts with Taylor, and her amazing dates with Riley. "Tell him that he doesn't owe me anything. Not an explanation, an apology, or... even a second chance to try this again. Tell him he doesn't owe me any of that, but... maybe he owes just a little bit of it to himself. Tell him... he knows where to find me when—or if he comes to that conclusion."

Ashley's eyes filled with tears, and she reached out and pulled Penelope into a hug. "I'm so sorry, Penelope... I will. I promise I'll tell him. I'll tell him a lot fucking more than just that, too. I swear I'll kick his ass into shape and back to you if I can."

Penelope pulled back and gave her a shaky smile. "Well... I don't know about all that, but... maybe some therapy might be a good idea?"

Ashley laughed a short, shaky laugh. "You better fucking believe it. I'm going to drag him by his stupid, gorgeous hair."

Penelope laughed then, but it was so close to a sob she thought it was probably time to leave.

She walked out to the car with Maria and climbed into the back seat on shaky legs. Then they were off, speeding down the dark streets towards home.

Frankie parked slightly more legally, and they all piled into the apartment. Diego guided Penelope to the couch while Frankie deposited the rabbit into her lap, and Maria ran into the kitchen to make "hot drinks, cold drinks, alcoholic drinks, and cookies."

As everyone moved around her, Penelope began to talk. She started at the beginning and told them about meeting Riley online and then seeing Taylor at the drag show. She told them about the parallel texting and dating app messages, she told them about the dates and late-night garbled phone calls. She told them about discovering her gender identity, sharing it with Taylor, withholding it from Riley, and getting very little in return from either of them. She even told them about the gender dysphoria moment the night before.

Then, she finally told them about tonight. About the awful, beautiful, terrifying moment when she realized the two people she had been interested in, more interested in than she'd ever been in anyone else before, were actually the same person. She told them how it had all gone awry when Taylor Riley had turned to fear instead of to Penelope. She cried on and off throughout the entire telling, and Maria cried with her, Diego paced around the apartment, and Frankie just held her hand through it all.

Finally, there was nothing left to say. She sat there petting the stupid rabbit that reminded her of Taylor Riley but also of her wonderful, loving roommate, and she cried more silent tears.

"What... do I do now?" Penelope finally asked into the silent room.

"You go to the beach with me," Maria said with such finality Penelope almost agreed immediately.

"Wait... what?" she asked, wiping the tears off her face with

Diego's borrowed shirt sleeve. She shot him an apologetic look, and he waved it off immediately.

"Crystal and I have been talking about going to the beach, because her family has a beach house, and I just texted her, and she said we can go tomorrow and stay for a week and a half. So. We're going to go to the beach. Frankie? Diego?"

"Sorry Maria, we have a drag brunch to run this weekend and the cafe the rest of the time, but—and before you say anything Lopi —we have it completely covered. The new person is starting tomorrow anyways. It's actually impeccable timing. We'll take care of everything while you're gone. Just make sure to email your work because you're going to the beach—uh, with a rabbit?" he said, looking down at the creature. Maria had brought out a handful of lettuce when she'd brought Penelope her five drinks, and the rabbit was just munching away.

"We need to name the dumb thing," Penelope said, stroking its ears fondly.

"Oh, he has a name. It's Sir Hopsalot, but I thought you would pretend to hate it even more than you pretend to hate him, so I didn't think it was worth telling you."

"Well, shit," Penelope said, looking down at Sir Hopsalot, "you ready to go to the beach S.H.?"

"Oh my god, you just learned his name. How have you already given him a nickname," Maria huffed.

"Yeahhhh, you do know if you didn't insist on going by nick-names, this probably wouldn't have happened," Frankie said fondly.

Penelope threw her almost empty plastic cup of alcohol at him.

"Too soon?" he joked as he tried to jump out of the way. She only felt a little bad when he ended up stepping right into its path, and pink liquid splashed down his stupid polo shirt.

(TAYLOR) RILEY

Riley woke up feeling decidedly masculine, decidedly hungover, and decidedly like the worst piece of shit human being who had ever lived. At least the masculinity felt slightly new and intriguing because usually, when he was this depressed, he felt a complete lack of gender.

He rolled over in bed and collided with Johanna, who then kicked her foot in protest and managed to nail Ashley in the face. Kim was safe for only a moment, having been lying behind Riley with her arms around his shoulders. However, when Ashley woke up in a panic, she flailed out and kneed Kim in the shin. To start Riley's morning perfectly, Kim then punched him in the face.

It was Friday morning the following week, and Riley hadn't been to work, eaten anything that wasn't directly placed in his mouth or drank much besides hot chocolate and alcohol in seven days.

His friends had left him alone all day the previous Saturday and most of Sunday, sending a few messages throughout the day but mostly giving him space to grieve. And grieve he did. He reread every single message he'd sent in the dating app, then deleted his profile, reread every single text message exchanged with Pen, and then blocked her number.

Ashley and Kim had shown up Sunday night with a new phone for him to transfer his old content to, takeout food, and six bottles of his favorite wine. Ashley had also brought a napkin with Penelope's number on it and a message from her that was so painful Riley fell to his knees in his kitchen when Ashley relayed it.

They'd sat with him on the floor as he sobbed, and then they'd wrapped themselves around him on the couch and held him until Monday morning. Monday afternoon, Johanna arrived and said she wasn't leaving until he was in therapy, quit his stupid job, and had won Penelope back.

Riley said he could do one of those and that she could just pick which one and get back to him, but that in the meantime he was going to go to sleep for the next year. He slept for about two hours before a pile of women was in his bed, and that's how the next five days had gone.

Ashley had managed to get him in to see a therapist, and the first session on Wednesday night had gone surprisingly okay. The therapist guided him through some basic questions about his mental health, gender, sexuality, and desires for therapy. He'd answered every question honestly, which was probably the first time he had ever told someone about his gender identity within the first, what, three months of knowing them?

They talked about that a little too, and they scheduled another session for that Friday afternoon and the following Monday and Friday. He was able to get out the bare bones story of what happened with Penelope, and then the therapist had added on an extra session for the following Wednesday as well. Riley was only mildly offended at this.

Riley cashed in all of his vacation time and wasn't set to return to work for another three weeks, and after that, he wasn't sure if he was going to return at all.

He tried not to talk about it often, except to Johanna, but he despised his job. He was good at it and made good money, but he worked with a bunch of prejudiced old assholes. They constantly made horrible, thinly veiled misogynistic, homophobic, and racist jokes, comments, and references. Every second Riley had to sit in the office with them was torture. It was something even worse than torture on the days Riley woke up as Taylor and the suit she was forced to wear felt like it cut off her air supply like a strait jacket.

When Riley brought this up over dinner Thursday night, River was actually the one to suggest he apply to new jobs with his preferred array of pronouns: she/they/he. If that meant he didn't get any interviews, then at least he would know there wasn't a space for him in this industry. Maybe then he'd have to try and make a career change, or maybe go back to school or literally anything that wasn't continuing to live the way he had been until now.

For some reason, these decisions to go to therapy and change jobs, had been haunting him for years, but he'd never been able to find the courage or motivation to do either. Single-handedly shattering his only chance at a happy relationship seemed to be the kick in the ass he finally needed.

His friends and sister took amazing care of him throughout the week. He would randomly burst into sobs, fits of anger, and self-hatred, and they would hold him and talk him through it all. They allowed him to berate himself on the first night, perhaps hoping he would get it all out of his system, but when it bled into the second and third nights, they put their collective foot down. The most poignant moment was when Kim asked, "So are you done with Penelope, and do you hate her because she's nonbinary and didn't tell you?"

Riley had frozen in horror and nearly yelled at Kim for asking such an awful question, but then he'd realized what she was saying. He'd walked out of the room to sit on the floor of his bedroom, staring into his gender-bending closet. Out of the blue, he remembered offering to share clothing with Pen and he smiled softly.

Of course he would never be done with or hate her for not opening up to him about her gender. He knew Kim was just trying to make him see that the same could possibly be said about him. He decided this was a great conversation to pay $150 an hour for with his therapist.

So, here he was, one bruised face and a broken heart later, sitting on the couch at his new therapist's office. He had spent the past forty-five minutes telling her his life story, starting in childhood, through college, dating and befriending Kim and Ashley all the way up through Penelope. He'd just begun to describe his past week when the therapist stopped him.

"I have a writing assignment for you, Riley. I want you to write yourself a series of letters. I want you to address it to yourself as a child, in college, while dating your friend Ashley, and while dating Penelope."

Riley blinked at her, already seeing where this was going and not liking it. "What, so... you want me to tell my child-self that it's okay your father is a bigot because you'll stay close with your sister? Tell my college self it might feel hard, but you'll realize you're gender fluid soon, and at least then you won't wake up hating yourself every day, just half the days. Tell myself with Ashley that it's okay. You'll finally learn that maybe you're better off not dating straight women who can't handle the fact that sometimes you're a woman too, but Ashley is going to become your fiercest advocate and ride-or-die friend in the end. And then. What. The fuck. Do you want me to say to myself with Penelope? Appreciate it while it lasts fucker, cause she's the best thing that ever happened or will happen to you, and because you're too weak and fragile to handle a few tough conversations, you're going to fuck it up with the only person you've ever actually started to plan a life with in your head—"

He stopped abruptly, snapping his mouth shut as he realized what he'd just said. His therapist was staring directly at him and somehow writing what looked like almost three pages of notes without looking down at her pad of paper. "Well, that sounds like a good place to start now, doesn't it? How did you see your life with Penelope?"

His heart ached every time anyone, including himself, used her name. "Happy," he finally said, dejectedly sinking back into the cushions.

"And why was it happy?" she asked.

"Because... she would have accepted me. The way Ashley, Kim, and Johanna do. She would... love me in a way I've never been loved before, and I'd love her too. I'd be able to wake up next to her in the morning, and no matter what gender, emotional state of mind, or *anything* I woke up as I would know that she would still be there."

"Have you ever let yourself want for things like that in the past?"

Riley's silence spoke volumes; he could tell this was true because his therapist's pen never stopped moving.

"Well then, Riley. Since you don't seem interested in writing the other letters I asked you to write, why don't you write a letter to your future self?"

"And say what...?" Riley asked skeptically.

"Why don't you ask yourself if you've gotten everything you wanted? Write it all out, friends, family, Penelope, job, a house, a yard, 2.1 kids, a pool, or a picket fence. I don't care what it is, just that it's real and it's really what you want. Write it all down, and then we'll talk about it on Monday."

So, that night Riley started writing. He wrote until three in the morning and didn't touch a drop of alcohol, not wanting to lose momentum or begin to write drunken musings. He was surprised that not all of it revolved around Penelope. Okay, most of it did, but several items didn't.

He wanted to be able to look in the mirror without feeling like he didn't know who he was. He wanted to be more playful with his clothing. He was more than just his gender; he wanted to reflect that in his clothes. He wanted a job where he could finally be his true self, and he wanted to talk to his mother about his childhood. He also wanted to be a better friend, being supportive, not just seeking support. Finally, he wanted some hobbies. He wanted there to be more to his life than work, movies, and Ashley's bar on Friday nights.

What he wanted with Penelope could have been summarized in eight words, but instead he let his mind wander and he wrote almost three pages worth. He wanted to talk to her as his true self, the way he had when he was Taylor, and thought Pen was just some nonbinary person she was getting to know over text. He wanted to be open with her but also have her be open with him. He wanted to finally have good sex, and it wouldn't just be good because it was her, and she was quite possibly the sexiest person he had ever met. He wanted it to be good because he would finally be honest about what he needed in bed.

He wanted to hang out with her and her friends and her brother. He wanted them to move in together and share a closet like they shared bottles of wine and nightly dinners. He wanted the stupid house and the stupid fence, with their obnoxious cat Oreo and maybe a dog if Penelope wanted. He even wanted kids if that was something she wanted. It would be hard for them to conceive with some of Riley's sex aversions, so maybe they wouldn't— or maybe they'd adopt, or maybe they'd just have animals, but whatever the configuration was, he wanted it with her. Because the eight words he wrote at the bottom of the letter, the words he underlined so much he ripped through the page, was: "I want a chance at forever with Nels."

TWELVE

PENELOPE

The week at the beach was a huge reprieve but it was also one of the hardest weeks of Penelope's life. She spent the first two days locked in her bedroom, rereading her texts with Taylor. Riley had apparently deleted his dating app profile, because when she logged into the dating app, it showed a big red error message that read: "this profile no longer exists; all messages have been deleted."

She read her messages with Taylor until she memorized them and realized how many clues she had missed.

After she fully reconciled everything she knew about Taylor with her perception of Riley, she did the opposite. She wrote down in a notebook every second of her dates with Riley that she could remember. She compared that with what she knew from her conversations with Taylor. When she was done, she had almost ten pages of notes, and she realized how much incredible depth there was to Taylor Riley.

When that was done, she just cried—a lot. On the third day, she finally let Maria and Crystal into her room, and they lay in bed all day watching Netflix and binging on funnel cake, fried Oreos, and boardwalk fries.

On the fourth day, they took her shopping, and she spent half a paycheck on fun, funky, and eclectic clothing. Some of the pieces were androgynous, some were very evidently men's clothes, and a select few were women's clothes that piqued her interest. Every five items she tried on, she allowed herself to wonder what Taylor Riley would have thought of them. In a moment of utter weakness, she texted just one photo of herself to Taylor's number. It was a photo of her in a silly Hawaiian shirt paired with a pair of men's swim trunks, wearing a flamingo pool floatie, while Maria wore a wetsuit and a swan pool floatie.

When the photo didn't send, she chalked it up to bad cell service and pocketed her phone until they left the store. When she rechecked it later, while walking on the beach, she saw that the text failed to deliver, a sure sign that her number was blocked. So, naturally, she chucked her phone into the ocean.

Sadly, her industrial strength case didn't save her phone this time, so they spent the next two hours sobbing in a phone store. Well, Penelope was sobbing. Maria and Crystal had a grand old time competing in angry birds on the display phones.

Penelope bought them both dinner to apologize for her antics, and they watched the sunset from a pier, feet dangling off the edge as they licked ice cream cones and talked about, strangely enough, the benefits of therapy.

Maria said she'd be happy to help Penelope find a therapist. Crystal recommended her therapist, who specialized in gender and sexuality, and Penelope was sold. She emailed and requested an appointment for the following week and was astounded when she got a confirmation on their walk back to the house.

"Ah yes," Crystal said sagely, "she is an expert in gender and sexuality. Work-life balance? Less so."

On the fifth night, she facetimed with Frankie and Diego, and they reported that her drag replacement had done an amazing job. They invited Penelope to attend the brunch as a guest the weekend after she returned. She hesitantly agreed, and they made plans for dinner afterwards.

On the sixth day and night she regressed a bit and stayed in her room while Maria and Crystal went snorkeling. She was flipping through channels on the TV when the movie series she'd marathoned with Maria and Riley came on TV. She cried into a box of cookies until the credits ran for the final movie. She threw away the soggy remnants of the box and made herself go for a walk on the beach.

She thought a lot about how hesitant she had been with Riley in the beginning of their time together. Initially, she had justified it as a way not to make him feel. Now though, she thought that maybe she'd just been too afraid of getting hurt. Too afraid to take a chance and fight for something she wanted. In doing so, she wondered if she had failed to let Riley know she *would* fight for him. If she had made it more obvious how interested she was in him, if she'd stopped providing him with outs and stopped giving herself excuses, maybe he would have been able to open up to her better. Hell, maybe she'd have been able to open up to him and start the gender conversation much earlier. Maybe if she'd provided him a safe space to share what he needed to share, this would never have happened.

She kicked at a shell, and it flew across the sand, narrowly avoiding a seagull pecking away at a piece of seaweed. She picked up the next shell she came across and tried to skip it into the water. When that worked pretty well, she did it again and then again. It was almost as satisfying as throwing her phone across the room, but not quite.

After throwing another dozen or so shells, she let out a sad sigh. There was no use thinking like this. She could have done many things differently, and so could Taylor Riley, but in the end, it just mattered what she did now.

———

They returned from the beach the following Wednesday night, and Penelope had a hard time readjusting to her daily routines. She ended up taking that Thursday and Friday off work to give herself just a little more time to process, but she found there was nothing left to process. She had found two amazing people that shook up her world and made her want to try to find love again. They'd turned out to be the same person, and that person didn't want to be with her.

Penelope wasn't ready to put herself back out there in the dating world, but she thought that maybe one day she would, now that she knew how badly she wanted to find someone for herself. She decided to work a full day shift at the cafe on Friday, and she, Maria, and Crystal attended the drag brunch on Saturday and Sunday.

The new MC was a gorgeous woman named River, who brought her own drag outfits to perform in. That weekend she was in a three-piece suit that had been tie-dyed with watercolors, and she tied her braids up under an equally colorful fedora. Her energy was different from Pen n' Wink's. River seemed to flow across the stage, like her name suggested, commanding the audience with an energy as powerful as raging rapids, but as subtle as a stream.

Something about her seemed familiar to Penelope, but she couldn't quite place her, and by the end of the second show, she had given up trying.

Penelope spent a lot of time that weekend, and much of the following week in Diego's closet as they worked on further detailing Penelope's style. Frankie flowed in and out of the conversation, admitting they still hadn't told their parents they were engaged.

"Well... after you told us your gender discovery, I kind of wanted to leave you space to talk to them—if you want to!— before completely taking over the narrative with our wedding planning," he finally admitted the following Wednesday night as they trooped up the stairs to his and Diego's apartment after a long dinner service.

"Oh jeez, no pressure, though," Penelope said glumly.

She'd had her first therapy session the week before and her second one just the night before. She'd spent both sessions discussing her gender and sexuality, which had been a nice change away from Taylor Riley, but really that had been what, and who, Penelope had wanted to talk about. Her therapist promised they would talk about Taylor Riley next time. She had given Penelope instructions to write her parents an email that she could choose to send or not, detailing the ways she felt they had dismissed her sexuality over the years.

"Truly no pressure! We're not thinking of having the wedding for another year or more, so there's no rush to tell Mom and Dad," he said breezily.

"You're being very blasé about the whole thing... do you really not mind if Mom and Dad don't know you're engaged to the love of your life?" she asked, causing Diego to blush and Frankie to grin.

"I really don't, big sis. But that's because I never sought their approval the way you did. It's an older sibling thing I think, but I was always happy just to do my own thing, cause my own trouble, and pave my way. You were their firstborn, so you felt all the pressure of their expectations, hopes, dreams, fears... I think they got it all out on you before I came along."

She thought about this for a moment and then asked if she could borrow Frankie's laptop. They helped her set herself up on the couch with tea and scones. She spent the next three hours writing two emails to her parents. The first was about her sexuality, and the second was about her gender. Frankie and Diego were in their pajamas by the time she finished, but they sat next to her and took turns reading the letters for her. Diego opted to be the one to edit her grammar and spelling so that Frankie could focus on the content of the letter.

By the time he finished, he had tears in his eyes, and he held her in his arms while she cried too. Maybe it was a late-night decision or maybe it was just what Penelope thought she just needed to get it over with, but at one a.m., she pressed send on both emails.

That weekend she attended the drag brunch again, but this time as staff helping out behind the scenes. She bustled around the back room with the queens and was nearly smothered to death by Sham Pain's pink boa as she held Penelope in a vice-like hug. They talked while Sham Pain did her makeup, and she was disappointed to hear that Taylor had completely disappeared on Penelope, but she told Penelope not to give up on her just yet. Penelope didn't tell her why she'd disappeared, of course. It was one thing to tell her best friend, her brother, and brother-in-law.

She'd never out Taylor Riley to anyone else in either of their lives.

Penelope looked over to where River was just starting to assemble her dozens of intricate braids on top of her head. They still hadn't spoken about the MC schedule, so she walked over to River slowly enough that she would see Penelope coming in the mirror.

"Hi! I'm uh—Penelope, also known as Pen n' Wink. I filled in as MC for the few weeks before we found you. First of all, I'd just like to say you're absolutely amazing up there. I never had the kind of natural presence you have—" she stammered and froze as River turned her chair around to face her.

"It's so lovely to finally meet you, Penelope. I've heard a lot about you from your brother and Diego, but also from Taylor Riley."

Penelope's heart constricted at the name, and she found herself taking a step back. "You... you came to brunch that first day with Taylor, didn't you..." She thought back to the woman sitting next to Taylor at that corner table. "You—well, you looked like you were having a great time," Penelope said, laughing suddenly.

"I was. Taylor was having a particularly hard week, and Kim—my partner—was otherwise engaged. So, I asked her to pick something fun for us, and she mentioned she had been to this show once or twice. I've been to many shows at different venues, but there was something about watching you on that stage. It inspired me. Actually—" she reached for her bag in a very unhurried manner.

Everything she did seemed unhurried, as if she was exactly where she wanted to be in this moment, with no need to be anywhere else. "You inspired one of my art pieces and also are the reason I am working here now. When I saw that the position was open, I applied, thinking it could help inspire some more of my art, but... since then, I have realized that it is in and of itself a beautiful art form in which I can express an entirely different side of myself. I'm having a wonderful time, but Penelope—Pen n' Wink—if you ever want to return, please do not hesitate on my behalf. Your brother told me you wanted to work one weekend a month, but if you wanted to do more, or if you wanted to co-MC, please just let me know."

River seemed to find what she was looking for in her bag, and she handed Penelope a business card with the name of an art studio on it. "The piece you inspired is being shown here for another few months if you are interested in seeing it."

Penelope was blown away by the woman and her words. She didn't know what to say so she just accepted the card. She had no idea Kim had a partner, but she could see these two together.

River was slowly turning back to the mirror, and Penelope knew she shouldn't do it, but she asked anyway. "How is Taylor doing?"

River didn't turn back around, instead, she went back to doing her makeup without a word. Penelope felt her shoulders slump, and she was about to walk away when River spoke.

"Ah, River. You have to do a better job of keeping up with your friends. I keep forgetting to text my dear friend Taylor. She's been so busy recently, looking for a new job where she doesn't feel the need to hide, going to therapy three times a week, and trying to heal some of her past trauma," River's voice was soft as if she really was speaking to herself in the mirror. Penelope felt like she wanted to run, pain shooting through her chest at this new information about Taylor Riley. She forced herself to stay rooted to the spot, not wanting to spook River from saying more.

River continued to work on her hair as she spoke directly to herself in the mirror. "I know it mustn't be easy to do all of that, but she is so lucky to have all of her friends here. I know her sister just left after being here for the past several weeks, so maybe this would be a good time for me to go see her, and perhaps I'll tell her about this amazing woman I met at drag brunch. She had a beautiful name, and she carried herself with the grace and poise of someone who has found themself and is just waiting to be found by others. Perhaps I'll share that she seemed, at least to me, to still be carrying a sadness around with her, like she was missing a very precious person. She also seemed to wish my dear friend all the best."

Penelope couldn't stop the tear that ran down her cheek as she stared at River in the mirror. River's eyes met hers in the mirror, and Penelope gave a sharp nod, and then she walked away.

Her first week back at work wasn't as bad as it could have been. She'd kept up with her emails at the beach so she wouldn't drown in them upon her return. Her project co-lead had stepped in to manage the project while Penelope was away, but he happily handed it all back to her when she returned. Greg gave her an entire forty-seven minutes back in the office before pouncing on her for details.

She told him the bare minimum, dating someone she thought she knew but didn't, she had been willing and excited to continue to date them and get to know them, but they had walked away. General heartbreak and sadness ensued, but now she was seeing a therapist and slowly doing better. Hesitantly, she asked him if he would get lunch with her later that week, and he agreed happily.

Her parents had called her over the weekend and spent several hours on the phone discussing her emails. Frankie had volunteered to join as a peacemaker. In the end, the conversation had gone about as well as she could have expected. They didn't understand why she needed to come out as nonbinary if she wasn't changing her pronouns or her name. Penelope said she reserved the right to change both of those things in the future, but that wasn't the point. They managed to meet in the middle, and her parents promised they'd discuss it again soon. The good news was they were finally referring to her as pansexual, so at least they'd ended that five-year battle. Now it just might take another five for them to recognize her gender identity.

It didn't leave her feeling exceptionally confident about coming out as nonbinary, but it gave her just the boost she needed to tell Greg over meatball subs. He excitedly shrieked and hugged her as she had secretly hoped he would. He immediately began researching nonbinary artwork. Feeling the first hint of excitement she'd felt in weeks, Penelope told him about River and her artwork, and they made plans to go to the gallery together later that week.

With her family, work, and Greg sorted out, Penelope was left with just one thing to do. Deeply dread her upcoming birthday.

She was turning thirty that next Friday, and it seemed like the universe was just trying to remind her that she was single and depressed about it. In absolutely no uncertain terms, she told Maria and Frankie that she did not want to do anything for her birthday except sit at home on the couch in her underwear and watch bad TV with takeout. She invited them to join her but said she'd be happy to do it alone. They agreed with her for several days, until suddenly they didn't.

"I'm so sorry, Lopi. We told the staff we're engaged, and now they want to throw us an engagement party. They didn't ask us about the date—seriously, we can cancel," Frankie said, as they sat together in the cafe at the "serious table" the Sunday before her birthday.

She'd been having such a good weekend. She'd gone to the art gallery with Greg and had bought a beautiful modern art piece in the nonbinary flag colors. She'd even seen River's piece about her. It was abstract, but Penelope could pick out the pinstripes from that first suit and top hat she'd worn.

"Let's just cancel," Diego agreed gravely.

"Yeah, this isn't the right time for a party—" Frankie continued to say.

"No! No, guys, stop. It's totally fine," Penelope interrupted, even though it definitely wasn't totally fine. She really didn't want to go to her brother's engagement party on her thirtieth birthday and have to pretend that she was happy and excited and totally okay. Well, she was the first two; she truly was the happiest she had ever been for her brother. It was pretending to be totally okay. That was going to be a stretch.

"I'm so happy for you guys to be engaged, and I want to celebrate with all of the staff—this will be great! You know what?" she said, standing up abruptly, and they both stared up at her. "A party is exactly what I need! I'll whip out a hot new outfit, hang out with all the drag queens and kings again, and it will be awesome. The fact that I just so happen to be turning thirty is a coincidence we will mention to absolutely no one. Understood?"

"Understood," they chorused back in unison, and she believed them. Of course, she should have known better.

TAYLOR (RILEY)

Taylor had given her two-week notice to her job, with her hair loose around her shoulders, her glasses placed proudly on her nose, and wearing a woman's skirt suit. She'd had to buy the suit since she didn't own one already, and she had to admit it didn't feel that much better than a men's suit, so maybe she just hated suits. She considered buying a business dress instead but realized it would probably be a waste of money since her new job was business casual.

Just thinking the phrase "new job" sent a thrill down Taylor's spine. Her new job, where she'd been asked her pronoun of the day at the beginning of both interviews and had been asked to provide pronouns for her staff profile on the website. She wanted desperately to tell Penelope about her new job, but then again, she wanted desperately to tell Penelope about everything.

After she'd written that stupid letter her therapist had told her to write, she'd started writing other letters as if she and Penelope were pen pals.

Taylor wrote about how she was doing really well in her therapy, despite her therapist's asinine letters, and how she had taken up rock climbing. She loved how it made her body feel strong and lean, yet somehow sensual, like a panther climbing a tree. Ashley finally succeeded in claiming Fridays at her bar as an official event in their lives. Still, she had immediately agreed to change the day if or "when," as she and Kim insisted, Taylor ever reunited with Penelope and Maria so as not to conflict with movie marathon night.

Taylor found herself doing this a lot, making life plans and trying to see how Penelope could or couldn't fit into them. Thus far,

Taylor hadn't found a single thing in her life that wouldn't be made better by having Penelope in it.

A few weeks into her self-imposed exile from Penelope, River came over, sat on the couch, and held Taylor's hand as she explained how she'd gotten a job at Penelope's younger brother's cafe. She had applied and been accepted as an MC before the "breakup" had happened, and she hadn't wanted to upset Taylor with the news until she knew if she was going to keep the job. River had also been hoping Taylor and Penelope would reconcile and it wouldn't matter.

Taylor admitted that she knew now that all she wanted was to be with Penelope again, but that she had a few more things to work through before then. River, of course agreed wholeheartedly that she should take all the time she needed but almost hesitantly, she admitted she had seen Penelope.

"She looked beautiful. So much more confident than the only other time I have seen her, at that first brunch, I'm sure you remember all too well. But she still has sadness in her. I think she still misses you terribly; she even asked after your well-being but... Taylor... she isn't going to wait forever. A confidence like the one she now has will attract potential partners to her, like bees to honey. I also do not think that she deserves to be kept waiting so long."

Taylor had felt like someone had thrown her off a building. She was falling, and she wasn't sure when she would hit the ground, but it could be any moment now. She wasn't ignorant; she knew there was a chance Penelope would move on and forget about her. It was probably what Taylor deserved after not only hiding the truth from her but then literally running away from it. Now that she was finally settling into her truth, she was only running and hiding from Penelope herself.

"If you are open to it, I think I might have an idea. It will take another week, so you have time to keep working on yourself, but I hope it also means you won't be too late," River offered, and Taylor listened with rapt attention and then increasing excitement as she proposed a plan.

THIRTEEN

PENELOPE

Penelope should have known something was up when Maria spent almost an hour helping her pick out an outfit to wear to the party.

Maria had shown a never-ending patience for Penelope's venture into fashion, but she typically had a finite amount of interest. Tonight, however, she had been almost obsessive about what Penelope chose to wear. She ended up in a black button-down made entirely of lace. She paired it with a camisole that perfectly matched her skin tone, and she felt sexy, feminine, and androgynous all at the same time. She wore a pair of fitted maroon slacks and pointy black men's oxford loafers. She fluffed out her hair with a brush and added a bit of a wave with a flat iron, and then she was ready to go.

Penelope *really* should have known something was up when she saw balloons around the entrance to the cafe that looked decidedly *not* engagement party themed. She shrugged it off as they entered the shop until a chorus of voices shouted, "SURPRISE!"

In a moment of panic and disorientation, Penelope wondered if this sort of thing would have been fun-scary or bad-scary for Taylor Riley. She shook her head to dispel the thought and looked around at all the familiar faces.

There was an assortment of staff, drag queens both in and out of drag, Greg, Maya, Frankie, Diego, and a smattering of other friends all spread out around the cafe. In the corner, she also saw River, Kim, and, to her surprise and delight, Ashley. They smiled at her happily as her eyes scanned over their faces, and she tried to keep the crushing disappointment off her face when there was no honey blonde in sight.

"Are you surprised?!" Frankie asked, bounding over to her, and he and Maria grinned at her like a pair of Cheshire cats.

"You know... I really shouldn't be after how long I've known the two of you, but I am." She pulled them both into a tight three-way hug. Diego ambled over and threw his arms around them.

"We have food, alcohol, lots of coffee, and cake, and Maria has a huge party game planned,"

Diego said, handing her a "Birthday Girl" sash with a "Thirty and Flirty" oversized pin stuck to it.

"Oh god, a game?" Penelope groaned.

"Yes, you love games. You always say you don't, but we know you do. Arcade games, board games, video games—... honestly, you probably like sex games too, but that's not something I need to know about you." All three of them spluttered indignantly as Maria just blinked at them.

"Alright, alright, I do like games. Shall we get drinks and food first? Say hello to everyone?" Penelope asked, trying to scrub the blush off her face with her hands.

"Of course! Right this way!" Maria said, magnanimously taking her arm and walking her around the room like she was her date.

"Where's Crystal? You did invite her, right? I would love for her to be here," Penelope said a bit nervously. She hoped Maria didn't purposefully not invite her so she could focus on Penelope all night.

"She's on her way! She got held up at work."

Maria led Penelope over to the corner where River, Kim, and Ashley were chatting amiably.

"Penelope, happy birthday!" River said with her liquid silk voice, enveloping Penelope in a hug. Kim and Ashley took turns exchanging greetings and how are you's.

"You're looking—thirty and flirty?" Ashley asked, reading her pin with raised eyebrows.

"Well, I'm definitely feeling thirty. I woke up this morning, and I swear my vision was worse," she said, squinting in an over-exaggerated manner, and everyone laughed. "Not feeling too flirty, though. I thought this was going to be my brother's engagement party." She caught Kim and Ashely exchanging a barely disguised look.

"Has your partner arrived yet?" River asked Maria, and vaguely Penelope wondered when the two of them had become friends.

"She's almost here, but until then, I am Penelope's designated date, and I have to make sure she says hello to everyone before we start the party game!" Maria said, and with that, she steered Penelope over to a small gathering of their other friends.

Penelope had lost touch with a few of these friends over the past several months of work and dating craziness, but seeing them all together now was amazing. They were the kind of friends she could probably go years without seeing, and the second they were all together again, it would be like no time had passed.

They took a never-ending stream of selfies, and as the alcohol and food flowed freely, the party became livelier, and someone turned music on over the cafe speakers.

Penelope was just finishing a conversation with Sham Pain and some of the other queens when Maria grabbed her arm. Crystal was there, and Penelope, slightly drunkenly, threw her arms around her in a huge hug. "Thank you so much for coming! It's great to see you."

"Yes, Penelope, it certainly has been too long since last night," Crystal said good-naturedly, hugging her back.

Crystal had been at their apartment almost every night this week, and Maria kept asking if it was too much, but Penelope adored the extra company. She was forever an extrovert at heart and loved being surrounded by people. A party had been precisely what she had needed.

"Yes, yes, lovely to see Crystal. Okay! It's time for your party game!" Maria hooted, steering Penelope over to a chair set up by the platform in the back of the cafe. During usual business hours, the platform housed a display of coffees and goods from around the world but on weekends, and right now, it was transformed into the drag stage.

"So, we all know that you're working on changing up your sense of style as you enter your thirties," Maria said, giving her a meaningful look but saying no more in front of the crowd of partygoers, "and we know that being single in your thirties can mean a lot of swiping. So! We wanted to combine the two to give you some practice. We're going to play a game, and the whole audience can play along on your phones as well—just go to the link I sent in your email invitation!"

Everyone began pulling out their phones, and Frankie stepped forward to hand Penelope a tablet. On the screen was what looked like a dating profile, but it was for an outfit. "The Heartbreaker" it said, and it was a maroon suit styled with suede boots and a white button-down.

"So, this is how the game is going to work. I'm going to read out the 'profile' of the outfit, and if Penelope approves, we'll ask one of our amazing volunteers to bring out the outfit to display on the stage. In the end, Penelope will get to choose her top three outfits, and she'll get to take them home with her! The rest we will return to the rental company."

Penelope was blown away and beyond touched by the gesture, and she had to admit the game sounded fun.

The game began, and Maria read out the full profile for "The Heartbreaker" while Penelope followed along on her screen. The audience voted, and Maria announced their votes, but Penelope knew she was swiping right. When she pressed the swipe right button, the screen filled with a green background and the text "swipe right." She held it up over her head, and the crowd screamed SWIPE RIGHT like they were at a rave.

The next outfit, "The Beach Bum" was an absurd Hawaiian patterned pantsuit paired with a flamingo pool floatie. "Please tell me you got these from the rental company. I will swipe right just to see this in real life," Penelope said, and when Maria nodded, she did so.

The audience was split down the middle on left or right, which made Penelope cackle. The outfit was brought onto the stage, and with a shriek, Penelope ran onto the stage and stole the flamingo floatie.

Maria shooed her off the stage, and Penelope returned to her seat wearing the floatie. She was able to rest the tablet against the floatie's head, so she counted it as a win.

The game continued like this for thirteen more outfits until the crowd had mostly dispersed, as those who were less fashion inclined made their way back to the bar and food. Penelope didn't mind though. She was having a great time with Frankie, Diego, River, Kim, Ashley, and Maria.

Maria had stopped reading the bios over the microphone, and they were chatting amiably amongst themselves about the outfits. Finally, after the fifteenth outfit was voted on, Penelope made to stand up to appraise the outfits on stage, but Maria stopped her with a hand on her shoulder.

"There's actually one more, Lopi, and it's a pretty long one, so we'll give you some time to read through it," Frankie explained.

"Also, please, for the love of god, give me the pool floatie; it clashes so badly with your gorgeous outfit," Diego burst out, looking like he'd been waiting over an hour to say this. Which, in all likelihood, he probably had been.

Penelope snorted but shimmied out of the pool floatie, exchanging it for the tablet again.

"We're going to go get drinks. Do you want anything?" Kim asked as they all began to walk to the bar together. Maria stayed by her side, and Penelope asked for a glass of wine.

Penelope settled back into her seat to check the final profile as the screen came back to life. Her breath caught when she saw the name at the top of the page.

"Taylor Riley" it read, and next to it was a large GF for Gender

Fluid. She looked up at Maria in shock, but she just pointed aggressively at the screen, and Penelope obediently looked back down.

There were probably almost thirty photos, comprised of a mix of the unbelievably beautiful Taylor in varying degrees of femininity and a younger version of her sweet Riley. Even though she and Maria had once stalked Riley's Facebook, she'd only seen a few of these photos. She'd never even bothered to look up Taylor, not knowing enough information about her to find her on Facebook, and now she knew she probably never would have found her.

The first and seemingly oldest photo was of Taylor when her hair was only down to the tips of her shoulders, and she was wearing frumpy sweatpants, a headband with a bow, and a college hoodie. In the next, she was wearing a baseball cap and a too-large t-shirt dress that was so big it looked like it was swallowing her up. As she kept scrolling through the photos, Taylor Riley aged before her eyes, growing into the femininely dressed Taylor and sharply dressed Riley she knew today. The profile was new as well. It read:

Hello, my name is Taylor Riley. I'm a gender fluid thirty-year-old who likes chocolate, wine, rock climbing, and, apparently, arcade games. I sometimes go by Taylor and she/her pronouns. When this is the case, I'm known to attend drag brunches, spend exorbitant amounts of money on clothing, and need to be on the go all the time. The rest of the time, I go by Riley and he/him pronouns. When this is the case, I spend more time at home, cuddling up with my cat or my loving friends, watching movies, and cooking nice meals.

I'm looking for a very special person to be my partner. I want someone who can not just fit into my life—because honestly my life has been kind of crappy up until very recently—but bring new energy, laughter, friends (specifically named Maria and Crystal) *bunnies, and love to my life. I promise to try and bring the same to yours (plus a cat named Oreo.)*

If any of this sounds appealing, your name is Penelope, Pen, Nels (or any variation thereof), and you're willing to give one exceptionally sorry and hopeful Taylor Riley a second chance... please swipe right now.

Also, I would hope this goes without saying, but if the words "you're too much; take up less space; why can't you just be ____" resonate with you in any way, PLEASE swipe left. You will hate me. I will hate you. It will be awful.

Penelope had to look away from the screen to blink back her tears, and she realized she was completely alone in the front half of the cafe. Her brother and Maria must have moved the party to the backroom to give her privacy. She wiped frantically at her eyes and then glanced back down at the dating profile.

She scrolled back up to the photos and touched the one of Riley holding Oreo. It was a selfie he had only sent to her, and she felt a fresh tear roll down her cheek. This was the only photo Penelope had of him, and it felt so strange seeing it on this larger screen when she'd been pining over it on her small phone screen for weeks.

She scrolled one more time back down to the profile and reread the words, some of which had been hers, some of which she would never have thought Taylor Riley would be brave enough to say or write. She scrolled to the very bottom of the page where the right and left buttons were.

She very purposefully pressed one of the buttons and stood up.

(Taylor) Riley

Riley was wondering if it was actually possible to die of anticipation. Well, maybe not just anticipation. Also, severe anxiety, nerves, and the feeling of impending doom as to what he would do if she said no.

He was behind the curtain, where he had once seen Pen n' Wink peeking out from. He could see Penelope perfectly from here, but she couldn't see him. He watched a series of emotions play across her face as she scrolled slowly through the profile.

Ashley and Kim had encouraged him to put as many photos as he could of himself when he was feeling and looking at his most Taylor and his most Riley. He regretted taking their advice now, though, because it took her almost ten minutes to review the full profile. He would have been sweating through his shirt, but the new depression medicine he was on had the strange side effect of making him sweat less. He had to be careful not to get overheated, but it played to his advantage at this exact moment.

He watched as Penelope pressed a button and stood up. She looked around the cafe in confusion, until her eyes settled on the curtain. She smiled wistfully and then held the tablet, displaying a garish green sign that read "swipe right" above her head.

Thankfully Riley's legs seemed to move of their own accord, because his brain had frozen. He stepped out onto the stage amidst the mannequins of beautiful clothing and walked to the end of the stage.

His hair was down, brushing softly against his shoulders as he moved. He wasn't wearing glasses because that was Taylor's signature, and he was trying to find a new signature for himself. He'd pierced his ears last week, and he liked how the studs looked with his hair up and down. He was wearing a women's lavender button-down that framed his shape in a soft way but still had all the intensity he enjoyed from dress clothes when he was feeling masculine. His jeans were black and slim cut, accentuating his long legs and tapering out over gray oxfords. He laughed to himself when he saw Penelope's shoes were similar but pointy and black.

Before he could speak, not that he had planned anything to say, she stepped forward, just a few feet away from him.

"So, I feel like I have a bit of an advantage here because I've gotten to read your profile, but you haven't gotten to read mine."

He froze and blinked a few times at her, uncertain of where she was going with this. She smiled and straightened her spine, so she was standing at her full height. He'd never really noticed before, but she tended to slouch down, curling her shoulders in as if to make herself less. She wasn't doing that now, though, and when he'd spotted her earlier in the party, when Crystal had helped sneak him in the back, she'd been standing tall then too.

"My name is Penelope. I'm pansexual, nonbinary, and I go by she/they pronouns, but reserve the right to change that at any point," she grinned at him, and he couldn't help but grin back as she continued.

"A few months back, I created a dating profile, thinking that I was open to the possibility of love, but... I think that I wasn't quite ready yet. I was still scared of fully opening myself up to another person, so I hedged my bets and said it was fine if all I got out of dating was friendship. Then I met an amazing woman, right over there, actually," she said, pointing to the corner where Taylor had sat during that first drag brunch. "She made me want more, but friendship was all she could give me. I started to learn more about myself through talking to her, figuring out things I guess I always suspected but never knew for sure. Through conversations with her and going on dates with an amazing guy, I realized that I am ready for love. I want it so badly and... that's why I'm here—er... on this dating app?" Her voice hitched up at the end in a question as she stumbled slightly over her imaginary dating profile. Riley bit back a smile and nodded.

Neither of them spoke, and then abruptly, she looked down at the tablet. She flicked her fingers across the screen for a few seconds, and Riley was momentarily confused until she handed him the tablet. The screen was on the bottom of some other profile, but she'd enlarged it, so it just said, "Swipe left" and "swipe right."

"You know... I'm pretty sure me being here right now, at your surprise birthday party that I helped plan, is me swiping right," he joked.

Her eyes widened, and her lips parted at the admission, but then the corners of her lips turned up, and she shrugged. "Thought it couldn't hurt to be thorough."

God, he'd missed her mouth, even when it was smirking sardonically at him.

Riley tapped the swipe right button and turned the tablet back around so she could see it. She held out both hands for the tablet, but when Riley handed it to her, she only used one hand to grab it and left her right hand extended out in front of her. Riley lifted an eyebrow but shook her hand anyway. Her hand was warm and just the tiniest bit sweaty, and that little physical admission of nerves was so beautiful to Riley that he could have cried.

"Hi. It's nice to officially meet you. Penelope, but you can call me Nels. She/they pronouns," she prompted, and Riley understood.

He cleared his throat and then said as clearly as he could, "It's lovely to meet you, Nels... My name is Taylor Riley. I go by both, but tonight you can call me Riley. He/him pronouns."

She nodded, and then her eyes filled with tears, and he felt panic rise in his chest for a moment, afraid he had upset her.

"It's so nice to finally see you," she said, and Riley noticed the change of words from meet to see, and it felt like the most perfect thing she could have said. She truly was seeing all of him for the first time. Her hand was still in his, and her eyes were roaming up and down his body, from his eyes to his hair, down his chest, legs, and back up.

He allowed himself just a moment to do the same, to truly see her too. Her shirt was unfairly glamorous, and her pants were perfectly fitted to her hips and legs in a way that had Riley's head spinning. He carefully pulled her by the hand up onto the stage with him.

"God, you're so beautiful..." he whispered, and then she was in his arms. She had her arms around his neck, and his arms were looped around her waist.

"Me? Look at you! Look at your hair!" she said as she fanned her fingers out through his golden locks. "I didn't get to appreciate it the last time I saw it down," she complained.

"Mmmmm," he hummed, savoring her warmth in his arms, "you're right. While I didn't have 'apologize for not giving you time to play with my hair while my world was falling apart' on my list of apologies, I will make sure to add it to the bottom of the list."

"Bottom? I've been wanting to play with your hair since the moment I met you. How about we add it to the middle of the list." She grinned at him, and he grinned right back, but then his smile faltered.

He slowly closed his eyes and leaned his forehead against hers.

"I'm sorry..." he started to say, but she slanted her head up and caught his mouth with hers.

His breath caught for an instant, and then he sighed into the kiss, and it felt like coming home. Like sinking onto his couch with hot chocolate and Oreo in his lap. He suddenly thought that if he could do this right and be the right person for Penelope, maybe she would be there too. Playing with his hair like she was doing now, holding onto him while he held onto her.

Their mouths gently brushed and nudged as if trying to remember each other. Then her lips parted, and he slid his tongue tenderly into her mouth. He found he hadn't forgotten even a moment of their previous kisses. He remembered the velvety softness of her tongue against his, and he remembered the shape of her mouth and the swell of her teeth against his tongue.

They stayed like this for an impossibly long time, giving and taking from each other, until his neck began to ache, and the pain superseded the pleasure. He pulled back, and for some reason, the words resurfaced. "I'm so sorry, Nels... I can't believe it took me so long—"

"Hey... none of that tonight, okay?" she said, silencing him by putting her entire hand over his mouth. He let his eyes fall shut for a moment, and he kissed her palm. "Tonight is only for happiness. No more apologies, okay? I think I have a few of my own too, but they can wait. It can all wait. I'd love for you to meet Diego and Frankie—... wait," she said, pulling back to squint at him in accusation.

His eyes flew open, and he felt himself blush red hot. "Oh... shit... uh... Am I allowed to apologize for this? I met them already... several times actually while planning the party. Uhm—I can pretend like I haven't, though, if you want?" he offered, biting his lip repentantly.

He wasn't sure if she would actually be mad about it or just mildly annoyed, but he hadn't expected her sunshine smile to break across her face. "I missed you and your utter absurdity... so much. Yes. I would like it very much if you could pretend you haven't met them before. And maybe anyone else I tell you to," she said with finality, but her smile was soft and affectionate as she took his hand and led him to the backroom.

When they walked in, all of their friends chatting amiably in the corner glanced up with varying looks of surprise, excitement, and pleasure on their faces. While Riley, who felt suddenly shy in the eyes of all of the party-goers, would have preferred to go to their friends first, Penelope tugged them in the opposite direction.

They slowly made their way around the room, and each time she gave the same introduction. "This is Riley, and we just started dating five minutes ago, and I'm quite fond of him." As they moved from person to person, Penelope added minutes to the number of minutes they'd been dating.

He got to meet her coworkers, Greg, an incredibly handsome black man, and Maya, who was absolutely glowing and nearly eight months pregnant. She patted him on the cheek and said it was lovely to finally meet him, and Riley marveled at the thought of being close enough with coworkers to share dating details.

Riley found himself blushing through almost all of the introductions, but none more so than when they finally reached Frankie and Diego. Frankie had an ecstatic look on his face, and he went to say something, but Penelope stopped him. "Frankie, I know you two have already met, but I would like to introduce you officially if that's all right?"

Frankie gave her a dubious look, but Diego elbowed him, and he agreed.

"Thank you. So," she said, looking up at Riley and then back to Frankie. "I have someone incredibly special for you to meet, both because of how special he is general, but also because of how important he is to me. Frankie, this is Riley. He is... one of the sweetest, most considerate, and most gentle people I have ever known. I'm so unbelievably excited to date him, and I want you to get to know him and... well, I think you guys are going to get along well." She was beaming, and Riley bit down hard on his lower lip to stop it from trembling as he reached out a shaky hand to Frankie. Frankie immediately pulled him into a bearhug, and Diego patted him lightly on the back.

"Welcome, Riley," Diego said softly, "it's a bit of a crazy ride with these two, but I promise, it's worth it."

"I'm sure I have no idea what you're talking about!" Frankie pouted, and Penelope latched back onto Riley's arm as he stepped back to her side.

They finally made it to their friends and were accosted from all sides by hugs, questions, congratulations, and pats on the back.

"Your hair is just exquisite, Riley," Maria said, beaming up at him.

"It's so nice to see you wearing it down more often," Kim said happily, and River and Ashley nodded their agreement.

Riley was introduced to a few more of Penelope and Maria's friends. They had been given the bare minimum of information, just that Riley had surprised her on her birthday by asking her out as part of the elaborate clothing game. They were all incredibly nice people, and Riley hoped they'd get to hang out more in the future.

"Oh! Penelope, you didn't end up picking the outfits you

wanted to keep, did you?" Ashley asked, a little loudly, as she had apparently been drinking, and Penelope's eyes widened.

"Oh shoot, you're right, and you said you have to return them—"

"Oh, I lied. We all chipped in to buy them, so they're all yours. Crystal and I are going to drink wine and pack them all up to take home later," Maria said dismissively.

Tears filled Penelope's eyes, and she threw her arms around Maria, then Crystal, and soon the whole group was hugging each other. Riley stood off to the side, allowing them to have their moment. He hadn't gotten her a physical gift because he was afraid if she said no tonight, he wouldn't know what to do with it. He planned to tell her later, but his gift was going to be an amazing first date experience, whenever they were ready for it.

After the hug was over, Penelope looked around the room briefly. "Well, I think you've met just about everyone—oh, you know what? There's still one very important someone I want you to meet!" she said, pulling him towards the exit.

"...oh?" he asked, a little confused, as everyone they passed waved goodbye to them, blowing air kisses and wishing Penelope a final happy birthday.

A fifteen-minute walk later, Riley was introduced to S.H., also known as Sir Hopsalot. He had to admit; he was just as adorable as Riley remembered. Penelope had seemingly forgotten that Riley had met the rabbit when Maria had picked him out, but he didn't dare remind her of that.

Instead, he made a big show of meeting the bunny for the first time, picking him up and giving him the Simba treatment, which he seemed unbothered by. He just continued to munch on his hay, which seemed to be accumulating in piles around their apartment.

His living arrangement was certainly an interesting choice to Riley, but he chose to keep that thought to himself as well.

"So..." Penelope said slowly, and he looked down at her expectantly.

There were so many ways she could finish that sentence. So we need to talk, so can we make out and not talk, so can we watch a movie and pet the rabbit, so I've reconsidered, and actually, I'm swiping left now.

Riley reminded himself that his therapist had been asking him to practice tamping down negative, self-harmful thoughts like those. He forced himself to wait as patiently as possible for her to continue.

"I would really like to talk about some things but... I'm also honestly still in a little bit of shock. Is there any way we could make plans to talk tomorrow?"

"Of course," Riley said, a little sadly.

He hadn't been ready to say goodbye so soon after getting Penelope back in his life, but he would never want to overstay his welcome. He reached into his pocket and pulled out his phone to call himself an Uber.

"Uhm—" Penelope said, reaching forward and resting her hand on his to stop his phone from rising any closer to his face, "you don't have to go quite yet if you don't want to. I was thinking on the walk over we could... change into sweats or something, maybe make some hot chocolate, turn on a movie and—uh... cuddle?" She looked so hopeful, and Riley was so overwhelmed with joy and relief from the day that he nodded immediately.

"It is your birthday, so... I feel like I have to do as you command." He gave a small bow and then switched into a curtsey halfway down. To finish it off, he took her hand and kissed the back of it, looking up at her through his long, fair lashes.

"Wow, you're pretty," she said, seemingly a little dazzled by his display.

He smiled widely at her and straightened up to press a soft kiss to her lips.

"Do you... want to handle hot chocolate, and I can find us some sweats? They might be a bit short on you, but otherwise I think I have something that will fit," she mused.

He agreed, and they split up to accomplish their tasks. He was just setting down the mugs of hot chocolate on the coffee table when she emerged from the bedroom.

"Okay, I set out the sweats on the bed so we can change, then we can..." she looked a little shy as she gestured to the couch. He gave her a quick kiss on the forehead as he walked into the bedroom.

He hoped his faux eagerness would hide his own nerves. He was eager, so incredibly eager, to cuddle with Penelope. It was just that they still hadn't talked about so many things, and while most of them truly could wait until the morning, there was one thing that really couldn't wait. It probably needed to be discussed, if not immediately, within the next five minutes.

He grabbed the pile Penelope pointed to and scurried into the bathroom. The mirror in here was blessedly small, so he could easily turn away as he changed. Penelope had given him a well-worn green camp counselor t-shirt and a pair of college-branded sweatpants that stopped just slightly above his ankles. Knowing that they were hers made him feel surprisingly soft and warm, even though they didn't fit. As he caught his reflection in the mirror, he realized he wasn't just feeling cozy, he could also feel his gender sliding. Okay, make that two things they needed to talk about tonight.

"Uhm, Nels, can we—" he started to ask as he emerged from the bathroom, but he stopped in his tracks as he caught sight of her naked back. He had no idea she would be changing in her bedroom while he was in the bathroom, or he would have knocked on the door before stepping outside.

She turned her head to look over her shoulder at him but didn't panic. She made a "whoops" face, and then gracefully pulled the t-shirt in her hands over her head and turned around. Riley felt like the image of her half naked in the dim light of her bedroom was going to be emblazoned on his retinas until the day he died, and he was pretty okay with that.

Last week he, Kim, and River had created a fake profile on Chasing Rainbows to research how to create the profiles for the clothing and for Riley. River had set the settings specifically so they would only find pansexual women, and to his surprise, Penelope had popped up almost immediately.

He had allowed himself to look through her photos twice while pulling quotes out of her bio to include in his. This meant that he had recently seen her tattoos and bare back in her bikini picture. It was nothing compared to her in real life, though.

Her hips were soft as they led up to her smaller waist and tapered back out to her slim shoulders. The tattoos ran from right below her neck to halfway down her back. He would have to ask her about them one day. He imagined stroking his fingers, and maybe his mouth, over each of the designs, and he felt himself shiver.

She seemed to pick up on this because she walked over and

wrapped her arms around his neck, and asked, a little sassily, "See something you like, sweetheart?"

He shivered again at the rumble in her voice, but he had to control himself, or they would never have this talk.

"Yes, absolutely, 100%. But... could we actually talk really quick? It's about me! Not you, but... I realized there are probably two things we need to talk about before we can keep hanging out and— uhm, cuddle tonight."

She immediately pulled back from him and nodded. She gestured to the living room, and they walked back out to sit near each other on the couch, not quite touching.

"So, I guess... I know you did some reading on gender fluidity?" he paused to let her nod before he continued. "So, let me start by reiterating that being gender fluid is not... black and white. Sometimes it's very clear to me when I'm a woman or when I'm a man, and sometimes it's a bit mixed. I like to think of it like I'm trying to listen to my body and place a pin on the gender scale where I'm currently feeling. Sometimes it feels more like I'm throwing a dart at it, and sometimes it feels like the scale is actively moving as I'm trying to pinpoint what I'm feeling for the day, it sort of slides back and forth. Does... that make sense?"

She nodded encouragingly.

"So... I try to check in with myself every morning. Typically this involves me purposefully looking in the mirror once per day and going through the exercise of putting a pin on the scale. On work days—well work days at my former job at least, where I had to constantly present as male, it just kind of gave me a sense of how much gender dysphoria I might have that day... but on weekends, it's more fun. It's like, 'okay what name am I using today? Should I put on my glasses and a dress or throw my hair up and wear something more neutral or masculine.' But—... jeez, sorry I'm realizing this is becoming a whole talk, and you didn't want to talk tonight... I'm sorry, forget it. We can just—"

"Riley," she said gently, and he couldn't stop himself from flinching.

She looked alarmed for a second, but then understanding dawned. She slowly reached forward and took his hand in hers, and he accepted her grasp willingly. "Okay... as clearly illustrated, I think I need you to finish explaining. I didn't want us to hash out *everything* between us," she said, gesturing lightly between the two of them with their joined hands, "but if there are some things you need to talk through to feel comfortable tonight, that's completely fine, sweetheart."

He nodded stiffly. "Uhm... Yes. Sorry. Uh—so... sometimes... it doesn't last the whole day—my gender identity, I mean, or sometimes I can't get a clear enough sense of myself in the morning, and it's almost like... I can feel myself slide between genders," he explained, swaying his head and shoulders back and forth to illustrate the slide. She nodded and squeezed his hand, but he didn't say anything for a moment.

"And... are you... I mean, did you just experience that? Did you... slide into Taylor?" she asked tentatively, and he had to smile.

"Uhm... I don't think I would have thought to phrase it like that but—yes actually. I think I 'slid' into feeling feminine and... if you... wouldn't mind switching pronouns...? And..."

"Calling you Taylor?" she asked as she smiled over at him.

He took in a deep breath and let it out. "Yes, please."

Taylor (Riley)

"Was... that hard to share with me?" Penelope asked, stroking her fingers softly up and down Taylor's arm.

Well, it definitely hadn't been easy, but there was more to it than that. Taylor often felt like she was taking a quiz each morning when she tried to figure out what gender she was. She felt a knot form in her stomach when she thought of Penelope having to take that same quiz. How often would she have to fail before she'd get frustrated or sad?

"Do you think... maybe it would be easier just to use they/them all the time? Then there's no real worry you'll use the wrong one?" Taylor mused.

Penelope sat there silently for a moment. "If that's what you want, I can totally do that, but... I don't want to do something because it's easy for me. Do you... like being gendered male or female when that's how you're feeling? Does it make you happy or make you feel more yourself?"

It did. It really did, but she didn't want to make Penelope ask her every day or even throughout the day. "I don't want you to feel uncomfortable like... I'm some kind of quiz you have to take," she said softly.

Penelope blinked at her. "Is... is that what you think I'm like?" her voice was hurt and a little angry.

"No! No, I..."

"Have you ever been with someone who was nonbinary or gender fluid?"

"Uhm... no, but I have a few nonbinary acquaintances."

"And is that how you feel about them? Like they're a quiz you could fail?"

Taylor's back stiffened, and she felt goosebumps crawl across her skin. "No. Never," she admitted.

"Okay... so if you don't think that's how I feel and that's not how you feel about another person... why is that how you feel about yourself?"

Taylor's hand flew to her throat, where a lump had lodged itself so deep, she was afraid she might be unable to breathe around it. Penelope lifted her hand and wrapped it around the nape of Taylor's neck, stroking her skin and massaging the place where her neck met her shoulders.

"Hey. It's okay. This is hard, I know. It's so hard, and it's going to be hard. But if we do the hard stuff up front, then I think we have a much better chance of it being less hard down the line?"

Taylor nodded and closed her eyes for a moment.

"So... in the past, you've changed your clothing and name so that everyone around you could recognize your correct gender. What if it was something like that but much simpler?" Penelope asked suddenly.

Taylor looked at her quizzically.

"Okay, so I have to be honest, I've spent a huge amount of time on gender queer Instagram reels, Tik Tok, and Reddit. So, this is not an original idea but... what if you had different gendered bracelets or necklaces or... I don't know, three pairs of fun, funky glasses or something? You'd never have to say anything out loud. I could just figure it out based on what you put on that day?"

Taylor pictured looking in the mirror each morning and grabbing the correctly colored bracelet, and... that would be it. She imagined walking into her apartment after work, and before getting caught up telling Penelope how her day was, she could switch bracelets if she needed to without even having to say a word.

"I... I think I'd really like that..."

Penelope smiled a little wryly. "Was it the funky glasses that did it? I know that's why you swiped right on my profile."

Taylor suddenly remembered the silly photo of Penelope in her profile, the one of her at a friend's wedding wearing gigantic glasses. "Oh my god, is that what you meant? I thought you meant, like, cute different-colored frames or something. Not fucking clown glasses!" She let herself laugh then. It was raw and a little shaky, but it felt so good to laugh with Penelope again. She'd truly thought she had lost this.

"I mean, either would work; I don't see the problem! We'd be cuddling, and you could just reach over and grab the pink ones or the blue ones. Super easy to tell," she said, still laughing *with* Taylor, never *at* her.

"I... I like the idea of bracelets. Maybe not... pink and blue, though. That feels a little..."

"Simplistic? Lame? Binary? Yeah, for sure. Sorry, I was just joking."

"No, no, I was just thinking maybe... Maybe something that spoke more to how I felt because I rarely feel all the way blue or all the way pink. Maybe... like lilac, eggplant, black, and white?"

Penelope nodded along until Taylor said black, then she got a pensive look on her face. "Would white be... you're feeling a little like everything? And black would be neither?"

Taylor nodded, smiling softly to herself. Penelope had clearly done some research. These were the colors of the gender fluid flag. She actually wondered if Penelope had talked to Maria about it. Maria knew her flags like she was studying for a world history class.

"Thank you, Penelope. You have... no idea how it feels to be seen like this. It's... scary. It is, but... maybe also a little exciting? To let you see this part of me? All of me?"

Penelope's eyes turned glassy, and she blinked four times in a row before she shook her head and brought their joined hands to her lips to kiss the back of Taylor's hand. Unfortunately, there was one more thing they had to discuss tonight.

"There is... one other thing though, and this one... might be harder... especially right now," Taylor said, shifting a little uncomfortably, but Penelope squeezed her hand supportively.

Taylor met her eye for the briefest of moments before she let it come out in a rush. "So again, please don't feel the need to discuss this right now, I just wanted to say I fully hear you about being careful with your chest, and I promise I will be. I will do my absolute best not to brush or bump your chest. I will try not to even look at it, if you don't want me to, and I won't mention it in any sort of sexual way."

Penelope blinked at her for a moment and then nodded slowly. "I... I think I do want to explore it a little further, but. Actually, yea I mean... yes. Yes, that sounds good for now. Thank you."

Taylor swallowed hard and then made her request. "Would... it be possible for you to do the same for... for me?" she said, gesturing down at her lap. "Uhm, not like always and forever; I—I have had sex and... uhm—" Taylor had to look up at the ceiling, suddenly feeling overwhelmed and a bit ill at the thought of it right at this moment.

"Taylor. It's okay," Penelope's hands had come up to cup her face, and Taylor glanced back down, and their eyes met. Penelope must have been able to see some of the turmoil Taylor was feeling because she took in a sharp breath. "Oh, sweetheart... it's okay. We're going to figure it all out together, I promise. Please just completely put sex out of your mind for right now. I told you. There are many ways for us to be intimate together, okay?"

Taylor bit her lip. "Non... heteronormative ways?" she asked, remembering Penelope's words.

Penelope's smile was big and maybe a little over-exaggerated to cheer Taylor up. "Exactly. Fuck that! Or—I guess maybe—let's not fuck like that?" she hedged, making a silly face that pulled a startled laugh out of Taylor.

"Okay," Taylor said shakily, unsure if what was bubbling in her chest was another laugh or possibly a sob. "Uhm so... just for now... I guess I'm just asking if we're cuddling or making out. Could you just..." she gestured again with her hand and grimaced.

Penelope nodded and then bit her own lip. "I—uh... have been trying to be careful when hugging you. I think a part of my subconscious brain figured it might be a dysphoria thing in some way, so I've been trying to leave some space between—" Penelope made her own gesture between them.

Taylor had noticed, and she had been eternally grateful for Penelope's innate understanding and kindness. "Ashley has been working for years to train that out of me. I do like full frontal hugs and— wow, that sounded dirtier than I wanted it to..." she made a face but continued, "And I think I'm almost starting to enjoy them. On top of that, I like... your body. A lot," Taylor admitted, blushing hard. Penelope's cheeks began to darken as well, and like a yawn, it seemed to spread back to Taylor, increasing the temperature of her face even further.

"Uhm, but with cuddling, maybe we should take it a little slow? Like... spooning, for example I'm not sure..." she looked away.

She would love absolutely nothing more than to have their top halves connected and finally hold Penelope in her arms, but it could be more challenging on the bottom half. "And again, I promise. There are some days when having... the parts that I was born with is totally okay with me. We can... maybe... find ways to, er, well, my therapist said at least—I mean I'm sure we'll figured something out —" she cut herself off, realizing she was spiraling a little bit.

Penelope had raised her eyebrows in question, but she seemed to be waiting for Taylor to finish.

"Uhm, so... I've been seeing a therapist. She has me on some antidepressants, which, actually, I think are starting to work. It's crazy, like, the world looks completely different now. Like is this how everyone else has always seen the world? It's almost surreal, but... sorry. Not the topic at hand. Er—so she specializes in gender and knows a fair amount about gender dysphoria. Uhm..." God, Taylor was really about to step in it now, but she'd come too far now to stop.

"So, when I decided I was going to try and... win you back. I told her that sex was essential to you and that if I ever wanted to be able to not just win you back for a moment but actually keep you, I'd have to figure out how to have sex and... And enjoy it, because... Because I want that with you. I—god, I really want you. I just—I just have some things I need to work out, but she—I mean she promised I probably could—" shit, she was crying now. Pretty hard, actually, the tears choking her throat as she tried desperately to get out what she needed to say.

Penelope's face was stricken. "Oh god, Taylor... I'm so sorry you —I mean, I'm so sorry I made you feel like that. I—oh man. Can I explain really fast?"

Taylor's hand shook as she wiped tears off her face.

"Wait—first, let's get you some comfort, okay?" Penelope said, and Taylor was confused by the sentence until Penelope grabbed a mug of the still-warm hot chocolate and leaned down to pick up S.H. off the ground. She plopped the rabbit in Taylor's lap and handed her the mug, reaching back over to pick up her own.

"...comfort..." Taylor said a little bemusedly. Penelope had wanted to pause their hard conversation and take a moment to make Taylor more comfortable. She let out another sob and reached up to scrub the fresh tears off her face.

"Oh, Taylor... okay. So, the only reason I ever said what I said about sex was that I feel like living with Maria for so long—" Penelope cut herself off and then took a deep breath. She lifted her gaze and met Taylor's eyes.

"The truth is, a part of me really just thought you were asexual and were afraid to tell me," she said, blowing angrily into her mug of hot chocolate. "Which is so, totally, my bad. I'm so sorry about that. I didn't mean to be so forceful about sex; I mean, honestly—sex can be kind of challenging for me too," she admitted looking straight down into her mug now.

Taylor gazed at her, trying to gauge how she was feeling by the slant in her familiar shoulders. It seemed like she was anxious and possibly a little embarrassed. Taylor brushed her slightly damp fingers over the top of Penelope's hand. Penelope glanced down at their hands but didn't look back up at Taylor as she spoke. "I want to keep working through those challenges with a partner, and so I just wanted to see if you were someone I could work things out with. I promise sex is not like this huge dealbreaker for me and—again. I almost prefer some of the less, er—part A goes into part B types of sex. It can be unpleasant for me at times, and... anyways... I'm sorry. I think you were trying to finish a thought, and I just stepped all over it?" Penelope looked embarrassed and a little dejected as she finally met Taylor's gaze.

"No, you didn't. You're fine. And here, before I continue—comfort," Taylor said, lifting S.H. and putting him in Penelope's lap. She laughed and began stroking his brown and black ears.

"Sorry, that sort of turned into a whole *thing*. What I was trying to say is that I talked to my therapist because I truly do want to explore sex as well, in a healthy way. My therapist... well, she gave me some strategies and some things we can talk about and work through when we're ready. And truly, I don't want a sexless marriage either. I want to be able to enjoy giving you pleasure and getting pleasure. I don't want—" Taylor froze at the funny look on Penelope's face. She played back her words quickly and then groaned. "Oh god, I said marriage, didn't I... Uhm—a sexless... relationship? Partnership?"

"You... want to get married someday?" Penelope asked almost reverently.

"I mean... yes? Do—do you?" she stammered.

"Oh, god, yes! I've already started pinning white wedding suits on my Pinterest boards!" Penelope said, and Taylor laughed, an ugly, wet, slightly high-pitched noise that made Penelope laugh in response.

They fell silent and, at his insistent foot thumping, Penelope lowered S.H. to the ground. As if drawn to each other by an invisible magnet, as Penelope sat back up they both leaned forward for a kiss. It was soft, much softer than their earlier kiss at the cafe, but just as sweet.

Taylor smiled into the kiss. "I feel like almost all of our kisses have tasted like chocolate."

Penelope's laugh ghosted out across Taylor's nose. "It does seem like we might be Pavlovian training ourselves. I think anytime I have hot chocolate now I'm going to want to kiss you."

Penelope reached forward, took the empty mug from Taylor's hands, and placed them both on the coffee table.

"Well, as long as it's not the other way around. If you want hot chocolate every time I kiss you, we might have to buy stock in a chocolate company," Taylor joked.

"Oh, you think we'll be kissing that much, huh?" Penelope teased, a devilish grin touching her lips, and Taylor rolled her eyes before leaning forward for another kiss.

Since it seemed like they'd gotten all of the hard stuff out of the way, for the time being at least, they turned on the first movie in Penelope's queue and settled back into the couch together. Taylor had her arm over Penelope's shoulder, and Penelope curled up into her side.

Taylor only caught the first twenty or so minutes of the movie before she fell asleep.

FOURTEEN

PENELOPE

Penelope was sure she was dreaming.

It had been a pretty straightforward dream. A thinly veiled surprise party, and a ridiculously obvious game to get her to swipe right on Taylor Riley's profile. The next part was a little harder to believe, that Taylor Riley was really back in her life, and not just that, but in her apartment, on her couch, and even against her side as she fell asleep.

Penelope sighed and wished she could force herself to fall back into the dream. She'd once read about lucid dreaming, where someone could teach themselves how to gain just enough consciousness during a dream to be able to control it and shape the outcome. She wished she could sink back into the dream now and maybe stay there for a while, but instead, she was awake at probably some godawful hour because that's what had been happening to her the past few weeks since their breakup.

She sighed again and shifted uncomfortably. Instead of finding relief in stretching out on the couch more, she collided with a warm, solid body. She gasped as her eyes flew wide and her arms flailed out, knocking Taylor Riley in the face, who startled awake and also flailed.

"Oh god—I'm so sorry, I... You're here," Penelope stammered, wiping at her eyes as if this whole thing might be a trick of the light.

They were curled up on the couch together, and the first hints of daylight were creeping in under the blinds. They must have fallen asleep together watching the movie.

Taylor Riley blinked dazedly. "Is... that a good thing?"

"Yes," she said. "Oh my god, Tayl—oh. Uh—" she stammered and bit her lip.

She had been referring to Taylor Riley as Taylor Riley in her head, using they/them pronouns for over a month now. Still, yesterday he'd been feeling masculine until they'd gotten into comfy clothes and been about to watch the movie. Then she'd been feeling feminine, and now Penelope wasn't quite sure what to do this morning.

"Oh, let's just use whatever I was last night—" Taylor said, flapping her hand in front of her face, "until I'm awake enough to even know what gender is. That's what I did with everyone else when they insisted on sleeping over the past month."

Penelope laughed and leaned up to close the two inches between them to kiss Taylor softly on the lips. "Well, we both know it's all just an epic construct anyways."

Taylor's eyes focused in on hers suddenly. "Nels... I can't believe... I mean... you're just so wonderful."

Penelope blushed fiercely as she buried her face in Taylor's messy hair. "Wow, I wake you up by basically punching you in the face, and you call me wonderful. You know how to spoil me, don't you?"

"Well... I would actually love to spoil you. I want to give you absolutely everything you've ever wanted and then some," Taylor said, nuzzling into Penelope's hair.

Taylor shifted around on the couch until they were settled against each other again and she was very clearly attempting to go back to sleep. Uh oh.

"So, uh... I guess this is something you should probably know about me..." Penelope hedged quietly. "Once I'm awake, I'm pretty much awake. I usually can't get back to sleep."

"Ughhh," Taylor groaned, burrowing somehow even deeper into Penelope's hair, "you're one of those people?"

Penelope felt a slight twinge in her gut. "Is that... a deal breaker?"

Without even a breath of hesitation, Taylor said, "Not in the slightest, darling. But you're just going to have to figure out how to entertain yourself because I am not leaving this couch until ten, at the absolute earliest."

"Darling..." Penelope mused. "I like that."

"Mmmm, good," Taylor said, placing her head on top of Penelope's head in a way that absolutely could not be comfortable for her neck, "because you are. My darling."

The words struck Penelope hard, almost like the feeling she'd gotten the first time she'd met Riley's gaze or laid eyes on Taylor.

At her silence, Taylor stiffened. "Sorry... was that... too much?"

"No, I... I like it. A lot. Is that... what you want?" Penelope asked as she pulled her head out from under Taylor's, and they locked eyes.

"You?" Taylor asked, her eyes bright and very much wide awake, despite what she'd said earlier.

"Me... to be yours?" Penelope clarified.

"I mean... if you want that too. I—well, I guess that's what I was trying to ask with the swipe yes or no, but I see now that maybe that was a bit contrived." Taylor got a thoughtful look on her face, pulling her bottom lip in between her front teeth.

"Maybe a little," Penelope laughed.

"Yes. I want you to be mine, and I want to be yours."

With a breathy "okay," Penelope pulled her in for a rough kiss.

It wasn't like in fairy tales where morning kisses were mythical things that featured perfectly coiffed hair, strangely fresh breath, and sexy lingerie. They were both pretty rumpled, Taylor had crease lines across her cheek, and they tasted like one does after a long night's sleep. Even so, it *was* a little magical. Just having Taylor here on the couch with her was magical.

"Ugh, I need a toothbrush. Desperately," Taylor groaned, pulling away from Penelope and leaning back into the couch.

"Wow, in one night, we reunited, started dating, had our first accidental sleepover, and now you're trying to leave a toothbrush at my place?" Penelope said, poking Taylor gently in the side. She squealed in a very undignified manner.

Penelope's eyes widened. "You're ticklish...?"

"Oh, darling, there is still a lot you don't know about me," she said as she curled up in the corner of the couch for protection.

"Well, should we get a jump on that today? Do you want to go somewhere for breakfast and talk?" Penelope asked as she stretched out the kinks in her neck and back.

Taylor smiled over at her. "Sure, but... I'll probably need a toothbrush, shower, and clothes. Should I... go home first, or...?"

Penelope felt an acute flash of panic at the idea of Taylor leaving her side for even a short trip home. "I mean... if you're okay with it, you're welcome to all those things here." Penelope reached over and grabbed one of Taylor's hands. Penelope could barely keep her hands off of her. She just wanted to hold and kiss and touch her like she hadn't been able to do for weeks. She kissed each of her knuckles one at a time, and Taylor just marveled at her.

"It seems like... you might be a very touchy person. I don't think I truly got to see this side of you before."

Penelope's smile turned guarded. "I am, yes. You said... you're a cuddly person after you get to know someone?"

"I am indeed," Taylor said, unfurling herself to pull Penelope back into her arms.

"Well. That's good because this household is pretty big on it, as you've probably noticed."

"Are Crystal and Maria cuddly? Also, they are together... right?"

"Yes, on both counts."

"Wow, that's amazing. I'm so glad they found each other. Crystal was lovely to me throughout planning your party, and she even picked me up from my apartment to bring me over last night."

Penelope felt her heart expand, grinch style. She was so happy Maria had found someone, and it felt like she and Taylor may have found a new friend as well.

"I guess I should probably get up and take a shower since you are clearly not letting me go back to sleep," Taylor said grudgingly, and they both got up and headed into the bedroom.

Penelope began to rummage through clothes, but suddenly she realized she didn't know what gender Taylor would end up feeling today. She thought about this for a moment and then set to work finding three different outfits for her. She now had a large selection of men's shirts, so she pulled out a navy-blue men's crew neck shirt as well as a more androgynous, slim-cut flannel. She reached deep into her closet and pulled out an eggplant cold-shoulder sweater. She didn't have much in the way of pants that would fit Taylor, so she grabbed her longest pair of jeans and a pair of leggings. She was reconsidering the androgynous shirt when Taylor walked out of the bathroom with her hair up in a bun and the shirt and sweats from last night.

Penelope observed her for a moment. "Until we find the bracelets, should I... assume if your hair is up, you're feeling masculine?"

Taylor had been studying the clothes on the bed, and she glanced over at Penelope. "Hm... I'm not sure if that's always going to be true, but for now, until we get the bracelets, yes, I think so. If I was at home, I'd tend to do hair down and glasses when feeling femme."

"And... last night, you had your hair down but no glasses, and were feeling masculine," Penelope noted thoughtfully.

Taylor just shrugged. "Yeah, not sure what to tell you about that one. It just felt right in the moment. You can always just ask if you want to know, though. I'll try to tell you as soon as I know. So. Today is feeling like Riley and he/him."

Penelope nodded and did a mental pivot. She pointed to the masculine-coded clothing. "I wasn't sure, so I picked out three different styles. Do any of these work? Er—I'm not sure about pants—"

"I think I'll just wear mine from last night. Thanks, Nels. I also have on the same underwear, but that certainly can't be helped," he said, laughing softly.

Penelope blushed suddenly and glanced away. "Uhm... actually... I thought that maybe I might like wearing boxers, so... I bought a pack, but I don't think I like them. Did you want a pair? They're new and clean, I promise."

Riley blushed and glanced away. "Uh, yeah, actually, that would be great. Can I ask—why you didn't like them?"

Penelope walked over to her dresser and began rifling through it. "I think I realized that while I may not like every part of my body, I like my legs and butt and I don't want to cover them up. Also, I'm not... male, per se. So, I don't necessarily want to dress in men's clothes just because they're men's clothes. I'm more interested in how men's style can play off the femininity I do feel, as well as androgyny?"

Penelope closed the drawer and turned around to hand him a pair of boxers, and he smiled appreciatively. "I will say, though, I liked the wide waistband peeking over my jeans look. I mean—" she groaned involuntarily, "when women wear sports bras and boxers with the waistband peeking out..."

Their eyes met, and they said in unison, "So hot."

Riley grinned at her, took the clothes, and grabbed his pants off the floor as he walked back into the bathroom. On a whim, Penelope decided to wear the more femme sweater today, and she paired it with the too-long jeans since they were already out.

She changed quickly and was kneeling on the ground, cuffing the jeans, as Riley walked out. He stepped up behind her as she stood up and gently placed his hand on her back, and she could feel the warmth through the sweater. "Where would you like to go for breakfast?"

"There's a cafe not too far from here. I've been wanting to try it, but I always feel like I'm cheating on Frankie and Diego. I think, in this instance, it's acceptable because it doesn't feel like we'll get much talking done if we go to drag brunch today."

They gathered phones, keys, and wallets and headed out.

They arrived at the only semi-full cafe and were seated quickly. Penelope took a little spiteful pride knowing that the drag brunch was sold out every weekend. It seemed the drag brunch might actually be pulling crowds from other cafes across the city. They ordered coffees, and Penelope took note of Riley's order, a mocha with caramel, and filed it away in her new and improved Taylor Riley drawer.

"So," Riley began, lifting his mug to his lips and momentarily obscuring his face in steam, "where should we begin?"

Penelope raised her own mug to her lips and blew. She had ordered a simple latte, but the smell of Riley's mocha was tantalizing. She eyed his mug with a bit of jealousy and was surprised when he held it out towards her.

"Would you like to try? I'm sure you're taking mental notes to report back to Frankie."

She smiled and gladly accepted the mug, handing him hers in return. She took a sip and let the sugar swirl around her tongue. "WOW, this is sweet," she exclaimed.

It almost smelled better than it tasted. She thought she would probably just stick with her latte, and based on Riley's pursed lips, he agreed, so they switched back.

With correct coffees back in hand, Penelope thought for a moment about Riley's question. "Why don't we start at the beginning? I mean—not, like, of time. But, of us? I feel like there were points throughout our time dating and our time texting that we were both obscuring parts of ourselves. Maybe we can start by clearing that up?"

So they began at the beginning, and Riley shared how Johanna had downloaded the app onto his phone because she was afraid he was going to end up alone in life. He admitted she had probably been right to worry, and that was how this whole thing had started. Penelope nearly spit out her coffee when he admitted she'd crafted his awful bio.

"You were actually the first person I swiped on," Penelope admitted. "I was so disappointed when it didn't immediately say we matched that I only swiped for a few more people, and then I let my friends and Frankie swipe for me."

Riley laughed but looked down into his coffee. "I swiped for a little while, but your profile really caught my eye. I think I messaged a few people, but you were the only one who responded, and then after our first date, I deleted my matches with everyone else."

Her eyes widened at that. "You actually did do that?"

"I did. I was serious when I said I just wanted to see if things would work out between us. But—well, I guess outside of you and me specifically, I also just wanted to see if I could actually have a relationship. It didn't seem like there was much point in figuring that out with multiple women at once if it turned out I just wasn't able to form a healthy relationship."

Penelope's mind stuck on the word women. "I just realized... you've never actually told me about your sexuality. Were you only matching with women?"

Riley pursed his lip. "Oh, wow, you're right. I'm sorry it was— well... to be frank, it can be a little hard to explain that I'm straight but also a lesbian without immediately outing myself as being gender non-conforming in some way."

Penelope blinked at him, and it all clicked into place. "That makes total sense actually, but wait, so... when you said you loved vaginas, that was—"

"Doubly true because I love them as both a man and a woman." He gave a slightly cheeky grin, but then his expression turned shy, and he looked down. "I have to admit, it truly was a huge help to me, mentally and emotionally, to know that you were pansexual. It made me feel like at least I wasn't withholding some pertinent piece of information about myself that would make you just fundamentally not be able to like me. Unfortunately... that was what happened with Ashley. I kept it from her, and we had some—well. I was going to say problematic sex, but I think catastrophic might be a more apt way of putting it."

Penelope's hands clenched so hard around her mug that the liquid inside trembled. She had a feeling she knew where this was going. The thought of how badly it must have hurt not just Riley but also Ashley had a knot lodging itself deep in Penelope's stomach.

Riley refused to look up at her as he went on. "We... had been dating for a little while, and I did the same thing I did with you. I was very closed off and didn't let her in, but she didn't give up, probably thinking once we got to know each other better, in other words, got more intimate, things would get better. We got a little too drunk one night, and we ended up in bed together. I'd had sex before, and sometimes it went... fine. But other times, like with Kim, I would just focus on the woman, completely denying them access to my body, and then when they were done... we would just be done. Ashley was insistent though that she didn't want to just receive, she wanted to give pleasure and..." He stopped again, taking a deep breath before continuing. "I thought, sure, I can probably do this, why not. Except halfway through, I just fully 'slid' sideways. Not even to a different gender it was—I mean, slid isn't even the right word for it; I think I dissociated. I... I had a panic attack and started sobbing while I was... inside..." Riley choked on his words, and he brought his free hand up to cover his face.

"Oh, sweetheart... I'm so sorry." Penelope reached across the table and wrapped her fingers gently around his arm.

"It... was awful. Just so awful, and it was completely my fault. I should have been honest upfront, but I was so scared of losing another person, and I mean—you've met her. Ashley is amazing, but I just... well. Obviously, I had to tell her after that. I told her everything, and she ended up holding me all night, and in the morning, she told me she wanted to still be friends and keep me in her life, but... She said she was very straight, and she fully supported me being gender fluid, but that meant she could never be with me because she just was not attracted, physically, mentally or emotionally to women."

Penelope nodded slowly. She completely understood now why Ashley had asked that prying question about sex. Another piece of the puzzle slotted into place. Riley's fingers were still tight around his mug. He had shifted his hand so his chin was resting in his palm, but he still wouldn't look at her.

"Tell me about our first date. What did you think when I totally ruined your plan to get there early?" Penelope prompted.

Her question had the desired effect because Riley looked up, and his eyes twinkled almost identically to how they had that first day. "That I was so fucking out of my league. I mean, I had to text you I was so nervous."

Penelope let out a startled laugh. "There is no way you were thinking that because that's what I was thinking. I mean, Riley, I blurted out that you were gorgeous within ten minutes of meeting you."

They spent the next fifteen minutes sharing their thoughts and impressions during their first date. When their food arrived, they used it as a natural transition to their second date. Penelope slowly realized that almost every question Riley had asked and the answers he'd given were his way of desperately trying to gauge if he could trust Penelope. He elaborated further on a few of his answers, reiterating that he would make it his life goal, if he could, to make sure Penelope never felt like a burden, and Penelope vowed never to let him feel unlovable.

They continued talking, and Riley shared how he had been so anxious after their second date that when Penelope had changed their third date, he had been almost glad, and that's how he had ended up at the drag brunch with River.

This was where Penelope had the most questions, and Riley did his best to answer all of them. He had meant everything he said to Penelope about not wanting to date more than one person, and that's why he had turned down "Pen." They both marveled at the utter absurdity that had allowed their mix-up to happen in the first place, let alone to go on for as long as it did.

Riley told her how amazing he'd felt holding her through the movie marathon, and Penelope admitted how she found herself falling for Riley's tenderness as well as his body and his touch while simultaneously falling for Taylor's bold, brash honesty. This seemed to shock Riley more than anything else. He admitted he had no idea Pen had been truly falling for Taylor and laughed again at his obliviousness.

Riley used every curse word in his repertoire to describe the day Oreo broke his phone. He had been going after a loaf of bread for almost the entire afternoon, and right when Riley had gone to snatch it away, the cat had smacked his phone off the counter, and it had soared across the room. Then that night, Penelope reminded him, Oreo had ended up eating the entire loaf of bread while he, as Taylor that day, had been on the phone with Penelope. Penelope apologized again for her behavior during the rainstorm, and they both laughed again at the absurdity of Riley's broken phone prolonging their mix up.

They slowly discussed the night it had all come out and reflected on how overprotective and yet unbelievably amazing Kim and Ashley were as his friends, and finally, they finished their food and paid the check.

As they walked back to Penelope's place, Riley told her all about what he had been doing the past month. She was ecstatic to hear about his job and that he was going to therapy and getting real help for his depression. He was down to one session a week now, and he shyly said that his therapist had asked to meet her if they ever ended up back together. Penelope immediately agreed.

She shared how she had spent nearly two weeks on the beach coming to terms with the fact that just because she was finally ready for a relationship didn't mean Riley would be. She was also seeing a therapist and was still working through some relationship anxieties of her own.

She told Riley about her years-long suspicions about Frankie and Diego and the fact that they were now engaged, and Riley let out an actual whoop. Finally, she told him how she came out to her parents, with moderate to low success.

Penelope was about to turn the key in her apartment's lock when she heard an unusual amount of noise coming from behind the door. She gave Riley a skeptical look, but he just shrugged.

"No more surprises from me, I promise. I'm done with surprises."

She turned back to the door and opened it slowly so as not to take out S.H. by accident.

A chorus of hellos and good mornings rang out from the room. River, Kim, and Ashley were sitting at the kitchen table holding mismatched mugs and munching on a plate of pancakes spread out before them. They were holding them in their hands like biscuits, which Penelope instantly approved of.

Maria was sitting in Crystal's lap on the couch, and they were chatting with Frankie and Diego, who was holding S.H. in his arms. Greg was chatting amiably with someone over by their window. With a start, Penelope realized it was Sham Pain but out of drag. She'd have to go over and introduce herself and Riley. But first.

"It's amazing to see everyone but... is there any particular reason you're all here?" Penelope asked, and Maria immediately jumped up and ran to her. She nearly knocked the wind out of Penelope with her hug.

"Well, last night we were supposed to be celebrating Frankie and Diego's engagement, but it was really a surprise for your birthday, which turned into you and Taylor Riley getting back together. So, last night, while very intoxicated I will admit, I invited everyone over for brunch to *actually* celebrate Frankie and Diego! They had already canceled the drag brunch in case everyone got too drunk at the party, so... here we are!"

Penelope blanched. "You... invited everyone over, except me?"

Maria's eyes went wide, and several of the room's occupants chuckled. "Well... In my defense! I didn't know Taylor Riley would be sleeping on our couch, and you'd be gallivanting around town so early in the morning! I'm not used to you being in a relationship. I didn't know the protocol!" Maria was getting herself worked up, so Penelope smooshed her back against her chest.

"I'm just joking, Maria! What a wonderful idea. I'm sorry we're late, but I'm happy we're here now!" She threw an apologetic, but also "this is clearly not my fault" look at her brother, who just waved her off.

Riley had meandered over to the table where his friends were eating pancakes, and they had completely enveloped him in their arms. Penelope's chest warmed seeing him surrounded by people who loved him so unconditionally

Penelope worked her way around the room, catching up with everyone more than she had been able to the previous night. She officially met Shiloh, who went by he/they pronouns when not in drag. She tried to send "he's amazing, you should make a move" messages to Greg with her eyes, but Greg was too busy staring dreamily at Shiloh to notice.

She spent a fair amount of time with Frankie, Diego, Maria, and Crystal. They pulled her onto the couch with them, and she ended up with her back resting on Maria and her legs sprawled across Frankie and Diego. She quickly caught them up on the previous night in a hushed voice, and they group-hugged her until she begged for air.

Eventually she made it over to Riley's friends, who showered her with congratulations, excitement, and so much love.

At last, she found Riley in the kitchen making two cups of coffee, which he was surreptitiously dumping a packet of hot chocolate into. "Oh god, please don't let Diego see you doing that; he might have a heart attack."

"Look. You have horrendous pod coffee here. I'm just doing what's necessary to survive." He smiled at her as he handed her a mug. "How is it that you have access to some of the world's best coffee at the cafe, and this is what you drink at home."

Penelope shrugged, trying a sip of the sugary brew. It was actually kind of nice, which she blamed on Riley's clear conditioning of her brain. As if on cue, he reached for her and pulled her in with an arm around her shoulder. He planted a soft kiss on her forehead, and she melted just a little.

"Well... I have a grinder and a French press at my place. Maybe I'll get you one to keep here, too. Then no matter where we choose to spend our time we'll have good coffee," he murmured into her hair.

They walked back into the living room, Riley's arm still secure around her shoulder. She took a moment to marvel at how things had turned out. Here they were, Riley's arm around her like they had been doing this for years, surrounded by their closest friends in the world. The people who truly knew them, sometimes even better than they knew themselves. One day, she hoped she would know Taylor Riley that well too. She knew they still had a lot more to talk about and so much more to do together, but at this moment, she was happy just to be here.

—Follow Penelope and Taylor Riley's continued adventures in the second book in the series *Just a Basic Binary*—

Acknowledgments

First, I'd like to thank my spouse and my best friend for being my sounding board, my never-ending support system, and my first and biggest fans. This book would never have become what it is today without you.

I'd like to thank my mom for always being willing to read and proofread my stories, and for always being open to learning and discussing new things.

A big thank you to my friends and family who continued to encourage me to pursue publishing even when it felt daunting and unachievable. Without you, there wouldn't be a book to write acknowledgements in.

A warm hello and big thank you to the community I've found through sharing a love of writing, reading, and telling meaningful queer stories. This story is really for you.

Finally, to my dear reader, whether you are a member of one of the groups above or not, I hope you enjoy.

ABOUT THE AUTHOR

Dawn Cutler-Tran is an avid board gamer and rock climber who lives on the East Coast of the United States but loves to travel to places near and far as often as she can.

Dawn has always identified as queer, but during the pandemic she finally discovered she was nonbinary (she/they pronouns) and came out to family and friends. This book was part of that process, and she has loved exploring different genderqueer identities like her own through her writing, reading, research, and countless hours watching reels and videos on social media.

When she's not reading or writing, or reading about writing, she dabbles in boxing, scrapbooking, cooking, and eating lots of new foods. She loves food so much that during the pandemic she wrote a cookbook with her spouse and best friends. This was what started Dawn down the path of writing and helped her get through the long dark days of the pandemic.

Her biggest hope in writing queer fiction is to provide at least one other person out there with characters and story lines that they can recognize themselves, or their friends and loved ones in.

Follow Dawn on Instagram at @dawncutlertranwrites